# The

# Red Cell

# Conspiracy

G W Grant

ISBN    978-1-936062-26-3

**Published by:**
**Desert Wind Books**
www.desertwindbooks.com

Visit G W Grant on the web at www.gwgrant.us

Comments are welcome

In memory of those that have perished while fighting to preserve our way of life. Your sacrifice will not be forgotten.

# CAUTION

This novel is of a graphic nature and contains profanity which may offend some readers.

NOT SUITABLE FOR YOUNG CHILDREN

# Chapter 1

The White House
Washington, D.C.

It was midday when thirty-five-year-old Colonel John Wilson, Commander of Strike Force Delta, arrived at the entrance to the secret underground tunnel that led to the White House. Dressed in his best suit and matching tie, he walked over to the keypad and scanned his presidential authorization identification badge. The door opened, and he entered the tunnel. The entrance door closed behind him, and he walked to the end of the tunnel and stood in front of the three and a half-foot thick see-through door. He showed the Secret Service agent that was standing guard his presidential authorization identification badge. The Secret Service agent punched in a code on the keypad that was on the wall, and the door slid open. Colonel Wilson stepped inside the entryway, and the see-through door slid closed.

Colonel Wilson walked through the remaining security checks without incident and was allowed to pass. He was met by General Thomas Richwood, Chairman of the Joint Chiefs of Staff. "John, how was your trip?" General Richwood asked as they shook hands. "I know this was short notice, but the president wanted you here."

"I understand, sir; I am at your disposal when you need me. Sir, do you have any idea what this meeting is about?"

"CIA Deputy Director Hicks is briefing President Elliot on the Iran issue. It seems that things are heating up over there."

"I've never met Deputy Director Hicks. What kind of person is he?"

General Richwood chuckled. "John, Deputy Director Hicks is a woman. The guys at Langley call her the Ice Queen. I call her the She-Devil."

"Oh," was all Colonel Wilson could manage to say. "I didn't know."

"That's one woman you want to stay clear of." General Richwood pointed out. "Enough with the questions; we need to get going."

"Yes, sir," Colonel Wilson acknowledged and followed General Richwood to the elevator. Once they were both inside the elevator, the door closed, and the elevator began to move upward. When the elevator stopped the door opened, and General Richwood exited the elevator, with Colonel Wilson following close behind him, and they headed toward the Situation Room.

When they arrived at the entrance to the Situation Room, the Marine, who was standing guard, dressed in his dress uniform and armed with a nine-millimeter Beretta M9-A1 side arm, snapped to attention and saluted the general. General Richwood returned the Marine's salute and him, and Colonel Wilson entered the Situation Room.

Colonel Wilson was quick to notice thirty-year-old CIA Deputy Director, Karen Hicks sitting at the table dressed in a tight-fitting skirt with a matching blouse. Her blonde color hair appeared to be wrapped in a tight bun and was secured to the back of her head with a hairpin.

General Richwood and Colonel Wilson walked over to where Deputy Director Hicks was sitting. "Deputy Director I would like to introduce Colonel John Wilson, Commander of Strike Force. He will be joining us for this briefing."

Deputy Director Hicks looked up at Colonel Wilson with her baby blue eyes and nodded. "I've heard of you Colonel."

"Nothing bad I hope."

"Nothing good, I might add," Deputy Director Hicks fired back.

*What a bitch.* Colonel Wilson thought while he followed General Richwood to the other side of the table and sat down in the chair next to the general.

Soon afterwards, President Elliot entered the Situation Room. The Marine guard who was standing outside the Situation Room closed the double-doors while at the same time, everyone in the room, jumped to their feet.

"Have a seat," President Elliot said while he walked over to the table and sat down. He waited for everyone to return to their seats before he continued. "I know everyone has a lot on their plate, so I'll get to the point. I've read the CIA report that Deputy Director Hicks dropped off last night." President Elliot looked directly at Deputy Director Hicks. "I must admit Karen that your report has a lot of holes in it. Is there anything you can tell me that I can't get from CNN news?"

"Mr. President, We believe that Al-Qaeda is planning something big in the Middle East," Deputy Director Hicks answered. "We also suspect that Al-Qaeda has been in contact with a Pakistani nuclear physicist named Yasin Abdul Zamani. It is believed..."

"Mr. President if I may," Colonel Wilson interrupted. "Sir, even though we suspect that Zamani is connected to Al-Qaeda, we have yet to prove that he has had any contact with anyone from Al-Qaeda."

"Mr. President," Deputy Director Hicks jumped in. "We..."

"Instead," Colonel Wilson continued, cutting Deputy Director Hicks off in mid sentence before she could finish. "It is believed, and proven that Zamani has been in contact with Iranian agents operating in Pakistan."

"Colonel, if you don't mind; I'd like to finish giving my presentation," Deputy Director Hicks snapped.

"By all means, please continue," Colonel Wilson shot back. "Why don't you tell us why Zamani hates the US?"

*That's my boy;* General Richwood thought. *Put the Ice Queen in her place.*

"I've not been briefed on that Colonel," Deputy Director Hicks fired back.

"Colonel Wilson, why don't you explain to me why you think Zamani hates the US?" President Elliot curiously inquired.

"My pleasure Mr. President," Colonel Wilson looked at Deputy Director Hicks and smiled before he continued. "Five years ago a CIA hit squad tried to assassinate Zamani in Gwadar, Pakistan and failed; instead, they killed Zamani's wife and son."

"Mr. President that's not true," Deputy Director Hicks pointed out. "That incident was proven to be an accident."

"So Colonel, what you're saying is that you suspect this Zamani fellow is working with the Iranians, and possibly working with Al-Qaeda to avenge his wife and son's death?"

"Yes, sir, I do," Colonel Wilson replied.

"Mr. President I would like to finish what I was saying before I was interrupted," Deputy Director Hicks said while she shot Colonel Wilson an evil look.

"Please continue Deputy Director," President Elliot said. "What else do you have for me today?"

"Mr. President, we believe, but have not yet confirmed that Iran is secretly working on its own uranium-enrichment program that will produce weapons-grade uranium two-thirty-five." Deputy Director Hicks began. "We're still gathering what intelligence, we can get our hands on, to determine if Iran is indeed, producing weapons-grade uranium two-thirty-five, and if so, where they are doing this."

"So you're not sure of anything are you?" Colonel Wilson inquired.

"Like I said, we're still processing the raw intelligence on this matter." Deputy Director Hicks fired back.

"So, in other words, you have jack-squat on this." Colonel Wilson shot back.

"The CIA is working hard to confirm that Iran is trying to produce nuclear weapons." Deputy Director Hicks pointed out. "We need to be sure of this first before we can recommend the appropriate action that should be taken to neutralize this threat."

Colonel Wilson could see that his remarks were agitating Deputy Director Hicks. "How long is that going to take? What are you going to do wait until they nuke someone for confirmation that they have nuclear capabilities?"

"All right, you two; let's not get into a pissing match over this." President Elliot intervened. "I want this Iran issue investigated. I expect some answers within forty-eight hours." President Elliot concluded as he got up from his seat, and everyone jumped to their feet. "I suggest the two of you put your petty differences aside and try to work on this one together." President Elliot walked over to the doors to the Situation Room. He opened them and left the room.

Deputy Director Hicks gave Colonel Wilson a dirty look.

"Is there something you want to say Deputy Director?" Colonel Wilson asked while he smiled back at her and winked.

"Men!" Deputy Director Hicks snarled. She picked up her things from the table and stormed out of the Situation Room.

"You know general; I think you were right about Hicks. That woman is a piece of work." Colonel Wilson commented. "What she needs is a good man to calm her ass down."

"Hold on Casanova," General Richwood remarked. "I hope you're not thinking of going after that."

"Hell no," Colonel Wilson fired back. "No, sir, not me."

General Richwood smiled; "Smart man; you wouldn't stand a chance in hell of getting through that hard shell she has around her heart. I pity any man who tries to."

Still, it would be a challenge; Colonel Wilson thought.

Colonel Wilson followed General Richwood out of the Situation Room. The Marine, who was standing outside, snapped to attention and saluted the general. General Richwood snapped the Marine a quick salute, and he and Colonel Wilson continued walking.

"Are you going back to Tinker tonight?" General Richwood asked while they walked back to the elevator to the secret tunnel.

"No, sir," Colonel Wilson answered. "I'll be spending the night at the Hay-Adams Hotel. I plan to fly back to Tinker in the morning."

General Richwood and Colonel Wilson stopped in front of the elevator. "Have a safe flight back to Tinker," General Richwood said as he pushed the button for the elevator. "I'll be in touch if I should need you for anything."

The elevator door opened, and they shook hands. "You know where to find me, sir if you should need me." Colonel Wilson pointed out while he stepped into the elevator. The elevator door closed and began to move downward.

The elevator stopped when it reached its destination, and the door opened. Colonel Wilson stepped out, and the door closed. He walked to the exit door and waited for the three and a half-foot thick see-through door to open. When the see-through door opened, he continued to the end of the tunnel and exited. He walked over to the vehicle that was waiting for him. The driver opened the back door, and Colonel Wilson climbed inside. The driver closed the door and hurried around to the driver's side; he opened the door and jumped in behind the wheel.

"Where to sir?"

"Drop me off at the Hay-Adams Hotel."

"Yes, sir," the driver acknowledged, and they drove off.

A few minutes later Colonel Wilson's vehicle pulled up in front of the Hay-Adams Hotel and stopped. The driver pushed a button on the dash, and the trunk popped open. The driver got out of the vehicle and closed the door. He hurried to the back of the vehicle where the trunk was located and retrieved Colonel Wilson's overnight bag from the trunk. He closed the trunk lid and hurried around to the backside of the vehicle where Colonel Wilson was sitting, and opened the back door.

Colonel Wilson stepped out of the vehicle, and the driver closed the door. "Pick me up at zero five-thirty," Colonel Wilson said as he took his overnight bag from the driver.

"I'll be here, sir."

Colonel Wilson walked to the entrance of the Hay-Adams Hotel while the driver got back into the vehicle and drove off.

"Good evening Mr. Wilson," the door attendant said as he opened the door for Colonel Wilson. "How are you today?"

"Doing good Mike," Colonel Wilson answered, and then he entered the hotel. He walked through the lobby over to the front desk.

"Good evening, Mr. Wilson," the man who was working the front desk said. "How long will you be staying with us this time?"

"Just for tonight; I'll be leaving early in the morning." Colonel Wilson signed the check-in register, and the desk clerk handed him his room keycard. He looked at the number on the keycard while he walked over to the elevator. The elevator door opened, and he stepped inside. He pushed the button for his floor, and the elevator door closed. Not long afterwards, he could feel the elevator move upward.

When the elevator arrived at the floor where Colonel Wilson's room was located, it stopped, and the door opened. Colonel Wilson stepped off the elevator, and the door closed. He walked to the room number that was on his room keycard and unlocked the door. He entered the room and closed the door. He placed his overnight bag on the bed and put the room keycard in his pants pocket before he sat down on the foot of the bed.

Colonel Wilson got up from the bed when someone knocked on his door. He walked over to the door and looked out the peephole, and saw a bellhop standing there. "Yes; who is it?"

"Mr. Wilson it's the bellhop, sir. I have a message that was left for you at the front desk."

Fearing that the message was important, Colonel Wilson flung open the door and took the message from the bellhop. He took out a five-dollar bill from his pants pocket and handed it to the bellhop. "Thanks; I appreciate you bringing this up to me."

"You're very welcome Mr. Wilson."

The bellhop walked back toward the elevator while Colonel Wilson closed the door. Colonel Wilson opened the message and quickly read its contents. "What the fuck." He said aloud and threw the message on his bed, and then hurried out of the room.

He checked his room door to make sure it was locked before he walked over to the elevator and pushed the call button. When the elevator arrived, the door opened, he stepped into the elevator, and the door closed. He pushed the button for the lobby, and the elevator began to move downward. A few minutes later the elevator stopped, and the door opened. Colonel Wilson stepped out of the elevator and walked through the hotel lobby to the hotel's lounge.

When Colonel Wilson entered the lounge, he saw Deputy Director Hicks sitting at a table in the corner; dressed in the same tight-fitting skirt and matching blouse that she was wearing earlier. Only this time her blonde hair hung freely to the middle of her back.

He carefully scanned the occupants in the hotel's lounge while he walked over to the table and sat down across from Deputy Director Hicks. He noticed a man and a woman sitting at a table a few feet away staring at them. When he looked closer, he could see the silhouette of a handgun under the man's jacket. "Don't say a word," he whispered to Deputy Director Hicks. "Meet me at the elevator." He got up from his seat and walked out of the lounge. He walked over to the elevator and waited for Deputy Director Hicks.

That man is a pain in my ass; Deputy Director Hicks thought as she got up from her seat at the table. She walked out of the hotel's lounge and hurried to the elevator where Colonel Wilson was waiting.

Colonel Wilson pushed the elevator call button on the wall, and the door opened. "Ladies first," he said to Deputy Director Hicks.

Deputy Director Hicks stepped into the elevator while Colonel Wilson looked back toward the hotel's lounge. He was quick to notice that the man and the woman, who were sitting at the table a few feet from where Deputy Director Hicks was sitting, were walking in their direction.

Colonel Wilson stepped into the elevator and looked at Deputy Director Hicks. "Are you armed?" He asked while he pulled out his Glock-19 from its holster, under his jacket.

"Of course, I am, why?"

Wilson readied his Glock-19 for action. "I suggest you do the same. It may be nothing, but I think you're being followed. Just follow my lead on this, okay?"

Deputy Director Hicks nodded in acknowledgment and removed her Beretta M9-A1 nine-millimeter from her purse. She placed the safety switch to its off position and moved to the back of the elevator while she hid the Beretta M9-A1 behind her back. "What if you're wrong?"

"Trust me, I'm not," Colonel Wilson fired back as he too hid his Glock-19 behind his back.

Wilson pushed the button for two floors above his floor and stepped back. The elevator door began to close when a woman yelled, "Please hold the elevator for us." He quickly reached forward and pushed the door open button. The elevator door reopened, and the man and woman entered.

"Thanks for holding the elevator for us," The woman said as the door closed.

"No problem," Deputy Director Hicks commented as the elevator began to move upward.

"Are the two of you married?" The woman asked.

"No, we're not," Deputy Director Hicks quickly answered.

"We're a couple," Colonel Wilson was quick to point out. "Maybe someday we'll get married."

*In your dreams' soldier boy*, Deputy Director Hicks thought.

The man looked at the woman and smiled, and then they faced the front of the elevator. Colonel Wilson noticed that the man hadn't pushed a floor number on the elevator's number panel. Without any warning, he pushed the emergency stop button on the elevator panel, and the elevator came to a sudden stop. The emergency alarm began ringing as Colonel Wilson spun the man around and slammed him up against the wall of the elevator. He placed his Glock-19 up against the right side of the man's ribcage. "Why are you following us?" He demanded to know.

The woman turned around to see what was going on, and discovered that Deputy Director Hicks was pointing her Beretta M9-A1 nine-millimeter at her. "Just keep your hands where I can see them."

"You got this all wrong," the woman fired back.

Without saying a word, Colonel Wilson removed the man's billfold from the inside breast pocket of his jacket. He took out the man's credentials and looked at it, and then shook his head in disbelief. "Say hello to Thomas Flowers from Homeland Security." He said while he removed his Glock-19 from the man's ribcage. He moved the safety switch to it's on position and returned it to its holster inside his jacket.

"And who might you be?" Deputy Director Hicks was quick to ask while she put the safety switch on her Beretta M9-A1 nine-millimeter to it's on position and returned it to her purse.

"Pamela Wells, also from Homeland Security," the woman answered. "We weren't following you. We..."

"I don't believe you." Colonel Wilson interrupted. "You better come up with something more convincing than that."

"I'm not at liberty to say." Pamela Wells shot back. "We weren't watching anyone, in particular."

"I think I know what's going on here." Deputy Director Hicks jumped in. She turned her attention to Colonel Wilson and continued. "I think they were watching the hotel's lounge for suspicious activity."

"Or, they're watching us, and they want us to believe otherwise." Colonel Wilson shot back. "I still don't believe that this was random."

"It was," Thomas Flowers assured them. "You got my attention the minute you entered the lounge. I got the impression that you were checking us out."

"I was, you dumbass."

"Oh my; Thomas, I think they wanted to keep their meeting a secret," Pamela Wells remarked. "I think they want to keep their relationship private."

"Yes we do," Colonel Wilson pointed out. "We don't want our colleagues to know about it right now; they wouldn't understand."

*You got that shit right;* Deputy Director Hicks thought. No one in their right mind would believe I'm screwing you.

Colonel Wilson pushed the emergency stop button again, and the alarm went silent. A few seconds later, the elevator began to move upward again while he pushed the button on the door panel for the next floor. When the elevator stopped, the door opened.

Flowers and Wells exited the elevator, and the door closed. "Wait until the guys at Homeland hear this one." Flowers remarked as they began to walk down the hallway.

"Yeah, they'll get a good laugh when they find out that Deputy Director Hicks and Colonel Wilson are doing it; won't they," Wells added.

"Who would have ever imagined Hicks and Wilson rolling around in the sheets?" Flowers snickered as they continued to walk down the hallway.

Meanwhile, Deputy Director Hicks looked at Colonel Wilson with fire in her eyes. "What were you thinking?" She asked as the elevator began to move upward. "Why did you tell them that we were a couple?"

"I had to tell them something." Colonel Wilson fired back while he pushed the button on the elevator panel for his floor.

"So, you don't believe any of what those two said?"

"Not a word of it."

The elevator stopped, and the door opened. Deputy Director Hicks followed Colonel Wilson down the hallway to his room. He took out his keycard and opened the door to his room. "Ladies first," he said with a smile on his face.

"What are you smiling for?" Deputy Director Hicks sarcastically asked as she entered the room, with Colonel Wilson following.

"I just thought of something funny," Colonel Wilson answered as he closed the door. He put the room keycard back into his pants pocket, and then he took out the radio frequency detector from his jacket pocket. He began to sweep the room for listening devices while Deputy Director Hicks walked over to the table that was in the room and laid her purse and briefcase down on the table. "No bugs," he reported after he finished scanning the room.

Deputy Director Hicks sat down in a chair at the table. "What was so funny?"

"The thought of you and I doing it," he answered while he walked over to the bed. He picked up the note from the bed and walked over to the table.

"That's all it's going to be too," she snapped back. "You just keep that thought in your head where it belongs."

"Your note said you had something important you needed to talk to me about." He said while he sat down at the table.

"Relax colonel; what do you have a hot date later?"

"Whether I do or not, is none of your business." Colonel Wilson fired back. "I got better things to do than waste my time playing your game."

"I see that you are indeed a hot head."

"I am not a hothead." Colonel Wilson snapped. "Now get to the point."

"Don't get your shorts in a knot colonel. President Elliot did say that he wanted the two of us to work together on this Iranian issue."

"I know what the president said." Colonel Wilson snapped back. "Get to the point of this meeting."

"I wanted to give you a copy of the material that I have on the situation in Iran," Deputy Director Hicks said as she opened her briefcase. She removed a folder from inside and closed her briefcase. "This is all the intelligence that the CIA has on what's going on over there," she continued as she handed Colonel Wilson the folder. "I was hoping you could find something that we might have missed."

"I'll look it over and get back to you on what I find," Colonel Wilson remarked as he placed the folder down on the table in front of him. "I still don't understand why we had to meet in secret?"

"I don't want anyone at the CIA to know that I gave you this file."

"Yeah, right; you just want me to do all the dirty work for you?"

"Look, Colonel, I set aside the fact that you embarrassed me earlier today in front of the president and came here with the hope that you and I can work together on this one." Deputy Director Hicks calmly answered. "I was hoping that we can find a peaceful solution to ease the tensions between Iran and Israel. I've already talked to General Richwood about this, and he suggested that you take the lead on this project."

"Who else knew that you were coming here to see me?"

"Just the two of us and General Richwood, why?"

"Good, let's keep it that way. Also, I would suggest you be more careful about who you talk to about this. I'm certain that someone is having you followed. Got any idea who that might be?"

"No, I don't."

"Well, just be careful who you talk to about this, and keep an eye out for anyone following you."

"I know how to spot a tail. I'm not new to this game."

"If you say so," Colonel Wilson sarcastically remarked. "Anyway, I'll snoop around a little and see what I can find out."

"So, when will I hear back from you?"

"When I find out something I'll let you know."

"Don't wait too long colonel; the clock is ticking on this one."

"Look, you're lucky I even agreed to do this so don't push your luck."

"I owe you one."

"You bet your ass you do."

"What do you mean by that?"

"Nothing," Colonel Wilson said as he got up from his seat. "Don't call me; I'll call you if I should come up with anything."

"Just keep me in the loop," Deputy Director Hicks demanded while she got up from her seat and picked up her purse, and the briefcase from the table. "And be quick about it," she continued while she walked to the door. "I need to know what you come up with." She opened the door and stepped into the hallway. "Have a nice day," she concluded before closing the door.

*What a bossy bitch;* Colonel Wilson thought while he got up from his seat. He walked over to the door and set the dead bolt on the door to its locked position. Afterwards, he walked over to the bed and sat down on the foot of the bed. He took out his cell phone from his jacket and flipped it open. He pushed the number three speed dial button and put the cell phone to his ear.

"Samantha Cooltrain," Lieutenant Cooltrain answered.

"Giggles, I need you to pull everything you can find on Thomas Flowers and Pamela Wells from Homeland Security. I'm going to need it when I get back tomorrow."

"I'll have it ready when you get here Wolverine."

"Good," Colonel Wilson acknowledged and closed his cell phone, to cancel the call. He put the cell phone back into his jacket pocket and got up from the bed; and walked into the bathroom. He turned on the shower and then took off his clothes; and stepped into the shower.

# Chapter 2

Gwadar, Pakistan

Yasin Abdul Zamani, a well-known Pakistani nuclear physicist, woke up at five-thirty A.M. like he had done for the past four years. He got out of his bed and walked over to his closet. He removed the suit that he was going to wear to his laboratory and laid it on his bed. He then walked over to his dresser, opened it and removed a pair of socks. He closed the dresser drawer and walked back over to his bed. He placed the socks near the edge of the bed and then put on his suit. Afterwards, he sat down on the edge of the bed and put on his socks. He then put on his shoes that were next to his bed.

Zamani sat on the edge of his bed and stared at the picture of his beloved wife and son, who were killed in a suspicious car accident five years earlier. A few minutes later, he suddenly jumped to his feet and walked back over to the dresser. He picked up his cell phone that was next to his wife and son's picture, and put it into the inside pocket of his suit jacket. He put his wallet in the back pocket of his trousers, and he put his keys and a few other items, in his front pockets.

He picked up the picture of his wife and son. "I will get those responsible for taking you away from me," he whispered in Farsi, his native language. "I promise you they will pay," he continued while he returned the picture to the top of the dresser.

Zamani looked at his watch and hurried down the stairs to the kitchen near the back entrance to his two-bedroom townhouse. He picked up the teapot that was on the stove. He put some water in the teapot and then placed the pot back on the stove. He turned the fire

14

on to heat up the water so he could make his morning cup of tea.

He walked to the front door and opened the door. He stepped out onto the front porch and retrieved the morning newspaper that was just delivered, and hurried back into the townhouse. He closed the door and walked back to the kitchen.

When he entered the kitchen, the teapot on the stove started whistling, indicating that his tea water was ready, so he laid the paper down on the table that was in the middle of the room. He took a cup out of the dish strainer and put in a fresh tea bag from the cupboard. He turned off the stove and poured some hot water into the cup.

Zamani removed a teaspoon from the dish strainer and stirred his tea. He then removed the tea bag from his cup and placed the used tea bag in the trash can at the end of the counter. He walked over to the kitchen sink, washed the teaspoon off, and placed it back into the dish strainer. He hurried back over to where he had left his cup of tea and carefully picked it up from the counter. He walked over to the kitchen table and sat down in a chair at the table. He took a drink of his hot tea and began to read his newspaper.

Twenty minutes later, there was a knock on the front door. Zamani set his cup of tea down on the table and laid the newspaper down in front of him. He got up from his seat and walked to the front door. He looked at his watch before he opened the door and found his supervisor from work, Yigal Allon standing on the porch.

"Yigal you're early," Zamani said in Farsi. "Is something wrong?"

"May I come in?" Allon asked who was also speaking in Farsi. "I rather not talk about it on your porch."

"Of course," Zamani commented and motioned for Allon to enter. Allon entered, and Zamani closed the door. "I was having my morning cup of tea. Would you like a cup? I'm sure the water is still hot enough."

"No, thank you, I'm fine. Something important has come up, and we need to talk."

"Very well, we can talk in the kitchen while I finish my tea."
Allon followed Zamani to the kitchen and sat down in a chair at the kitchen table while Zamani sat back down in his chair. He took a sip of his tea and waited for Allon to tell him what was so important that it couldn't wait until later.

"Are you sure you don't want a cup of tea?"

"I'm fine," Allon assured Zamani. "Yasin, I don't want you to take this the wrong way, but I've been approached by some people who say you've been in contact with several Al-Qaeda members. Is this true?"

Zamani looked at Allon in dismay. "Certainly not," he fired back. "Who's saying this?"

"I believe they said they were from Interpol, and that they were working with the American CIA. They said that you were meeting with these people secretly."

"Whatever would give them the idea that I would associate with Al-Qaeda?"

"I do not know my friend. I just thought I'd give you a heads-up on this new development."

"I assure you Yigal; I have had no contact with any Al-Qaeda members. I do not want anything to do with those people."

"I believe what you're saying to be true, but the CIA won't give up on you that easily. They're probably going to follow you to see who you meet with."

Zamani chuckled and took the last drink of his tea. "I believe it's time to go to work," he continued to say while he got up from his seat. He walked over to the kitchen sink and washed out his teacup. He placed it in the dish strainer and turned to face Allon. "The Americans can watch me all they want; I have nothing to hide."

"Still, I would be careful if I were you."

"Yeah, I know what you mean. Now let's go to work."

Without saying another word, Zamani left the kitchen, and Allon followed him. He opened the front door, and they stepped out onto the porch. Zamani locked the front door and closed it tightly. He turned the doorknob to make sure that the door was indeed locked.

Zamani followed Allon to his silver tone Toyota RAV4 that was parked in front of his house at the curb. Zamani got in on the passenger's side while Allon got in on the driver's side. Allon started the car, and they drove off.

Ten Hours Later

The sun began to disappear over the horizon, and the day turned into night. Yigal Allon and Yasin Abdul Zamani pulled up in Allon's silver tone Toyota RAV4 and parked in front of Zamani's two-bedroom townhouse. Allon noticed a Metallic Blue Mercedes-Benz G550 SUV parked across the street. He had never seen this car parked on the street before. He looked closer and could clearly see the two occupants, a husky man and a red-haired woman in the front seat looking at a road map.

"What are you looking at?" Zamani asked when he noticed that Allon was checking out a blue Mercedes parked across the street. "Do you know them?"

"No, I don't; I guess they're lost."

"They're probably some tourists who got lost."

"Yeah, I guess you're right," Allon agreed. "Well, I best be getting home. I'll see you tomorrow."

"I won't need a ride tomorrow. Remember, I'm taking the day off," Zamani reminded Allon.

Allon looked at Zamani sadly. He had forgotten that tomorrow was the anniversary of the day Zamani's wife and son died in their car accident. He nodded his head in acknowledgment, and Zamani opened the car door and exited the vehicle. He closed the door, and Allon drove off.

Zamani walked up the walkway to his front porch. He hurried up the steps while he removed his keys from his pants pocket. When he reached the front door, he unlocked it with his key and entered. He closed the door and walked up the steps to his bedroom.

He entered his bedroom and walked over to the window. He pulled the curtain back a little and saw that the Metallic Blue Mercedes-Benz G550 SUV was still parked across the street. *That's odd;* he thought. *If you were tourists, you would have been gone by now. No matter; you can watch me all you want. It does not matter to me.*

Zamani changed into his bedclothes and turned on the television that was in his room. He laid on his bed and drifted off to sleep.

The next morning Yasin Abdul Zamani woke up early from a restless night's sleep. He got out of his bed and walked over to the window. He pulled back the curtain to let in the sunlight, and noticed the Metallic Blue Mercedes-Benz G550 SUV was still parked across the street. *Good morning my watchdogs,* he thought. *I hope you enjoyed spending the night in your car.*

He closed the curtain and walked over to his closet. He removed a large travel bag and a small travel bag from the closet. He placed the large travel bag on his bed and walked into his bathroom with the small travel bag. He opened it and packed a few necessities. He zipped the bag closed and returned to the bedroom. He placed the small travel bag on the bed and opened the large travel bag. He carefully placed several pieces of clothing into the bag and then placed two large brown envelopes that were on his nightstand, along with the picture of his late wife and son on top of his clothing, and zipped the bag closed.

He picked up both bags from his bed, one in each hand, and walked down the stairs to the back door of his two-bedroom townhouse, and placed them next to the door.

He started to walk to the kitchen when he heard a tapping sound coming from the laundry room located next to the back door. He hurried into the room and removed a floor panel, exposing a tunnel. A man of Pakistani descent emerged from the tunnel; Zamani quickly motioned for the man to be silent. They embraced each other in friendship, and then he motioned to the man to follow him.

The man followed Zamani upstairs to his bedroom. Zamani pointed to the window and whispered in Farsi, "That Metallic Blue Mercedes has been parked out there since last night. I think they're watching me."

The man looked out the window and saw the Metallic Blue Mercedes-Benz G550 SUV that Zamani mentioned. "They're watching you all right," the man whispered in Farsi. "Any idea who they might be?"

"I'm not sure who they are," Zamani whispered back. "They're most likely CIA. Do you think they know about our plan?"

"I doubt it, but we need to go. Everything has been arranged."

Zamani followed the man out of the bedroom and back downstairs. They walked back to the tunnel entrance, and the man hurried down the ladder. Zamani handed the man his two travel bags and proceeded down the ladder. When he was half-way down the ladder, he grabbed the floor panel and put it back into place while he slowly continued down the ladder into the tunnel.

Once in the tunnel, Zamani laid the ladder on its side. He grabbed his two travel bags and followed the man down the narrow tunnel. Using flashlights, they continued to navigate the narrow tunnel. At the end of the tunnel, a silver tone Suzuki Alto (GF) GLX hatchback, and two of their friends were waiting for them. The driver pressed a button on the dash, and the hatchback opened. Zamani put his travel bags into the back of the car and closed the hatchback. Zamani and the man got into the backseat, and they drove off.

They drove to the waterfront and stopped in front of the dock where the Iranian cargo vessel Al-Jasourah was berthed.

"You must hurry in case we were followed," the man who was sitting next to Zamani in the backseat said in Farsi. "This will get you on board the freighter," he continued while he handed Zamani an envelope. "Give this to the man who will greet you on the ship. He will take care of the rest."

With the envelope in hand, Zamani got out of the vehicle and walked to the back. The driver pressed a button on the dash and the hatchback opened. Zamani retrieved his travel bags from the back of the vehicle and closed the hatchback. He hurried up the gangplank while the Suzuki Alto (GF) GLX hatchback drove off.

"Welcome friend," the man who was standing at the top of the gangplank said in Farsi.

"It is good to be here," Zamani remarked in Farsi while he handed the man the envelope that he was given earlier.

The man removed the contents from the envelope and quickly scanned through its contents. "Everything appears to be in order," he said while he put the papers back into the envelope and handed the envelope back to Zamani. "Follow me and I will show you to your living quarters."

Zamani followed the man into the lower decks of the ship where his living quarters were located. When they reached his living quarters, the man opened the door. "It's not much, but it's only for a couple of days," the man said in Farsi. "I will be back after we leave port to show you around the ship."

Zamani nodded that he understood what the man had said and

entered his living quarters. He looked around the small room and saw how shabby his accommodations were. *I'm glad this is only a two-day trip;* he thought.

The man closed the door while Zamani walked over to the bunk style bed. He put his travel bags on the backside of the bunk next to the wall and sat down on the bunk. "I've slept on worse," he muttered.

Zamani grabbed the raggedy pillow that was on the bunk and rolled it up to form a stiffer pillow. He kicked off his shoes and stretched out on the bed, resting his head on his newly formed pillow. "Praise the Prophet Muhammad; I made it on board this ship undetected." He mumbled. "I will have my revenge on those who have taken so much from me." He closed his eyes and drifted off to sleep.

Meanwhile, CIA operative Samuel Cain, a husky twenty-six-year-old man and CIA operative Kate Livingston, a red-haired thirty-year-old woman, sat in their Metallic Blue Mercedes-Benz G550 SUV, in front of Zamani's townhouse.

"This doesn't feel right," Samuel Cain commented. "The sun has been up for over two hours, and Zamani hasn't left for work yet."

"Maybe he took the day off."

"I'm telling you Kate; this doesn't feel right. I think we should take a closer look."

"I think we should let HQ know what's going on," Livingston suggested while she took her cell phone out of her purse. "Our orders were to watch and report; so, let's report this and let HQ decide what action we should take."

"Yeah, I guess you're right."

Livingston looked at Cain and smiled. "Don't you hate it when I'm right?"

"Just make the damn call," Cain snapped.

"Okay, Sam don't get your knickers in a knot," Livingston said while she flipped open her cell phone and pressed a speed dial button. She put the cell phone to her ear and waited for someone on the other end to answer.

"Code in please," the person that answered the call said.

"Alfa three one Delta," Livingston said in a calm voice.

"Situation?" The man on the other end asked.

"We haven't had eyes on the target since he entered his residence fourteen hours ago; request authorization to take a closer look."

"Proceed with extreme caution."

"Roger that," Livingston acknowledged. "We'll be careful." Livingston flipped the cell phone closed to end the call.

"Now can we go and see what's up?" Cain sarcastically asked while he turned on his earwig and put it in his ear.

Kate Livingston shot Cain an evil look. "Yes, I guess we can," she snapped back. She turned on her earwig and put it in her ear while she opened the car door. She got out of the vehicle and slammed the door shut.

Cain shook his head in disbelief. He got out of the vehicle and followed Livingston toward Zamani's townhouse. As they approached the front entrance, Cain sensed that something wasn't right. He removed his forty-caliber Glock twenty-two pistol from his shoulder holster. He loaded a round into the firing chamber and flipped the safety to its off position.

Without questioning Cain's reason for readying his weapon, Livingston removed her Beretta M9-A1 nine-millimeter pistol from her purse and readied it for service.

"It's too quiet," Cain pointed out. "You stay here, and I'll go around back. I'll let you know if I should find anything."

Livingston gave Cain the thumbs up, and Cain proceeded to the back of the townhouse. When he reached the back door, he turned the door handle, and the door opened. Cain carefully opened the door a few inches. He listened and heard no activity inside. He took a closer look and saw what appeared to be some kind of a trip-wire.

"Kate, don't open the front door," Cain said while he quietly closed the door.

"What's up," Livingston asked.

"Just don't open that door," Cain said in a loud voice. "It might be booby-trapped."

"Oh my," Livingston gasped.

"Hang tight Kate, I'll be there in a couple of minutes."

Cain heard a noise coming from behind him. He swung around with his forty-caliber Glock twenty-two pistol ready to take action. He was surprised to see CIA operative Harry Wheeler; a tall middle-aged man who has been with the CIA for over fifteen years and his young partner Robert King, standing there.

"Woo, Sam, easy my friend," Wheeler said.

"Harry, you know better than to sneak up on someone like that," Cain pointed out while he lowered his weapon. "I could have shot both of you."

"Sorry Sam," Wheeler calmly remarked. "We heard what you said to Kate over the earwig; just thought we'd offer you our assistance."

"No one's home," Sam informed Wheeler. "Zamani must have somehow slipped out without us seeing him, and the back door is booby-trapped. No telling, how many more booby-traps are inside."

"There's no way he got past us without us seeing him," Wheeler was quick to point out.

"Well, he didn't get past us either," Cain fired back.

"Then where is he?" King asked. "He couldn't have just disappeared into thin air."

Cain looked at Wheeler, and they both said at the same time, "A tunnel."

"That makes sense to me," Cain heard Livingston say over his earwig.

Cain thought for a moment, "Kate, call Headquarters; tell them that Zamani has flown the coop."

"You got it," Cain heard Livingston acknowledge over his earwig.

"Wheeler, I want you and King to wait here," Cain ordered. "Whatever you do, don't go inside, it's too dangerous right now."

Wheeler gave Cain the thumbs up, indicating that he understood what Cain had said to him. "We'll be right here waiting."

Cain hurried back to the front where Livingston, who was on her cell phone, was standing. He stood next to her and waited for her to get done with her call.

"I understand," Livingston acknowledged, "I'll pass it on to the others." Livingston flipped her cell phone closed to end the call, and then returned it to her purse.

"Well," Cain impatiently inquired.

"We're to keep a low profile and proceed with caution."

"Wheeler, I want you and King to remain where you are. Kate and I will breach the front and work our way to the back."

"Roger," Cain heard Wheeler acknowledge over his earwig. "Be careful in there Sam."

"Always,' Cain assured Wheeler.

Cain walked up to the front door and turned the doorknob; it was unlocked. He slowly opened the door a few inches and saw that it was booby-trapped just like the back door was. "Another trip-wire," Cain was quick to point out to Livingston.

"I got a pair of wire cutters in my purse if you need them," Livingston commented.

Cain looked at Livingston and smiled. "What don't you have in that purse of yours?"

"I always like to be prepared for the unexpected," Livingston answered while she looked through her purse. "Oh, here it is," she continued and pulled the wire cutters from her purse. She walked over to Cain and handed him the wire cutters. "What would you do without me?"

Cain shook his head in disbelief and took the wire cutters from Livingston. "I guess I would have walked back to the car and got a pair out of the back."

"Smart ass," Livingston fired back and backed away from the door.

Cain stooped down, and cut the trip-wire, and then he pushed the door open. He readied his forty-caliber Glock twenty-two pistol and entered Zamani's residence. Without hesitation, Livingston followed Cain's lead and readied her Beretta M9-A1 nine-millimeter pistol for action, and proceeded to follow Cain inside.

Livingston carefully searched the bottom floor of the townhouse while Cain walked over to the back door and began to disarm the booby-trap that was on the back door. With the first floor secure, and with no sign of Zamani, or any other booby-traps, Livingston headed up the stairs to the second floor.

Livingston entered Zamani's bedroom and looked through the dresser drawers. She found nothing out of the ordinary, so she walked into the bathroom. She started to open the medicine cabinet while she looked down at the trash can next to the sink. "What do we have here?" She mumbled while she bent over and removed an empty box for Dramamine, a drug used to help with motion sickness, from the trash can. "Why would you need to take this shit?" she mumbled again while she stood back up and examined the empty Dramamine box closer.

"Kate, did you find something?" Livingston heard Cain ask over her earwig.

"Nothing yet," she replied. "I still have one more room to check out."

"Meet me back down here when you're done."

"I shouldn't be much longer," Livingston said and tossed the empty Dramamine box back into the trash can. She left the bathroom and walked to the other bedroom. She opened the door with extreme caution while she checked for a trip wire and found none. She pushed the door open the rest of the way and entered.

Meanwhile, Cain finished disarming the booby-trap that was on the back door. He opened the back door, and Wheeler and King entered. "I don't think we missed anything, but be careful anyway," Cain warned Wheeler and King. "You never know what might still be in here."

"Where's Livingston?" King asked.

"She's upstairs," Cain answered.

"Guys, you need to see this," Everyone heard Livingston say over their earwig. "You're not going to believe this shit."

"What did you find?" Cain asked.

"Just bring your ass up here."

Cain hurried over to the stairs with Wheeler and King following close behind him. They hurried up the steps, with Cain leading the way.

When Cain reached the room where Livingston was waiting, he entered. He looked around the room and was stunned by what he saw. The walls in the room were papered with photos of Zamani's late wife and son, along with newspaper clippings about their accident. "Kate I want you to take pictures of everything," Cain instructed Livingston. "Don't miss anything."

Livingston took her digital camera from her purse and began to take pictures while Cain, along with Wheeler and King, looked through some papers that were on the desk in the corner of the room.

When she finished taking pictures of everything on the walls, she put her digital camera back into her purse. She started to walk over to the desk to join the others when her cell phone rang. She took her cell phone out of her purse and flipped it open before putting it to her ear. She listened for a few minutes and then flipped her cell phone shut, ending the call. "I think I know where Zamani is heading," she replied while she put her cell phone back into her purse. "He was seen this morning boarding the Iranian cargo vessel Al-Jasourah bound for Jask Iran. That explains the empty Dramamine box I found in the bathroom trash can."

"Are you sure?" Wheeler asked.

"Yes, I am," Livingston shot back.

"Sorry, I asked," Wheeler remarked.

"All right enough," Cain jumped in. "Wheeler, I want you and Livingston to head back to the safe house. King and I are going to hang here for a few minutes and try to locate the tunnel that Zamani used to elude our surveillance."

"You two be careful," Wheeler warned.

"We will," Cain assured Wheeler.

Wheeler and Livingston left the room. They hurried down the stairs and exited Zamani's townhouse through the back door. They walked back to Wheeler's vehicle, and Wheeler got in on the driver's side and closed the door. Livingston hurried around to the passenger's side and opened the door; she jumped in and closed her door. Wheeler put the key in the ignition. He started the vehicle, and they drove off.

King and Cain searched the rest of the room before going back downstairs. "What now?" King asked.

"We need to find that tunnel," Cain answered. "We might just find out where, he really went off to."

"I'll look in the kitchen while you look out here," King suggested.

"Be careful," Cain warned. "You never know what might be lying around."

King carefully made his way to the kitchen. He saw a laptop sitting on the kitchen table and walked into the kitchen. He took three steps and heard a loud click. He knew that he had stepped on a pressure plate to an explosive device. A split second later, the explosive device went off, killing King and Cain almost instantly and destroying the townhouse.

# Chapter 3

Gwadar, Pakistan
CIA Safe House

CIA operative Harry Wheeler parked his vehicle next to another vehicle in the driveway, in front of the safe house. He quickly got out of the vehicle and hurried inside; with CIA operative Kate Livingston, following close behind him. Wheeler and Livingston were met in the entryway by twenty-eight-year-old CIA operative Jacob Calhoun. "Thank God you're both all right," Calhoun said, excited to see that Wheeler and Livingston were unharmed.

"What the hell are you talking about?" Wheeler asked.

"You mean you don't know?"

"Know what?" Livingston inquired.

"The Zamani residence exploded a few minutes ago," Calhoun answered. "It's all over the local news."

*Oh my god,* Livingston thought as tears began to flow from her eyes, and run down her cheeks.

"Where's Cain and King?" Calhoun asked. "Aren't they with you?"

"They stayed behind to search for more clues as to where Zamani went off too," Wheeler sadly answered. "One of them must have triggered a booby trap that we didn't find."

"Oh my," was all Calhoun could say.

Wheeler and Livingston followed Calhoun into the living room and sat down. Wheeler and Livingston sat in silence while Calhoun went into the other room that was used as a radio room, so he could notify CIA headquarters in Langley Virginia of the news about Samuel

Cain and Robert King.

Livingston pulled herself together and looked at Wheeler. "What do we do now?"

"We find this son-of-a-bitch, and we put him down," Wheeler fired back.

"No, we don't," Calhoun, who had emerged from the radio room, said. "We've been ordered to close up shop here and return to London."

"So, we're just going to let Zamani get away?" Livingston curiously asked.

"Headquarters has a team already in place in Iran to hunt down Zamani," Calhoun pointed out. "Zamani isn't going to get away from us that easily."

"When do we leave for London?" Wheeler inquired.

"You and I are to leave immediately after the cleaners arrive to clean up the place," Calhoun answered. "Kate, after the cleaners finish up here you will call a cab and go to the airport. You can pick up your ticket at the British Airways ticket counter."

"I'm not going back to London with you and Wheeler?" Livingston curiously asked.

"Not this time love," Calhoun answered. "You'll find out your destination when you pick up your ticket." The doorbell rang, and Calhoun walked over to the door and opened it.

"Good day, sir," the man standing on the front step said. " Bluebird sent us here to clean up the bird cage."

"Please come in," Calhoun offered. "We have been expecting you."

The man entered and was followed by three other men who were pushing large laundry carts. They followed Calhoun into the radio room and began to pack up the equipment that was in the room. Wheeler and Livingston got up from their seats and went to their rooms, and began packing for their upcoming trip. A few seconds later, Calhoun hurried out of the radio room and into his room to pack up his personal items.

When Calhoun finished packing his things, he returned to the living room where Wheeler and Livingston were sitting. Wheeler grabbed his bag and jumped to his feet.

"We are to take separate cars to the pickup point," Calhoun pointed out to Wheeler. "It's best if you follow me."

"No problem," Wheeler acknowledged. He followed Calhoun outside and got into his car. He waited for Calhoun to leave before he backed out of the driveway and began to follow Calhoun.

When the cleaners finished packing up the radio room, they left. Kate Livingston took out her cell phone from her purse and called the local taxicab company. She gave them the address and then canceled the call. She returned her cell phone to her purse and paced back and forth until a taxicab pulled up out front and blew his horn. With her bag in hand, Livingston hurried outside to where the taxi was parked and placed her bag into the open trunk. The driver closed the trunk lid while Livingston got into the back of the cab.

The driver hurried around to the driver's side of the cab and got in behind the wheel. "Where to Miss?" He asked in English, with a strong Pakistani accent.

"International Airport," Livingston answered.

"Yes, Miss," the driver acknowledged, and he drove off, heading toward the airport.

When Livingston's taxi cab arrived at the airport the cab parked in front of the main entrance; she paid the driver and got out of the cab. The cab driver jumped out and hurried to the back of the cab; and opened the trunk. He removed Livingston's bag and handed it to her. He closed the trunk and walked to the driver's side of the cab while Livingston entered the airport. She walked over to the British Airways ticket counter and sat her bag down in the opening to check her bag.

"My name is Kate Livingston; I believe you're holding a ticket for me."

The ticket clerk looked at Livingston and smiled. "That we are," she cheerfully said. "Would you like for me to check your bag?"

"Yes, please do."

The clerk checked Livingston's bag and handed Livingston her ticket and a small brown envelope. Livingston looked at the ticket and shook her head. *What the hell am I going to do in Washington DC?* She thought. She looked at the clerk and asked, "What gate does this flight board at?"

"Gate A-17," the clerk replied. "You still have a couple of hours before they start boarding. You can wait in the Sky Lounge if you wish."

"Thanks; I think I'll do just that," Livingston commented while she put the small brown envelope and her ticket into her purse. She walked away from the ticket counter and headed for the Sky Lounge. She stopped a few feet from the security checkpoint and looked through her purse for her FBI credentials when her cell phone beeped, indicating that she had received an important text message.

She walked over to an empty bench and sat down. She took her cell phone from her purse and retrieved the text message.

> (Kate – danger – you need to get rid of the photos you took at the Zamani house before you go through the security checkpoint. My note enclosed in the small envelope will explain everything – M.)

Livingston erased the message from M on her cell phone and got up from the bench. She hurried into the Ladies room and entered the first stall; and closed the door. She fastened the lock and pulled out her digital camera from her purse. She flipped through the pictures on her cell phone and thought. *What is so damn important about these photos?*

She sat down on the toilet and pulled out her iPod and USB patch cord from her purse. She downloaded the photos from her digital camera to her iPod and then deleted the pictures from her camera. She then downloaded some pictures from her iPod that she took a few days earlier with her digital camera, replacing the ones that she had taken earlier at the Zamani house.

She removed the small brown envelope from her purse and opened it. She took out the piece of paper and read the message.

> (Kate – the explosion at the Zamani house was not caused by Cain or King missing something; they were both too good agents to miss a booby trap. Send the pictures to the e-mail address below. She'll know what to do with them when she gets the pictures. Destroy this letter when you're done – M.)

Livingston activated the Bluetooth on her iPod and connected it tothe Internet. She opened her e-mail program and typed in the e-mail address that was on the paper. She typed in a brief message and attached the pictures to the e-mail; and sent the message. She deleted the Zamani photos and the e-mail she had just sent from her iPad and put everything back into her purse.

She stood up and flung her purse over her shoulder. She dropped the letter into the toilet and watched it dissolve in the water before flushing the toilet. She unlocked the door and left the Ladies room.

Livingston walked over to the security checkpoint for VIPs and got in line. As she proceeded closer to the security checkpoint, she reached into her purse and removed her FBI credentials. When it was her turn to be processed through the security checkpoint, she handed her FBI credentials to the security guard.

The security guard looked at Livingston's credentials. He then motioned to the two ISI agents who were standing nearby, and the two men walked over to the security guard. The security guard handed Livingston's credentials to one of the men. "I believe this is the person you're looking for," the security guard said in Farsi.

"Miss, you need to come with us," the man instructed Livingston in perfect English. "We have a few questions for you," he continued to say as he showed Livingston his credentials.

"I've done nothing wrong," Livingston declared.

"Please come with us," the man insisted while he took Livingston's credentials from the guard. "This will only take a few minutes, and you'll be on your way."

Livingston gave in and followed the two ISI agents to an interrogation room. She sat down at the table while one of the men sat across from her, and the other closed the door. The man who sat across from Livingston stared at her while the other ISI agent stood behind her. Livingston kept her cool and stared back at the man.

"First off I must tell you that I know that you're with the American CIA, and not the FBI," the man began; speaking in perfect English.

"You're mistaken," Livingston fired back. "I have no ties with the CIA."

"I know the truth about you," the man insisted. "You can deny it all you want, but it won't do you any good. You're a spy operating here in Pakistan, and you got caught."

"I'm telling you; you're mistaken," Livingston fired back.

"I'll get right to the point," the man continued, ignoring what Livingston had said. "A woman fitting your description was seen leaving the residence of Yasin Abdul Zamani minutes before his house exploded," The man looked Livingston square in the eyes before he continued. "Tell me; why were you there?"

"Who the hell is this Yasin Abdul Zamani?" Livingston calmly answered. "I know no one by that name."

"Dump out her purse," the man said in Farsi to the other ISI agent. "Let's see what this bitch is hiding."

*These assholes don't know that I can understand everything they're saying;* Livingston thought. *I might be able to use this to my advantage.*

The ISI agent snatched Livingston's purse from her shoulder. A sharp pain shot down her arm. She sat at the table in pain while the ISI agent dumped the contents of her purse on the table.

"Hey, you can't do that," Livingston shouted. "I'm an American, and I demand to see a representative from my embassy."

"She wants to see a representative from the American embassy," the man sitting across from Livingston said in Farsi to the other man who was busy searching through her things. "I ought to put a bullet in her head and be done with this nonsense." Both men laughed at the same time.

*Oh my,* Livingston thought. *I don't like the sound of this.*

"Yeah, I know what you mean, but the boss wants her alive," the other man pointed out. He picked up Livingston's digital camera from the table and handed it to the other ISI agent.

"Did you take any photos while you were in the Zamani house?" the man asked in a harsh tone.

"I don't know anyone named Zamani," Livingston fired back. "The only pictures you'll find on my camera are some last minute photos I took of some historic sites before I came to the airport."

"Look what we have here," the other ISI agent commented in Farsi while he held up Livingston's iPad for his fellow agent to see. "I bet we find what we're looking for on one of these devices."

*Now M's message makes sense;* Livingston thought. *These assholes are looking for the photos I took at the Zamani house; but how do they know I had the photos?*

"Go right ahead," Livingston shot back. "I don't have what you're looking for."

The ISI agent looked at the pictures that were on Livingston's camera while his partner looked on her iPad. Both were discouraged when they didn't find what they were looking for. The ISI agent who was sitting across from Livingston got up from his seat. "Put everything back in her purse," he said to his partner in Farsi. "We'll sort through it later."

His partner gave him the thumbs up while he walked around where Livingston was sitting. He pulled her hand behind her back and placed handcuffs around her wrists while his partner threw Livingston's things back into her purse. "This isn't over yet," he whispered into Livingston's ear while he pulled her to her feet. He placed a burlap bag over her head and escorted her out of the room, with his partner following close behind him.

When they got to the ISI agent's car, he opened the trunk and held Livingston's body close to his. His partner handed him a hypodermic syringe filled with a strong sedative. He inserted the syringe at the base of Livingston's neck and pushed the plunger down, delivering the full dose of the sedative into Livingston's blood stream. Moments later, Livingston's body went limp in his arms. The two ISI agents carefully placed Livingston into the trunk and closed the trunk lid. They climbed into the car and drove off.

A few hours later, Kate Livingston opened her eyes. Unaware of her surroundings, she found herself lying on a cold hard surface. At first, her vision was blurry; all she could see was the shadow of someone sitting across from her. She sat up and blinked her eyes a few times, and her vision began to improve.

"Easy Kate," a familiar voice said.

"Wheeler, is that you?" Livingston asked. Seconds later, her vision returned to normal, and she saw Wheeler sitting on the bunk across from her.

"Yes, Kate, it's me; Calhoun and I were ambushed a few kilometers from our rendezvous point. We were gassed and ended up here."

"Where are we?"

"I don't know," Wheeler answered. "It looks like we're in some kind of holding area."

"Where's Calhoun?"

"He didn't make it," Wheeler sadly replied. "The sons-of-a-bitches killed him shortly after we got here. Kate, they're looking for those photos you took in that room in Zamani's townhouse."

"What's the big deal about the pictures I took at Zamani's townhouse?"

"Apparently, there was something in that room that they don't want anyone to know about, and you took a picture of it."

"I never left Zamani's townhouse with those pictures. I gave Cain the memory card before we left that room, and he put the memory card in his pocket." Livingston got up from her bunk and made her way to the entrance door to the cell. She turned to face Wheeler. "Whatever was on that memory card was lost in the explosion."

"I didn't see you hand Cain anything before we left."

"Well, I did," Livingston fired back. "If I remember correctly, the room was papered with photos of Zamani's late wife and son, along with newspaper clippings about their accident."

"There had to be something else in that room that you took pictures of," Wheeler pointed out. "We're not here, and Calhoun isn't dead, because of some newspaper clippings."

"Whatever it was; it was destroyed in the explosion." Livingston turned back to face the cell entrance when the door to the holding area opened, and the two ISI agents from the airport, along with two other men dressed in military uniforms entered. *Now, what?* She thought.

"These are the two Americans we told you about," one of the ISI agents said in Farsi.

The men looked at the ISI agents and nodded. "We will take it from here," one of the men said in Farsi. "You may return to your duties."

The two ISI agents left the room. A few minutes later, six men, dressed in Pakistani military uniforms and armed with the Pakistani-made Heckler & Koch G3-A3 assault rifle, entered the room. One of the soldiers was carrying two hoods and two sets of shackles.

The soldiers walked over to the holding cell and stopped a few feet from the door. They readied their G3-A3 assault rifles, except for the soldier who was carrying the two hoods and two sets of shackles, and pointed their weapons at the holding cell.

Wheeler jumped to his feet and stood next to Livingston. "I don't like this Kate," Wheeler whispered in Livingston's ear.

"Back away from the door and get on your knees," the soldier who was carrying the two hoods and two sets of shackles ordered, speaking in almost perfect English. "You make one wrong move, and it will be your last."

Wheeler and Livingston dropped to their knees as instructed while one of the soldiers opened the cell. The soldier entered the cell with his G3-A3 assault rifle trained at Wheeler and Livingston. The soldier who was carrying the two hoods and two sets of shackles followed.

"Stand up," the soldier who was carrying the two hoods and two sets of shackles ordered.

Wheeler and Livingston complied with the soldier's request and stood up. The soldier put a belt around their midsection and secured it tightly. They remained still while he placed the shackles on their feet, and secured their hands to the metal ring that was on the front of the belt. He then put a black color hood over each of their heads.

The soldiers escorted Wheeler and Livingston out of the holding cell area and to a windowless van that was waiting outside. Once Wheeler and Livingston were secured in their seats, a soldier closed the sliding door, and the van drove off.

* * * * *

Strike Force Delta Command
Tinker Air Force Base
Oklahoma City, Oklahoma

Colonel Wilson sat at his desk going over some intelligence reports that had come in while he was in Washington. His personal assistant, Second Lieutenant Samantha Cooltrain, nicked named Giggles, entered the office carrying two folders in her hand. "Good morning Wolverine," she cheerfully said.

"Good morning Giggles," Colonel Wilson commented.

"I have those files on Thomas Flowers and Pamela Wells from Homeland Security that you requested," Lieutenant Cooltrain continued while she walked over to Colonel Wilson's desk and put the folders that she was carrying down on his desk. "Is there anything else you need?"

"No, not at this time."

"Very well," Lieutenant Cooltrain acknowledged and headed toward the exit.

"You can leave the door open," Colonel Wilson said and returned to what he was doing before Lieutenant Cooltrain had interrupted him while Lieutenant Cooltrain left his office, leaving the door open.

When he finished going over the intelligence reports that had come in while he was in Washington, he turned his attention to the folders that Lieutenant Cooltrain had left for him. He opened the folder on Thomas Flowers and began to read through the folder's contents. *Very interesting;* he thought while he put everything back into the folder. He closed the folder and opened the other folder on Pamela Wells. He scanned through its contents, and when he was finished, he put both folders in the bottom right side drawer of his desk.

"Now why were the two of you following Deputy Director Hicks?" he mumbled while he turned on his computer. He opened his e-mail program and discovered that he had a new message waiting to be read from an unknown sender. He opened the message and saw that it was from Deputy Director Hicks. He quickly read the message and then moved it to his private in-box that only he could access. "This woman is a pain in my ass," he said out loud.

"Who's a pain in the ass?" Captain Hale asked who was standing in the office doorway.

"CIA Deputy Director Hicks."

"Oh; you mean you got the She-Devil ragging your ass?" Captain Hale asked while he entered Colonel Wilson's office.

"That woman is worse than an ingrown hair on my ass."

"You got that shit right," Captain Hale commented. "I hear that she's a hand full."

"Yeah, and the bitch of it all is that President Elliot wants me to work with her on getting him some answers on the situation brewing in Iran."

"You're going to have your hands full working with that woman," Captain Hale pointed out while he closed the door. He walked over to the chair that was in front of Colonel Wilson's desk and sat down.

"Maybe, but I have a bigger problem to deal with."

"And what might that be?" Captain Hale inquired.

"I think someone is following Deputy Director Hicks."

"How can you be certain that she's being followed?"

"She came to see me at the hotel's lounge, and I spotted a man and a woman following her."

Captain Hale smiled. "Any idea who they were?"

"When we left the lounge and headed back to my room. They followed us into the elevator. I confronted them, and they claimed to be Thomas Flowers and Pamela Wells from Homeland Security."

"Why the hell would Homeland be following Deputy Director Hicks?"

"That's what I need to find out."

"So what did you and the She-Devil do in your room?" Captain Hale curiously asked.

"It was all business," Colonel Wilson fired back. "Get your fuckin' head out of the gutter, Bulldog. There's no way I'd ever think about nailing that ass."

"If you say so," Captain Hale calmly said. "I believe you."

Colonel Wilson shot Captain Hale a nasty look. "Yes, I say so." He waited a few seconds before he continued, "Without shaking up the Hornets' nest, I need you to try to find out why Homeland is following Deputy Director Hicks."

"I'll get right on it," Captain Hale said while he got up from his seat. "You know; I was only kidding you about you and Deputy Director Hicks."

"I know, but shit like that is how rumors get started. I don't need that kind of a headache. You can leave the door open on your way out."

Captain Hale left Colonel Wilson's office. *Wilson and Hicks fucking;* he thought, *No fucking way.* He shook his head and then laughed as he continued on his way.

# Chapter 4

Washington, D.C.
The White House
0730 Hours Local Time

President Elliot sat behind his desk in the Oval Office reading over the recent intelligence reports that he had received from the CIA and NSA about the construction of a top-secret research facility, a few kilometers outside of Iranshahr, Iran. He looked through the satellite photographs carefully, paying attention to every detail.

The satellite photographs showed clearly that the research facility consisted of several concrete steel-reinforced bunkers. A twelve foot electrified fence surrounded the entire facility with razor ribbon wire attached to the top. High-powered halogen lights were strategically placed on top of the fence, and on telephone poles inside the facility.

Iranian Zulfiqar-3 tanks, along with ground forces were strategically deployed around the outside perimeter; ready to repel any ground assault mounted against the facility. For added security, several Raad Air Defense Systems were deployed nearby to provide air defense in case of an aerial attack on the facility.

President Elliot read the note that was attached to each of the satellite photographs. According to British Intelligence MI-6 division, security at the main gate to the facility was extremely tight. Six Iranian soldiers dressed in full combat dress, and armed with the Khaybar/KH-2002 Iranian assault rifles stood guard at the main gate at all times. Access was restricted to research personnel and certain military vehicles. Special identification papers had to be presented at the main gate before entry was allowed. All vehicles were searched before entering and leaving the facility. At the end of each shift, all research personnel were searched before they were allowed to exit the facility.

When President Elliot finished going over the intelligence reports, he put everything back into its perspective folders. "Enter," He said when there was a knock on the side door of the Oval Office.

The door opened, and White House Chief of Staff, Howard Gordon, entered. "I apologize for the intrusion Mr. President, but Director Müller and Director Parkinson are in the Situation Room waiting for you, sir."

"Very well," President Elliot acknowledged while he got up from his seat from behind his desk. He picked up the folders from his desk that contained the intelligence reports, and then he followed Gordon out of the Oval Office.

Howard Gordon closed the door to the Oval Office and walked back toward his office while President Elliot walked toward the Situation Room. When President Elliot reached the entrance to the Situation Room the Marine, who was standing there dressed in his dress uniform and armed with a nine-millimeter Beretta M9-A1 side arm, snapped to attention and saluted President Elliot.

"As you were Marine," President Elliot said and then entered the Situation Room.

CIA Director Robert Müller and NSA Director Jack Parkinson immediately jumped to their feet. President Elliot walked over to the table and sat down in the seat at the head of the table while the Marine guard closed the double-doors and returned to his post.

"Have a seat, gentlemen," President Elliot commented and waited until Director Müller, and Director Parkinson returned to their seats. "I know that you both have a lot to do, so I'll get right to the point. I have gone over the reports that the two of you sent me. I must say that I have a lot of questions about this new research facility in Iranshahr, Iran." He laid the folders down on the table in front of him. "We need to know what this new research facility in Iranshahr is researching, and why it's so heavily guarded."

"Mr. President, I have no real assets in the area," Director Müller was quick to point out. "Getting information out of Iran has become difficult over the past few years."

"Sir, all we have to go on is our satellite surveillance of the area," Director Parkinson added.

"Enough with the excuses," President Elliot fired back. "Israel claims that Mossad has proof that this research facility is more than what meets the eye."

"Mr. President, the Israelis will say anything to get what they want," Director Müller pointed out. "I wouldn't put too much faith in what the Israeli Mossad has to say."

"Regardless of what the Israelis say, I need answers," President Elliot snapped back.

"Mr. President, our only option at this time would be to send in a surveillance drone; we might get a better idea about what's going on there." Director Parkinson was quick to point out.

"Sending a drone into Iran could make the situation worse," Director Müller was quick to point out. "The Iranians might not take too kindly to us invading their airspace."

"It's safer than sending in a surveillance team," Director Parkinson fired back.

President Elliot pounded his fist on the table. "Enough of this bickering. I don't care what you have to do, but get me some answers, and fast. The clock is ticking on this one gentleman." President Elliot picked up the intelligence reports from the table in front of him and got up from his seat.

"Yes, Mr. President," Director Müller acknowledged while he and Director Parkinson jumped to their feet. "We'll get right on it, sir."

President Elliot walked over to the double-doors and opened one of them. He exited the Situation Room. The Marine standing outside snapped to attention. Without saying a word, President Elliot walked back to the Oval Office and entered through the side door.

He laid the intelligence reports down on his desk and sat down. He opened the center drawer to his desk and put the folders in the drawer. He closed the drawer and then removed the key from his pants pocket. He locked the drawer and returned the key to his pants pocket.

President Elliot was startled when there was a knock on the door. The door opened, and his personal secretary, Mrs. Wyatt, entered. "Good morning, Mr. President," she said while she closed the door and walked over to the president's desk.

"Yes, it is for some," he commented.

Mrs. Wyatt looked at the president confused. "Are we having a bad day, sir?"

He smiled at Mrs. Wyatt. "Has Israeli Ambassador Shamir arrived yet?"

"Yes, he has Mr. President. He's waiting outside."

"Good, you can show him in."

"Yes, Mr. President," Mrs. Wyatt said and walked over to the door. She opened the door and stood in the doorway. "Mr. Ambassador, the president, will see you now."

Ambassador Shamir entered the Oval Office with his briefcase in hand, and President Elliot got up from his seat. He walked over to greet the Ambassador while Mrs. Wyatt closed the door.

"Mr. Ambassador, it's nice to see you again," President Elliot said while they shook hands. "Please, have a seat." He continued to say, motioning to one of the sofas in the middle of the room.

"I appreciate you taking the time to see me Mr. President," Ambassador Shamir commented while he sat on the sofa, and President Elliot sat on the other sofa across from him. "I must say Mr. President that I was surprised when I was brought to your office," the ambassador continued. "I've never met any president here in the Oval Office before today."

"I find it more comfortable here in the Oval Office than in the Diplomatic Room," President Elliot pointed out.

"Mr. President, I know that you're a busy man, so I'll get right to the point," Ambassador Shamir began while he placed his briefcase on his lap and opened it. He took out a folder and closed his briefcase. He placed the briefcase on the floor next to his feet and then handed the folder to President Elliot before he continued. "Prime Minister Pelossof wanted me to give this to you. He said to tell you that when you go through this material, you will see that based on Mossad's latest report. Iran is producing weapons-grade uranium-two-thirty-five at their top-secret research facility, a few kilometers outside of Iranshahr. It is also believed that Iran has acquired the technology to manufacture nuclear weapons and that they are doing so at this top-secret facility."

"Are you sure about this?" President Elliot asked, shocked by what he had just heard. "I've heard nothing about Iran producing weapons-grade uranium-two-thirty-five or nuclear weapons at their facility outside of Iranshahr."

"Yes, we are sure, Mr. President."

"If that's the case, then why haven't you shared this information with the CIA?"

"The CIA was notified about this last week. I'm surprised that you have not heard about this." Ambassador Shamir paused before he continued. "Mr. President, Prime Minister Pelossof wanted me to reiterate his position on this Iranian matter. Israel will not allow Iran to possess nuclear weapons. If the United States does not do something about this, then Israel will."

"Surely you're not saying what I think you're saying?"

"Mr. President, Iran has been stonewalling everyone. We are running out of options. Prime Minister Pelossof has declared that Israel will protect itself against any kind of aggression regardless of the consequences."

"Tell Prime Minister Pelossof that I look forward to talking to him some more about this when we meet at the NATO summit in Brussels in a couple of days."

"Prime Minister Pelossof will not be attending the NATO summit in Brussels. Minister of defense Begin will be attending in his place."

"I see; then please notify the Prime Minister that I'm asking him to give me some time to look into this. Keep in mind that Israel won't be the only one that will suffer if you go to war with Iran."

"I will inform Prime Minister Pelossof of your request," Ambassador Shamir commented while he got up from the sofa.

President Elliot stood up and shook hands with Ambassador Shamir and then walked over to his desk while Ambassador Shamir left the Oval Office and closed the door. He laid the folder down on his desk and sat down.

He opened the folder and carefully looked through its contents. When he was finished, he closed the folder and picked up the telephone receiver from the telephone on his desk. He put the telephone receiver to his ear while he dialed the extension number to Vice President Conrad's office; after a few rings, Vice President Conrad answered.

"Jim, can you step into my office for a minute?"

"Yes, Mr. President. I'm on my way."

President Elliot returned the telephone receiver to the telephone on his desk. A few minutes later Vice President Conrad entered the Oval Office.

"Pull up a chair Jim," President Elliot said, motioning to the chair next to his desk.

Vice President Conrad grabbed the chair next to President Elliot's desk. He placed the chair in front of the desk and sat down. "What's up?"

"I have something that you need to take a look at," President Elliot answered and handed Vice President Conrad the folder that Israeli Ambassador Shamir had given him a few minutes earlier. "You're not going to believe this shit."

Vice President Conrad opened the folder and looked through the contents. When he was finished, he handed the folder back to President Elliot. "Is any of that true?" He asked.

"That's what we need to find out," President Elliot answered while he placed the folder down on the desk in front of him. "I talked to Director Müller, and Director Parkinson earlier, and they mentioned nothing about this."

"That's strange," Vice President Conrad remarked.

"I think Director Müller and Director Parkinson know more than what they're telling me," President Elliot pointed out. "I get the impression that they don't want me to know anything about this."

"Mr. President, I'm sure Director Müller and Director Parkinson have a good reason for not mentioning this to you. After all, the Israelis have been wrong about their intelligence before," Vice President Conrad pointed out. "They might have wanted more proof before mentioning this to you."

"Even a hint that Iran is manufacturing nuclear weapons should have been brought to my attention," President Elliot fired back. "I want you to follow up on this while I'm attending the NATO summit in Brussels. I want some answers when I get back."

"I'll get right on it, Mr. President," Vice President Conrad said while he got up from his seat. "I'll have it taken care of before you get back from the NATO summit," he continued to say while putting the chair back where it belonged. "You have a safe trip sir, and I'll see you when you get back."

"Thanks, Jim."

Vice President Conrad left the Oval Office and closed the door on his way out. President Elliot removed the key from his pants pocket and unlocked the center drawer to his desk. He picked up the folder that Israeli Ambassador Shamir had given him earlier and put the folder on top of the folders that he had gotten earlier from Director Müller and Director Parkinson, and closed the drawer. He then locked the drawer and returned the key to his pants pocket.

He pushed the intercom button on the telephone on his desk. "Mrs. Wyatt, please have the Secret Service bring my car around; I'm going out for a while."

"Yes, Mr. President," Mrs. Wyatt acknowledged. "Shall I tell them your destination sir?"

"Just tell them I'll be there in about five minutes." President Elliot shot back and then he pushed the intercom button to end the intercom call.

President Elliot got up from his seat and left the Oval Office through the side entrance. He walked down the hallway toward where his car was waiting with two Secret Service men following.

$$* * * * *$$

The Pentagon
General Thomas Richwood's Office

General Richwood sat at his desk drinking a cup of coffee when there was a knock on the office door, and the door opened. His assistant, thirty-three-year-old Major Emily Harris, entered the office carrying a cup of coffee in one hand, and some papers in the other. "I brought you another cup just in case you wanted it, sir," Major Harris remarked while she closed the door and then walked over to the general's desk.

The general smiled and took the cup of coffee from Major Harris. "I sure can use another cup," He remarked while he threw his empty cup into the waste paper basket next to his desk. He took a sip from the cup that Major Harris had brought him and then sat it down on his desk. "Are those papers for me?" The general asked, referring to the papers that Major Harris was holding in her hand.

"It's a list of supplies that Strike Force needs," She cheerfully answered and handed the list to General Richwood. "I need your signature of approval before I can process it."

General Richwood glanced over the list before he signed it and handed it back to Major Harris. "Is there anything else?"

"No, sir, not at the moment."

Before General Richwood could say another word his office door opened, and President Martin Elliot entered. General Richwood jumped up from his seat, and he and Major Harris snapped to attention and saluted the president.

President Elliot smiled and walked over to the general's desk and sat down in the chair that was in front of it. "Please general have a seat."

"Yes, Mr. President," General Richwood acknowledged and sat back down in his chair while Major Harris left the office and closed the door.

"General, I need your help."

General Richwood looked at President Elliot confused. "Mr. President, I'd be glad to help any way I can."

"Earlier today I met with Israeli Ambassador Shamir," President Elliot began. "The Israelis claim that Mossad has uncovered information that Iran has acquired the technology to produce nuclear weapons, and that they are doing so in secret."

"If that's true, that would upset the balance of power in the Middle East," General Richwood was quick to point out. "It could turn out to be a bad situation for everyone. Especially, if al-Qaeda gets their hands on this technology."

"So you've heard nothing about this?" President Elliot calmly asked.

"Mr. President, if Colonel Wilson and his people had found out about something like this we would have both heard about it by now. Sir, what's the CIA and NSA say about this?"

"I met with Director Müller, and Director Parkinson earlier to discuss the top-secret research facility the Iranians built a few kilometers outside of Iranshahr. They never mentioned anything about

Iran having the technology to produce nuclear weapons," President Elliot replied. "Could the Israeli Mossad be wrong on this one?"

"That's a possibility," General Richwood answered.

"General, I need answers," President Elliot fired back. "It seems that no one is certain what is going on at this facility. I would like Colonel Wilson and his people to look into this and see what they can find out."

"I'll have them look into this immediately," General Richwood assured President Elliot.

"General, we need to keep this between us," President Elliot said, and then he stood up. "Let me know the minute you have something."

General Richwood jumped to his feet. "Yes, Sir, Mr. President I will."

President Elliot walked over to the door and opened it, and left General Richwood's office. One of the Secret Service agents who was standing outside of the office closed the door.

General Richwood returned to his seat and picked up the telephone receiver from the telephone on his desk. He dialed the number for Colonel Wilson at Strike Force Delta Command while he put the telephone receiver to his ear.

Colonel Wilson was sitting behind his desk in his office going over the new duty roster when the telephone on his desk rang. He picked up the telephone receiver from the telephone on his desk and put it to his ear, "Wilson here."

"Wilson, I'm sending you a top-priority message," General Richwood began. "I want you to handle this one very carefully. This comes directly from the top."

"What's our time frame on this one, sir?"

"I need answers A-sap."

"I understand, sir."

"Wilson this one could turn out to be a powder keg so keep your eyes open at all times."

"Affirmative, sir..." Colonel Wilson abruptly stopped talking when he realized that General Rich-wood had hung up the telephone on his end.

He returned the telephone receiver to the telephone on his desk just as thirty-two-year-old Captain Nathan Hale, nicknamed Bulldog, and second in command of Strike Force Delta, entered his office carrying a brown folder.

"I have the readiness reports that you asked for," Captain Hale said while he closed the office door. He walked over to the Colonel's desk and sat down in the chair in front of the desk before he handed Colonel Wilson the folder. "Is there something going on?"

"Not that I know of," Colonel Wilson answered. "I just want to make sure that we're prepared in case something does come up." Colonel Wilson pointed out while he opened the folder and looked through its contents. When he was finished, he closed the folder. "I like what I see. Looks like we're in good shape and ready in case we're called upon."

Without any warning, Second Lieutenant Samantha Cooltrain, nicknamed Giggles, entered the office carrying a piece of paper in her hand and hurried over to Colonel Wilson's desk. "Wolverine, I have a message from GS one-O-three in London," she said while she handed the paper to Colonel Wilson. "It's top-priority, your eyes only."

"Who the hell is GS one-O-three?" Captain Hale curiously asked.

"Thanks, Giggles," Colonel Wilson commented.

"Is there anything else?" Lieutenant Cooltrain inquired.

"Yes, there is," Colonel Wilson answered. "I'm expecting a top-priority message from General Richwood. I want you to bring it to me the moment it comes in." Colonel Wilson paused for a brief moment before he continued. "Please close the door on your way out."

"I'll bring it to you the moment it arrives," Lieutenant Cooltrain assured Colonel Wilson.

Colonel Wilson remained silent and waited until Lieutenant Cooltrain left the office and closed the door before he answered Captain Hale's question. "GS one-O-three is my contact in the CIA field office, in London. He's been feeding me information on the movements of known terrorist in Pakistan for the past few months."

"I never knew that you had a contact at the CIA field office in London," Captain Hale commented.

Colonel Wilson looked at Captain Hale, smiled, and then read the message from GS one-O-three. "Well, this is interesting," He remarked.

"What's up?" Captain Hale asked.

"Zamani has disappeared from his home in Gwadar, Pakistan two days ago," Colonel Wilson answered. "CIA operatives entered Zamani's residence when he failed to go to work. Two hours later, Zamani's residence exploded, killing both operatives who were inside at the time. The London field office believes that he might have boarded an Iranian cargo vessel Al-Jasourah that was bound for Jask, Iran."

"So, they're not sure where Zamani went off to are they?" Captain Hale inquired.

"No, they're not," Colonel Wilson answered.

Without warning, the office door opened, and Lieutenant Cooltrain entered carrying a piece of paper in her hand. She walked over to Colonel Wilson's desk. "Wolverine, I have the message you were expecting from General Richwood," she said while she handed the message to Colonel Wilson.

"Thanks, Giggles; that'll be all for now," Colonel Wilson commented. He read the message from General Richwood while Lieutenant Cooltrain left the office and closed the door. "It seems that Iran has constructed a top-secret research facility a few kilometers outside of Iranshahr, Iran," Colonel Wilson began. "Both the CIA and the NSA have no idea what's being researched at this new facility. All that is known for sure is that this facility is heavily fortified against an air or ground assault."

"Do you think it has anything to do with why Zamani is supposedly heading to Iran?" Captain Hale asked.

"That's what we need to find out," Colonel Wilson answered. "We need to get to the bottom of this shit before it blows up in our faces, and we find ourselves in the middle of a shooting war. The president has asked us to get him some answers so put as many people as you need on this one. We need to find out what's going on at this facility and if Zamani is there, and if so, why."

"I'll get right on it," Captain Hale said while he got up out of his seat. He left Colonel Wilson's office and closed the door.

Colonel Wilson removed his cell phone from his shirt pocket and dialed a number, and then put the cell phone to his ear. After a few rings, a man answered. "We need to talk," Colonel Wilson said. "Meet me in our usual place in one hour."

Before the man on the other end could say a word, Colonel Wilson pushed the end call button on his cell phone. He turned off his cell phone and returned it to his shirt pocket. He got up from his seat and hurried out of his office.

Colonel Wilson left the building and walked to the Humvee that was parked at the curb. He jumped in behind the wheel and started it up, and drove off. He left the Strike Force facility and drove to the parking lot near the main gate to the base where his black colored Cadillac Escalade was parked. He parked the Humvee next to the Escalade and got out. He got into the Escalade on the driver's side, started it up, and drove off.

He drove out of the main gate and headed toward the Oklahoma City airport. When he arrived at the airport, he pulled into the long-term parking area and parked next to a vehicle where a man was standing. The man opened the front passenger door and climbed into Colonel Wilson's Escalade and closed the door. "This better be important," the man said.

"Oh, it is," Colonel Wilson assured him. "We believe that Zamani is in Iran and that he's overseeing Iran's uranium-enrichment program to produce weapons-grade uranium-two-thirty-five. We believe that Iran is close to having a working bomb which might put a nuke in al-Qaeda's hands."

"I was afraid of that," the man commented. "What do you need me to do for you this time?"

"I need to know why our intelligence agencies are telling the president that Iran doesn't have the technology to build a nuke," Colonel Wilson answered. "I need to know if Iran is close to having a nuke, and I need to know A-sap before Israel does something stupid."

"You know you could be wrong about Zamani's whereabouts," the man pointed out.

"What if I'm not wrong?" Colonel Wilson shot back.

"I see your point; give me twenty-four hours, and I'll see what I can come up with," the man said while he opened the car door. "Call me around this time tomorrow. I should have some answers by then."

The man got out of Colonel Wilson's Escalade and closed the door. He waited until Colonel Wilson backed out of his parking space and drove off before he got back into his vehicle.

Colonel Wilson drove back to Tinker Air Force Base and stopped at the main gate. He showed the guard his credentials and was allowed to continue. He drove to the parking lot and parked next to the Humvee. He got out of his Escalade and got in the Humvee on the driver's side. He took his cell phone out of his pocket and turned it on before he started up the Humvee, and headed back to the Strike Force facility.

When Colonel Wilson arrived at the main gate to the Strike Force facility, he showed his identification badge to the guard and was allowed to proceed. He parked the Humvee in front of the main building and got out. He entered the building and hurried to his office. He walked over to his desk and sat down in his chair. He looked at the crisis board on the wall across from him that was used to track terrorist activities, and to identify possible hot spots worldwide. He noticed that while he was gone, Iran had been marked a hot spot, and a point of interest.

"I've been looking all over for you," Captain Hale, who was standing in the doorway, said. "I tried to call you, but all I got was your voicemail."

"I had to step out for a few minutes," Colonel Wilson answered. "Do you have anything new on that facility Iran built a few kilometers outside of Iranshahr?"

"As per your directive I had our Looking-glass' (satellite) re-tasked so they would spend more time over the facility near Iranshahr," Captain Hale answered while he entered the office, and closed the door. He walked over to Colonel Wilson's desk and picked up the controller for the wall size plasma screen that was located on the wall behind Colonel Wilson's desk. "I had the Looking-glass (satellite) photos loaded onto the plasma screen," he continued and then pushed the button on the controller to display the first satellite photo onto the plasma screen.

Colonel Wilson stood up and turned to face the plasma screen. With his back to Captain Hale, he stared at the photo. He stepped closer to the plasma screen; he touched a section of the screen and the area where he touched enlarged, displaying a larger view of the facility. "That's an awful lot of firepower around that facility," he pointed out. "That's got to be more than a research facility. Colonel Wilson turned

*49*

to look at Captain Hale; "What's the CIA or NSA say about this?"

"They're not saying anything," Captain Hale replied. "If they know something, and I'm sure that they do, they're not telling anyone."

"Or, they're not sure what's going on there," Colonel Wilson was quick to point out, and then he turned back to face the plasma screen. "What else do you have for me to look at?"

"The rest of the photos from the first Looking-glass (satellite) didn't show much more than this one does," Captain Hale answered. "However," he continued as he pushed the next button on the controller, and the next photo appeared. "When the second Looking-glass (satellite) passed over the area a few mikes (minutes) later using its inferred ground-penetrating radar, we got an excellent picture of what's beneath that facility."

Colonel Wilson studied the picture for a few minutes. "So they're working on something underground," he commented.

"Yeah, but what, is the magical question?"

"You can bet that whatever they're working on, it's not good for us," Colonel Wilson said while he examined the photo more closely. "What does the CIA have to say about this underground network?"

"According to the most recent reports the CIA mentioned nothing about anything being under the surface," Captain Hale answered. "I took the liberty of tapping into their Looking-glass (satellite) when it passed over the area and found that their Looking-glass (satellite) picked up everything ours did. However, the CIA and NSA directors didn't report it to the president this morning when they briefed him on the Iranian situation."

"That's odd?" Colonel Wilson remarked as he turned around to face Captain Hale. "I want you to stay on this, and keep digging. Check with our outside sources and see what they have on this. We got to find out what they're doing there."

Captain Hale placed the controller for the wall size plasma screen on the desk. "I'll get some people on it right away."

"Good; let me know the minute you come up with some answers," Colonel Wilson instructed Captain Hale. "We got to get ahead of this before it bites us on the ass."

Colonel Wilson picked up the controller for the plasma screen from his desk while Captain Hale left the office and closed the door.

He pushed the power button on the controller and turned off the plasma screen. He sat down behind his desk and put the controller to the plasma screen in the center drawer. He logged onto his computer and began working on his daily intelligence report.

# Chapter 5

CIA Headquarters
Langley, Virginia

CIA Deputy Director Hicks sat at her desk in her office finishing up some important last minute paperwork when there was a knock on her office door. Seconds later the door opened, and her personal assistant, twenty-five-year-old Carla Garcia, entered the office carrying a thumb-drive in her hand. "I apologize for the intrusion," She said while she closed the office door.

Deputy Director Hicks could tell by the look on Garcia's face that something was bothering her. "Carla, what's wrong?"

"I have something you need to see," She answered as she walked over to Deputy Director Hick's desk. "I was on my way out when I got an important e-mail came in addressed to you," she continued while she walked over to the chair that was in front of the desk and sat down. "I downloaded it to this thumb-drive for you," she concluded while she offered the thumb-drive to Deputy Director Hicks.

Deputy Director Hicks took the thumb-drive from Garcia and plugged it into her computer. "Did you read any of this?" She asked while she waited for the file on the thumb-drive to open.

"I read enough to wish that I hadn't read any of it." Garcia sadly replied.

When the thumb-drive finished loading into the computer, the cover note opened. Deputy Director Hicks was stunned by its content.

(I took these pictures at Yasin Abdul Zamani's

townhouse a few hours before it exploded.

I was instructed by M to send these to you – Kate Livingston.)

Deputy Director Hicks opened the rest of the file. She scanned through the photographs in the file, examining each one with a watchful eye, paying close attention to every detail in each of the photographs on the thumb-drive. When she had finished examining the pictures, she sat at her desk in silence. After a few seconds of silence, she looked at Garcia. "Who else knows about this file?"

"Just you," Garcia answered. "I've told no one else about this."

"Good; let's keep it that way," Deputy Director Hicks instructed Garcia. "I'll look into this, but for now, I want you to go back to your desk and delete everything about this from your computer. Do you understand?"

"Yes, I understand," Garcia said as she got up from her seat. "Good night Deputy Director," she concluded, and then she walked over to the office door and opened it, and left the office, closing the door behind her.

Carla Garcia hurried back to her office and sat down behind her desk, and logged onto her computer. *What's so damn important about these photographs?* She asked herself while she opened her e-mail program, and then opened the file that Kate Livingston had sent her. She carefully scanned through the photographs one by one, paying close attention to every detail. *Oh my god,* she thought when she was done. *Kate, what have you stumbled into?*

She opened a new message template and typed the e-mail address for Colonel Wilson, commander of Strike Force Delta, in the addressee part of the message, and then attached each photograph as a file attachment. She wrote a quick note in the message area and then pressed the send button.

Garcia waited for confirmation that the message was sent before she deleted the message she had just sent to Colonel Wilson, and then she deleted the message from Kate Livingston, along with the photographs. Afterwards, she closed her e-mail program and logged off her computer. She opened the bottom right drawer of her desk and retrieved her purse. She closed the drawer while she got up from her seat. She left the office, locking the door on her way out.

She walked to the elevator and pushed the call button. A few minutes later, the elevator door opened, and she stepped inside. She pushed the button for the secured parking lot that was located in the basement. The elevator door closed, and the elevator began to move downward.

When the elevator stopped, the door opened, and Garcia exited the elevator. She walked to her car, a Cherry red Ford Mustang while she removed her car keys from her purse. She unlocked the door on the driver's side and opened the door. She got in behind the wheel and a few seconds later, she drove off.

Forty-five minutes later Carla Garcia pulled her Ford Mustang into the driveway in front of her two-story brick house. She got out of her car and walked to the front door. She unlocked the door with her key and opened the door, and went inside.

She closed the door and turned on the light in the entryway. She returned her keys to her purse and put her purse on the table by the front door. She kicked off her shoes and walked to the kitchen. When she turned on the light in the kitchen, she found a woman sitting at the kitchen table. Without saying a word, Garcia took a couple of steps backward, and someone grabbed her from behind. She struggled to free herself, but failed. "Who the hell are you?" She shouted. "What are you doing in my house?"

"Relax Carla," the woman at the table said while she pulled out her credentials from her inside jacket pocket. "I'm Pamela Wells, and the man behind you is Thomas Flowers, Homeland Security. We're here to ask you a few questions, so have a seat."

Thomas Flowers released his hold on Garcia. "Questions about what?" Garcia calmly asked while she walked over to the table and sat down across from Wells. "You know I can't talk about my work."

Wells revealed her Glock-19 with a silencer attached that she had hidden under the table. She pointed the Glock-19 at Garcia while Thomas Flowers walked over to the table and stood next to Garcia. "Put your arms on the arms of the chair," Wells demanded.

"Is this really necessary?" Garcia asked while she placed her arms on the arms of the chair as instructed.

"Yes, it is," Flowers answered while he zipped tied each of

Garcia's arms to the chair arms.

Wells placed her Glock-19 on the table in front of her. "Now tell me what did you do with the pictures that Kate Livingston sent to you?"

"I don't know any Kate Livingston," Garcia answered. "I know nothing about any pictures."

"Don't insult my intelligence," Wells shot back. "I know Kate sent you some pictures."

"You're wrong; I received no pictures from anyone."

Wells signaled Flowers; he placed a plastic bag over Garcia's head and held it tightly. After a few long seconds, Flowers removed the plastic bag, and Garcia gasped uncontrollably for fresh air.

"Why are you doing this?" Garcia screamed. "I don't have the answers you're looking for."

"I believe you do," Wells fired back. "Tell me what I want to know, and we'll leave."

"I don't know anything about any pictures," Garcia said as tears began to form in her eyes. "Who are you people?"

"I told you; we're from Homeland Security," Wells calmly replied. "Now, tell me..."

"There's no way you're from Homeland Security," Garcia interrupted. "Who the hell are you?"

"Just..." Wells stopped talking when her cell phone began to ring. She took out her cell phone from her jacket pocket and answered the call. She listened for a few minutes before she canceled the call and returned her cell phone to her jacket pocket. "So you sent Kate Livingston's pictures to Colonel Wilson at Strike Force."

"I didn't send Wilson anything," Garcia was quick to answer.

"The computer log at Langley says you did," Wells fired back. "Stop lying to me."

"I'm not lying to you."

"Did you tell your boss about any of this?" Wells pressed on. "Has Hicks seen Livingston's pictures?"

"As far as I know, Deputy Director Hicks knows nothing about any pictures."

"It's time to put an end to this," Wells commented.

Flowers placed the plastic bag over Garcia's head; only this time, he held the bag tightly around her head. Garcia frantically struggled for air while she tried to free herself, but failed. Seconds later her body went limp, and twenty-five-year-old Carla Garcia was dead.

"Lying bitch," Wells said as she got up from her seat at the table. She stared at the lifeless body of Carla Garcia for a few moments and then picked up the Glock-19 from the table. She removed the silencer and returned the Glock to her shoulder holster, and she put the silencer in her jacket pocket. "Let's get out of here."

Flowers removed the zip ties that bound Garcia to the chair and the plastic bag from around her head. He put them in his jacket pocket and followed Wells out of the house. They walked down the street where their car was parked, and Flowers got in on the driver's side while Wells got in on the passenger's side. He pulled out a remote control device from his inside jacket pocket.

He extended the small antenna on the remote control device and looked at Wells, and she nodded. He flipped the switch on the remote control device to activate it and then pushed the red button that was on the front of the remote control device. Seconds later, Carla Garcia's house exploded into an enormous fireball.

"We need to be going," Wells commented. "Our job here is done."

Flowers started the car, and they drove past the burning house that use to be Carla Garcia's residence. Seconds later, the first responders were beginning to arrive as Flowers and Wells continued down the street and disappeared into the darkness.

* * * * *

Residence of CIA Deputy Director Karen Hicks

**D**eputy Director Karen Hicks tossed and turned all night. All she could think about was the pictures on the thumb-drive that her personal assistant; twenty-five-year-old Carla Garcia gave her. Realizing that she wasn't going to be able to go back to sleep, she sat up on the edge of her bed. She took a cigarette from the pack of Marlboro Lights that was on her nightstand next to her Beretta M9-A1 nine-millimeter.

She picked up the lighter that was lying on top of the pack of cigarettes and lit up her cigarette.

When Deputy Director Hicks was finished smoking her cigarette, she crushed it out in the ashtray on the nightstand. She got up from her bed and quickly made her bed. Afterwards, she walked over to her closet and picked out a pair of slacks and a blouse. She picked out a jacket that would go with the outfit that she was going to wear to work, and then laid everything on her bed.

She walked into the bathroom and took a quick shower. A few minutes later, Deputy Director Hicks returned to her bedroom dressed in a towel. She sat down in front of her make-up mirror and put on her make-up. When she was done, she got up from her seat and walked over to the bed, and got dressed for work.

She secured her Beretta M9-A1 nine-millimeter to her waste under her jacket. She put her cigarettes and lighter in the outside jacket pocket and her credentials and cell phone in the other pocket. She picked up the thumb-drive that Carla Garcia had given her the night before from the nightstand, and put the thumb-drive in the inside jacket pocket.

Deputy Director Hicks hurried out of the bedroom and walked to the kitchen. She put the correct amount of water and coffee in her Hamilton Beach Flex Brew Single-Serve Coffeemaker to make a single cup of coffee. She placed her coffee cup in place and turned on the power switch.

She walked to the front door and opened it, and retrieved the morning newspaper. She closed the front door and walked back to the kitchen. She removed the coffee cup from the coffee maker and walked over to the kitchen table, and sat down.

She opened the newspaper; "Oh my God," was all she could manage to say when she saw that the incident at Carla Garcia's residence was on the front page. She continued to read the article while she drank her cup of coffee. The more she read about what happened at Carla Garcia's residence, the more she was convinced that it was not an accident. She laid the newspaper down on the table and finished her coffee. "Gas explosion my ass," she mumbled.

Deputy Director Hicks got up from her seat at the kitchen table and hurried into her study that she used as a home office. She walked over to the desk and sat down, and turned on the computer monitor, and then her computer. She pulled out the thumb-drive that Carla Garcia had given her the night before from her inside jacket pocket, and connected the thumb-drive to the USB port on her computer and waited for the file to open.

When the file opened, she began to go back over the pictures on the thumb-drive. Most of the pictures were of old newspaper clippings, but two of the pictures contained documents that caught her attention. She read the documents twice to be certain that she understood its content. *So it's not a myth,* she thought. *Red Cell does exist, and they're in cahoots with the Iranians.*

Deputy Director Hicks removed the telephone receiver from the telephone on her desk and put it to her ear, and dialed the telephone number for Colonel Wilson's office at Strike Force Delta Command. After a few rings, she looked at her watch; *Shit it's 0537 there. Wilson won't be in his office,* she thought while she returned the telephone receiver to the telephone on her desk.

She sat at her desk and thought about her next move, and who she could trust with the information that Red Cell did indeed exist. She knew that if she talked to the wrong person about her findings that she could meet the same faith as Carla Garcia.

She closed the file and removed the thumb-drive from her computer. She returned the thumb-drive to the inside pocket of her jacket and then turned off her computer and the computer monitor. She got up from her seat from behind her desk and walked toward the door. She opened the door and left her office.

Deputy Director Hicks walked down the entryway and grabbed her car keys from the table next to the door on her way out. She locked the front door and walked to her silver-tone Chevy Cobalt that was parked in the driveway. She unlocked the driver's side door and got in, and closed the door. She started the car and backed out of her driveway, and drove off.

Forty minutes later, Deputy Director Hicks arrived at the main gate to CIA Headquarters in Langley Virginia. "What the hell," she commented when she saw the line of cars waiting to clear security. "I don't have time for this shit."

Twenty minutes later, Deputy Director Hicks reached the front of the line. She pulled her silver-tone Chevy Cobalt to the guard shack and stopped. She was quick to notice that the guard who usually worked the main gate was different.

"Identification, please."

She pulled out her credentials from her jacket pocket and handed it to the guard. "Where's Harry?"

"Don't know, ma'am."

She looked around and saw several men dressed in full combat dress standing guard with their M-16-A4 assault rifles ready for action. "What's up with all the security?"

"Not sure, ma'am, director's orders," The guard replied as he looked at Deputy Director Hicks credentials, and then he handed it back to her. "You may proceed Deputy Director. Have a nice day ma'am."

Deputy Director Hicks smiled and then hung her identification card around her neck, using the long chain that was attached to it. "You do the same," she remarked, and then she proceeded through the main gate. She drove to the parking garage and parked her silver-tone Chevy Cobalt in her assigned parking space located on the first level.

She got out of her car and walked to the entrance that was used by high-ranking CIA personnel. Using the scanner on the wall next to the door, she scanned her identification card. The red light on the scanner turned green, and the door opened, and she entered.

She walked to the elevator and pushed the call button. A few minutes later the elevator door opened, and she stepped inside. She pushed the button for the floor where her office was located. The door closed, and the elevator began to move upward. A few minutes later, the elevator stopped, and the door opened. She stepped off the elevator, and the door closed.

Deputy Director Hicks walked to her office and entered the reception area. She fought with all her being to hold back the tears that were forming in her eyes as she walked past Carla Garcia's desk. She couldn't help but notice that Garcia's desk had been cleared out. It was as if she had never been there. She opened the door to her office and stepped inside. She left the door open and hurried over to her desk, and sat down in the chair behind her desk.

She was startled when the telephone on her desk began to ring.

She removed the telephone receiver from the telephone on her desk and put it to her ear. "Hicks here."

"Karen, can you step into my office for a minute?" CIA Director Robert Müller said. "We need to have a talk."

"On my way," Deputy Director Hicks acknowledged, and she returned the telephone receiver to the telephone on her desk. She got up from her seat and left her office. She walked to Director Müller's office and entered the reception area.

"You can go on in," Director Müller's assistant, twenty-eight-year-old Mary Roberts said. "The director is expecting you."

Deputy Director Hicks smiled at Roberts and walked over to the door to Director Müller's office; and opened the door. When she entered Director Müller's office, she found forty-eight-year-old Eric Michal, Director of Homeland Security sitting in a chair, in front of Director Müller's desk. "I'm sorry, sir. I didn't mean to interrupt your meeting."

"You're not interrupting anything," Director Müller assured Deputy Director Hicks. "Please close the door and have a seat." Director Müller paused while Deputy Director Hicks closed the door and walked over to the other chair next to where Director Michal was sitting and sat down. "Karen we had a security breach, and it's believed to have come from your office."

"Are you sure about that?"

"I'm afraid so," Director Michal answered. "We believe that your assistant, Carla Garcia, was passing classified information to the Iranians."

"You're both wrong," Deputy Director Hicks fired back. "I don't believe this. Carla hasn't been dead twenty-four hours, and you're accusing her of being a traitor."

"Believe what you want," Director Müller fired back. "We know that recently she received an important encrypted file from one of our operatives that was on the Zamani surveillance team in Gwadar, Pakistan. Shortly afterwards two team members were killed, and the rest of the team disappeared."

"And you believe that Carla had something to do with this?" Deputy Director Hicks asked sarcastically. "You're nuts."

"At this time we're not sure," Director Michal answered. "The encrypted file she received is still missing. I have two of my top people looking into this."

"You mean the two that was following me around the other day?" Deputy Director Hicks calmly asked, trying to keep her temper under control. "I found that very intrusive. What I do on my time off is my business; not yours."

"That has nothing to do with this," Director Michal pointed out. "I apologize for that. Please pass my apologies on to Colonel Wilson."

"Do you know anything about this missing file?" Director Müller inquired.

"I have no idea what you're talking about," Deputy Director Hicks answered. "Carla never mentioned anything to me about any file."

"I want you to take a couple of days off while we look into this," Director Müller suggested. "I'm sorry Karen; you're too close to this."

"This is bullshit, and you know it," Deputy Director Hicks commented. "If there's a security leak, I can assure you it wasn't Carla."

"Enough," Director Müller shot back while he slammed his hands down on his desk, and then jumped to his feet. "Go home Karen. I'll call you in a couple of days."

Deputy Director Hicks got up from her seat and walked to the door. She turned to face Director Müller and Director Michal. "Keep in mind, gentlemen, I'm not going to let you pin this on Carla." She turned around and opened the door and left the office, and slammed the door closed.

She hurried back to her office and entered the reception area. She walked into her office and closed the door. She walked over to her desk and sat down in the chair that was behind her desk. "Fuckin' assholes," she mumbled.

She grabbed her briefcase that was sitting on the floor next to her desk and placed it on her desk, and opened the briefcase. She collected a few items from her desk and put them inside and closed it. She got up from her seat and grabbed her briefcase. She left her office and closed the door.

# Chapter 6

Strike Force Delta Command
Colonel Wilson's Office

Colonel Wilson poured himself a cup of coffee and sat behind his desk. He turned on his computer and the computer monitor, and waited for everything to warm up before he logged onto the system. He opened his e-mail program and began to read his messages.

When he got to the e-mail from Carla Garcia, he curiously opened the message. He read the cover message, and then he opened the attached file that contained several photographs. He loaded the images onto the wall size plasma screen on the wall behind him, and then he picked up the controller for the plasma screen from his desk. He got up from his seat and sat on his desk; and faced the plasma screen. He drank his coffee while he scanned through the pictures several times until he finally stopped on the last photograph. "This doesn't make any sense," he mumbled while he turned off the plasma screen, and then placed his empty coffee cup and the controller for the plasma screen down on his desk.

"What doesn't make sense?" Captain Hale asked, who was standing in the doorway.

Startled by Captain Hale's sudden appearance, Colonel Wilson jumped off his desk and turned to face Captain Hale. "How long have you been standing there?"

"Long enough to see that those pictures you were looking at has you stumped," Captain Hale commented as he entered Colonel Wilson's office. He walked over to the coffee maker and poured himself a cup of coffee. With the coffee pot in hand, he turned to face Colonel Wilson. "Need a refill boss?"

"That's not a bad idea," Colonel Wilson commented. He picked up his empty coffee cup from his desk and walked over to Captain Hale.

Captain Hale filled up Colonel Wilson's coffee cup and returned the pot to the coffee maker. "Want to fill me in on what's got you stumped about the pictures you were looking at?"

"What's got me stumped is why someone would send me those pictures in the first place," Colonel Wilson answered. "Most of the pictures are copies of newspaper articles about the accident that killed Yasin Abdul Zamani's wife and son. The last two are pictures of documents written in English about some terrorist group known as Red Cell."

"Do you think Red Cell and Zamani are connected?"

"It's a possibility," Colonel Wilson replied as he walked back to his desk. "However, what I don't get is what's so important about the other pictures, and why did someone go through the trouble of sending them to me?" He set his cup of coffee down on his desk and sat down in the chair behind his desk. "I want you to quietly look into the possibility that this Red Cell and Zamani are connected. Until we find out what this is all about, I want you to tell no one about any of this or these pictures, understood."

"Roger that," Captain Hale acknowledged. He finished his cup of coffee and placed the empty cup on the counter next to the coffee maker, and left Colonel Wilson's office.

Colonel Wilson turned his attention to the stack of recent intelligence reports in front of him on his desk. He drank his coffee while he read through them. "Same old bullshit," he mumbled when he finished reading the last report, and placed them on the front corner of his desk. He finished his cup of coffee and sat the empty cup down on his desk.

"Good morning," Second Lieutenant Samantha Cooltrain remarked while she entered Colonel Wilson's office. "I hate to bother you Wolverine, but there's someone at the security building waiting for you in the conference room. I was told that it was important and that it can't wait. I have a car waiting outside."

"Very well, lead the way," Colonel Wilson commented. "Let's find out what's so damn important."

He followed Lieutenant Cooltrain out of his office and closed the door. They exited the building and walked to the vehicle that was waiting. Colonel Wilson opened the back door and got in while Lieutenant Cooltrain got in on the driver's side, and they drove off. A few minutes later, they arrived at the security building, and Lieutenant Cooltrain stopped the vehicle near the front entrance.

"I'll have someone waiting here to give you a ride back," Lieutenant Cooltrain pointed out.

"Sounds good to me," Colonel Wilson remarked and then exited the vehicle. He walked up the walkway to the main entrance where an armed guard was standing and handed him his credentials.

"Sir, your visitor, is waiting for you in the conference room," the guard said as he handed Colonel Wilson his credentials back and then opened the door.

"Thank you," Colonel Wilson said and entered the building. He walked down the hallway to the conference room where another armed guard was standing. The guard opened the door, and Colonel Wilson entered the conference room.

"I don't believe my eyes," Colonel Wilson said when he saw his old friend Joseph Samson, whom he hadn't seen in years, sitting at the table in the middle of the room. "What the hell have you been up to?" He asked while he walked over to where Samson was sitting.

"Same old shit," Samson replied as he got up from his seat, reached across the table, and shook hands with Colonel Wilson. "I have something that you need to see," he continued, referring to his briefcase on the table. "I hate to bring you bad news, but there's a world of shit coming your way my friend."

"Every time I see or talk to you, you never have any good news for me," Colonel Wilson said as he sat at the conference table across from where Samson was standing. "I hope someday you might bring me some good news for a change," he continued to say while Samson returned to his seat.

"I got a call from our mutual friend," Samson began. "He said that you asked him to look into the whereabouts of Yasin Abdul Zamani?"

"Yes, I did," Colonel Wilson answered. "He's supposed to get back to me on that."

"I told him that I would take care of your request personally," Samson said as he opened his briefcase. He pulled out a folder and handed it to Colonel Wilson. "Yasin Abdul Zamani is in Iran."

"That's not good," Colonel Wilson replied while he laid the folder down on the table in front of him.

"I came here to warn you that Zamani is overseeing the Iranians secret uranium-enrichment program at their new research facility near Iranshahr," Samson continued. "It is believed that the Iranians are producing weapons-grade uranium two-thirty-five and that Zamani is working hard to put a nuke in their hands, but that's not all of it."

"You mean there's more?" Colonel Wilson dared to ask.

Joe Samson looked at Colonel Wilson and nodded. "Yes, there is my friend. Have you heard of a terrorist group called Red Cell?"

"Recently Red Cell popped up in one of our investigations," Colonel Wilson answered. "I've not seen anything yet that would indicate that they're a threat to anyone."

"Take it from me, they're a threat. I have reason to believe that with the support of the Iranian government, Red Cell, is planning to set off a nuke right here in the United States."

"Joe, are you sure about this?"

"If I wasn't sure, I wouldn't be here. It's all in that folder," Samson said, referring to the folder that was lying on the table in front of Colonel Wilson. "I tried to pass this information onto your CIA, but they told me to mind my own business," he continued while he closed his briefcase.

"The CIA is hard to deal with sometimes. They don't like it when someone points out that they missed something."

"Any way you look at it; the proof is there my friend. Iran has the ability to produce nuclear weapons, and they're going to use Red Cell to attack the United States. You know I wouldn't be here if I wasn't one-hundred percent sure about this."

"Surely the Iranians must know that we would figure out that they were behind such an attack and unleash holy hell on them," Colonel Wilson was quick to point out. "In the long-run, they would be writing their own death warrant."

"I believe, but can't prove that someone high up in your

government is working with the Iranians."

Colonel Wilson was stunned. He couldn't understand what Samson had just said. "Are you saying what I think you're saying?"

"I'm afraid so, someone in your upper government is a traitor to your people. This traitor is going to get a lot of your people killed."

"Got any idea who it might be?"

"Not yet. However, I was told that you had a back channel to your president. I was hoping that perhaps you could get this information to him before all hell breaks loose."

"I don't know about having a back channel to President Elliot, but I'll see what I can do. I can't promise that he'll listen to me, but I'll give it my best shot."

"That's all I'm asking. I know if you can help me get this to your president it will benefit everyone." Samson got up from his seat with his briefcase in hand. "I hate to end our meeting, but I need to be going. I want you to keep the file," he said, referring to the folder he gave Colonel Wilson. "Maybe if you go back over the material with a closer eye you might find something that was overlooked. Just don't tell anyone where you got this information and watch your back. Be extra careful who you tell about this."

"I understand," Colonel Wilson said while he got up from his seat. "I'll see what I can do," he continued while he shook hands with Samson. "Be careful my friend. I hope to see you again someday."

"Until we meet again," Samson remarked, and he walked over to the door. He opened it and stepped into the hallway. "You may escort me back to my vehicle at the main gate now," he said to the guard that was standing there.

Colonel Wilson picked up the folder from the table, walked over to the opened door, and left the room. He stood in the hallway and watched as Samson followed the guard out of the building. Colonel Wilson waited for a few minutes, then exited the building, and walked over to the vehicle that was waiting. As he approached, a woman dressed in an Air Force uniform opened the back door, and he got in. She closed the door, walked around, and got in on the driver's side. A few seconds later, they drove off.

"Where to, sir?"

"Drop me off at the facility's gate."

"Yes, sir," the driver acknowledged, and they drove off.

When they arrived at the Strike Force facility, Colonel Wilson got out of the vehicle. The vehicle drove off while he walked over to the guard at the gate and showed him his credentials.

"Sir, I have a Humvee waiting," the guard said while handing Colonel Wilson his credentials back, and then pointed to a Humvee a few feet away. "The driver will take you to your office, sir."

"Very well," Colonel Wilson said and walked over to the Humvee that was waiting for him with its engine running and jumped in on the passenger side.

The driver put the Humvee in gear, and they drove off. A few minutes later, the vehicle stopped in front of the main building. Colonel Wilson got out of the Humvee and entered the building. He walked to his office and sat down in the chair behind his desk.

He opened the folder that Samson left with him and started going over the material that was inside. When he was finished going back over the folder's contents, he put everything back into the folder. He turned on his computer and began typing up his report that he would send to the president.

When he was finished with his report, he pressed the print button on his keyboard and got up from his seat, and walked over to the printer. He retrieved the printout of his report and walked back over to his desk, and sat down. Colonel Wilson quickly read back over his three-page report. He wanted to be certain that he had covered everything that Samson discussed with him earlier, except for the part that someone high up in the government was working with the Iranians.

Satisfied with his report, he pressed the encryption key on his keyboard and then saved the encrypted message that only he could decrypt on his computer. He got up from his seat, with the unencrypted version of his report in hand, and walked over to the encryption machine next to the printer. He set up the encryption machine to encrypt his report so that General Richwood and President Elliot's trusted staff would be the only ones who could decrypt it.

He scanned the unencrypted version of his report into the encryption machine and the encrypted version printed out on the printer. He retrieved the encrypted printout of his report and walked back over to his desk, and sat down. He opened the left-side bottom drawer of his desk and removed a bright-red folder from inside, and closed the drawer. He opened the folder and put the three-page encrypted report in the folder, and closed it.

Colonel Wilson placed the folder on his desk in front of him and picked up the telephone receiver from the telephone on his desk. He put the telephone receiver to his ear while he dialed the extension number for Captain Hale's office. After a few rings, he realized that Captain Hale was not in his office, so he canceled the call. He then dialed the pager number for Lieutenant Cooltrain, waited for it to beep, and then returned the telephone receiver to the telephone.

Seconds later, the office door opened, and Lieutenant Cooltrain entered carrying a folder in her hand. "A message came in from GS one-O-three while you were gone." She said while she walked over to Colonel Wilson's desk. "I think you should look at this," she concluded and handed Colonel Wilson the folder.

Colonel Wilson opened the folder and read the message from GS one-O-three. The message confirmed most of what Joseph Samson had told him earlier. "Interesting," he remarked while he closed the folder and laid it down on his desk next to his report.

He picked up his encrypted report from his desk and handed it to Lieutenant Cooltrain. "I want you to take this report to the Communication Center and have it sent to the President and General Richwood immediately. Tell them to mark it urgent, their eyes only," he instructed her. "You're to wait for confirmation that the com-centers at the White House and the Pentagon have received it."

"Right away," Lieutenant Cooltrain acknowledged and then hurried out of the office.

Colonel Wilson once again picked up the telephone receiver from the telephone on his desk. He put the telephone receiver to his ear while he dialed the extension number for Captain Hale's office. After a few rings, he realized that Captain Hale still wasn't in his office, so he canceled the call. He then dialed the pager number for Captain Hale. He waited for it to beep, and then returned the telephone receiver to the telephone.

A few seconds later, his telephone rang, and he pushed the speaker button on the telephone. "Wilson," he said in a strong voice.

"Wolverine, the messages you wanted me to send have been sent and received," Lieutenant Cooltrain reported. "However, the president is onboard Air Force One, so the vice president acknowledged receipt of the message. He said he would pass it on to the president."

"Very well," Colonel Wilson acknowledged and pushed the speaker button on the telephone to cancel the call.

Twenty minutes later the telephone on Colonel Wilson's desk rang again. He picked up the telephone receiver from the telephone and put it to his ear. "Wilson."

"Wilson, I just finished reading your report," General Richwood said. "Are you sure about this?"

"General, it's been confirmed by two separate sources."

"How soon can you get your ass to Washington?"

"I can be there in a few hours,"

"Leave at once. I'll meet you at Andrews when you get here," General Richwood said, and then the line went dead.

Colonel Wilson waited for a dial tone, and then he dialed the extension for the pilot assigned to Strike Force's Gulfstream G550 twin-engine jet aircraft. He waited for the pilot to pick up, and then said, "This is Wilson. I'll be leaving for Washington within the hour."

"The aircraft will be ready for departure when you get here," the pilot assured Colonel Wilson.

"Good; I'll see you in about an hour," Colonel Wilson concluded, and then he returned the telephone receiver to the telephone on his desk.

Ten minutes later, Lieutenant Cooltrain entered Colonel Wilson's office with the encrypted copy of his report that she had just sent out to President Elliot and General Richwood. She walked over to his desk and handed it to Colonel Wilson.

"That'll be all for now."

"Roger that," Lieutenant Cooltrain acknowledged, and then she left Colonel Wilson's office.

Colonel Wilson got up from his seat behind his desk with the encrypted report in hand and walked over to the paper shredder. He shredded the report and walked back to his seat, and sat down behind his desk just as Captain Hale entered his office. "You paged me Wolverine?"

"Yes, I did," Colonel Wilson answered. "Have a seat."

Captain Hale sat in the chair, in front of Colonel Wilson's desk. Colonel Wilson picked up the folder that contained his unencrypted three-page report from his desk and handed it to Captain Hale. "You need to read this."

Captain Hale opened the folder and carefully read the report. When he was done, he closed the folder and handed it back to Colonel Wilson. "Iran making nukes. That's not good."

"Oh, that's not all," Colonel Wilson pointed out.

"You mean there's more?"

"I'm afraid so; there's a lot that I didn't put in my report."

Captain Hale looked at Colonel Wilson surprised. "Like what?"

"Like the fact that the terrorist group, Red Cell is a threat to our way of life; and that Red Cell may have ties to al-Qaeda."

"Are you sure Red Cell is working with al-Qaeda," Captain Hale curiously asked.

"I'll bet a year's pay that Red Cell is working with al-Qaeda or the Iranian government," Colonel Wilson fired back.

"If you're so sure of this, then why did you leave that information out of your report? I've never known you to hold back information like that."

"I didn't put it in my report because I have reason to believe that there is at least one high-ranking official in our government that's helping Red Cell smuggle a nuke into the country. My gut tells me that they intend to set it off somewhere here in the US." Colonel Wilson paused for a brief moment before he continued. "I don't know who I can trust with this."

"Surely you don't think that General Richwood is involved in this?"

"No, I don't. I think it's best I tell him in person. That way there's no paper trail for whoever is involved in this attack to find."

"So what's our next move?" Captain Hale inquired.

"General Richwood has ordered me back to Washington. I'll fill him in on this when I get there. What I want you to do is put two units on standby, just in case they're needed. I'll have more information when I get back. I want you to keep this between us. Tell no one about any of this."

"I'll get right on it," Captain Hale acknowledged while he got up from his seat and then hurried out of Colonel Wilson's office.

Colonel Wilson picked up his report from his desk and got up from his seat. He walked over to the paper shredder and shredded his report. Afterwards, he walked out of his office and closed the door.

* * * * *

CIA Headquarters
Langley, Virginia
Director Robert Müller's Office

**D**irector Robert Müller was sitting behind his desk going over the latest report on the mishap at the Yasin Abdul Zamani residence in Gwadar, Pakistan. He was startled when his office door suddenly opened, and his personal assistant, twenty-eight-year-old Mary Roberts, entered the office carrying a red folder in her hand.

"The counter-terrorist unit sent this up a few minutes ago," Roberts said while she walked over to Director Müller's desk. "They said that you wanted to see their findings on the incident in Gwadar, Pakistan."

"That was quick," Director Müller commented. He took the folder from Roberts and laid it down on his desk in front of him. "Is there anything else?"

"No, sir," Roberts answered. "I'll be at my desk if you should need me," she concluded and walked out of Director Müller's office, and closed the office door.

Director Müller opened the folder and began to thumb through the information contained inside. He read the first page of the two-page document and stopped. "Holly shit!" He said and then continued to read the next page of the report. Afterwards, he examined the satellite photographs that were taken of the area on the day Samuel Cain, and Robert King were killed.

He was startled when the intercom on the telephone on his desk beeped. He pushed the intercom button. "Yes."

"Sir, Thomas Zachery is here. He says he has a situation, and he needs to see you."

"Send him in," Director Müller said; and then he pushed the intercom button on the telephone to end the intercom call.

Director Müller's office door opened, and thirty-one-year-old Thomas Zachery, entered, and closed the door. "I'm sorry to bother you, sir, but I have an update on our people that went missing in Gwadar, Pakistan." He continued while he walked over to Director Müller's desk. "Sir, it appears that our people were taken by a group of Pakistani ISI personnel that are working with the Iranians."

"Are you sure about this?"

"Yes, sir, I am, but that's not why I'm here."

Director Müller looked at Zachery confused. "Then why are you here?"

Zachery hesitated for a moment before he answered. "Our people were turned over to Iranian intelligence that was operating in the area, and they're on their way to Iran. They'll be crossing the Iranian border shortly."

"Any idea why the Iranians want our people?"

"I don't know for sure. I think our people might have stumbled onto something at the Zamani townhouse that the Iranians don't want to get out."

"That's possible, but what?

"I'm still trying to figure that out."

"I want you to keep looking into this and find out where the Iranians are taking our people," Director Müller said in a strong voice. "There's got to be more to this than what we're seeing. We need to find out what the Iranians are hiding before it bites us on the ass."

"I'll get my team on this immediately," Zachery assured Director Müller. "I'll let you know the minute we find out something."

"Tread lightly on this one," Director Müller warned. "We need to get our people back in one piece."

"Understood, sir," Zachery acknowledged. He walked over to the door and opened it. He left Director Müller's office and closed the door.

Director Müller turned his attention back to the counter-terrorist unit's report he was going over before he was interrupted. He put everything back into the folder and laid the folder on top of the pile of folders on his desk. Without warning, his office door swung open, and

Vice President James Conrad entered. The vice president closed the door and walked over to Director Müller's desk.

"Mr. Vice President," Director Müller said while he jumped to his feet. "It's nice to see you again, sir."

"Relax Robert," Vice President Conrad said, and then he sat in the chair that was in front of Director Müller's desk.

"What brings you to Langley, sir?"

"The president asked me to stop by and have a chat with you."

"A chat about what?"

"About your intelligence reports on Iran's capability to produce nuclear weapons," Vice President Conrad replied. "The president received a report from the Israelis about what they think is going on in Iran. The Israelis believe that Iran has nuclear capabilities. Is this true?"

"The Israelis are guessing," Director Müller fired back.

"I saw the report myself," Vice President Conrad shot back.

"I'm telling you the report is wrong," Director Müller insisted. "You know as well as I that it's no secret that the Israelis have been itching for a fight with Iran for years."

"President Elliot wants answers," Vice President Conrad fired back. "You need to get to the bottom of this Iran situation, and fast." Vice President Conrad got up from his seat. "He expects your report on this Iranian situation to be on his desk when he returns from the NATO summit in Brussels."

"Inform the president that I don't have all the facts yet, but I'm working on it. I hope to have some answers shortly. I don't want to speculate about any of this and be wrong." Director Müller got up from his seat. "I'll have my report sent over to the White House before the president gets back."

"I'll pass it on to the president," Vice President Conrad commented while he walked over to the office door. He opened the door and left Director Müller's office with Director Müller following. Director Müller stood in the doorway to his office and watched Vice President Conrad leave the reception area.

"Is there something you need sir?" Mary Roberts asked.

Director Müller smiled at Roberts. "Not right now," he answered and stepped back into his office. He closed the door and walked over to his desk, and sat down in the chair behind his desk.

# Chapter 7

Iranshahr, Iran

Samir Hamidi and Amos Adler, both Iranian nationals, had been monitoring the activity at the research facility, since its construction. From their position that overlooked the research facility, and with the aid of their high-powered binoculars, they could see everything that was going on inside the research compound.

Hamidi and Adler watched while the sun slowly disappeared behind the mountains, and the research facility faded away into the darkness. It was a moonless night with a slight breeze coming down from the mountains, bringing a chill to the night air. The facility remained in darkness, except for a few lights that were turned on around the steel-reinforced concrete bunkers.

"Something's not right," Samir Hamidi commented. "Why haven't they turned on the lights?"

"I don't know," Amos Adler replied. "They should have turned them on by now."

Before Samir Hamidi could say what he was thinking, the Raad Air Defense Systems came to life and fired two Iranian-made Taer missiles into the night sky. Seconds later, the Taer missiles slammed into their intended target, creating an enormous fireball in the darkened sky.

"What the hell did they just shoot down?" Samir Hamidi asked.

"My guess is that it must have been a surveillance drone," Amos Adler answered.

"Scratch one drone," Samir Hamidi commented. "They can kiss that one goodbye."

"That's for sure," Amos Adler concurred.

A few minutes later, the High-powered halogen lights were turned on, lighting up the compound like it was daytime. Several military vehicles left the compound and headed in the direction of the crash site to inspect the wreckage.

Samir Hamidi looked at his watch. "We need to get going so we can meet with our contact in the city," he pointed out. "He's supposed to have some information for us about what's actually going on inside this facility."

"I'm right behind you," Amos Adler acknowledged.

Hamidi handed Adler his high-powered binoculars, and they hurried back to where they had parked their four-door Iran Khodro Samand LX sedan. Samir Hamidi jumped in on the front driver's side and closed the door. Amos Adler opened the trunk lid and put their high-powered binoculars in the secret compartment that was located in the bottom of the trunk, and then closed the trunk lid shut. Hamidi fired up the vehicle while Adler climbed in on the front passenger's side and closed his door.

Hamidi put the Iran Khodro Samand LX sedan in gear. He gave it some gas and sped off toward the main road, where he turned on the headlights and proceeded toward Iranshahr at a normal speed.

When Samir Hamidi and Amos Adler arrived in town, Samir Hamidi parked the four-door Khodro Samand LX sedan in front of the local bar and turned off the car. He and Amos Adler got out of their vehicle and went inside. They walked over to the bar and sat down.

The bartender walked over to Samir Hamidi and Amos Adler. "What can I get you?" He asked in Farsi.

"We'll both have a beer," Samir Hamidi answered back in Farsi.

The bartender drew two glasses of beer from the tap and placed them on the bar in front of Samir Hamidi and Amos Adler. "Can I get you anything else?"

"We're okay for now," Amos Adler replied.

Samir Hamidi and Amos Adler slowly drank their beer while they waited for their contact to arrive. A few minutes later their contact, Javad Yousef, entered the bar. He walked over to his usual table in the corner and sat down.

Samir Hamidi was quick to notice that two men entered the bar a few seconds after Javad Yousef. They sat down at a table a few feet from where Javad Yousef was sitting. *This doesn't feel right,* he thought. Amos Adler started to get up from his seat at the bar, but stopped when Samir Hamidi grabbed his arm. "Something's not right," Hamidi whispered to Adler. "We need to get out of here now."

Samir Hamidi and Amos Adler started to get up from their seats at the bar when the bartender walked over to them carrying a medium-sized brown paper bag. "Your dinner order is ready," he said to them in a normal tone of voice, and then he placed the bag down on the bar in front of Samir Hamidi. "I'm sorry it took so long. The cook's a little slow today. I'm sure you'll find your dinner to be everything you were expecting it to be."

Hamidi understood exactly what the bartender was trying to say to him. "Tell your cook, I understand," He said as he picked up the bag of food from the bar and handed it to Amos Adler. "Tell your cook, I hope his day gets better."

"I'll pass it on," the bartender acknowledged. "You gentlemen have a nice day."

"See you later," Samir Hamidi remarked and then he and Amos Adler left the bar and hurried back to their four-door Khodro Samand LX sedan parked outside. Hamidi jumped in on the front driver's side and closed the door. He fired up the vehicle while Adler climbed in on the front passenger's side; and closed his door.

"What the hell was that all about?" Amos Adler asked, "I don't remember us ordering any food."

Samir Hamidi shook his head in disbelief as they pulled away from the curb and headed back out of town. "Are you that stupid? That bartender back there just saved our asses."

Amos Adler looked in the bag. "Hey, there's actually food in here."

"What a dumbass," Samir Hamidi remarked. "You know, sometimes I wonder if you got any brains in that head of yours. Of course, there's food in that bag, and there's probably something else in there too. I'm hoping that Yousef had the bartender pass us the information that he had for us."

Amos Adler looked over at Samir Hamidi and smiled, "Of course; I knew that, but I'm getting hungry; aren't you?"

Samir Hamidi chuckled as he pulled the car over just outside of town. He reached over and opened the glove box. He removed the radio frequency detector and turned it on, and got out of the car. He walked around the car scanning for tracking devices and found none.

He turned off the radio frequency detector and got back into the car. He put the radio frequency detector back into the glove box and closed the glove box. "Now we can go to the safe house and find out what's really in that bag."

Samir Hamidi pulled the car back on the road and headed out of town. He turned down the first side road they came to and continued to the house at the end of the road. He parked the Khodro Samand LX sedan behind the house and turned off the engine.

Hamidi and Adler got out of the vehicle. Adler followed Hamidi to the back door with the bag of food in hand. They entered the house and walked into the kitchen area. Adler sat the paper bag down on the table while Hamidi sat down in a chair at the table.

Samir Hamidi's wife, Myra, entered the kitchen and gave her husband a quick peck on the cheek. "Did everything go as planned?"

"Not exactly," Samir Hamidi answered. "I think Yousef was being followed. I believe he had the bartender pass his information to us in the food that he gave us."

Adler opened the paper bag that the bartender had given them and carefully removed three trays of food from the bag. He placed the food trays side by side on the table. He removed the package that contained two small loaves of fresh baked bread and opened the package. He inspected each loaf of bread and found that one of them had a hole at one end. "I think I found something," Adler said as he ripped off the end of the loaf of bread. "Bingo," he commented when he found a thumb-drive hidden inside the end of the loaf of bread. "I got it," he continued while he held up the thumb-drive for Hamidi and Myra to see.

"Clever," Myra commented.

Samir Hamidi got up from his seat and grabbed the thumb-drive out of Amos Adler's hand. "I'll take care of that," he pointed out and walked out of the kitchen, and into the sitting room, with Myra and Amos Adler hot on his heels.

Hamidi pushed the sofa back and exposed the hidden trapdoor that was in the floor. He opened the trapdoor that led to a room that was hidden beneath the sitting room. He walked down a couple of steps and flipped a switch to turn on the lights that illuminated the entire room below, and continued down the steps, with Myra following close behind.

Amos Adler closed the trapdoor and went into his bedroom. He turned on his computer and began to watch the live camera feed from the cameras that were strategically placed around the outside of the house; and along the road leading to the house,

Samir Hamidi and his wife Myra walked over to a small table in the corner of the room that had a computer terminal sitting on top of the table. Hamidi sat down in the chair, and Myra stood at his side. He turned on the computer and waited for it to warm up before he placed the thumb-drive into the computer's USB port.

The files on the thumb-drive appeared on the monitor, and Hamidi began to scan through them. After scanning through a small portion of the material that was on the thumb-drive, Samir Hamidi looked at Myra. "We need to send this information to our people back in the US at once."

"That we do," Myra agreed.

Hamidi looked at the clock on the table that they used to keep track of when the satellite would be in position to receive their transmission. "We need to get everything ready to transmit. We only have five minutes before the satellite is in position to receive our transmission."

"That's not much time," Myra pointed out.

Hamidi looked at Myra. "We have plenty of time my dear," he pointed out and then he proceeded to open the encryption program. He entered the encryption key-code, so he could encrypt the contents of the thumb-drive; and prepared the file for transmission. When he finished encrypting the file on the computer, he removed the thumb-drive and put it in his pants pocket. He looked at the clock on the table. "See, we got two minutes to spare," he remarked. "Damn, I'm good."

"Smart ass," Myra commented while she walked over to the radio transmitter that was on the other end of the table. She grabbed the coax cable that was attached to the radio transmitter and attached the other end to the box that sat on top of the computer, which was wired directly into the computer. "We're all set," she informed Hamidi.

"Good," Hamidi acknowledged. He used his mouse to position the mouse pointer on the computer monitor to the send button, and waited as the clock counted down the seconds. When the clock reached zero, he clicked the send button, and the file was sent to the satellite that was passing over their position. A few minutes later, he received a message that his transmission was received. "Transmission has been sent and received. We're to stand by for further instructions."

"I wonder what they want now," Myra remarked. "We've done everything they've asked of us."

"You never know," Hamidi commented. "They could..." Hamidi suddenly stopped talking when the computer beeped, indicating that an incoming message had been received.

"That was fast," Myra was quick to point out.

"Yeah, it was," Hamidi said while he opened the message. He quickly entered the correct encryption key-code and a few seconds later, a readable message appeared on the screen.

(Destroy all computers, transmitters, and encryption key-codes at your location. Then proceed with caution to extraction point Delta for extraction in twelve hours. God speed, and good luck.)

"Look on the map and see how far it is to point Delta," Hamidi suggested.

Myra walked over to the table behind them and looked at the map that was laid out on the table to see where point Delta was located. "We got about five-hundred kilometers to cover to get to point Delta. I don't understand why they didn't use point Charlie or point Bravo; they're closer to us than point Delta."

"I'm sure they have their reasons for using point Delta," Hamidi pointed out. "Whatever their reasons might be, it doesn't matter. We have our orders." He got up from his seat and faced Myra. "We need to destroy everything down here and upstairs."

Hamidi walked over to the toolbox that was on the shelf next to the table where he was standing. He removed a large ball-peen hammer from the toolbox while Myra grabbed two one-gallon bottles of hydrochloric acid from the shelf beneath the toolbox.

He hurried over to the transmitter, and with the use of the ball-peen hammer, Samir Hamidi broke the radio transmitter into several unusable pieces. When he was done, he laid the ball-peen hammer down on the table, and Myra handed him one of the gallon containers of hydrochloric acid. He opened the container and poured the entire bottle of hydrochloric acid over the pieces from the radio transmitter. Hamidi and Myra stood there and watched while the hydrochloric acid dissolved the pieces from the radio transmitter to an unrecognizable pile of junk.

Satisfied that the radio transmitter was destroyed, Hamidi picked up the ball-peen hammer from the table, and he and Myra returned to the table where the computer and the monitor were sitting. Without hesitation, Hamidi used the ball-peen hammer to demolish the computer and the monitor into several pieces.

Myra handed him the last bottle of hydrochloric acid, and he poured the hydrochloric acid on the pieces from the computer and the monitor. They watched as the hydrochloric acid dissolved everything into an unrecognizable pile of junk.

Hamidi hurried over to the table behind him and folded up the map, and then stuck it into his pants pocket. He walked over to where he had gotten the two one-gallon bottles of hydrochloric acid from and grabbed the last bottle from the shelf. He handed the bottle of hydrochloric acid and the ball-peen hammer to Myra. "I want you to go upstairs and let Amos know what's going on, and then destroy what needs to be destroyed up there. I'll be up in a couple of minutes."

Myra looked at Hamidi confused. "Okay," She commented and then walked over to the steps, and stopped. After a few brief seconds, Myra walked up the steps and opened the trap door, and entered the sitting room.

She hurried over to the room where Amos Adler was and entered. "We've been ordered out," she informed him. "Samir wants everything in this room destroyed," she continued and set the bottle of hydrochloric acid down on the desk; and handed Adler the ball-peen hammer. "You know what needs to be done. Samir doesn't want any evidence left behind that could indicate what we were doing here."

Amos Adler smiled. "No problem," he commented. He used the ball-peen hammer to demolish the computer and the monitor into several pieces. He laid the ball-peen hammer down on the desk, and Myra handed him the gallon container of hydrochloric acid. He opened the container and poured the entire bottle of hydrochloric acid over the pieces from the computer and the monitor. This should take care of it," he pointed out while he and Myra watched as the hydrochloric acid dissolved everything into an unrecognizable pile of junk. Satisfied that their task was completed, Myra and Amos Adler hurried out of the room and walked into the sitting room where they found Samir Hamidi sitting on the sofa.

"Everything in the other room has been destroyed," Myra reported.

"Great," Hamidi commented as he jumped to his feet. "Let's get the hell out of here while we still can."

Myra and Amos Adler followed Samir Hamidi out of the sitting room and into the kitchen, and out the back door. They walked to the four-door Khodro Samand LX sedan that was parked nearby. Hamidi got in on the front driver's side and closed the door. Myra got in on the front passenger's side while Amos Adler got in on the rear passenger's side of the vehicle and closed the door.

Hamidi fired up the Khodro Samand LX sedan and put it in gear. He pushed the fuel pedal downward a little to give the engine some gas, and they drove off. When they reached the main road, Hamidi turned onto the road, and they continued, traveling at a normal rate of speed.

They traveled several hours before Hamidi turned off the main road onto a side road a few kilometers outside the town of Nikshahr. "We need to find a place to pull over so we can check in and let the extraction team know that we're on our way," he pointed out while they continued down the road. "This will do," Hamidi commented when he spotted a wide spot on the side of the road and pulled over. He stopped the Khodro Samand LX sedan and turned off the headlights. Hamidi got out and walked toward the back of the vehicle while Amos Adler and Myra got out of the vehicle on the passenger's side.

Hamidi opened the trunk lid. He removed the satellite radio transmitter that he had hidden in a secret compartment located in the sidewall of the trunk. Myra walked to the front of the vehicle and watched the road for approaching traffic while Amos Adler hurried to the back to help Hamidi set up the satellite radio-transmitter.

When the satellite radio-transmitter was ready for use, Hamidi plugged the telephone receiver into the front of the satellite radio-transmitter. He turned on the power, and then he put the telephone receiver to his ear. He pushed the transmit key and said, "Eagle Nest, this is Sparrow, do you copy?" Hamidi said in perfect English.

The radio cracked to life. "Sparrow, this is Eagle Nest, go ahead, over."

Samir Hamidi pressed the transmit key again. "Eagle Nest, We are Oscar Mike and on time, over."

"Roger that. Proceed to extraction point Delta, Eagle Nest, out."

Hamidi handed the telephone receiver to Adler. "Take care of the radio," He said to Adler and then walked to the front of the vehicle where Myra was standing.

"It's so dark out here tonight," she commented.

"We'll be continuing on in a few minutes," Hamidi informed Myra as he kissed her on the cheek, and then he walked back toward where he had left Adler.

When he reached the back of the vehicle, Hamidi was surprised to see that Amos Adler had grabbed his backpack from the trunk and put it on his back. He was quick to notice that Adler had removed one of the M16-A4 assault rifles and ammunition belts from the trunk. Adler had the ammunition belt around his waist, and the M16-A4 assault rifle hung on his shoulder.

"Amos, what are you doing?" Hamidi asked.

"This is where we part company," Adler replied as he closed the trunk lid. "Your work here is finished, my friend, but mine has just begun."

Myra overheard Hamidi and Adler talking, and she hurried over to Hamidi. She stood next to him, and they held hands. "What's going on here?"

"Amos isn't coming with us," Hamidi answered.

"Amos, is this true?"

"You will be continuing on without me."

"Will we ever see you again?" Myra asked while she fought back her tears.

"The world is a small place," Adler answered. "If it is the will of Allah, we will meet again."

Myra let go of Hamidi's hand and hugged Amos Adler. "You take care of yourself my brother."

"That I will," Adler assured Myra as they broke their embrace, "May the prophet Muhammad walk with you and Samir on the rest of your journey."

"Where will you go?" Samir Hamidi asked while he and Amos Adler shook hands.

"I have friends nearby that will assist me on my quest. Now go, you don't want to be late."

Samir Hamidi and Myra got back into the Khodro Samand LX sedan. Hamidi started the motor and turned the vehicle around, and drove off back towards the main road. When they reached the main road, they continued in the direction that they were previously traveling.

Amos Adler walked down the darkened road in the opposite direction that Hamidi and Myra had traveled. He walked down the road a few kilometers when he heard a vehicle coming up the road from behind him. He hurried to a ditch that ran alongside the road and took cover. Seconds later, a two and a half ton military cargo truck drove by and pulled off to the side of the road, and stopped a few feet from where he was hiding.

Adler carefully watched while the two men in the front seat of the truck got out and walked to the back of the truck. The two men lit up a cigarette, and the light from their lighters provided just enough light so that Adler could see that they were Iranian military personnel.

"Sure is dark out here tonight," one of the soldiers remarked in Farsi.

"No shit," the other soldier fired back. "Do you have any idea where we are at?"

Adler cautiously watched and listened while the two men argued about whose fault it was that they were lost. He glanced across the road for a second and saw two mussel flashes. Seconds later, both men slammed against the back of the truck and dropped to the ground.

"Amos," a man's voice called out in Farsi.

"Javad is that you?" Adler asked when he recognized the voice that was calling out to him.

"It sure is," the man answered. "Little Joe sent me here to meet you and bring you to him."

"How did you know where to find me?"

"I've been following you ever since you left the house with Samir and Myra," Javad Yousef answered while he walked closer to the ditch where Adler was hiding.

"How the hell did you get here?" Adler asked as he aimed his M16-A4 assault rifle at Javad Yousef, who was approaching him in the darkness.

"Woo now," Yousef said when he heard Adler slide back the loading mechanism on the M16-A4 assault rifle. "When those two clowns passed me and stopped here, I parked my car a few meters down the road behind a sand dune. I hurried up here to see what those two were up to, and when I saw you hiding in that ditch; I knew that I had to neutralize them before they discovered you."

"Come closer so I can get a good look at your face," Adler instructed the man who claimed to be Javad Yousef. "You better be who you claim to be."

Yousef shouldered his weapon and walked closer to Adler, so he could see that it was indeed him. "See Amos, it is me, so point that weapon somewhere else, okay?"

"It is nice to see you again Javad," Adler commented while he lowered his M16-A4 assault rifle. "I thank you for helping me."

"Any time; now come, we must get going. Little Joe is expecting you." Javad Yousef helped Amos Adler out of the ditch, and they walked down the road to where Yousef had left his vehicle. Yousef looked at Adler bewildered. "I know I parked my car here."

"Then where the hell did it go?" Adler inquired as he started to walk to the spot where Yousef had claimed to have parked his vehicle.

"Wait," Yousef said as he grabbed Adler by the arm. "Something does not feel right." He pulled a mini flashlight from his jacket pocket and turned it on, and shined the beam of light toward the spot where the vehicle was parked. "What the hell," Yousef commented when he saw the top part of his vehicle sticking out of the sand. "I do not believe this shit; my car just sank into the sand."

"It sure did," Adler agreed. "Now what do we do?"

Yousef and Adler watched as Yousef's vehicle disappeared beneath the sand. "I guess we head back to where the truck is and get the hell out of here while the gettin' is good," he pointed out. He turned off his mini flashlight and put it back into his jacket pocket. "Follow me."

Adler followed Yousef back to where the two and a half ton truck was parked. He was quick to notice that the two dead soldiers were no longer lying on the ground at the rear of the truck. He removed his M16-A4 and readied his weapon for action. "Something is not right here," he informed Yousef as he scanned the area and saw nothing. "Somebody has been here and has removed the two dead soldiers that were here."

"Stand down," a familiar voice shouted from within the darkness,

Adler looked at Yousef; "Is that who I think it is?"

"Well, it certainly is not the boogie man," a man's voice said as he and three other men emerged from the darkness.

"Little Joe, how did you find us?" Javad Yousef curiously asked as he and Amos Adler greeted Little Joe.

"I tracked you down by using the GPS that was in your car," Little Joe answered. I feared the worst when your GPS went dead; what happened?"

"I parked my car down the road to come help Amos. When we walked back to where I parked the car, we found out that the car had sunk into the sand."

Little Joe and the other three men laughed. "Come we must leave this place," Little Joe suggested. "Our people are not far away. If we hurry, we can be there by morning."

Javad Yousef and Amos Adler started to walk toward the truck.

"We are not taking the truck," Little Joe pointed out. "It is too easy to track."

"Yes, of course," Amos Adler commented.

Amos Adler and Javad Yousef followed Little Joe and the other three men, and they disappeared into the darkness.

# Chapter 8

US Naval Intelligence Center
The Pentagon
Arlington County, Virginia

Admiral Rick Williams was going over his daily radio traffic, when there was a knock on his office door. "Enter!" Admiral Williams commanded.

The door opened, and the admiral's Yeomen, twenty-six-year-old Petty Officer Second, Class Mandy Hill, a brown-haired woman, entered the room carrying a large envelope in her left hand. She marched over to the front of the admiral's desk and snapped to attention. "Sir, this envelope just arrived by special courier," she pointed out to the Admiral. "Sir, it's marked your eyes only."

"That'll be all," he said while he took the envelope from her. "Dismissed."

"I I sir," she acknowledged. She did an about-face, and then left the room, closing the door on her way out.

Admiral Williams opened the envelope and removed its contents. He read the cover page that was attached to the document.

> (Rick-The information in this report is sensitive and should be kept secret. I fear that some members of our government are involved in a plot to bring down President Elliot. Be extra careful who you talk to about what you're going to read. I will be in Washington tomorrow. I will call you when I have

time to do so. I'm going to need your help on this one to prevent a disaster that's heading our way.- John Wilson.)

He quickly read Colonel Wilson's report. When he finished, he sat there thinking about what he had just read. *Wow,* he said to himself as he put the report back into the envelope. He opened the bottom right-hand drawer of his desk and placed the envelope inside. *This is some serious shit;* he thought as he closed the desk drawer. "Enter," Williams said when there was a knock on his door.

"The door opened, and Petty Officer Hill entered. She walked up to the admiral's desk, snapped to attention and said. "Sorry to disturb you, sir, but there's a gentleman outside wanting to see you."

"I'm busy," Admiral Williams snapped at her. "Tell him to come back later."

"Sir, he's from the CIA."

"Very well, show him in."

"I I sir," she acknowledged. She did an about-face, and then left the room.

A few seconds later, a man entered the room and closed the door. He walked up to the admiral's desk. "Admiral, my name is Jim Benson, CIA," the man said while he took out his CIA credentials and then flashed it for the admiral to see. "I'm here to talk to you about a package you received today from Colonel Wilson."

"I see, and what does this have to do with the CIA?" The admiral curiously asked.

"I was sent here by my director to tell you that everything in that report is incorrect."

"I have never known Colonel Wilson to act on anything that he wasn't sure of," the admiral was quick to point out. "I think he's gotten a hold of something that you don't want to get out."

"That's not so," Benson shot back. "The CIA is not hiding anything."

"Yeah, right," the admiral remarked. "You being here is proof enough for me that Colonel Wilson has gotten close to something, and you're trying to cover your ass."

"This is a sensitive matter that is not open for debate." Benson pointed out. "If this bogus intelligence should get out, and be exploited by the media, it can cause unnecessary panic and undermine our foreign and domestic policies."

"What a crock of shit," Admiral Williams fired back.

"Admiral, if you know what's good for you, you will distance yourself from this," Benson suggested.

"Who in the hell do you think you are?" The admiral shouted as he pounded his fist on the desk. "No one comes in my office and threatens me," he shouted at Benson while he got up from his seat. "Get your ass the hell out of here while you can still walk."

Benson was stunned by the admiral's reaction. "You haven't heard the last of me." Benson left the office and then slammed the door shut.

*Fuckin' asshole*, Admiral Williams said to himself while he sat back down.

Thirty Minutes Later

The door to his office suddenly opened, and the Secretary of the Navy, John Forsythe entered. Admiral Williams jumped to his feet. "Mr. Secretary. It's nice to see you again, sir."

"Admiral this isn't a social call," Secretary of the Navy, John Forsythe, pointed out. "I just got my ass chewed out by Vice President Conrad. He's not happy about how you handled that Benson fellow from the CIA that came to see you not long ago. What the hell were you thinking?"

"Sir, he came in here and threatened me."

"About what?" Secretary Forsythe quickly asked.

"About a report that Colonel Wilson sent me," Admiral Williams replied.

"I heard all about that report of Colonel Wilson's from the vice president," Secretary Forsythe shot back. "I have to agree with the vice president. That report is based on unreliable information and has no merit."

"Mr. Secretary, I've known Colonel Wilson for a long time. He's not one to jump the gun unless he's convinced it's legit."

"That's not our main concern right now," Secretary Forsythe

snapped back. "I'm telling you to back off admiral. We need not go any further on this issue. It's not our problem. Do I make myself clear?"

"Yes, sir, Mr. Secretary. I understand, sir," Admiral Williams acknowledged.

Secretary Forsythe left Admiral Williams office and slammed the door on his way out.

*Fuckin' asshole*, Admiral Williams thought to himself as he returned to his seat behind his desk. He pushed the intercom button on his telephone console and waited for Petty Officer Hill to answer.

"Yes, sir," Petty Officer Hill said over the intercom.

"Have Captain Jones report to me A-sap," Admiral Williams said.

"I I sir," she acknowledged.

Admiral Williams canceled the intercom call and continued going over his radio traffic while he waited for Captain Jones to arrive.

"Enter," Admiral Williams said when there was a knock on his office door.

The door swung open, and Navy Captain Jones entered. He walked over to the admiral's desk and snapped to attention while Petty Officer Hill closed the door.

"The Admiral wishes to see me."

"Have a seat," Admiral Williams said, motioning to the chair that was in front of his desk.

"I I sir," Captain Jones acknowledged, and then he sat down in the chair that was in front of the admiral's desk.

"Captain, what I'm about to tell you is to stay between us," Admiral Williams began. "You are not to talk about this with anyone. Is that Clear?"

"Yes, sir, crystal clear, sir."

"I want you to look at something and tell me what you think," Admiral Williams said while he opened the bottom right-hand drawer of his desk. He removed the envelope that Colonel Wilson had sent to him. "This just came in a few minutes ago," he continued while he removed Colonel Wilson's report from the envelope, and then he handed the report to Captain Jones.

Captain Jones began to read through Colonel Wilson's report. When he finished, he laid the report down on the admiral's desk. "So, Red Cell does exist?"

"Yes, they do, and they're planning to strike here in the US," Admiral Williams remarked.

"I take it that you know something that wasn't in this report, sir?"

"I'm afraid so. There's more to this than what's in that report." Admiral Williams answered. "Colonel Wilson has reason to believe that there are Red Cell members in our own government."

Captain Jones was stunned by what Admiral Williams had just said. "Sir, does Colonel Wilson know who in our government is Red Cell members?"

"As far as I know, he's still looking into it." All I do know for sure is that he must be getting close to the answers because I have the brass crawling up my ass about this."

"You don't think Sec-Nav is involved in any of this do you?" Captain Jones curiously asked.

"I don't know. That's why I want you to look into this Red Cell group without raising too many red flags and see what you find out. This is to be kept off the books."

"Sir, if I may," Captain Jones jumped in. "Any report that suggests a terrorist threat against the US is without question something to be concerned about, especially if someone in our own government is involved."

"I agree," Admiral Williams said. "Like I said, the brass has been crawling up my ass about this report. Sec-Nav has ordered me to stay out of this. I'm not ordering you to investigate this. I'm asking you to look into this Red Cell thing and see what you find. So Captain, are you up to the task?"

"I'll do it, sir."

Admiral Williams grinned. "I need to know what you find A-sap."

"I I Sir," Captain Jones acknowledged, and then he jumped to his feet. "I'll get it done, sir." Captain Jones got up from his seat and left Admiral Williams' office, and closed the door behind him.

Admiral Williams put Colonel Wilson's report back into the envelope. He placed the envelope back into the opened bottom right-hand drawer of his desk and closed the desk drawer. He took the key from his pants pocket and locked the drawer. He got up from his seat from behind his desk and put the key in his pants pocket. He walked over to the door and opened it. Petty Officer Hill, who was sitting behind her desk, jumped to her feet and snapped to attention.

"I'll be out for the rest of the day," Admiral Williams informed Petty Officer Hill.

"I I Sir," she acknowledged.

Admiral Williams walked to the door that led to the main hallway and opened the door. He exited the office and closed the door while Petty Officer Hill returned to her seat.

* * * * *

Air Force One
Somewhere Over The Atlantic Ocean

President Martin Elliot sat behind his desk reading a book while on his way to a NATO summit in Brussels. He hated flying, but reading helped pass the time, and helped him relax from the stress of being President of the United States.

He was startled when his secretary, Mrs. Joan Wyatt's voice came over the intercom. "Mr. President, I'm sorry to bother you, sir, but Secretary Maxwell would like to see you."

"Send him in," President Elliot was quick to answer and then pushed the intercom button on the telephone to cancel the call.

A few seconds later, Secretary of State, George Maxwell, entered. "Mr. President, I'm sorry for the intrusion, but I have an updated intelligence report fresh off the decoding machine from Colonel Wilson sent by General Richwood. It just came in a few minutes ago," he said while he walked over to President Elliot's desk and sat down in the chair next to the president's desk. "It's marked your eyes only and urgent."

President Elliot marked his place in the book he was reading with a piece of paper from his desk. He put the book down on his desk and took the report from Secretary Maxwell. He placed the report on the desk in front of him and began to read the three-page report. He read every page carefully, not wanting to overlook anything. When finished, President Elliot leaned his chair back a little. After a brief moment of silence, he continued. "So, General Richwood sent this report?" He asked while he leaned his chair forward to its proper sitting position.

"Yes, sir, he did."

"I wonder why Vice President Conrad didn't send me this report when it got to the White House."

"I wondered the same thing myself, so I called Vice President Conrad a few minutes ago, and I asked him why he didn't forward Colonel Wilson's report to you the moment he received it. He said he read the report and decided that it was best not to bother you with this until you returned from Brussels. He said it wasn't important enough to bother you with it; because Colonel Wilson's report has no merit."

"Not important enough," Elliot snapped. "Who in the hell does he think he is to determine what is or isn't important enough to tell me? That's not his decision to make."

"I agree Mr. President," Secretary Maxwell said, trying to calm down President Elliot. "I'm sure the Vice President meant no disrespect, sir."

"Have you read any of this?"

"No, Mr. President, I haven't."

"Here read this report," President Elliot remarked as he handed Secretary Maxwell Colonel Wilson's report.

Secretary Maxwell began to read Colonel Wilson's report. When he was finished, he laid the report down on President Elliot's desk. "I don't understand why Vice President Conrad says that this has no merit," Secretary Maxwell answered. "Just the implication that Iran has nukes, and that they're planning to set one-off on American soil is reason enough to be concerned. If this is true, we have a serious problem to deal with."

"You damn right we do," President Elliot fired back. "It looks like the Israelis were right about Iran having a nuke. We need to get ahead of this before it blows up in our face."

"Sir, what if Colonel Wilson's report is wrong?"

"What if it isn't?" President Elliot shot back. "We need to take this threat seriously."

"I see your point," Secretary Maxwell said. "However, I suggest we proceed with caution until we know one way or the other."

"I agree," President Elliot concurred. "Tell only those you think you can trust. We don't need this leaking to the press,"

"Yes, Mr. President; I understand, sir."

"Is there something else you need?"

"Mr. President, Kate Livingston is missing."

"What do you mean she's missing?"

"It would appear that Kate was part of a surveillance team that was watching Yasin Abdul Zamani. A Pakistani nuclear physicist in Gwadar, Pakistan that the CIA believed was working with the Iranians. When they went into Zamani's home, it exploded a few minutes later, killing two CIA operatives. Kate and another operative returned to their safe house unharmed. A few hours later, they left their safe house for the airport, and they haven't been heard from since."

"Does Director Müller have any idea what happened to Kate and the other operatives?"

"He believes that Pakistani ISI detained them before they could get out of the country and turned them over to the Iranian Intelligence Agency. He's confident that they're somewhere in Iran."

"Does Director Müller have any idea where in Iran?"

"He's not sure."

"My God. Does the First Lady know about Kate?"

"I don't think so."

President Elliot picked up the telephone receiver from the telephone on his desk in front of him. He put the telephone receiver to his ear while he punched a few numbers on the telephone keypad and waited for the pilot to answer. "Pilot, turn us around. We're going back to Andrews." When the pilot acknowledged his order, President Elliot returned the telephone receiver to the telephone.

"Mr. President, what about the summit meeting?"

"Inform them that I will not be attending."

"Yes, Mr. President. I'll get right on it, sir," Secretary Maxwell got up from his seat and left the room, closing the door on his way out.

A few minutes later, there was a knock on the door. The door opened, and the First Lady, Amanda Elliot, entered while Mrs. Wyatt closed the door.

"Martin is something wrong? I heard that we're returning to Andrews."

"Kate is missing."

"I don't understand. How could Kate be missing?"

"That jackass Müller sent Kate on some mission in Pakistan, even after I told him to keep her in the US. The CIA is looking into this."

"Does the CIA know where she might be?"

"All I know is they're working on finding her."

"Does my sister know that Kate's missing?"

"No, she does not know, and for now, we can't tell anyone that Kate is missing. I promise you I will do everything in my power to find her."

"Martin, I don't like this one bit," the First Lady, Amanda Elliot remarked as tears began to appear in her eyes. "But I promise I won't say anything about Kate missing until you tell me it's okay to do so." Amanda Elliot walked over to the door and stopped. With tears running down her face, she turned to face President Elliot. "Martin, please find Kate."

President Elliot jumped up from his seat and hurried over to the First Lady. He took the First Lady in his arms and held her tight against his body. She wept uncontrollably for a few long seconds until she got her emotions under control. "I will find Kate," he assured the First Lady as they broke their embrace. He took his handkerchief from his suit pocket and handed it to her, and she dried her eyes with it, and then she handed it back to him.

President Elliot opened the door for the First Lady, and she exited the office. Mrs. Wyatt looked at President Elliot confused. "She'll be fine," President Elliot assured Mrs. Wyatt. "She just got some bad news that's all."

"Is there something you need Mr. President?"

"I'm fine." President Elliot smiled at Mrs. Wyatt and stepped back into his office. He closed the door and walked back over to his desk, and picked up the book he was reading from the desk. He leaned back in his chair and opened it to the page where he had left off at, and began reading his book.

* * * * *

Iranian Secret Detention Center
10 Kilometers east of Khash, Iran

The windowless van that was transporting CIA operatives Kate

Livingston and Harry Wheeler crossed the Pakistan-Iran border. The van continued down a dirt road until it reached its final destination and stopped.

The driver and the passenger got out of the van and hurried to the cargo side door. The driver opened the door, and he and his companion removed Livingston and Wheeler from the van. They walked a few yards and stopped.

Kate Livingston listened carefully to the driver, and the passenger's conversation that they were having with an unknown man in Farsi.

"These are the two American pigs you asked about," the driver said. "Give us our money and we'll be on our way."

"Have they said anything to you while on their way here?" The man asked.

"They won't talk," the passenger answered.

"We'll see about that," the man commented. "We have plenty of ways to get them to talk."

*I don't like the sound of that,* Kate Livingston thought.

"Take these two to their cells while I settle with our friends," the man ordered.

Livingston felt someone grab her arm and squeese it hard, shooting a sharp pain up her arm. "Move," a man said in perfect English.

"I won't resist," She assured the man and complied with the man's order. He began to escort Livingston when two shots rang out. "Wheeler," Livingston called out.

"I'm okay, but I don't think the other two guys are," Wheeler answered.

Livingston and Wheeler were escorted into a building a few feet away while the lifeless bodies of their transporters were loaded into the van, and the van drove off. They were escorted to the cellblock area that was located two levels beneath the surface and put into separate cells across from each other. Afterwards, the restraints which bound their hands, and the hoods that were over their heads were removed.

Kate Livingston slowly opened her eyes to give them time to adjust to the bright light in the cell area. When her eyes had adjusted to the light, she could clearly see Harry Wheeler in the cell across from hers. "I got a bad feeling about this Harry."

"So do I," Harry Wheeler agreed. "I don't see how we're going to get out of this one."

The lights in the cell area dimmed, and a man's voice came over the loudspeaker system in the cell area. "The two of you need to get some sleep," the man's voice said in perfect English. "We will talk later."

"We better do as the man says," Wheeler pointed out.

"I don't think we have much choice in the matter," Livingston remarked while she walked over to the cot that was in her cell and sat down. She kicked off her shoes and stretched out on the cot. She laid her head down on the pillow and started too drift off to sleep when she heard the sound of a man screaming. She sat up on the edge of the cot and listened to the horrible screams that were coming from the cellblock down the hall. "Harry, are you awake?"

"That I am," Wheeler answered. "Who can sleep with that going on?"

The lights in their cellblock came on, and the cellblock door opened. A man, who was accompanied by two soldiers dressed in full combat dress and armed with the Pakistani-made Heckler & Koch G3-A3 assault rifle, entered the cellblock. The man walked over to Livingston's cell and stopped a few feet from her cell while one of the soldiers closed the cellblock door, and stood at the cellblock entrance.

"Welcome to your new home," the man sarcastically said in perfect English. "I hope you're comfortable."

"Go to hell," Livingston shot back. "You and I both know that you don't give a rat's ass about our comfort."

"I'm sorry you feel that way. I promise you Miss Livingston that I do care about your comfort."

"What are you doing to that poor man down the hall?" Livingston demanded to know.

"That man is of no concern to you," the man replied as he motioned to one of the soldiers who was standing at the cellblock entrance. The soldier walked over to the man and snapped to attention. The man whispered something in the soldier's ear.

"Yes, sir," the soldier acknowledged, speaking in Farsi. "Right away, sir." The soldier walked to the cellblock door, and the other soldier opened the door and closed it when his companion left the cellblock.

A few minutes later, the man who was screaming from the cellblock down the hall let out another scream that sent a cold chill down Livingston's spine. *My god, what are they doing to that poor man?* She asked herself while she glanced over at Wheeler and saw the fear in his facial expression. Suddenly, a shot from a small-caliber weapon rang out, and the man stopped screaming. Livingston looked back at the man and shook her head in disbelief.

"Now, where was I?" The man said in English. "Oh yes, Miss Livingston, my name is Major Alizadeh al-Shirazi with the Iranian Intelligence Agency. I was sent here to interrogate you and your friend. I know that you took some pictures when you and your other CIA friends violated the sanctity of Yasin Abdul Zamani's townhouse."

"I don't know anything about any pictures," Kate Livingston fired back.

"I know you do," Major al-Shirazi pointed out. "I also know for a fact that you sent the pictures to Carla Garcia, the personal assistant to CIA Deputy Director Hicks. I know that this Carla Garcia sent the pictures to a Colonel Wilson and that she gave her boss, Deputy Director Hicks a copy of the pictures."

"You're full of shit," Livingston shouted. "If what you say is true, then we wouldn't be of any use to you, and we'd sure as hell be dead by now."

"You are very important to me, Miss Livingston," Major al-Shirazi assured Kate Livingston. "However, your friend is not." Major al-Shirazi turned to the soldier who was standing by the cellblock door and nodded, and then he faced Kate Livingston. The soldier walked over to Harry Wheeler's cell. He drew his Colt forty-five sidearm and pointed it at Harry Wheeler; and waited for further instructions from Major al-Shirazi. "You will tell me what I want to know, or your friend will die," Major al-Shirazi pointed out. "The choice is yours."

"Kate, don't tell them anything," Wheeler shouted. "He's going to kill us both when he gets what he wants from us."

Major al-Shirazi looked over at Wheeler. "Perhaps I should send you to our interrogator down the hall. I'm sure he will enjoy interrogating you."

"That won't be necessary," Livingston jumped in. "What do you want to know?"

Major al-Shirazi turned his attention back to Kate Livingston. "I want to know who this Colonel Wilson is."

"I don't know anyone by that name," Livingston calmly answered.

"You are lying," Major al-Shirazi shouted.

"No, I'm not. I don't know anyone named Colonel Wilson."

"I know for a fact that you do know this Colonel Wilson fellow and that the American President is your uncle. You could be extremely useful to me later. However, Mr. Wheeler is of no use to me," Major al-Shirazi concluded and signaled the soldier who had his Colt forty-five sidearm trained on Harry Wheeler, and the soldier pulled the trigger. The bullet shot out from the soldier's Colt forty-five and slammed into Wheeler's forehead, killing him instantly. The soldier holstered his Colt forty-five sidearm and turned to face Major al-Shirazi, and stood at attention.

*My god,* Kate Livingston thought while she sat on her cot in shock. "You murderer," she shouted at Major al-Shirazi. "Harry was no threat to you. You didn't have to kill him."

"That is what you get for lying to me," Major al-Shirazi was quick to point out. "You left me no choice."

"Bullshit. You didn't have to kill Harry. I hope you rot in hell."

"Such language from such a lovely woman; perhaps I should pass you around to my soldiers. Maybe that would make you a little more cooperative."

"You can rape me all you want. It still won't change anything."

"Maybe not, but it would be an experience that you will never forget."

Without warning, the door to the cellblock swung open, and a soldier entered. The soldier hurried over to Major al-Shirazi and snapped to attention. "Sir, headquarters is calling," the soldier said in Farsi. "They say it is urgent."

"Clean this mess up," Major al-Shirazi instructed the soldiers in Farsi, and then he hurried out of the cellblock.

Tears poured from Kate Livingston's eyes while she watched one soldier open the cell that contained the lifeless body of Harry Wheeler. The soldier and his companion drug Harry Wheeler's body from the cell and closed the cell door. They drug Harry Wheeler's body out of the cellblock and closed the cellblock door.

A few minutes later, the lights in the cellblock were turned off, and Kate Livingston laid back down on her cot and cried herself to sleep.

# Chapter 9

Strike Force Delta Command
Office Of Captain Nathan Hale

Captain Hale sat behind his desk and turned on his computer. He picked up the remote control for the plasma screen that was located on the wall in front of him from his desk, and pushed the power button. He loaded the pictures that Kate Livingston took at Yasin Abdul Zamani's townhouse onto the plasma screen. The same pictures that Carla Garcia had sent to Colonel Wilson. He laid the remote control down on his desk and stared at the plasma screen. He knew that he had to figure out what was so important about the pictures, and why Carla Garcia had sent them to Colonel Wilson in the first place.

Suddenly, the office door swung open, and encryption specialist, twenty-three-year-old Second Lieutenant Betty Williams, nicknamed Raven, entered.

"Is there something you need Raven?"

"I'm sorry; I didn't mean to interrupt you. If you're busy I can come back later."

"No, that's all right. I was just trying to figure something out."

Lieutenant Williams looked at the plasma screen. "Is there anything I can help you with?"

"I don't know," Captain Hale answered. "Someone sent these pictures to Wolverine. We're not sure what meaning they have yet. Got any ideas?"

Lieutenant Williams stepped closer to the plasma screen and looked at each picture closely. "Where were these pictures taken?"

"They were taken at Yasin Abdul Zamani's townhouse in Gwadar, Pakistan before it blew up. Why do you see something that Wolverine, and I didn't see?"

"I think so," Lieutenant Williams commented as she looked at the pictures again. "Yes, I'm certain that I've seen this before. I have no doubt that these newspaper articles are being used as an Encryption code-key."

"Are you sure?" Captain Hale said as he got up from his seat from behind his desk. "Are you saying that Zamani is using this code to communicate with his terrorist friends?" He asked while he walked over to where Lieutenant Williams was standing.

"Yes; I am," Lieutenant Williams fired back. "If you look at each article closely you will notice that they're different. Also, if you look at the bottom of each article, you will see that there are numbers and letters written on them. The numbers and letters will be the first set in the message so whoever receives the message will know what article to use. The rest of the message will be a group of numbers that will indicate the line number and word in the article."

"Well, I'll be damned," Captain Hale remarked as he looked closer at the pictures. "Any idea what the last two pictures refer to?"

"I would say that they're a list used to reference a certain person with a certain word," Lieutenant Williams pointed out. "Bulldog, I'm certain that we are looking at the encryption code-key that Yasin Abdul Zamani is using to send and receive messages. We now have the resources to decrypt any message that he might send or receive."

Captain Hale was stunned by what Lieutenant Williams had just said. "I wonder why he left this behind when he disappeared," he continued as he turned to face Lieutenant Williams. "Zamani must have known that we would figure it out eventually."

"Maybe he thought the pictures would be destroyed when his townhouse blew up," Lieutenant Williams was quick to point out. "I don't think he gave any thought to the fact that someone would take pictures of his encryption code-key and send it to us. He probably thought it would be safe to leave it behind, and that no one would make the connection."

"You could be right, or he left his encryption code-key behind because he no longer needed it, and he wanted us to know who he was communicating with." Captain Hale paused for a moment before he continued. "You said you've seen this code before?"

"Yes, I have. We intercepted several messages that were sent to, or sent from Zamani in the past few months. We've been trying to figure out what encryption code-key he was using. That is until now."

"How long will it take you to decrypt those messages?" Captain Hale asked while he walked over to his desk.

"A couple of hours."

"I want you to decrypt those messages, and tell no one about this," Captain Hale said as he grabbed an ink pen from his desk. He wrote the filename and password that Lieutenant Williams would need to get access to the file on the computer on a piece of paper. He picked up the paper and walked back to where Lieutenant Williams was standing. "You're going to need this to access the file," he said as he handed Lieutenant Williams the paper. "When you're done bring them to me."

"Roger that," Lieutenant Williams acknowledged while she folded the paper in half, and then she left Captain Hale's office and closed the door.

Captain Hale walked back to his desk and sat down in the chair behind his desk. He terminated the computer feed to the plasma screen, and the plasma screen went dark. He reached for the remote control for the plasma screen, so he could turn it off when the telephone on his desk began to ring. He turned off the plasma screen and laid the remote control back on his desk.

Captain Hale picked up the telephone receiver from the telephone on his desk and put the it to his ear. "Bulldog."

"Bulldog, we just received a satellite transmission from Sparrow," Lieutenant Cooltrain said. "Do you want me to take it to Raven so it can be decrypted?"

"No, bring it to me. I'll decrypt it myself.

"Okay," Lieutenant Cooltrain acknowledged.

"Thanks, Giggles," Captain Hale said, and then he returned the telephone receiver to the telephone on his desk, and waited for Lieutenant Cooltrain to bring him the material from Samir Hamidi.

A few minutes later, Lieutenant Cooltrain entered Captain Hale's office carrying a thumb-drive that contained the material that was received from Samir Hamidi in her hand. She walked over to Captain Hale's desk and gave him the thumb-drive.

"That was quick," Captain Hale commented.

"Is there anything else you need?"

"No, I don't think so."

"Roger that," Lieutenant Cooltrain said, and then she left Captain Hale's office and closed the door.

Captain Hale turned on his computer monitor, and then he connected the thumb-drive to the USB port on his computer, and waited for the file on the thumb-drive to open. When the file opened, Captain Hale activated the decryption program. When prompted, he entered the location assigned to the thumb-drive, the file name, and the decryption code-key name that he needed to decrypt the file. Satisfied the information he entered was correct, he clicked the process key.

A few minutes later, the entire file was decrypted and translated into English, and then displayed on Captain Hale's computer monitor. He saved the decrypted file on his computer under a new file name, and then he closed the decryption program. He removed the thumb-drive from his computer and opened the top middle drawer of his desk. He placed the thumb-drive in the pencil tray and closed the drawer.

"Now, let's see what Sparrow has for us this time," Captain Hale muttered as he began to read through the material from Samir Hamidi, code-named Sparrow, with a keen eye. He didn't want to take a chance that he would miss something important. *This is unbelievable,* he thought while he continued to read on.

When he was done reading the file's content, he password protected the decrypted file so that only he could open it. He closed the decrypted file and turned off his computer monitor and computer. He got up from his seat and left his office. He closed the office door and proceeded to walk to the communications center, and entered.

Captain Hale walked over to the situation board that covered one wall. He stared at it for a few seconds to see if anything had changed while he was out. *I know you're going to strike, but where?* He thought.

"Bulldog, we've just received word that President Elliot has ordered Air Force One back to Andrews," one of the communication specialist said. "They should be landing in a few hours."

"What's the status on Popeye and his team?"

"They're still at Sandbox (a training center somewhere in Saudi Arabia). They're due to rotate out today."

"Get Popeye on the horn A-sap," Captain Hale ordered. "Put him on the Plasma," he continued as he turned to face the wall size plasma screen. A few seconds later, First Lieutenant Mathew McDonald, nicknamed Popeye, appeared on the plasma screen.

"Popeye, I know that you and your people were scheduled to pull out of there today, but something has come up, and I need you to stay there a little longer."

"What's up?" Lieutenant McDonald curiously asked.

"I'm not sure. I haven't talked to Wolverine yet. It could turn out to be nothing."

"Roger that Bulldog. We'll be standing by until notified otherwise."

Captain Hale hand-signaled the communication specialist, and the screen went blank. "I'll be in my office if you should need me," he informed the communication specialist and left the communication center. He walked to his office and entered. "How long have you been here?" He asked encryption specialist, Lieutenant Williams, who was in his office.

"Not long," Lieutenant Williams answered. "I decrypted the messages that you asked for," she continued, referring to the folder she was holding in her right hand.

"You could have just left it on my desk."

"What's in these messages is too important to leave lying around," Lieutenant Williams pointed out. "We've hit the jackpot on this one." She continued while she handed the folder to Captain Hale. "Take a look and you'll see what I'm talking about."

Captain Hale opened the folder and began to scan through its contents. After the third page, he stopped and closed the folder. "You are to tell no one about the contents of this folder."

"Roger that," Lieutenant Williams acknowledged.

"Wolverine needs to know about this. He won't be back here until sometime tomorrow, so I want you on the next flight to D.C. You are to hand deliver a copy of this to him at the Hay-Adams Hotel."

"I will leave at once," Lieutenant Williams said, and then she left Captain Hale's office and closed the door.

Captain Hale walked over to his desk and sat down in the chair that was behind his desk. He laid the folder down on his desk in front of him and opened it. He read each page in the folder, and then he closed the folder. He opened the bottom left drawer of his desk and placed the folder inside. Captain Hale removed his keys from his pants pocket and locked the drawer. He returned the keys to his pants pocket and got up from his seat from behind his desk. He left his office and locked the door on his way out.

\* \* \* \* \*

Bandar Beheshti Iran

Under the cover of darkness, Samir Hamidi and Myra drove through town and parked their four-door Iran Khodro Samand LX sedan in a secluded area near the waterfront. Samir Hamidi got out of the vehicle and closed the door while Myra got out on the passenger's side. "Are we early?" She asked while she closed the door.

"I believe so," Hamidi answered. "They should be here shortly. Let's get our gear ready, so we can be ready to move out when they get here," he continued while he walked toward the back of the vehicle. "I don't want to be here any longer than necessary."

Myra joined Hamidi at the back of the vehicle. Hamidi opened the trunk lid, and they each removed a backpack from the trunk and put it on their backs. They each grabbed one of the M16-A4 assault rifles and one ammunition belt from the trunk. They secured the ammunition belt around their waist, and the M16-A4 assault rifle hung on their shoulder. Hamidi picked up the high-powered binoculars and hung it around his neck.

"I think we got everything we need," Myra pointed out.

Hamidi nodded his head in agreement. He reached into the trunk and pushed the button on the left side of the trunk; and closed the trunk lid. "Let's move out. I want to put some distance between us, and the car before it incinerates."

Myra nodded and followed Hamidi down the trail that led to the beach. When they reached the sea, they could hear the faint sounds of the incineratery devices in the trunk ignite. Myra looked back to where they had parked the four-door Iran Khodro Samand LX sedan and saw that it was on fire.

"That's going to draw some attention," Myra was quick to point out.

"It's a signal."

"A signal for whom?"

"Don't move," a man's voice said in Farsi from behind them. "Put your hands up, and turn around."

"Where the hell did they come from?" Hamidi remarked as he and Myra put their hands up in the air. "Don't shoot," He called out in Farsi. "We're your friends," he continued as he and Myra slowly turned around and found three Iranian soldiers pointing their Pakistani-made Heckler & Koch G3-A3 assault rifle at them.

"Sparrow, hit the dirt," someone yelled out from the water in English.

Hamidi grabbed Myra, and they dove for the sand. Hamidi laid on top of Myra to protect her while the sounds of muffled automatic gunfire filled the night air. When the gunfire stopped, Hamidi sat up and looked at the three Iranian soldiers who lay dead in the sand not far away. He jumped to his feet and helped Myra up from the ground. Hamidi and Myra looked toward the shoreline and watched as several men, dressed in black scuba suits emerged from the water.

"Sparrow, I'm Blue Jay," one of the men said while he walked over to where Hamidi and Myra were standing. "Come, we must go."

Myra and Hamidi followed Blue Jay to a black Zodiac Zoom two-sixty inflatable boat that was waiting and climbed into the boat. Blue Jay and his team members turned the Zodiac Zoom two-sixty inflatable boat around and climbed in. The boat operator engaged the Mercury two-hundred and sixty horsepower boat motor, and they headed out to sea.

Not long afterwards, they reached international waters and continued to the rendezvous point where they were to meet the USS Nevada, SSBN-733 an Ohio-class nuclear-powered submarine. When they arrived at the rendezvous point, the boat operator turned off the Mercury two-hundred and sixty horsepower boat motor and handed

Blue Jay the satellite radiotelephone. "Big fish this is Blue Jay. We are at the rally point and awaiting pickup. Do you copy?"

Without any warning, the USS Nevada surfaced directly underneath the Zodiac Zoom two-sixty inflatable boat, lifting it safely out of the water. Shortly afterwards, several crewmen from the Nevada were on deck dismantling the Zodiac Zoom two-sixty inflatable boat while Blue Jay and his team escorted Hamidi and Myra to an open hatch not far away. They carefully made their way down the ladder that led into the submarine, and the hatch was secured.

A man dressed in the Navy's NWU (Navy Working Uniform) walked up to Hamidi and Myra. "Welcome to the Nevada," the man said. "I am the Chief Petty Officer of the Boat. Everyone just calls me COB. If you would follow me, I'll show you to your quarters."

Hamidi and Myra followed the COB down the passageway to where a sailor was standing and stopped. The sailor opened the door, and Hamidi and Myra entered, with the COB right behind them. The inside of the room was small but cozy. There were two single bunks along one wall, and a set of lockers and a writing desk along the other wall. The room was also equipped with its own washroom with full facilities.

"You Submarine guys have some setup here," Myra commented.

The COB chuckled. "Ma'am, this is our VIP stateroom. Not all our staterooms have the luxury that this one has."

"This will do," Hamidi remarked.

"If you should need anything, the sailor outside will assist you," the COB pointed out. "You are not allowed to roam the boat without an escort."

"How long will we be here?" Myra asked.

"We should rendezvous with the Eisenhower battle group in a few hours," The COB answered. "Now, if you'll excuse me, I need to return to my duties." The COB walked out of the room and closed the door.

"I'm tired," Myra commented as she walked over to one of the bunks. "I don't know about you, but I'm worn out," she continued while she sat down on the bunk.

Myra laid down on the bunk while Hamidi turned out the light in the room and walked over to the other bunk, and laid down.

# Chapter 10

Joint Base Andrews
Camp Springs
Prince George's County, Maryland

Colonel Wilson's Gulfstream G550 twin-engine jet aircraft landed at Joint Base Andrews and taxied on the runway for a few minutes before the pilot shut down the aircraft's engines. He looked out the window and saw General Richwood standing next to a limousine that was parked a few feet away from the aircraft. *What the hell is he doing here?* He thought while he exited the aircraft, and then he hurried over to where General Richwood was waiting. "It's nice to see you again, sir. I wasn't expecting you to greet me when I arrived."

"Something has come up that couldn't wait," General Richwood commented. "We have a lot to talk about so let's get moving," he continued while he opened the back door to the limousine.

General Richwood climbed into the limousine and then closed the door. Colonel Wilson walked around to the other side of the limousine and opened the door. He got into the back next to General Richwood and closed the door. The driver started the limousine, and they drove off.

"John, I took the liberty of sending your report directly to the president on board Air Force One," General Richwood began. "He was moved by its contents."

Colonel Wilson looked at General Richwood confused. "Sir, I sent my report to the White House when I sent yours. I was led to believe that Vice President Conrad was going to pass it onto President Elliot."

"Well, he didn't, and the president is pissed. John, are you sure about the accuracy of the information in the report you sent me?"

"Yes, sir, I am one-hundred percent sure of its accuracy. General, my sources have never been wrong before. They have put their asses out on the limb to get this information to me."

"I hope so. I would hate to find out later that you were wrong about this."

"I thought the president was going to Brussels?"

"He was until he read your report. He ordered Air Force One back to Andrews. He landed thirty minutes ago. The president is waiting for us. He's called a security meeting to determine what our course of action should be, and how we should proceed."

Colonel Wilson stared out his window without saying a word. When the limousine reached the front gate to Joint Base Andrews, the limousine turned in the opposite direction that would have taken them to the White House. He looked at General Richwood confused. "I thought we were going to the White House, sir."

"We're not going to the White House," General Richwood pointed out. "The president wants to meet in the War room at the Pentagon."

The limousine made its way to the Pentagon and entered the underground parking structure that was only used by high-ranking officials that visited the Pentagon. The limousine stopped in front of a set of doors that were guarded by two Marines dressed in full combat dress and armed with the M16-A4 assault rifle. The driver got out and walked to the back of the limousine. He opened the rear driver's side door, and General Richwood exited the vehicle with Colonel Wilson following.

As General Richwood and Colonel Wilson approached the entrance, one of the Marines opened the door while the other Marine stood at attention. Colonel Wilson followed General Richwood down the hall, and they stopped at the double-door entrance to the War Room where two more Marines, dressed in full combat dress and armed with the M16-A4 assault rifle stood watch.

"I thought we were going to your office, sir."

"Not today," General Richwood remarked.

Each Marine opened a door, and General Richwood and Colonel

Wilson entered the War Room. Colonel Wilson scanned the room and was quick to notice that President Elliot was sitting at the head of the rectangular table that was in the room.

CIA Director Müller sat next to Deputy Director Hicks and to his left was Admiral Williams. Sitting next to Admiral Williams was Secretary of the Navy, John Forsythe. NSA Director, Parkinson was seated next to Secretary Forsythe.

"Deputy Director Hicks I thought you took some time off," Colonel Wilson commented.

"That's what you get for thinking," Deputy Director Hicks fired back.

"Well, it's nice to see you again anyway," Colonel Wilson remarked while he and General Richwood walked over to the table and sat down at the table across from CIA Director Müller. "I was sorry to hear about what happened to Carla Garcia. I know what it's like to lose a close friend."

"We were co-workers Colonel, not friends," Deputy Director Hicks was quick to point out.

"Well, excuse me. I stand corrected," Colonel Wilson shot back. *What a fuckin' bitch,* he thought.

"All right now," President Elliot jumped in. "Let's get down to business."

"Mr. President, I would like to start out by saying that I believe Colonel Wilson's report should be looked at more closely," Deputy Director Hicks began. "I believe that there are some points in his report that needs to be explored further."

"So, you agree that we're facing a bigger threat than we have before?" President Elliot asked.

"Yes Mr. President I do," Deputy Director Hicks answered. "I believe that any hint of an attack on our soil is worth looking into."

*Damn the bitch finally agrees with me on something,* Colonel Wilson thought. *It's going to rain for sure.*

"Mr. President, I disagree with Deputy Director Hicks," Director Müller jumped in. "There is no evidence to support that Colonel Wilson's information is even close to being accurate."

"I agree with Director Müller," Director Parkinson added. "Mr. President we need to look into where this information came from to determine if it has any merit."

"Are the two of you nuts?" Colonel Wilson remarked. "We need to act upon this information now before it's too late. The clock is ticking, and the time to act is now. Any delay could have devastating results."

"Mr. President, I believe that Colonel Wilson is jumping the gun on this one," Secretary of the Navy, John Forsythe, calmly pointed out. "If this threat is real, then why haven't our intelligence agencies picked up on this?"

*What a dickhead,* Deputy Director Hicks, thought as she looked at Secretary Forsythe and shook her head in disbelief. "Maybe they have, and chose to ignore it."

*Damn, she has a set on her,* Colonel Wilson thought as he studied the expressions on everyone's faces. When he made eye contact with Admiral Williams, the admiral nodded his head but remained silent.

"Karen, that is all uncalled for," Director Müller snapped. "I think you're forgetting who you work for."

"I'm fully aware of who I work for," Deputy Director Hicks pointed out. "I meant no disrespect. I was simply making an observation; that's all."

"Admiral Williams, I've been told that you've read Colonel Wilson's report. "What's your opinion on this?" President Elliot inquired. "What's your gut telling you?"

"I believe that even though the origin of the information may be questionable. The bottom line is that we can all agree that the existence of the terrorist group called Red Cell has been known to us for quite some time. Any hint that they're planning some kind of an attack against us should be investigated," Admiral Williams answered. "Not doing so could come back and bite us later."

"Mr. President," Secretary Forsythe began.

"I've heard enough," President Elliot interrupted. "I think we need to find out for sure if this Red Cell group is working with the Iranian Intelligence Agency. Director Müller, I want you to work with Director Parkinson and find out if there is an attack coming our way, and if so, I want to know how and when."

"Yes Mr. President," Director Müller acknowledged.

"Secretary Forsythe, I want a carrier task group in the Gulf of

Oman at all times," President Elliot continued. "I also want another surveillance drone sent into Iran. The target will be the uranium-enrichment facility that we know they have at Iranshahr."

Mr. President, I already have a carrier task group in the Gulf of Oman," Secretary Forsythe pointed out. "We've already launched two surveillance drones to that area, and they were both shot down before we could get close enough to see anything."

"Mr. President, I would advise against sending in another surveillance drone," Director Müller was quick to point out.

"And why is that?" President Elliot snapped.

"Sir, sending in another surveillance drone might rattle the Iranian High-Command. They might fire on our ships in the Gulf of Oman in retaliation because we continue to violate their airspace."

"Send in the surveillance drone and put the carrier task group on alert," President Elliot ordered. "Let's see if they have the balls to pick a fight with us." President Elliot got up from his seat, and everyone in the room jumped to their feet. "General Richwood I would like to have a word with you in your office."

"Yes, Mr. President," General Richwood replied, and then he turned to Colonel Wilson. "Don't go anywhere yet. I might need you."

"Yes, sir," Colonel Wilson replied. He watched General Richwood and President Elliot exit the War Room before he walked over to where Deputy Director Hicks was standing. "Deputy Director would you like to have a few drinks with me later at my hotel?" He boldly asked.

"In your dreams soldier boy," She snapped at him. She walked over to where Director Müller and Director Parkinson were standing, and they departed the War Room, with Secretary Forsythe close behind them.

*Fuckin' bitch,* Colonel Wilson said to himself. *But what an ass.*

"Wilson, are you nuts?" Admiral Williams asked, who was standing behind Colonel Wilson. "Surely you got better things to do than fuck with that."

"I was just trying to be friendly," Colonel Wilson answered as he turned to face his old friend. "I meant no harm."

"Yeah, right," Admiral Williams remarked while he shook hands with Colonel Wilson. "I've known you too long to believe that."

Colonel Wilson smiled. "You got to admit she's got a nice ass on her."

"I hate to break up the party, sir, but General Richwood wants to see you in his office," General Richwood's Assistant, Major Emily Harris, who was standing in the doorway said. "You can talk about Deputy Director Hick's ass later."

"Damn Wilson, she has you pegged."

"I ought to sir; we were married for four years," Major Harris pointed out. "Now follow me, Colonel; the general is waiting. If you promise to behave yourself, I might wiggle my ass a little for you."

"Damn," Admiral Williams commented.

"Take care, my friend," Colonel Wilson said, and he followed Major Harris out of the War Room.

He walked behind Major Harris and watched as she wiggled her ass with every step. After a short walk, they reached the outer office to General Richwood's office and entered. Major Harris walked over to the door to General Richwood's office and opened the door. She smiled at Colonel Wilson as he entered the general's office. Major Harris closed the door and returned to her normal duties.

Colonel Wilson froze when he saw General Richwood sitting behind his desk and that President Elliot was sitting in a chair, in front of General Richwood's desk. "Mr. President, I wasn't expecting you to still be here."

"I'm sorry for my quick exit earlier, but I had something to run by General Richwood before I talked to you about it," President Elliot pointed out.

"Mr. President, before we go any further there is something that I need to tell you that wasn't in my report."

"I don't understand," President Elliot commented. "What could be that delicate that you had to tell me face to face?"

"Sir, I have reason to believe that at least one person high up in our government is connected to Red Cell and that Red Cell is plotting to take you down."

"Are you sure about this?" General Richwood snapped. "When in the hell were you going to tell me about this?"

"I thought that something of this nature was best not sent in a message or talked about over the telephone," Colonel Wilson was quick to answer. "I wanted to limit the knowledge about this information until I was certain who is involved with Red Cell."

"Wilson," General Richwood began.

"He's right general," President Elliot jumped in. "For now, the less people that know about this the faster we can flush this person out. You got any ideas, Colonel?"

"I got my best people working on this. I should have a solution soon," Colonel Wilson answered.

"I'll leave it in your capable hands; just keep me and the general in the loop."

"Yes, Mr. President."

"General could you give us the room?"

"Yes Mr. President," General Richwood said and got up from his seat from behind his desk. "I'll be right outside if you should need me, sir."

President Elliot waited for General Richwood to exit the office. "Colonel, the reason I asked you here is because I need a big favor from you," President Elliot began. "My niece has fallen into the hands of some people who may try to use her to influence my decisions on certain matters. She was a member of the surveillance team in Gwadar, Pakistan that was watching Yasin Abdul Zamani, a well-known Pakistani nuclear physicist whom the CIA suspected of working with al-Qaeda or the Iranians. Somehow, the mission went sideways, and two agents were killed when Zamani's townhouse exploded. Shortly afterwards, my niece and the other two agents went missing."

"Your niece's name wouldn't happen to be Kate Livingston would it?"

"Yes. Do you know her?"

"No, sir, I don't. I recognized the name from the report I read about that mission. I didn't know that she was your niece until now. Does the CIA have any idea who has taken them and where they're being held?"

"Director Müller told me that Kate and the others were detained by some Pakistani ISI agents who are working for the Iranians before they could get out of the country. The ISI agents turned them over to the Iranian Intelligence Agency. He's confident that they're somewhere in Iran by now. Colonel, I don't care what you have to do, but please find Kate and her friends, and bring them back home safely."

Colonel Wilson looked at President Elliot confused. "Sir, you do realize what you're asking me to do?"

"I know the risks. That's why I'm asking you to do this, not ordering you," President Elliot paused for a moment then continued. "So, Colonel, will you do this for me?"

"Yes, sir, I will," Colonel Wilson quickly answered.

The door suddenly opened, and Secretary of Defense; Mark Roberts entered. "Mr. President, we have a situation. Sir, you're needed in the War Room. Everyone is assembled and waiting for you.

"What's up?" President Elliot dared to ask.

"Sir, someone just set off a nuke in Brussels."

"My God, who would do such a thing?" President Elliot inquired.

"We're not sure yet."

"Colonel, come with me," President Elliot instructed Colonel Wilson as he got up from his seat and then hurried out of General Richwood's office to the outer office where General Richwood was waiting.

General Richwood and Colonel Wilson followed President Elliot out of the office. They walked down the hall to the double-door entrance to the War Room where two Marines, dressed in full combat dress and armed with the M16-A4 assault rifle stood watch. Each Marine opened a door, and General Richwood and Colonel Wilson followed President Elliot into the War Room.

All the plasma screens that hung on the walls in the War Room were displaying the map of the Brussels area and the area affected by the nuclear fallout. Two more Marines, both dressed in full combat dress and armed with the M16-A4 assault rifle, stood at the inside entrance.

President Elliot walked over to the rectangular table and sat down at the head of the table while everyone else sat down in their prospective seats. "Where's Vice President Conrad and National Security Advisor, John Haig?"

"Vice President Conrad is on his way back from visiting his family on the west coast," Secretary of Defense, Mark Roberts, answered.

"What about John Haig?" President Elliot asked again.

"Mr. President, John and some of his staff were in Brussels setting up your schedule for the summit meeting," Secretary of State, George Maxwell, sadly answered. "Sir, they were there when the bomb went off."

"My God," President Elliot gasped. "Any idea who's behind this?"

"We don't know yet," CIA Director, Robert Müller, answered. "No one has yet to claim responsibility for the bombing."

"Casualties," President Elliot fired back.

"Mr. President, the body count could exceed two- million," NSA Director, Jack Parkinson, sadly said.

"Mr. President, I suggest that we put our military on high alert until we get to the bottom of this," Secretary of Defense, Mark Roberts, suggested.

"There's no need to go that far," CIA Director, Robert Müller, jumped in. "We should find out who did this and go after them. Mr. President, raising our military readiness could send the wrong signal to the rest of the world."

"Bull," Secretary Roberts fired back. "Raising our military readiness would show that we're taking this threat seriously and that we're ready to take the fight to the perpetrators of this attack."

"I agree with Director Müller," Director Parkinson jumped in. "We shouldn't react too harshly without knowing who did this. Mr. President, a show of force could send the wrong message."

"You're both nuts," Secretary Roberts remarked. "We need to act now, not later. We need to show the world that we're ready to act if the situation calls for it."

"Mr. President, I agree with Secretary Roberts." Secretary of the Navy, John Forsythe jumped in. "We need to be ready for whatever comes next."

"I've heard enough," President Elliot jumped in. "Director Müller, is there any proof that this was an isolated incident?"

"No, sir, not at this time."

"Director Parkinson, what about you?"

"We're not sure at this time."

"General Richwood, what's your opinion on this?" President Elliot inquired.

"Mr. President, I don't see where a show of force would hurt," General Richwood, Chairman of the Joint Chiefs of Staff answered.

"The situation warrants, that we take some kind of action."

"Okay, this is how we're going to handle this," President Elliot began. "I want the CIA and NSA to pursue the investigation on who did this. I also want our military readiness raised to FAST PACE (DEFCON 2) immediately," President Elliot concluded as he got up from his seat. "The clock is ticking people. Get me some answers, and be quick about it."

Everyone in the room jumped to their feet, except for General Richwood and Colonel Wilson, who remained seated. One by one everyone else proceeded to exit the War Room. When Deputy Director Hicks walked past Colonel Wilson, he cracked a smile.

*Really,* Deputy Director Hicks thought and continued walking. *Grow up Wilson.* She continued to think as she exited the War Room.

General Richwood looked at Colonel Wilson. "Wilson, what are you doing?"

"What do you mean, sir?"

"Don't give me that shit. I see the way the two of you look at each other," General Richwood fired back. "What's going on between you and Deputy Director Hicks?"

"Nothing, Sir."

"Is there a problem general?" President Elliot asked while he returned to his seat.

"No, sir. I was just talking to Colonel Wilson about something."

"I see." President Elliot smiled. "It wouldn't have anything to do with Deputy Director Hicks would it?"

"Mr. President, I assure you that there's nothing going on between Deputy Director Hicks and myself. We are colleagues and nothing else. Our relationship is strictly a professional one."

"Petty," President Elliot remarked.

"Excuse me Mr. President," Press Secretary, John Mitchell said when he entered the War Room and hurried over to where President Elliot was sitting. "Mr. President, the press has been assembled in the Press Room. Sir, they're getting a little restless."

President Elliot got up from his seat, and General Richwood and Colonel Wilson jumped to their feet. President Elliot walked over to Colonel Wilson. "Colonel, Find Kate, and find out who set off this nuke."

"Yes, Mr. President," Colonel Wilson acknowledged.

"General, keep me updated on Colonel Wilson's progress."

"Yes, Mr. President."

President Elliot followed Press Secretary, John Mitchell out of the War Room and rejoined his Secret Service protection team. General Richwood and Colonel Wilson walked out of the War Room not long afterwards and headed back to the general's office.

# Chapter 11

The Gulf OF Oman
USS Nevada, SSBN-733

Myra awakened when Samir Hamidi turned on the television set in their stateroom. She sat up on her bunk and waited for her eyes to adjust to the light in the room. "What's up?" She asked as she walked over to the table in the middle of the room where Hamidi was sitting.

"Someone set off a nuke in Brussels. President Elliot is expected to make an announcement soon."

"Do they know who did it?" Myra asked while she sat down at the table next to Hamidi.

"If they do, they're not saying," Hamidi answered. "But I got a pretty good idea who did it."

"Yeah, me too," Myra remarked. "It's only going to get worse from here on out."

Samir Hamidi and Myra watched the news broadcast on the television about the devastation in Brussels. A special news bulletin flashed on the screen, and they watched as President Elliot stepped up to the podium, in the Pentagon News Room.

"A few hours ago, a nuclear device was detonated at the NATO Headquarters in Brussels, Belgium," President Elliot began. "It is estimated that millions of innocent people have perished in this cowardly attack. I would like to take this time to express my utmost sympathy to the people of Belgium. I promise that the United States will hunt down and punish those responsible for this cowardly attack, using the full force of the US military if necessary." President Elliot paused and then continued. "We will not rest until the perpetrators involved in this attack are hunted down and brought to justice." President Elliot stepped away from the podium and hurried out of the Pentagon News Room.

"Come in," Myra said when there was a knock on the door. Samir Hamidi picked up the remote control from the table and turned off the television. The door opened, and the COB entered carrying two life vests and two safety harnesses, along with two pairs of headphone ear protectors. "Hello COB," Myra cheerfully said.

The COB walked over to the table where Samir Hamidi and Myra were sitting. "The two of you are to put on a vest and a safety harness, and hearing protection," he informed Samir Hamidi and Myra. He laid the two life vests, and two safety harnesses, along with two pairs of headphone type ear protectors on the table. "A helicopter from the Eisenhower is inbound to pick the two of you up. It will be here shortly."

"I didn't know that you could land a helicopter on a submarine," Hamidi commented as he got up from his seat.

"You can't," the COB said. "The helicopter will hover over us, and you will be lifted up into the helicopter by a cable."

"Isn't that dangerous?" Myra asked as she too got up from her seat.

"A little," the COB commented. He helped Hamidi and Myra put on their life vests, and safety harnesses. "Now please we must hurry. They're waiting for you topside," he said while he finished checking their life vests, and safety harnesses to ensure that they were wearing them properly. "The helicopter can't stay here long when it gets here."

Satisfied that Hamidi and Myra were wearing their life vests, and safety harnesses properly the COB helped them put on their ear protectors, and then he escorted them out of the stateroom. The Sailor outside of the stateroom closed the door and followed Hamidi and Myra down the passageway, with the COB leading the way.

They walked to an exit hatch not far away. The COB climbed up the ladder first, and then he stood at the top of the ladder; and helped Hamidi and Myra onto the deck of the Nevada. The COB pointed to a Sikorsky SH-60H Seahawk helicopter fast approaching. "We will be sending you up one at a time," he shouted, loud enough for Hamidi and Myra to hear him.

Shortly afterwards, the Sikorsky SH-60H Seahawk helicopter hovered above the Nevada, and a cable was lowered. The COB hooked the cable to Myra's safety harness and gave the thumbs up. Hamidi watched as Myra was hoisted on board the helicopter, and the cable was lowered again. The COB hooked the cable to Hamidi's safety harness and once again, he gave the thumbs up, and Hamidi was hoisted on board the helicopter.

The helicopter crew helped Hamidi and Myra strap into their seats. Hamidi glanced out the small side window and watched as the Nevada disappeared beneath the ocean surface. The Sikorsky SH-60H Seahawk helicopter proceeded towards the USS Eisenhower aircraft carrier that was waiting two-hundred miles away.

Traveling at top speed, it wasn't long before the Sikorsky SH-60H Seahawk helicopter touched down on the flight deck of the USS Eisenhower. The flight deck crew immediately proceeded to secure the helicopter to the flight deck while the helicopter pilot and copilot shut down the rotor blades. Within minutes, the Sikorsky SH-60H Seahawk helicopter was safely secured to the deck of the Eisenhower and Samir Hamidi, and Myra were escorted to a Bell Boeing V-22 Osprey aircraft that was waiting.

Once the aircraft's crew had Hamidi and Myra securely strapped into their seats, the Osprey's pilot and copilot throttled up the Osprey's two Rolls-Royce Allison T406/AE 1107C-Liberty turbo shaft tilt-rotor engines, and lifted off the flight deck of the USS Eisenhower. The Osprey quickly climbed to its cruising altitude of nine thousand feet before leveling off and continuing on its flight plan.

Hamidi was quick to notice a man, First Lieutenant Mathew McDonald, sitting across from them, dressed in an all-black combat uniform, and wearing a pair of headphone ear protectors. *I wonder why he's here,* Hamidi thought while he tapped Myra on the thigh.

Myra looked down and saw Hamidi's finger pointing to the other side of the aircraft. She looked in the direction he was pointing, and she too saw Lieutenant McDonald sitting across from them. She turned toward Hamidi and shrugged her shoulders.

Lieutenant McDonald saw that Hamidi and Myra were getting restless by his presence, so he removed his seat restraints and stood up.

He walked over to where Hamidi and Myra were sitting and sat down next to Myra. He removed his headphone ear protectors and put on a pair of headphones that had a boom microphone attached to it that was hanging from the ceiling of the aircraft. He then motioned Hamidi and Myra to do the same.

Hamidi and Myra removed their headphone ear protectors, and they each put on a pair of headphones that had a boom microphone attached to it that was hanging from the ceiling of the aircraft.

"We are on a secure com-link that only we can hear what's being said," Lieutenant McDonald pointed out. "All you have to do is talk normal; the headset will do the rest."

"Who are you?" Myra asked.

"Everyone calls me Popeye."

"Where are we heading?" Hamidi inquired.

"We are heading to a secured facility that we refer to as Sandbox. Its location is classified."

"We were supposed to be heading back to the US," Hamidi was quick to point out. "Why the sudden change?"

"All I know is that my orders are to see to it that you arrive at Sandbox safely," Lieutenant McDonald answered. "Now if you'll excuse me, I need to have the pilot let Sandbox know that we're heading their way." Lieutenant McDonald removed his com-set and put it back where he had gotten it from. He put his headphone ear protectors back over his ears and walked toward the cockpit of the Osprey aircraft.

"Something has changed," Hamidi commented as he took Myra's hand in his.

"Whatever it is, it isn't good," Myra added. "I just hope that we can help."

Hamidi nodded, and they sat there holding hands.

Meanwhile, Lieutenant McDonald entered the cockpit and closed the door. He removed his headphone ear protectors and hung them up on a hook on the back of the door. He removed a Headset com-link from the adjacent hook. He put it on and then plugged the headset into a jack on a panel that was located next to the co-pilot. "I need to contact Strike Force Delta Command," he said to the co-pilot. "Can you get me a secure line?"

The co-pilot flipped a switch on the panel next to him. "Your com-link is open."

"Eagle Nest, this is Foxfire. Do you copy, over?"

"Foxfire, this is Eagle Nest; we copy, over."

"Eagle Nest, the package has been picked up, and we're proceeding to Sandbox, over."

"Roger that Foxfire; proceed to Sandbox and standby, over."

"Roger that, Foxfire standing by, over and out." Lieutenant McDonald unplugged the headset com-link from the panel and hung it back on the hook. He removed the headphone ear protectors and placed them back over his ears. Lieutenant McDonald exited the cockpit area and sat down in the seat he was sitting in before. He fastened his seat restraints and looked at Hamidi and Myra, who were holding hands and smiled.

\* \* \* \* \*

US Naval Intelligence Center
The Pentagon
Arlington County, Virginia

Navy Captain, Mark Jones was standing in front of the printer and watched as his two-page report about his findings on the report that Colonel Wilson had sent to Admiral Williams was printing out when a man and a woman entered his office. He quickly turned to face them.

"Captain Jones, my name is Thomas Flowers, and this is my partner Pamela Wells; Homeland Security," the man stated, while he and Pamela Wells took out their Homeland Security credentials and flashed them for the captain to see.

"Don't you people knock before you enter someone's office?" Captain Jones fired back.

"Captain, we have some questions about your inquiries into Red Cell," Pamela Wells said, ignoring what Captain Jones had asked. "We want to know why you're looking into Red Cell. Does this have something to do with the Brussels bombing?"

"I have no idea if they were involved in the Brussels bombing," Captain Jones quickly answered. "There's nothing going on here that concerns Homeland."

"We want to know why the sudden interest in Red Cell." Flowers pressed. "Why is the Navy looking into Red Cell? We know that Admiral Williams asked you to look into this."

*How the hell do they know that?* Captain Jones asked himself. "I don't know what the hell you're talking about. Now if you don't mind, I have a lot to do today, and don't let the door hit you on the ass on the way out. Now get out before I call security."

"Stop looking into Red Cell captain," Thomas Flowers remarked. "You're wasting your time."

Thomas Flowers and Pamela Wells left Captain Jones' office and closed the door. Captain Jones removed his two-page report from the printer and walked over to his desk and sat down in the chair behind his desk. He laid his report down on his desk and picked up the telephone receiver from the telephone on his desk. He dialed the extension number for the Pentagon Security Office while he put the telephone receiver to his ear.

"Security," a woman's voice said when Captain Jones's call was answered. "How may I help you?"

"Yes, this is Captain Jones from the Naval Intel office. I need a security team to do a security check in my office A-sap."

"Are you declaring a security breach?"

"Not at this time. It's a precautionary measure."

"Very well captain, a security team is on its way."

"Thanks," Captain Jones said and returned the telephone receiver to the telephone on his desk.

A few minutes later, there was a knock on the office door. The door opened, and three technicians entered. The men were carrying a medium-sized silver case and a handheld radio frequency detector. They quickly motioned for Captain Jones to remain silent.

They closed the door and began to scan the office using the handheld radio frequency detectors. They each scanned the office area and found nothing until one of the technicians scanned around Captain Jones's desk, and his handheld radio frequency detector began to beep.

The technician honed in on the source of the transmission that was coming from Captain Jones' desk. The closer the technician got to

Captain Jones' telephone the louder his handheld radio frequency detector beeped. He lifted Captain Jones' telephone from the desk. He turned it over and found a radio-transmitting device attached to the bottom of the telephone. He placed the silver box on Captain Jones's desk and opened the box. He then removed the radio-transmitting device and placed it in the silver box, and closed the case.

"Your office is secure," the technician who found the listening device declared.

"Any idea how long that device was there?" Captain Jones asked.

"Your last security check was six days ago."

"Is there any way to find out where it was transmitting to?"

"I would say somewhere in the building. Captain, this is a security breach that must be reported."

"I understand, but first I want you to follow me," Captain Jones instructed them while he got up from his seat. "I want Admiral Williams' office checked."

Captain Jones grabbed his report from his desk and walked over to the door. The technician, who was standing by the door, opened the door. Captain Jones exited the office, and the technicians followed. He locked the office door and walked toward Admiral Williams' office with the technicians following close behind.

When Captain Jones arrived at Admiral Williams' office, he entered. Petty Officer Hill jumped to her feet; Captain Jones motioned for her to be silent while the technicians began to scan the room.

"This room is clear," one of the technicians declared.

"Is the admiral in?" Captain Jones asked.

"No, sir; he's attending a security meeting with Sec-Nav," Petty Officer Hill answered. "He'll be back shortly."

Captain Jones walked over to the door that led into Admiral Williams' office and opened the door. The technicians entered the office and began sweeping the room for listening devices. Captain Jones stepped inside and walked over to the Admiral's desk, and laid his report down on the desk where the Admiral would see it when he returned.

When the technicians completed their scan of the room, a listening device was found on the chair that was in front of the admiral's desk. The listening device was placed in a silver box, and the room was declared secured.

"I want to know where these listening devices came from," Captain Jones ordered. "I will inform the admiral about this security breach. I'm sure he will want answers."

"We'll let you know what we find out," one of the technicians said as they left the admiral's office.

"Captain, what the hell is going on here?" Admiral Williams demanded to know, who was standing in the doorway. "What were those security techs doing in my office?" he asked while he closed his office door.

"Sir, we've had a security breach. The techs found a listening device on my office phone and one in your office."

Admiral Williams walked over to his desk and sat down in the chair behind his desk. "How did that happen?"

"Don't know yet, sir."

"What in the world ever made you suspect that we were being bugged?"

"A Thomas Flowers and Pamela Wells from Homeland Security visited me in my office a few minutes ago. One of them mentioned that you asked me to look into this Red Cell business. I knew that there was only one way they could have known about you asking me to look into this Red Cell thing. I was certain that my office or your office was bugged, and that they were sent here to find out what we knew."

"That was quick-thinking captain."

"Thank you, sir."

"So what did you find out?"

"I believe that Colonel Wilson's report is right on the money. My report is on your desk."

"What are your thoughts on this Brussels bombing?"

"Sir, I believe that when all the facts are in it will be clear that Red Cell, with help from the Iranian government, was behind the bombing in Brussels."

"I agree. Good work captain." Admiral Williams looked at his watch and then continued. "It's getting late. We'll go over your report in the morning before I pass your report onto Sec-Nav so he can brief the president."

"I I sir," Captain Jones acknowledged and left Admiral Williams' office and closed the door. Petty Officer Hill, who was sitting behind her desk, jumped to her feet and stood at attention. "Carry on Petty Officer," Captain Jones remarked as he opened the outer door.

"I I sir," Petty Officer Hill acknowledged and returned to her seat.

Captain Jones stepped into the hallway and closed the door. He walked down the hallway and past his office to the exit door to the parking garage, and entered. Unknown to Captain Jones, Thomas Flowers, and Pamela Wells watched from the parking lot across the street with their high-powered binoculars as he walked over to where his car was parked. He removed his keys from his pants pocket and unlocked the driver's side door, and opened the door. He got in behind the wheel and closed the door. He put on his seat belt, and then he inserted the ignition key into the ignition. Captain Jones turned the ignition key to start the car, and it exploded into a fireball, killing him instantly.

"Well, that takes care of that," Flowers commented while he put his pair of high-powered binoculars back into its carrying case and threw the case into the backseat. He started up the vehicle that he and Pamela Wells were sitting in, and put the vehicle in drive. "It's been a long day," he commented.

"That it has," Wells agreed as she too put her pair of high-powered binoculars back into its carrying case and threw the case into the backseat.

Flowers drove off while Wells removed her cell phone from her purse. She pushed one of the speed dial numbers and put the cell phone to her ear.

"Report," someone said when the call was answered.

"Target neutralized," Wells reported.

"Carry on," the person on the other end of the telephone remarked, and the line went dead.

"Where to now?" Wells asked as she put her cell phone back into her purse.

"I figure that we'll head on back to the office and wait for the boss to figure out his next move."

"Sounds like a winner to me," Wells agreed.

Flowers maneuvered their car onto the interstate highway and headed toward Washington.

# Chapter 12

The Hay-Adams Hotel
Washington, D C


Colonel Wilson sat on the edge of the bed in his room wrapped only in a towel. He picked up the television remote that was lying on the bed next to him, and turned on the television. He flipped through the channels until he got to the CNN channel. He watched carefully and listened while the news commentator reported on the situation in Brussels.

"We now go to Thomas Horn, who is reporting live from NATO Regional Headquarters in Berlin, Germany," the man on the television said. "Thomas, does anyone know for sure who did this, or how they got the nuclear device into the city?"

"No one has yet to claim responsibility for setting off the nuclear device. It's unclear at this time how the perpetrators got the device into the city," Thomas Horn reported. "However, I have learned from an anonymous source that the United States and NATO, along with several other countries, have put their Armed Forces on high alert. Thomas Horn, reporting live from NATO Regional Headquarters in Berlin; back to you Jim."

"What a crock of shit," Colonel Wilson mumbled. He grabbed the remote control for the television from the bed next to him and started to turn off the television when the news about the bombing at the Pentagon came on. "Holy shit?" He said as the pictures of the bombing were displayed on the television screen. "This shit is getting out of hand," he commented as he turned off the television and tossed the remote control in the chair across from him.

He got up from the bed and started to walk to the bathroom when someone knocked on his door. Colonel Wilson hurried over to the door. He looked out the peephole in the door and saw thirty-year-old, CIA Deputy Director, Karen Hicks, standing there with her hair let down and dressed in her usual skirt and blouse. *What the fuck does she want,* he thought while he tightened the towel around his waist, and then he opened the door. "Deputy Director Hicks, what a pleasant surprise."

"Cut out the pleasantries' colonel," Deputy Director Hicks said while she entered Colonel Wilson's room with her briefcase in hand. "I'm not here on a social call,"

Colonel Wilson shook his head in disbelief and closed the door. "Then why the hell are you here?"

"Do you always greet your guests dressed that way? You could have at least put on something more appropriate than a towel wrapped around you before you answered your door."

"Never mind how I'm dressed. What do you want Deputy Director?"

"I wanted to talk to you about the incident in Brussels and the bombing at the Pentagon," Deputy Director Hicks replied while she walked over to the small table next to the window. She sat down in the chair and put her briefcase on the table.

"All I know is what I saw on CNN," Colonel Wilson pointed out while he walked into the bathroom. He dropped the towel to the floor and put on his bathrobe, not realizing that Deputy Director Hicks could see him in the mirror on the wall. "You probably know more about what's going on than I do," he continued to say as he stepped out of the bathroom.

"Next time, Colonel, you might want to close the door before disrobing," Deputy Director Hicks pointed out. "You know there are mirrors in every bathroom."

Colonel Wilson stood there with a dumbfounded look on his face. "I meant no disrespect; I..."

"Relax Colonel; you're not the first man I've seen butt-ass-naked. *Imagine that,* Colonel Wilson thought. *The bitch is human after all.*

"Colonel, do you mind if I smoke?"

"It is a smoking room," Colonel Wilson pointed out. "I'll get an ashtray."

Colonel Wilson walked over to the nightstand next to the bed and retrieved the ashtray. He dumped the contents into the trashcan next to the nightstand. He lost his grip and dropped the ashtray into the trashcan. With his back to Deputy Director Hicks, Colonel Wilson bent over and picked the ashtray out of the trashcan.

Deputy Director Hicks cracked a smile. *Yum, yum; nice ass*, she thought. *That would make a nice snack;* she continued to think while she kicked off her shoes. She ran her tongue across her lips while she unbuttoned a couple of buttons on her blouse, revealing the top part of her perfectly shaped breasts.

Colonel Wilson returned to the table with the ashtray in hand. He placed the ashtray in the middle of the table and sat down in the chair across from Deputy Director Hicks. *Now that's not a bad view;* he thought when he noticed that the top part of her breasts was exposed. *I bet those babies are a mouth full.*

Deputy Director Hicks opened her briefcase and removed a pack of cigarettes and a Bic lighter. She removed a cigarette from the pack and put it to her lips. She lit up the cigarette and took a long draw from it, and then exhaled the smoke. "Would you like one Colonel?" She offered.

"Please call me John," Colonel Wilson said while he took a cigarette from Deputy Director Hicks.

"Very well John; you may call me Karen for now."

*I've called you worse than that*, Colonel Wilson thought while he picked up the Bic lighter from the table and then lit his cigarette. He took a draw from the cigarette and quickly exhaled the smoke. "So tell me Karen, why are you here?"

"Did you get a file from Carla Garcia that contained some pictures?"

"Yes, I did," Colonel Wilson answered. He took another draw from his cigarette and quickly exhaled the smoke. "I have no idea what those pictures are supposed to mean, or why she sent them to me."

"Carla died in a house fire the same night she sent you those pictures." Deputy Director Hicks paused for a moment to get her emotions under control. "They said it was an accident, but I think she was murdered. Carla was a good person and a friend. She didn't deserve to die like that."

"Are you telling me that someone had this Carla Garcia murdered over these pictures?"

"I know it sounds crazy, but yes I am."

"How can I help?"

"I was hoping that you could check into this and see what you can find out." Deputy Director Hicks shot back.

"Who else have you told this to?"

"You're the first person that I told about my suspicions. Please don't tell anyone where you got this idea from," Deputy Director Hicks said while she crushed her cigarette out in the ashtray. "We need to keep this between us for now."

"All right, I'll look into it for you," Colonel Wilson said. He took a draw from his cigarette and then exhaled the smoke. "I'll let you know if I find anything of interest." He continued as he crushed his cigarette out in the ashtray.

Deputy Director Hicks started to get up from her seat. "Hold on Karen," Colonel Wilson said while he grabbed her by the arm and pulled her back down to her seat.

Deputy Director Hicks looked Colonel Wilson in the eye and smiled. "You can let go of my arm John."

Without any warning, Colonel Wilson stood up and leaned over the table. He kissed Deputy Director Hicks on the lips and after a few short seconds, she pushed Colonel Wilson away. "Not so fast cowboy," Deputy Director Hicks softly said.

"I'm sorry; I don't know what came over me," Colonel Wilson said while he sat back down in the chair. *What, the fuck was I thinking?* He thought.

Deputy Director Hicks stared at Colonel Wilson and grinned. She could feel the uncontrollable desire building inside her for him. She got up from her seat and leaned over the table. She kissed Colonel Wilson passionately on his lips until this time he pushed her away.

Colonel Wilson got up from his seat. *Holy shit,* he thought and rushed into the bathroom and closed the door. *This is not a good idea John;* he continued to think while he paced around the bathroom.

He waited a few minutes, and then he opened the bathroom door and walked back into the room. He was stunned by the sight of Deputy Director Hicks lying on the bed butt-ass-naked with her legs spread wide, exposing herself to him. *Jesus Christ, what have I gotten myself into now?* He thought to himself. *This can't be happening to me. Not with the Ice Queen.*

"Like what you see soldier boy?" Deputy Director Hicks asked, and then smiled.

Colonel Wilson walked over to the foot of the bed and stared at the nude woman who was lying on his bed. "You bet your ass, I do," He said while he opened his robe and then let it fall to the floor. He crawled on top of Deputy Director Hicks, and they kissed. After what seem like a few long minutes, he broke his embrace with her, and they began to make love.

When Colonel Wilson got to the point where he could no longer continue, he rolled off from on top of Deputy Director Hicks and laid on his back next to her. *You did it now John,* he thought. *You melted the Ice Queen.* He looked over at Deputy Director Hicks, and she smiled back at him.

Deputy Director Hicks quickly kissed Colonel Wilson on the lips and jumped out of bed. She hurried into the bathroom and closed the door.

Meanwhile, Colonel Wilson laid on the bed. It took all the strength he had left to sit up on the edge of the bed. He got up from the bed when Deputy Director Hicks opened the bathroom door and entered the room. Colonel Wilson hurried into the bathroom and closed the door.

He walked over to the mirror and stared at his reflection. *You just couldn't keep your dick in your pants could you John?* He thought. *You got to work with this woman. You should have known better dumb ass.*

Meanwhile, Deputy Director Hicks walked over to the table and took out a cigarette from the pack. She put the cigarette in her mouth, picked up the Bic lighter from the table, and lit her cigarette. She put the Bic lighter down on top of the pack of cigarettes and picked up the ashtray from the table. She walked back over to the bed and sat down. She placed the ashtray on the nightstand and continued to smoke her cigarette.

The bathroom door opened just as Deputy Director Hicks put her cigarette out in the ashtray. Colonel Wilson walked over to the bed and picked up the bathrobe on the floor. He put on the robe and stood there looking at the still bare ass Deputy Director Hicks sitting on the edge of the bed.

"What's wrong?" Deputy Director Hicks asked.

"Nothing," Colonel Wilson answered. "I was just thinking; why don't we get dressed and go grab a bite to eat, my treat?"

"Great idea," Deputy Director Hicks said and jumped to her feet. She began to round up her clothes when there was a knock on the door. "Are you expecting anyone?" She asked while she finished picking up her clothes from the floor.

"No, I'm not."

"Wilson, are you in there?" They heard General Richwood say.

"I'll be right there, sir," Wilson said in a loud voice. "I need to put something on first."

"Hurry up Wilson. I don't have all day."

"Hide," Colonel Wilson whispered.

"Hide where?"

"In the closet," he suggested.

"Are you nuts?"

"Look, Karen, General Richwood can't find you here."

"I know that, but the closet?"

"Just do it before the general blows a gasket."

"All right," Deputy Director Hicks said. She hurried over to the closet and opened the door. She stepped inside and closed the door.

Colonel Wilson walked over to the door and opened it. "Sorry, it took so long, sir."

"What the hell Wilson," General Richwood barked while he entered. "You know better than to keep me waiting."

"I apologize for the delay sir," Colonel Wilson said and closed the door.

"Wilson, I stopped by to let you know that the Ice Queen is looking for you." General Richwood walked over to the table and noticed the briefcase that Deputy Director Hicks left on the table. The general looked at the briefcase closer and saw the Deputy Director's name engraved on the outside. "I see the She-Devil has already been here. Where is she now?"

"Sir, Deputy Director Hicks, left a few minutes ago," Colonel Wilson was quick to point out. "She must have left her briefcase. I'm sure she'll be back for it, sir."

"Wilson, that's one woman you don't want to fuck with. She'll eat you for breakfast and spit your ass out before lunch."

Colonel Wilson smiled. "Roger that, sir."

"What did the Ice Queen want anyway?"

"I don't know, sir. She got a call on her cell and left in a hurry.

General Richwood glanced down at the floor next to the bed and saw a pair of woman's panties lying on the floor with the initials KH monogrammed on the waistband. *You fuckin' liar,* he thought. *I hope you know what you're fuckin' doing.* He glanced back at Colonel Wilson and asked. "When are you going back to Strike Force Delta Command?"

"I'll be leaving around thirteen hundred tomorrow."

"Why so late?"

"Bulldog is sending me something by special courier in the morning. I need to be here when the courier arrives."

"Any idea what's so important that it couldn't wait until you got back to Strike Force Delta Command?"

"He didn't say, sir. He just said it was too important to wait, and that it was too sensitive to talk about it over the telephone."

General Richwood picked up the pair of woman's panties from the floor and handed them to Colonel Wilson. "I hope you know what the fuck you're doing," he whispered.

Colonel Wilson cracked a grin. "Me too, sir," he whispered back as he took the pair of woman's panties from General Richwood.

"Well, I best be heading home," General Richwood remarked. "The wife is probably wondering what's keeping me."

"Give Mrs. Richwood my regards, sir."

"Carry on Colonel," General Richwood said as he walked to the door. "Good luck with the Ice Queen."

"Roger that, sir."

General Richwood opened the door and stepped into the hallway. Colonel Wilson walked over to the door. He closed the door and set the dead bolt. Deputy Director Hicks flung the closet door open. "The Ice Queen," she snapped. "Who the hell does he think he is anyway?

I'm no She-Devil. I do my job in the utmost professional manner."

"Calm down Karen. The general is just being, well, himself." Colonel Wilson pointed out while he twirled the pair of panties with his finger.

Deputy Director Hicks smiled. "He knew I was here?"

"He sure did."

"Am I that hard to get along with?" Deputy Director Hicks asked. She threw her clothes on the floor and stood there with nothing on. "You don't think that of me do you?"

Colonel Wilson tossed the panties on the pile of clothes that were on the floor and walked over to Deputy Director Hicks. He took her into his arms, and they kissed. "You can't help but be who you are," He answered. He swept her off her feet and carried her to the bed. "Let's skip dinner," he said as he laid Deputy Director Hicks down on the bed and then removed his robe. "I'm not hungry for food; if you know what I mean."

Deputy Director Hicks smiled, "You read my mind." She took Colonel Wilson by the hand and pulled him closer. "We can always order room service later." Colonel Wilson climbed on top of Deputy Director Hicks, and they began to make love again.

Colonel Wilson's excitement grew by the moment. He tried to control the inevitable, for as long as he possibly could but failed. Afterwards, he rolled off of Deputy Director Hicks and laid on his back next to her. Seconds later, they both drifted off to sleep.

* * * * *

Baltimore International Airport

The Boeing seven-fifty-seven that carried Second Lieutenant, Betty Williams, from Oklahoma City, landed safely on the ground and taxied to the terminal gate. After a brief wait, while the ground crew secured the aircraft, the passengers were allowed to disembark. She exited the aircraft with her briefcase in hand and hurried to the airport's main entrance to catch a cab.

Lieutenant Williams opened the door and climbed into the cab. "Hay-Adams Hotel, " she instructed the cab driver while she closed the door, and the cab drove off.

The sun began to break over the horizon as the taxi pulled up in front of the Hay-Adams Hotel. The taxi driver stopped the cab at the main entrance, and the doorman opened her door while Lieutenant Williams paid the cab driver. She got out of the cab, and the doorman closed the cab door, and the cab drove off. The doorman hurried to the entrance door and opened it. Lieutenant Williams entered the hotel and walked to the front desk.

"Good morning," the young lady behind the desk said. "How may I help you?"

"I'm a colleague of John Wilson, and I need to know what room he's in."

"I'm sorry miss, but I can't give out that information. It's hotel policy."

"Look, I don't give a rat's ass about your hotel policy," Lieutenant Williams snapped. "I need to speak with Mr. Wilson. This is urgent business that can't wait. If you can't give me the information I'm asking for, then go find someone that can, and do it now."

The young lady stepped back from the counter and signaled the hotel manager to assist her. The hotel manager walked over to where the young lady was standing. "She wants Mr. Wilson's room number, and she won't take no for an answer."

"I'll handle this," the hotel manager said. "You can go help someone else." The hotel manager stepped up to the counter. "What is your name miss?" He inquired while he looked up Colonel Wilson's information on his computer.

"Betty Williams."

"I'm sorry, Miss Williams, but Mr. Wilson has asked not to be disturbed, which means that I can't call him to verify that he knows you," The hotel manager pointed out. "Therefore, I cannot give you his room number."

"Fuck it. I guess I'll have to call the White House and see if they know Wilson's room number," Lieutenant Williams commented and began to look for her cell phone in her purse.

"There is no need to call the White House;" The hotel manager gave in. "He is in room fifteen-twenty-five."

"Now that wasn't so hard was it?" Lieutenant Williams said

sarcastically. *Fuckin' asshole,* she thought as she walked away from the counter. She walked over to the elevators and pushed the call button. The elevator door opened, and she stepped inside. Lieutenant Williams pushed the button for the fifteenth floor. The elevator door closed and began to move upward.

Meanwhile, Deputy Director Hicks woke up when the morning sun began to shine on her face. She sat up on the edge of the bed on her side. She looked over at Colonel Wilson, who was sound asleep and smiled. She giggled softly when Colonel Wilson began to snore.

She got dressed and walked over to the table. She put her cigarettes and lighter back into her briefcase and sat down in the chair. She took out one of her business cards and an ink pen from the briefcase. She wrote on the back of her business card; *John, Sorry I had to run. Give me a call when you get the time, Karen.*

She returned the ink pen to her briefcase and put on her shoes. With her briefcase in hand, Deputy Director Hicks got up from her seat and walked over to the door, and opened it.

At the same time, Lieutenant Williams arrived on the floor where Colonel Wilson's room was located. She stepped out of the elevator and saw Deputy Director Hicks leave Colonel Wilson's room and shut the door. Deputy Director Hicks tried the door to make sure it was locked before she headed for the elevator.

"Good morning," Deputy Director Hicks cheerfully said to Lieutenant Williams as they passed each other in the hallway.

Lieutenant Williams stopped. *Oh my god,* she thought. *The rumors are true. Wilson is fucking Deputy Director Hicks.* She watched as Deputy Director Hicks entered the elevator before she continued to Colonel Wilson's room. She knocked on Colonel Wilson's door and waited.

"Karen, did you forget something?" Colonel Wilson asked as he opened the door with only a towel covering his man parts. "Raven, I'm sorry. I thought you were someone else."

"I'm not Karen, sir," Lieutenant Williams was quick to point out. "She just left, and she had one hell of a smile on her face."

"Hang on. Let me get dressed," he said and closed the door. A few minutes later Colonel Wilson opened the door with his clothes on. "I'm sorry about that Raven. I meant no disrespect towards you."

"None taken, sir," she commented as she entered Colonel

Wilson's room. "It's not my place to judge." Lieutenant Williams continued while she walked over to the table. She placed her briefcase down on the table and sat down. She opened the briefcase and removed a stack of papers that she had brought with her, and sat them on the table. She closed her briefcase and sat it on the floor next to her feet.

"I would like to keep what you saw between us," Colonel Wilson commented.

"Keep what between us, sir?" Lieutenant Williams asked and then smiled. "I have no idea what you're talking about."

"All right, what's so important that it couldn't wait until I got back?"

"It's about those pictures you received from Carla Garcia."

"What about them?"

"The news articles in those pictures were actually an encryption code-key."

"That's interesting; go on."

"I'm convinced that Yasin Abdul Zamani was using this code to communicate with the Iranians and Red Cell. Sir, Brussels, was just the beginning." Lieutenant Williams paused while she removed a paper from the stack of papers in front of her. "This is a list of participants I drew up from the messages I've decrypted so far," she continued while she handed Colonel Wilson the list. "Everyone on that list has been in contact with Zamani, and they're working with the Iranian Government."

Colonel Wilson looked at the list. "Holy shit," was all he could say. "Are you sure about this?"

"Without a doubt; the people on that list are conspiring to assassinate President Elliot and take control of our government. I'm sure that the incident in Brussels was an assassination attempt on President Elliot that failed."

Colonel Wilson handed the list back to Lieutenant Williams. He picked up Deputy Director Hick's card from the table while he removed his cell phone from his pants pocket. He opened his cell phone and dialed the cell phone number that was on the card. He put it to his ear and waited for Deputy Director Hicks to answer.

"Deputy Director Hicks."

"Karen where are you?"

"Already missing me are you?"

"Where are you?"

"I'm getting ready to get in my car. What's up? You sound serious."

"You need to get back up here. We have a situation."

"I'm on my way," Deputy Director Hicks said and then the line went dead.

Colonel Wilson dialed the number for General Richwood's office at the Pentagon and General Richwood's Assistant, Major Harris, answered. "Emily, this is John. I need to talk to General Richwood."

"General Richwood is at the White House attending a security briefing," Major Harris pointed out. "I can get a message to him if it's important and can't wait."

"That'll work."

"What's your message?

"Tell the general that I need to talk to him A-sap."

"That's it?"

"That's it Emily. Let the general know that I'll be leaving here within the hour."

"Roger that," Major Harris acknowledged.

Colonel Wilson closed his cell phone to cancel the call. He thought for a few short seconds before he opened his cell phone again. He pushed the auto-dial number for Captain Hale and put the cell phone to his ear.

"Hale," Captain Hale answered.

"Bulldog, has Popeye left Sandbox?"

"No, he hasn't. I ordered him to remain there until I heard from you."

"Good. I want you to send Maverick and Crazy Horse over there. Raven and I will be flying back this afternoon. I'll brief you more on this when I get there."

"Roger that Wolverine," Captain Hale acknowledged. "I'll see you when you get here."

Once again, Colonel Wilson closed his cell phone to cancel the call, but this time he returned the cell phone to his pants pocket. He looked at Lieutenant Williams and could see the fear in her eyes.

"Don't worry Raven; it's just a precautionary measure."

Before Lieutenant Williams could say a word, there was a knock on the door. Colonel Wilson walked over to the door and looked through the peephole before he opened the door.

"What's wrong;? Didn't you get enough of me last night?" Deputy Director Hicks asked as she entered the room. "I was on my way to the White House to attend a security briefing, so this better be good soldier boy."

"Deputy Director Hicks, this is my encryption specialist Raven," Colonel Wilson was quick to point out. "I believe the two of you met earlier."

"Briefly," Deputy Director Hicks remarked. "Now, what's up?" Deputy Director Hicks asked. "You said we had a situation."

"We do," Colonel Wilson fired back. He took the list of names from Lieutenant Williams and handed it to Deputy Director Hicks. "Everyone on that list has been in constant contact with Zamani, and they're working with the Iranian Government."

Deputy Director Hicks looked at the list; she was speechless. *This is bigger than I've dreamed of;* she thought. *Much bigger.*

"We need to be careful what we say around these people," Colonel Wilson was quick to point out.

"Does President Elliot know about this?" Deputy Director Hicks inquired while she looked at the list again.

"He will before the end of the day," Colonel Wilson assured Deputy Director Hicks. "For now, we need to act as though we know nothing of this."

"Yes, of course," she agreed as she handed Colonel Wilson the list back.

"Are you all right Deputy Director?" Lieutenant Williams asked.

"I'm fine," she replied. "Now, if you'll excuse me. I need to get going." Deputy Director Hicks walked over to the door and opened it. She exited the room and closed the door.

"She looked a little rattled," Lieutenant Williams pointed out. "Are you sure we can trust her?"

"We don't have much choice in the matter," Colonel Wilson answered. "At least now we know who we can trust and who we shouldn't trust." Colonel Wilson removed his cell phone from his pants pocket. He opened the cell phone and pushed the auto-dial number for the pilot of his aircraft that was at Joint Base Andrews. He put the cell phone to his ear and waited for the pilot to answer. "This is Wilson. Is the aircraft ready?"

"Yes, sir; fueled and ready," the pilot answered.

"Good, I'll be there shortly." Colonel Wilson closed his cell phone to cancel the call and returned the cell phone to his pants pocket. "Raven put those papers back into your briefcase. We're leaving."

Lieutenant Williams picked up the briefcase next to her feet and sat it down on the table. She opened it and placed the stack of papers inside. She closed her briefcase and got up from her seat at the table.

Colonel Wilson quickly packed his belongings and headed for the door when there was a knock on the door. Startled, Colonel Wilson looked through the peephole and saw General Richwood standing there. He quickly opened the door. "General, I was told that you were at the White House attending a security briefing."

"I was until I got your message," General Richwood remarked as he stepped inside the room. "Major Harris said it sounded important," he continued while Colonel Wilson closed the door.

Lieutenant Williams opened her briefcase and removed the list of names. She handed the list to Colonel Wilson and closed her briefcase.

"Sir, Raven broke the Zamani code. We now have a list of all Red Cells members," Colonel Wilson pointed out as he offered the list to General Richwood.

General Richwood took the list from Colonel Wilson and looked at it. "Are you sure about this list?"

"Yes, sir, I am," Lieutenant Williams answered.

"Good work you two," General Richwood said while he continued to look over the list. "When are you leaving?"

"Raven, and I are heading to Andrews," Colonel Wilson answered. "The aircraft is waiting for us."

"I'll be in touch," General Richwood said as he walked to the door. "Carry on Wilson," he continued while he opened the door. The general stepped outside into the hallway and closed the door.

Colonel Wilson did one last check of the room to be certain that he hadn't forgotten anything before he and Lieutenant Williams exited the room.

# Chapter 13

Washington, D.C.
The White House

President Elliot sat behind his desk in the Oval Office and began going over the latest report on the car bombing at the Pentagon that was lying on his desk. When he was finished reading the report, he put the report back into the folder that it came in. He picked up the folder and noticed that the folder was sitting on top of a piece of paper. He picked up the piece of paper and laid the folder back down on his desk, and read what was on the paper.

> Mr. President:
> Resign, or we will set off another nuke. This time it will be in the US.
> You have forty-eight hours to comply.
>
> PS
> Don't forget we still have Kate. Do as we say, or she too will die.

President Elliot felt a cold chill shoot up his back as he sat there in shock. He quickly snapped back to reality when there was a knock on the office entry door. He folded the piece of paper several times, and then he stuffed the piece of paper into his shirt pocket. "Enter," he said in a calm voice.

The door opened, and Vice President James Conrad entered the Oval Office. "I'm sorry to bother you Mr. President, but I was told that you wanted to see me," he said while he closed the door and walked toward the president's desk. "I was told that it was important," he concluded as he sat in the chair located next to the president's desk.

"Yes, it is important," President Elliot remarked. "I want to know why you didn't tell me about the intelligence report you received from Colonel Wilson."

"I didn't see any reason to bother you with it. The report came from an unreliable source."

"Says who?" Elliot shot back.

"Mr. President, if there was a real threat, the CIA, and the NSA would have picked up on this."

"Not necessarily," President Elliot was quick to point out. "I should have been told about this the minute you found out. Do you know what would have of happened if I hadn't of turned Air Force One around?"

"Yes, sir, I do. You would be dead, and I would be president."

President Elliot stared at Vice President Conrad. *You arrogant asshole,* he thought.

"Is there anything else you need Mr. President? I have a full schedule today."

"From now on something like this needs to be brought to my attention immediately," President Elliot snapped back. "I make the decisions here, not you. Your job is to assist me in these matters. If you can't do your job, then resign, and I'll find someone else that can." President Elliot paused for a brief moment then continued. "Now get back to work and get me some answers."

"Yes, Mr. President," Vice President Conrad said as he got up from his seat and hurried out of the Oval Office, and closed the door.

President Elliot pushed the intercom button on the telephone on his desk and waited for Mrs. Wyatt to answer.

"Yes, Mr. President."

"I need you to find General Richwood and tell him I have a security issue I need to discuss with him."

"Yes, Mr. President."

President Elliot pushed the intercom button on the telephone to end the intercom call. A few minutes later, the door opened, and Mrs. Wyatt entered. "Mr. President, Secretary Roberts is here. He says it's important."

"Send him in."

Mrs. Wyatt left the Oval Office and Secretary of Defense, Mark Roberts, entered. He walked over to the chair next to the President Elliot's desk and sat down while Mrs. Wyatt closed the door to the Oval Office.

"Any news on who set off the nuke in Brussels?" President Elliot inquired.

"Preliminary reports say that the plutonium used in the nuke was from an unknown source."

"So we have no idea where it came from."

"That's correct, sir. We're trying to pin down where the plutonium was refined."

"If you had to guess, where would you say the bomb came from?"

"My best guess would be Iran."

"Why Iran?"

"Sir, we know that Iran has a uranium-enrichment program that's capable of producing weapons-grade plutonium," Secretary Roberts was quick to point out. "We also know that Iran hates everything we stand for. It wouldn't surprise me if they had something to do with the bombing in Brussels."

"I see your point, but do we have any proof that Iran is manufacturing nuclear weapons?"

"None that I know of Mr. President."

"I need to know what the Iranians are up to before we find out the hard way," President Elliot instructed Secretary Roberts. "If they're behind the Brussels bombing, I want to know."

"Yes, I agree, but every time we send in a surveillance drone the Iranians shoot it down," Secretary Roberts pointed out. "The Iranians already warned us that if we send in another drone they will consider it an act of war and that they will act accordingly."

"They're bluffing," President Elliot remarked.

"What if the Iranians aren't bluffing?"

"We need to find out what they're doing at Iranshahr."

"Sir, maybe you should have a talk with Director Müller about this. I'm sure the CIA can get you what you're asking for quicker than I can."

"Lately, Director Müller has been slow with his intelligence reports. I don't have time to wait on his ass, so Mark do you have any ideas?"

Secretary Roberts thought for a moment. "There is one possibility," he began. "For the past four months, Northrop Grumman has been testing a specially modified RQ-4 Global Hawk surveillance drone that is equipped with stealth technology. It might be possible to send this drone into Iran and bring it back out safely without the Iranians knowing we were even there."

"Where's this drone at now?"

Secretary Roberts smiled. "It's still on the Eisenhower, and the Eisenhower is parked three-hundred miles off the coast of Iran."

"I want you to oversee this personally, and tell no one here in Washington what you're doing. You are to report your findings to me, and me only. We need to keep this between the two of us."

"Are you sure that's a good idea?" Secretary Roberts curiously asked.

"Mark, you're the only one I trust with this. I need your findings within twenty-four hours."

"Yes, Mr. President. I understand," Secretary Roberts acknowledged as he got up from his seat. "I'll have everything in motion within the hour." He walked over to the exit door and opened the door. He exited the Oval Office and closed the door.

A few minutes later, there was a knock on the side entrance. *Now what,* President Elliot thought. "Enter," he said and the side door of the Oval Office opened. General Richwood entered, followed by two technicians. Each technician carried a medium-sized silver case and a handheld radio frequency detector. General Richwood motioned for President Elliot to remain silent while the technicians began to scan the Oval Office with their handheld radio frequency detectors. After a few minutes, the technicians had completed their scan and found no electronic listening devices in the room.

"The room is clear, sir," one of the technicians reported.

"Very well, return to your normal duties."

"General what's this all about?" President Elliot demanded to know as he got up from his seat. "Surely you don't think that someone has the balls to bug my office," he continued. "This office is checked twice a day for electronic listening devices."

"Mr. President, I can explain," General Richwood began as the two technicians exited the Oval Office and closed the door. "Sir, due to the fact that some offices in the Pentagon were bugged. I took it upon myself to have this office checked again," he pointed out while he walked over to the president's desk.

"Does this have anything to do with the car bombing at the Pentagon earlier?" President Elliot asked.

"I believe so, but Mr. President, that's not the real reason why I'm here," General Richwood said. He removed the list that Colonel Wilson had given him earlier from the inside pocket of his uniform. "Using the information supplied to Colonel Wilson from Kate, his encryption specialist has broken the Zamani code." General Richwood handed President Elliot the list. "The names on that paper are everyone who has had contact with Zamani over the past few months."

President Elliot looked at the list as he flopped down in his chair. "Are you sure about this?" He asked while he laid the list down on his desk. "Could this be some kind of a trick to shake things up here in Washington?"

"That's what I thought of first, but Mr. President, I'm sure that the list is genuine. I believe that the people on that list have been working with the Iranians and Yasin Abdul Zamani for quite some time now."

"My god, this is a political nightmare," President Elliot mumbled. "I know most of the people on this list." President Elliot got up from his seat and walked over to one of the sofas in the middle of the room, and sat down. "Have a seat general," President Elliot said while he motioned to the other sofa across from him. "We have a lot to talk about."

General Richwood walked over to the sofa and sat down. "Mr. President, Colonel Wilson and I believe that the bombing in Brussels was an attempt to assassinate you and several other key heads-of-state."

"Do you think the people on that list were involved?"

"I would say it's a good chance they knew about it beforehand," General Richwood replied.

"Is Colonel Wilson still in town?"

"No, sir; he's on his way back to Strike Force Delta Command."

"I want you to send Colonel Wilson a message. Tell Colonel Wilson, he has forty-eight hours to finish what I asked him to do for me. Tell him that if it can't be done in this time frame I understand."

"Wilson's going in after Kate isn't he?"

"Yes, he is. I authorized him to do what needs to be done to ensure Kate's safe return." President Elliot paused, "I found this on my desk a little while ago," he said as he took the note from his shirt pocket and handed it to General Richwood. "It must have been placed on my desk while I was at the Pentagon."

General Richwood unfolded the note and quickly read it. "What course of action would you like to take, sir?"

"Well, I'm not going to resign if that's what you're asking," President Elliot shot back as he got up from the sofa and snatched the note out of General Richwood's hand.

"I would hope not, sir," General Richwood commented as he jumped to his feet.

"Tell no one about this note," President Elliot ordered while he walked over to his desk and sat down behind the desk.

"Yes, sir, Mr. President." General Richwood acknowledged. "Is there anything else you need sir?"

"Nothing that I can think of."

"Very well, sir. Good day Mr. President."

"Good day general."

General Richwood exited the Oval Office through the side entrance while President Elliot folded the note and returned it to his shirt pocket.

President Elliot picked up the list that General Richwood had given him and read the names to himself. Afterwards, he opened the center drawer of his desk and placed the list inside, and closed the drawer. He took out his keys from his pants pocket and locked the drawer. He returned the keys to his pants pocket, and then he got up from his seat behind his desk and exited the Oval Office through the side door.

\* \* \* \* \*

Home of Thomas Flowers and Pamela Wells

Thomas Flowers pulled into the driveway of the house that he and Pamela Wells shared together and turned off the ignition. He opened the door and got out while Pamela Wells got out on the passenger's side and closed the door. They met at the front of the vehicle, and together they walked to the front door. Flowers inserted the house key into the door lock and unlocked the door. He removed the key from the door lock and returned his keys to his pants pocket. Pamela Wells stepped inside the house, and Thomas Flowers followed.

"I was wondering when the two of you were going to show," Deputy Director Hicks said, who was hiding behind the door. "We're going to have a little talk," she continued as she slammed the door shut.

Thomas Flowers and Pamela Wells turned to face Deputy Director Hicks and found that she had her Beretta M9-A1, with its silencer attached, in her hand, and was pointing it in their direction. "What's the meaning of this?" Flowers demanded to know. "Have you gone nuts?"

"Shut up," Deputy Director Hicks fired back.

"What are you going to do, shoot us?" Pamela Wells inquired.

"If I was going to shoot the two of you, I would have done it by now dumbass," Deputy Director Hicks answered. "What I want is for the two of you to slowly drop your weapons to the floor and don't try any stupid shit."

"We better do as she says," Thomas Flowers remarked, and he slowly removed his Colt forty-five from his shoulder holster, and then he dropped it to the floor.

"My weapon is in my purse," Pamela Wells pointed out, and she dropped her purse to the floor.

"Don't forget your backup weapon," Deputy Director Hicks instructed.

Flowers and Wells removed their ankle holsters and laid them on the floor. "Now move your asses in the front room."

Flowers and Wells entered the front room as instructed. "What's with the chairs?" Wells asked when she saw two metal chairs in the middle of the room with handcuffs fastened to the arms and legs.

"I want each of you to sit in a chair and handcuff yourself to it," Deputy Director Hicks ordered.

Flowers and Wells complied with Deputy Director Hick's demands, and they sat down in a metal chair and handcuffed themselves to it.

"Now that wasn't so hard was it," Deputy Director Hicks said while she sat down on the sofa across from Thomas Flowers and Pamela Wells.

"What do you want?" Pamela Wells demanded to know.

"I want to know why you killed Carla Garcia." Deputy Director Hicks fired back. "She was no threat to you."

"Who the hell is Carla Garcia?" Thomas Flowers asked.

Deputy Director Hicks jumped up off the sofa and walked over to Thomas Flowers, and stood in front of him. "She's the woman that one of you killed the other day."

"Oh, that squeally ass little bitch." Flowers fired back.

Deputy Director Hicks punched Thomas Flowers in his mouth with the butt of her Beretta, and his lip began to bleed. "Carla was a good person. You have no right to talk about her like that."

"You bitch," Flowers shouted.

Deputy Director Hicks sidestepped and stood in front of Pamela Wells. "What about you?"

"What are you going to do if I don't answer, punch me in the mouth with your Beretta," Wells smarted off.

"That's not a bad idea," Deputy Director Hicks remarked, and then she punched Pamela Wells in her mouth with the butt of the Beretta, and Well's lip began to bleed. "Now smart ass, answer my question before I start putting bullets in one of you."

"We were ordered to," Pamela Wells began. "I..."

"Shut up Pam," Thomas Flowers interrupted. "Don't tell her anything; the bitch is going to kill us anyway."

Deputy Director Hicks picked up the roll of Duck Tape that was on the floor between Flowers and Wells. She tore off an eight-inch piece of tape and put the Duck Tape back down on the floor. She stood in front of Thomas Flowers and placed the piece of Duck Tape over his mouth.

"There that will shut you up while Pam and I have a little talk," she commented while she turned her attention back to Pamela Wells. "Now sweetie, what were you saying before you were rudely interrupted."

"Nothing, so if you're going to kill us do it now and get it over with."

"I see," Deputy Director Hicks remarked. "Tell me are the two of you a couple?"

"What?"

"Are the two of you fucking?"

"That's none of your business."

"So, if I put a bullet in him, you wouldn't care."

Pamela Wells looked at Thomas Flowers with tears in her eyes. "I love you," she said without making a sound, and then she looked back at Deputy Director Hicks. "Won't matter to me."

Deputy Director Hicks pointed her Beretta at Thomas Flowers's right foot and pulled the trigger. The bullet shot out of the Beretta and tore into Flowers's foot. Flowers screamed out in pain, but the Duck Tape on his mouth prevented the sound of his outcry from being heard.

"Tell me what I want to know, or I'll shoot the other foot."

"Please stop," Pamela Wells pleaded while she desperately tried to fight back her tears. "We only did what we were ordered to do."

"By whom?"

"Our director."

"Are you telling me that the Director of Homeland Security, Eric Michal, ordered you to kill Carla Garcia?"

"Yes; he did," Pamela Wells replied as tears rolled down her face uncontrollably. "We were ordered to find out if she sent Colonel Wilson the pictures that Kate Livingston sent her."

"What about Captain Jones at the Pentagon?"

"Director Michal ordered that too."

"I've heard enough." Deputy Director Hicks pointed her Beretta at Thomas Flowers's head and pulled the trigger. The bullet shot out of the Beretta and tore into Flowers's head, killing him almost instantly.

She then pointed the Beretta at Pamela Wells' chest. "This is for Carla." She said and pulled the trigger twice, shooting Pamela Wells in the chest with each shot. "Go to hell the both of you," Deputy Director Hicks said as she watched Pamela Wells take her last breath.

Satisfied that Thomas Flowers and Pamela Wells were no longer a threat to her, Deputy Director Hicks removed the silencer from her Beretta and put it in the front pocket of the jacket she was wearing. She placed the Beretta in the small of her back and pulled the jacket over the Beretta to conceal the weapon.

She walked over to Thomas Flowers and removed his wallet from his inside jacket pocket. She searched through the wallet and found nothing useful, so she tossed the wallet to the floor and removed his cell phone from his outside jacket pocket. *This might prove useful;* she thought. She powered down the cell phone and put it in her jacket pocket.

She searched the room and came up empty-handed. She walked into the entry and over to where Pamela Wells had left her purse. She dumped the purse's contents out onto the floor. "Damn you carried a lot of junk around with you," she commented while she searched through the items lying on the floor.

She picked up Pamela Wells' cell phone from the floor and powered it down, and then tossed the cell phone into the empty purse. Deputy Director Hicks picked up the purse from the floor and headed down the hallway to the dining room while she removed Thomas Flowers' cell phone from her jacket pocket and put it into the purse.

She sat the purse down on the dining room table and entered the room adjacent to the dining room. She walked over to the desk and found a laptop computer sitting on top of the desk. She opened the laptop. "Damn," she commented when the laptop asked for a password. Deputy Director Hicks started to pick up the laptop when she noticed a small three-ring notebook next to the laptop. She picked up the notebook and thumbed through the pages. "Jackpot," she said when she realized that the notebook had value.

She grabbed the laptop from the desk and walked back into the dining room. She picked up the purse from the table and put the three-ring notebook inside. "Thanks for the purse Pam," she commented as she hung the purse on her shoulder.

Deputy Director Hicks walked to the back door and opened the door. She stepped onto the back porch and closed the door. She walked across the back yard to the alley and continued through the alley to the street where her silver-tone Chevy Cobalt was parked.

She removed her car keys from her jacket pocket and unlocked the driver's side door. She got in behind the wheel and inserted the key into the ignition while she closed the door. She turned the key and started the vehicle, and drove away as if nothing had happened.

# Chapter 14

Oklahoma City, Oklahoma
Tinker Air Force Base

The Gulfstream G550 twin-engine jet aircraft landed and then taxied to the hangar entrance where Captain Hale was waiting with a Humvee. The pilot shut down the aircraft's jet engines, and the door to the aircraft opened. Colonel Wilson and Lieutenant Williams departed from the aircraft. Colonel Wilson was surprised to find Captain Hale waiting for them. "Sit-rep," Colonel Wilson inquired.

"Condition two has been implemented as ordered by President Elliot," Captain Hale reported. "Everyone is at their post and standing by."

"Excellent," Colonel Wilson commented. "Is there anything else?"

"I got a message for you from General Richwood. It's marked urgent," Captain Hale said as he handed the message to Colonel Wilson.

Colonel Wilson took the message from Captain Hale and read the message. "This is bullshit."

"Something wrong Wolverine?" Captain Hale dared to ask.

"We have been ordered to locate Kate Livingston and free her from her captors, and we only have forty-eight hours to pull this off."

"That's not much time," Captain Hale pointed out.

"Has Maverick and Crazy Horse left yet?" He asked while he folded the message, and then stuffed it into his pocket.

"Yes, they have," Captain Hale answered.

"I want a video conference with them the minute they arrive at Sandbox," Colonel Wilson ordered while he walked to the front passenger's side door and opened the door.

"I'll get right on it," Captain Hale acknowledged as he walked over to the driver's side of the Humvee, and then opened the door.

Colonel Wilson jumped into the Humvee and closed the door while Lieutenant Williams opened the back passenger's side door and climbed in, and closed the door. Captain Hale climbed behind the wheel. He closed the door and started up the Humvee. He put it in gear, and they drove off in the direction of the Strike Force Delta compound.

When they arrived at the entrance to the Strike Force Delta facility, Captain Hale stopped the Humvee in front of the chain-linked fence type gate and rolled down the driver's side window. The guard, dressed in full combat dress and armed with the M-4 assault rifle, walked out of the guard shack and over to the driver's side of the Humvee. The guard looked inside and recognized everyone in the Humvee. He signaled the other guard inside the guard shack, and the gate opened.

Captain Hale put the Humvee in gear and drove through the gate. He continued to the command building and stopped in front of the building. Colonel Wilson was the first to exit the Humvee, "I'll be in the com-center if you should need me," he said as he closed the door; and then hurried inside.

Lieutenant Williams exited the Humvee and closed her door while Captain Hale did the same. He looked at Lieutenant Williams. "What the hell has Wolverine all fired up?"

"I don't know," Lieutenant Williams casually answered. "Maybe Wolverine got lucky while he was in Washington."

"Spit it out Raven. What don't you know?"

"All I can say is that when I went to Wolverine's room, someone whom we both know was leaving."

"Who was it?" Captain Hale curiously asked.

"I promised Wolverine that I wouldn't tell anyone about who I saw leaving his room. I've already said more than I should have," Lieutenant Williams politely concluded, and then she walked toward the entrance to the command building and entered.

"Women," Captain Hale muttered.

"Yeah, they can be a pain in the ass," Second Lieutenant, Daniel Shea, nicknamed Hammer, who was standing next to Captain Hale, pointed out.

"Jesus Christ Hammer," Captain Hale said, startled by Lieutenant Shea's sudden appearance. "What are you trying to do, give me a heart attack?"

"Damn Bulldog, you've been out of the field too long."

"Is there something you need Hammer?" Captain Hale snapped.

"Yes, there is;" Lieutenant Shea answered. "I wanted to let you know that the new people are ready if you should need them."

"Add the new personnel to the duty roster and give it to Wolverine," Captain Hale shot back, and then he walked to the entrance to the command building and entered.

*What a fuckin' dickhead,* Lieutenant Shea thought as he walked back toward the training building.

$$* * * * *$$

Sandbox
Location Classified

The Bell Boeing V-22 Osprey aircraft landed safely on the ground. The Osprey's pilot and copilot throttled down the Osprey's two Rolls-Royce Allison T406/AE 1107C-Liberty turbo shafts tilt-rotor engines. When it was safe to exit the aircraft, the back cargo door opened.

Lieutenant McDonald was the first to exit the aircraft with Samir Hamidi and Myra a few steps behind him. They followed Lieutenant McDonald into a hangar a few yards away where they were met by the rest of Lieutenant McDonald's strike team. "Everyone this is Samir Hamidi and his wife, Myra. They are not to leave this hangar without an escort." Lieutenant McDonald turned to face Hamidi and Myra. "It is for your own safety that you don't wonder off. Please follow me, and I'll show you to your quarters that we have set up for you in the back of the hangar."

Hamidi and Myra followed Lieutenant McDonald to a room at the back of the hangar and entered. There were two single bunks along one wall and a table and chairs in the middle of the room. "I know it's not much, but it's the best we could do on such short notice," Lieutenant McDonald pointed out.

"This will do just fine," Myra assured Lieutenant McDonald. "We've had worse."

"I..."

"Popeye, I have an incoming message from Strike Force Delta Command," Terminator, the unit's communications operator interrupted, who was standing in the doorway holding the message in his hand. "You need to see this."

Lieutenant McDonald took the message from Terminator and quickly read its contents. He learned that Second Lieutenant Roger Milestone and Second Lieutenant Rick Johnson, along with their assault teams were heading their way. "I want everything ready before Crazy Horse, and Maverick get here."

"I'm on it," Terminator acknowledged and hurried off. Lieutenant McDonald turned his attention back to Samir Hamidi and Myra. "I need the two of you to follow me, please."

Samir Hamidi and Myra followed Lieutenant McDonald out of the room. They walked across the hangar to the command tent that was set up in the far corner of the hangar, and entered. "Sit-rep," Lieutenant McDonald ordered.

"Coms are up and running," Terminator reported. "We have video and audio links with the Strike Force Delta Command Center, and the Situation Room at the White House."

"Very well," Lieutenant McDonald acknowledged.

"Impressive," Myra remarked as she looked around the tent and saw that there were two plasma screens set on tripods along one side of the tent. In front of each plasma screen was a desk and chair, with a laptop on top of each desk. "You got some setup here," she continued while she and Hamidi walked over to the large plotter-board that was in the center of the tent.

"I see that you have an electronic map of the area on your plotter-board. Are you planning something?" Hamidi inquired.

"Terminator, this is Samir Hamidi and his wife, Myra," Lieutenant McDonald said, ignoring Hamidi's question. "They will be staying with us for a while."

"Pleased to meet you," Terminator said and gracefully nodded his head in respect. "I believe someone would like to talk to you."

A few seconds later, Amos Adler appeared on the plasma screen in front of Myra. "Hello, Myra."

"Amos," Myra remarked as she looked at the image of Amos Adler on the screen while she positioned herself in front of the camera that was attached to the top of the plasma screen. "I have been worried sick about you."

"I'm fine," Amos Adler assured Myra. "I was delighted to hear that you and Samir got out safely."

"Is Little Joe nearby?" Lieutenant McDonald interrupted as he stepped in front of the plasma screen next to Myra.

"Be safe Amos," Myra said, and then she stepped away from the screen.

"I'm right here Popeye," Little Joe said as he appeared on the screen next to Amos Adler. "Is Sparrow there with you?"

"Yes, I'm here," Samir Hamidi acknowledged as he stepped in front of the plasma screen next to Lieutenant McDonald.

"I am so pleased that you and Myra are safe," Little Joe commented. "May Allah keep both of you safe, and watch over you wherever your journey may take you."

"Thank you my friend," Samir Hamidi said, and then he walked over to where Myra was standing. "Amos will be fine," he assured Myra.

"Little Joe, have you had any luck locating the CIA operatives that the Iranians are holding captive?" Lieutenant McDonald inquired.

"I have my best people out there looking, but they have come up empty-handed," Little Joe answered. "I will continue to look for them."

"Let me know the minute you find them."

"That I will," Little Joe said, and the screen went blank.

Lieutenant McDonald walked over to where Samir Hamidi and Myra were standing. "If you would follow me, I'll take you back to your quarters."

"Popeye, there's an incoming video transmission from Strike Force Delta Command," Terminator said.

Lieutenant McDonald hurried back over to the plasma screen. A few seconds later, Colonel Wilson appeared on the screen. "Wolverine, everything here is ready, and awaiting your orders."

"Has Sparrow arrived yet?"

"Yes, he has. In fact, he's standing a few feet away." Lieutenant McDonald motioned for Hamidi to step in front of the camera that was attached to the top of the plasma screen.

"Sparrow, it's nice to see you again my old friend," Colonel Wilson commented when Samir Hamidi stepped into his view on the plasma screen. "I take it life has been treating you well."

"Nice to see you again Wolverine," Samir Hamidi said. "I have been well, thank you," he continued while Myra stood by his side.

"Myra, you're looking prettier than ever," Colonel Wilson remarked.

Myra smiled. "I bet you say that to all the ladies."

Colonel Wilson chuckled at Myra's remark. "If the two you should need anything you let Popeye know, and he'll get it for you."

"We have everything we need," Hamidi assured Colonel Wilson. "However, I am curious as to why we were brought here?"

"I was hoping that you could shed some light on what's going on at Iran's research facility at Iranshahr," Colonel Wilson pointed out.

"I sent that information in right before Myra, and I left the safe house," Hamidi was quick to point out. "Didn't you read my report?"

"I haven't seen it yet. It must still be in the process of being decrypted. Is there anything I should know about?"

"All that is known for sure is that the facility at Iranshahr is indeed producing weapons-grade material and that most of the work is being done underground," Hamidi began. "My man inside has informed me that a terrorist group known as Red Cell is working with Yasin Abdul Zamani; who in turn is working with the Iranian government to develop nuclear weapons. It is believed that these weapons could be used against Western targets."

"So, what you're saying is that the Iranians have no clue that Zamani is working with Red Cell, and Red Cell has no idea that Zamani is working with the Iranians."

"It appears so," Hamidi answered. "I would also like to point out that if the Brussels bomb came from Iran, the Iranian government had nothing to do with it. It would seem that someone wants us to believe that Iran was responsible for the Brussels bombing. I think that

Zamani is the key to all of this."

"Yes, I see your point," Colonel Wilson commented. "What about the CIA operatives that are missing and presumed held in Iran. Do you have any idea where they might be detained at?"

"I have no clue where they are being held. However, I just talked with Little Joe; he said that he has people out looking for them."

"Excellent. With a little luck, he might just find them." Colonel Wilson pointed out. "For now, I want you and Myra to relax a little while I work on getting you back here."

"Very well, my friend," Samir Hamidi said before the screen went blank.

Colonel Wilson turned to face Captain Hale. "In my office now," he ordered, and then he stormed out of the Operation Center and slammed the door shut.

*Oh boy, he's pissed,* Captain Hale thought as he opened the door and left the Operation Center. He closed the door and hurried off to catch up with Colonel Wilson.

Colonel Wilson entered his office, with Captain Hale a few seconds behind him. "Close the door," he snapped as he turned to face Captain Hale.

"Wolverine, I can explain," Captain Hale said while he closed the door.

"Bulldog, what the fuck is going on here?" Colonel Wilson demanded. "I should have been informed about Sparrow's report the minute it came in."

"Wolverine, with all the excitement that's been going on around here I forgot about the report from Sparrow. I have it encrypted on my computer."

"You forgot; what kind of lame-ass excuse is that?" Colonel Wilson shouted. "When I'm not here, I depend on you to keep me apprised of new developments as they come in," he continued in a lower tone of voice. "The clock is running out on this one."

"Wolverine, I assure you that this will never happen again."

"See to it that it doesn't," Colonel Wilson snapped. "The President is counting on us to get the answers that he so desperately needs."

The door to the office swung open, and Second Lieutenant Samantha Cooltrain entered. "I'm sorry to bother you Wolverine, but

General Richwood is on the secure line."

"Clear the room," Colonel Wilson ordered while he walked over to his desk and sat down in the chair behind his desk. He waited until Lieutenant Cooltrain and Captain Hale had left the room, and his office door was closed before he picked up the telephone receiver from the telephone on his desk. He put the telephone receiver to his ear and pushed the flashing button on his telephone. "General, it's nice to hear from you, sir."

"Wilson, I got a text from the Ice Queen a few minutes ago. She wanted me to tell you to look east of Khash. Whatever the hell that means."

"I have a pretty good idea what she's talking about," Colonel Wilson pointed out. "Tell me, sir, how is Deputy Director Hicks these days?"

"How the fuck would I know. The last I heard she was taking some time off."

"That's odd," Colonel Wilson commented. "She didn't mention anything to me about taking time off."

"Wilson, I know it's none of my business, but are you banging the Ice Queen?"

"With all due respect general you're right, it's none of your business."

*Holy fuck,* General Richwood thought. "Wilson, I didn't mean to pry into your personal life. I apologize if I offended you."

"Sir, is there anything else you wanted to talk to me about?" Colonel Wilson asked, hoping to change the subject.

"Do the names Thomas Flowers and Pamela Wells ring a bell?" General Richwood asked.

"Yes, sir, they do. If I'm not mistaken, they were on the list."

"That they were," General Richwood concurred. "I just thought that you would like to know that a few hours ago the two of them were found murdered in the house they shared. Local police are saying that they must have walked in on a robbery in progress. Anyway, that's two less traders that we have to deal with."

"Yes, sir, I'll remove them from the list. Is there anything else, sir?"

"No, I think we've covered everything. Let me know, the moment you find something that I can take to the president."

"Yes, sir, I..." Colonel Wilson stopped talking when he realized that General Richwood was no longer on the line. "I wish he'd stop doing that shit," Colonel Wilson mumbled. "That's fucking annoying," he continued to mumble while he returned the telephone receiver to the telephone on his desk.

Colonel Wilson got up from his seat and left his office. He walked to the Communication Center and entered. He closed the door and walked over to the technician who was in charge of positioning the satellites. "Is there a Looking-glass (satellite) that passes east of Khash, Iran?"

"Yes, there is," the technician answered. "It's due to pass there in a few mikes (minutes)."

"Do you have time to set the Looking-glass to scan with inferred and for heat signatures?"

"Yes, there's time, but there's nothing in that area."

"Just do it," Colonel Wilson ordered. "I want you to put the feed up on the large plasma, and record everything."

"You're the boss," the technician commented as he did what Colonel Wilson had ordered.

"That I am," Colonel Wilson said as he walked over to the wall size plasma screen.

"We've been over that area several times," Captain Hale was quick to point out as he stood by Colonel Wilson's side.

Colonel Wilson watched closely at the satellite feed on the screen when suddenly, something caught his eye. "Hold that," he said as he pointed at the screen.

"What's that green dot?" Captain Hale curiously asked. "It wasn't there before."

"It's a distress beacon," Colonel Wilson answered. "Blow up the area around that green dot."

"On it," the satellite technician acknowledged.

Seconds later, the area around the green dot was enlarged on the plasma screen and revealed several heat signatures in what appeared to be an old military installation of some kind.

"That's our target area," Colonel Wilson commented.

"How the hell did we miss that?" Captain Hale barked out. "We've been over that area several times, and this never showed up before."

"They must be using a satellite cloaking device, similar to the one we use here and at Sandbox. I think that when the distress beacon was activated, it punched a hole through their cloaking system, wide enough for us to see what's there," Colonel Wilson pointed out. "The distress beacon must have been activated recently. That would explain why we couldn't see this before."

"It could be a trap," Captain Hale pointed out.

"Yes, it could be a trap," Colonel Wilson agreed. "Get me Little Joe, priority-one."

"Coming up in five seconds," the technician responsible for video communications reported.

"Wolverine, what's up?" Little Joe asked when his image appeared on the plasma screen.

"What do you know about a facility located ten kilometers east of Khash?"

"It was abandoned until a few months ago," Little Joe answered. "I believe the Iranian Intelligence Agency reopened it and is using it to detain and interrogate prisoners."

"How far are you from that installation?"

"About a hundred kilometers. "I could have my people there in a couple of hours."

"I want you to get your people there as quickly as possible and stay out of sight. You are to assess the strength of the garrison there and report back to Popeye. He will fill you in on the particulars later."

"Roger that," Little Joe acknowledged, and the screen went blank.

"Get me Popeye at Sandbox; priority-one," Colonel Wilson ordered.

"Wolverine what's up?"

"I'm sending you an encrypted file. You will need to use the Charlie Mike encryption code-key to decrypt the file." Colonel Wilson paused while the file was sent to Lieutenant McDonald. The communication technician gave Colonel Wilson the thumbs-up to indicate that the file was sent and received. "Everything you need to know is in that file. Little Joe will send you the rest of the information you'll need shortly. This is going to be a rescue mission. Extract the package and take a few prisoners if you can."

"Affirmative," Popeye acknowledged and the screen went blank.

"Bulldog, I'll be in my office," Colonel Wilson said as he walked to the door and opened it, "Keep me apprised of the situation."

"Affirmative Wolverine," Captain Hale acknowledged as Colonel Wilson exited the Communication Center, and then he closed the door.

# Chapter 15

Gulf Of Oman
The USS Dwight D. Eisenhower CV-69
300 Nautical Miles Off The Coast Of Iran

The flight deck crew worked frantically to prepare the stealth modified Northrop Grumman RQ-4 Global Hawk surveillance drone for takeoff. Every detail, no matter how small, had to be checked to ensure that the surveillance drone was ready for launch before launch control, which was located in the Combat Information Center, was given permission to launch the surveillance drone.

Navy Commander John Young, the officer on duty in the Combat Information Center, stood next to the petty officer in charge of operating the surveillance drone. He watched while the petty officer did his final systems check to ensure that the surveillance drone would function properly while in flight. One by one, each light on the drone control panel turned from red to green. It only took seconds before all the lights on the drone control panel were green, which indicated that the surveillance drone was ready to be launched.

"All systems are go for launch," the petty officer reported.

"Very well," Commander Young said as he put on the Sennheiser HMD 281 pro single-sided communications headset that was hanging on the control panel in front of him. He plugged the headset into the control panel and pushed the button for flight operations. "Ops; CIC; everything is green here for launch," he said and waited for a reply."Roger that CIC; stand by."

"Standing by," Commander Young acknowledged.

Without warning, the door to the Combat Information Center opened, and thirty-three-year-old, CIA operative, Robyn Morris, entered. "Who authorized this launch?" She demanded to know.

Commander Young placed his hand over the headset microphone. "Authorization came from the White House through the Secretary of Defense," Commander Young was quick to point out.

"Oh," Robyn Morris commented as she walked over to the control panel and stood on the other side of the petty officer.

"CIC; Ops; you are clear to launch."

"Roger that," Commander Young acknowledged. He pushed the button on the control panel to disconnect from Flight Ops Control. "All right petty officer, it's all yours."

Commander Young and CIA operative, Robyn Morris turned their attention to the monitor screen that hung from the ceiling and watched as the surveillance drone launched from the Eisenhower and proceeded toward the Iranian coast.

"Radar, what do you have on your scope?"

"Nothing, Commander," the radar operator reported. "The drone's stealth is functioning at one-hundred percent."

"Very well; keep me informed of any changes in the drone's stealth."

"I I sir."

"Commander, we're coming up on the Iranian coast," the petty officer in charge of the surveillance drone reported.

Commander Young and Robyn Morris watched as the stealth modified Northrop Grumman RQ-4 Global Hawk surveillance drone flew over the Iranian coast undetected and proceeded inland to its intended target.

"Where is the intended target area?" Robyn Morris asked when she noticed that the surveillance drone wasn't heading to Iranshahr.

"We are going to take a look at an area ten kilometers east of Khash."

"What the hell is there to look at?"

"It is believed that the Iranian Intelligence Agency is holding Kate Livingston hostage in an old abandoned Army post there. We've been ordered by Secretary of Defense Roberts to investigate and report our findings back to Sandbox."

"Coming into range," the petty officer in charge of operating the surveillance drone reported.

"Start recording," Commander Young ordered. "Transmit everything the drone picks up to Sandbox."

"I I Commander," the petty officer in charge of operating the surveillance drone acknowledged. "Transmitting now, sir."

Commander Young and Robyn Morris watched the live feed on the monitor as the surveillance drone passed over the area. When the surveillance drone passed over the main building of the compound, a green dot appeared on the screen. The drone made two passes over the area and then headed back toward the coast.

"What was that green dot that kept popping up?" Commander Young inquired.

"That's a distress beacon," Robyn Morris answered. "Kate must have recently activated hers."

"You don't say," Commander Young commented. "Anyway, I counted about forty heat signatures if not more," he pointed out. "I hope..."

"Commander, we have detected several missiles launched from land-base missile launchers along the coast," The Electronic Warfare Officer (EWO) interrupted.

"Radar, status on the destination of those missiles," Commander Young ordered.

"I have nothing on radar, sir," the petty officer monitoring the radar system console reported. "Wait, no, it's nothing."

"Well, radar what is it? Do you, or don't you have contact?"

"Commander, I'm not sure. One second I have contact with something, and then it disappears off the scope. Sir, whatever it is, it's heading our way. It appears to be skimming the waves."

"Shit," Commander Young commented as he turned back to the control panel. "How long before we retrieve the drone?"

"The drone is landing as we speak," the petty officer answered.

"Good," he commented, and then he pressed the button for the bridge. "Bridge, CIC; we have detected a land-base missile launch, and we have an unknown number of inbounds heading our way," Commander Young calmly reported.

Unknown to Commander Young the captain was sitting in his chair on the bridge enjoying the view when his call rang out over the bridge intercom. The captain retrieved the telephone type receiver that was next to his chair. He put it to his ear and pushed the button on his chair for the Combat Information Center. "This is the captain speaking," He said as he got out of his chair. "How far out are the inbounds?"

"Unknown, sir; they're coming in close to the water to confuse our radar."

"Activate the Phalanx system," the captain ordered.

"Weapons, activate the Phalanx," Commander Young shouted to the weapon's officer.

The weapon's officer flipped the switches on the weapon's fire-control panel in front of him to activate the four-block 1B Phalanx CIWS twenty-millimeter six-barreled M61 Vulcan Gatling Guns; each capable of firing forty-five-hundred rounds per minute. "Phalanx activated," The weapon's officer reported.

"Phalanx activated," Commander Young reported to the captain.

"Very well," The captain acknowledged and pushed the button on his chair for the Combat Information Center to cancel the call. He returned the telephone type receiver to its resting place and removed his binoculars from the side of his chair. "All ahead flank," he ordered while he walked over to the side of the bridge facing the direction of the inbound threat. "Officer of the deck, sound general quarters. Set condition one. This is not a drill."

"I I captain," the officer of the deck acknowledged and sounded the alarm. "Set condition one throughout the ship," he said over the ship's 1MC (shipboard public address system). "This is not a drill."

The captain watched through his binoculars as the Phalanx weapon system sprung into action, filling the sky with twenty-millimeter projectiles while the ship began to pick up speed. *This isn't good;* he thought as six Iranian Shahab-3 long-range missiles were destroyed, and three more continued toward the ship. "Right full rudder," he ordered, but it was too late. Two of the Shahab-3 missiles slammed into the side of the Eisenhower just above the water line while the third slammed into the superstructure just below the bridge, killing everyone on the bridge.

\* \* \* \* \*

Washington, D.C.
The White House
0228 Hours Local Time

President Elliot was sound asleep in his bed in the presidential residence when he was awakened by the telephone ringing on his night table. He sat up on the bed and turned on the lamp that was on the night table. He picked up the cordless telephone receiver and pushed the answer button, and then put it to his ear. "Yes."

"Mr. President, we have a situation," White House Chief of Staff Howard Gordon reported.

"What happened?"

"Sir the Iranians fired several Shahab-3 missiles at the Eisenhower, three-hundred nautical miles off the coast of Iran. The Eisenhower took three direct hits and is still afloat. However, she is severely damaged."

"Casualties?"

"Unknown at this time, sir."

"Wake everyone up and have them meet me in the Situation Room. I'll be there as soon as I get dressed."

"Yes, Mr. President."

President Elliot pushed the end call button on the cordless telephone receiver and tossed it on the night table. "Damn it."

"What's wrong Martin?" First Lady Amanda Elliot asked as she sat up on her side of the bed.

"The Iranians just put three missiles into the Eisenhower. If it's a war they want. I'll give them a war they won't forget."

"I'll make some coffee," Amanda Elliot said while she got out of bed.

"I don't have time for coffee."

"Then make time," Amanda Elliot snapped. "You need to calm down some before you go do something you will regret later."

"Yes, dear," President Elliot said and then smiled, "a cup of coffee sounds good to me."

Amanda Elliot put on her robe and hurried into the kitchen area, and began making a pot of coffee while President Elliot quickly got dressed. She set the dining room table and plugged in the coffee pot warmer that was on the table. When the coffee was ready, she placed the coffee pot on the warmer and sat down at the table.

A few minutes later, President Elliot entered the dining area and sat down at the table across from Amanda Elliot. The First Lady poured the president some coffee in his cup, and then poured herself one. "Have you heard anything about Kate?" She asked.

"Nothing yet," the president answered as he picked up his coffee cup. "I have Colonel Wilson looking into it." He took a sip of his coffee and then placed the cup back down on the table. "I have faith that he'll find her."

The First Lady looked into President Elliot's eyes. "You don't think they've harmed her do you?"

"No, I don't," President Elliot answered while he looked at his watch, and then finished off his cup of coffee. "I got to go. Thanks for the coffee," he said as he got up from his seat. "It was just what I needed." President Elliot walked to the entrance to the presidential residence and opened the door.

"Good morning, Mr. President," the Secret Service agent who was on duty said when President Elliot stepped out into the hallway.

"Not for some," President Elliot commented and began to walk toward the Situation Room.

*Bad choice of words,* the Secret Service agent thought while he closed the door and remained at the entrance to the presidential residence.

When the president arrived at the entrance to the Situation Room the Marine, who was standing guard, dressed in his dress uniform and armed with a nine-millimeter Beretta M9-A1 side arm, snapped to attention and saluted President Elliot. The president returned the Marine's salute and entered the Situation Room. The room fell silent, anyone who was seated around the table jumped to their feet. The Marine closed the double-doors to the Situation Room and returned to his post outside.

"Okay everyone, let's get started," President Elliot said while he walked over to the table and sat down. "Status on the condition of the Eisenhower?" he asked while everyone sat down at the table.

"Mr. President, the Eisenhower has sustained heavy damage. The fires on-board are under control, and she's still afloat," Secretary of the Navy, John Forsythe reported. "It's still unclear at this time how many sailors were lost in the attack."

"I say let's nuke the sons-of-bitches back into the Stone Age," Vice President, James Conrad commented.

"I agree," Secretary of State, George Maxwell added. "We need to present a show of force. Who knows what they're planning to do next."

"Mr. President, I disagree with Vice President Conrad and Secretary Maxwell," A man sitting next to Secretary of Defense, Mark Roberts jumped in. "I don't think shooting off nukes is a good idea. There are other ways to show our outrage over this incident."

"Who the hell are you?" Vice President Conrad asked.

"I am Senior CIA analyst, Thomas Zachery. "I am here at Director Müller's request."

"An analyst," Vice President Conrad said in a raised voice. "You have no idea what you're talking about."

"I assure you Mr. Vice President, I know exactly what I'm talking about."

"Okay, let's move on," President Elliot jumped in. "Thomas, what do you recommend we do?"

"I think we should take out the missile installations that fired on the Eisenhower with Tomahawk cruise missiles before they start firing on the remaining ships that we have in the area."

"With the Eisenhower out of action, we don't have enough firepower in the area for such an attack," Secretary Forsythe shot back.

"Oh, but we do," Thomas, Zachery was quick to point out. "We can use the Tomahawk cruise missiles that are onboard our ships in the area, or we can use the one-hundred and fifty-four Tomahawks that the Ballistic Missile Submarine Ohio is carrying."

"I see that you've done your homework," President Elliot commented. "Gentlemen, Mr. Zachery has a point. We need to retaliate, and the missile batteries that fired on the Eisenhower is a good place to start."

"Mr. President, I'd like to point out that if we attack those missile sites the Iranians might escalate their hostilities towards us," Vice

President Conrad pointed out. "This could start a war."

"They practically blew the Eisenhower out of the water," President Elliot snapped. "They drew first blood. If they want a war, I'll sure as hell give them one."

"We should at least try to open up some kind of communication with them."

"That's not going to happen," President Elliot shot back. "John, do we have anything nearby that we can send into the area?" President Elliot asked Secretary of the Navy, John Forsythe.

"Yes we do,' Secretary Forsythe answered. "At top speed, the Washington, and her battle group can be there in five hours."

"Make it happen."

"Yes, sir," Secretary Forsythe acknowledged.

"I have one last thing to go over before we close," President Elliot continued. "Do we know where the Brussels bomb was manufactured, and who is responsible for putting it there?"

"I've personally talked to Director Müller and Director Parkinson about this last night. They told me that everything they've had found so far points to Iran," Secretary of State, George Maxwell replied.

"So, I'm to believe that Iran did this with no outside help from anyone?" President Elliot calmly asked.

"That's what our intelligence is telling us," Secretary Maxwell answered.

"John, when the Washington and her battle group arrive in the area, I want you to have the Ohio move in close to the Iranian shore and take out those missile sites that fired on the Eisenhower," President Elliot instructed Secretary of the Navy, John Forsythe. "The next move after that will be up to the Iranians."

"So we wait?" Vice President Conrad remarked. "I don't think that's a good idea."

"We wait," President Elliot fired back.

"Mr. President, the longer we wait, the more time Iran has to plan its next move," Secretary of the Navy, John Forsythe pointed out.

"I agree," Vice President Conrad added.

"I said we wait," President Elliot snapped back. "Mr. Zachery, tell your boss that I want indisputable proof that Iran was behind the Brussels bombing. Tell him to work fast."

"Yes, Mr. President," Thomas Zachery acknowledged.

"General, I want to see you in my office," President Elliot commented as he got up from his seat at the table. "The rest of you need to get me some answers," he concluded and walked over to the double-doors. He opened one of the doors and exited the Situation Room. The Marine outside snapped to attention and saluted President Elliot. "As you were Marine," he said and continued to walk toward the Oval Office.

"What's your opinion about all this general," Vice President Conrad asked General Richwood.

"I don't have an opinion, sir," he answered as he got up from his seat. "I don't question the president's decisions." General Richwood walked over to the doorway and exited the Situation room. The Marine standing outside the Situation Room snapped to attention and saluted the general. The general returned the Marine's salute and walked down the hallway to the Oval Office. He knocked on the open door and waited.

"Come in general," President Elliot ordered, "and close the door."

General Richwood stepped into the Oval Office and found President Elliot sitting behind his desk. He closed the door and walked over to the president's desk.

"Have you heard anything from Colonel Wilson about Kate's location?" President Elliot asked. "I'm running out of time."

"Colonel Wilson believes that he has located her and is in the process of preparing to go in after her."

"Sounds good," President Elliot remarked. "Keep me in the loop."

"Yes, sir, Mr. President. Is there anything else you need?"

"No, I think that covers it."

"Good day, Mr. President," General Richwood said and walked over to the office door. He opened the door and stepped outside, and closed the door.

President Elliot opened the left middle drawer on his desk and removed a five by seven frame picture he had of Kate Livingston, and closed the drawer. "Hang in there Pickles," he said as he put the picture on his desk. "My boys are coming to get you."

# Chapter 16

Sandbox
Location Classified

The specially modified Lockheed Martin C-130J Super Hercules aircraft, with its four Rolls-Royce AE 2100 D3 turboprop engines, touched down and taxied to the hangar where Lieutenant McDonald was waiting. The C-130J came to a complete stop a few feet from the entrance. The pilot shut down the aircraft's engines, and the back cargo door opened.

Second Lieutenant, Rick Johnson, nicknamed Maverick, and Second Lieutenant, Roger Milestone, nicknamed Crazy Horse, along with the rest of their Strike Force team exited the aircraft. Lieutenant Johnson hurried over to where Lieutenant McDonald was standing while Lieutenant Milestone led the Strike Force team into the hangar.

"Welcome to the Sandbox," Lieutenant McDonald said as he shook hands with Lieutenant Johnson.

"Is it true that the Iranians fired on the Eisenhower?" Lieutenant Johnson asked.

"Yes, it's true," Lieutenant McDonald answered. "We're going to have to move fast on this one."

"We're ready," Lieutenant Johnson assured Lieutenant McDonald. "We've been going over the operational plan that Wolverine sent. We'll have no moon tonight, so I don't think we'll have any problems with this mission. We should be in and out of there in a matter of minutes. I would like to bug out of here at sundown."

"That's not a..." Lieutenant McDonald stopped in mid sentence when Lieutenant Milestone approached.

"Wolverine is on video com," Lieutenant Milestone reported.

Lieutenant McDonald, with Lieutenant Johnson and Lieutenant Milestone following, walked across the hangar to the command tent that was set up in the far corner of the hangar, and entered. They positioned themselves in front of the camera that was attached to the top of the plasma screen and waited for Terminator, Lieutenant McDonald's communications operator, to activate the video link with Colonel Wilson. Seconds later, Colonel Wilson appeared on the plasma screen.

"Gentlemen," Colonel Wilson began. "The president has green-lighted the operation. A C-130J aircraft will be landing there within the hour to pick up Sparrow and his package. You are to load all your excess equipment and supplies onto the aircraft. You won't be returning to Sandbox, understood."

"Yes, sir," Lieutenant McDonald acknowledged.

"Little Joe and his people will have the landing zone secured by the time you arrive," Colonel Wilson continued. "Maverick, you are in command of the assault. Crazy Horse, you will assist Maverick. Popeye, you are the operational commander. I want you and your team to provide security for the aircraft while it's on the ground. Any questions?" Colonel Wilson waited a few seconds before he continued. "You may proceed when you're ready. Good hunting gentlemen, and watch your six over there."

"Terminator, you best get cracking," Lieutenant McDonald snapped when the screen went blank. "You don't have much time to get this shit ready," he concluded, and then he left the command tent.

"I wonder what crawled up his ass," Lieutenant Johnson commented.

"I think he's pissed because Wolverine gave you command of the assault force instead of him. Don't worry, he'll get over it."

"Yeah, you're probably right," Lieutenant Johnson commented. He walked over to the exit and stepped into the hangar, with Lieutenant Milestone a few steps behind him.

Badger, one of Lieutenant Johnson's unit members, walked over to Lieutenant Johnson. "Is it true Maverick?"

Lieutenant Johnson looked at Badger confused. "Is what true?" He asked. "What in the hell are you talking about?"

"Is Popeye and his team coming with us?"

"Yes, we're all going in," Lieutenant Johnson answered. "Everyone will be briefed on the mission when we're in the air. I suggest you check your gear and be ready to move out in a few."

Badger walked back over to where the rest of the assault team was assembled with Lieutenant Johnson and Lieutenant Milestone not far behind him.

"Okay, listen up," Lieutenant Johnson began. "The president has given us the green light to continue this mission. We will be leaving here as soon as our aircraft is fueled. Popeye and his team will be accompanying us on this mission."

"Are you ready to go kick some ass?" Lieutenant Milestone shouted.

"Hooah," everyone shouted back at the same time.

Lieutenant McDonald, who was standing at the hangar's entrance next to Samir Hamidi and Myra, smiled. "Hooah," he softly said as he looked up into the blue sky. "Here comes your ride," he said to Samir Hamidi and Myra as he pointed to a C-130J Super Hercules aircraft that was approaching.

The C-130J Super Hercules aircraft touched down safely on the runway and taxied over to the hangar where they were standing. The aircraft came to a complete stop a few feet from the hangar entrance. The pilot powered down the aircraft's engines, and the back cargo door opened.

Lieutenant McDonald stepped back into the hangar. "Listen up," he said in a raised voice so he could be heard. "I want everything that we don't need for this mission loaded on the aircraft. Don't leave anything behind. We won't be coming back here after the mission."

Lieutenant McDonald walked back over to the hangar entrance where Samir Hamidi and Myra were standing. "When they're finished loading the aircraft you will be leaving for the states. A few hours after that, you'll be stateside."

"Why couldn't we have used the other aircraft instead of waiting for this one?" Samir Hamidi asked, referring to the Strike Force assault aircraft that was being fueled a few feet away.

"That aircraft is our assault aircraft," Lieutenant McDonald answered.

"My that's a large aircraft," Myra commented. "Are you sure you can penetrate the Iranian's radar defenses without being detected?"

"That won't be a problem. Our assault aircraft is equipped with stealth technology," Lieutenant McDonald pointed out. "We won't have any problem getting in without anyone knowing."

"Interesting," Samir Hamidi remarked.

Lieutenant McDonald, along with Samir Hamidi and Myra, stood at the hangar's entrance. They watched while the aircraft was being loaded. When the aircraft was loaded, Lieutenant Johnson and Lieutenant Milestone walked over to where Lieutenant McDonald was standing. "The aircraft is loaded and ready to take off as soon as Samir and Myra are on board," Lieutenant Johnson reported.

"Very well," Lieutenant McDonald acknowledged. "Maverick, I want you to escort Samir and Myra to their seats."

Myra grabbed Lieutenant McDonald's arm. "Mr. Popeye, I..."

"Please, ma'am, just call me, Popeye," Lieutenant McDonald interrupted.

"I meant no disrespect."

"None taken ma'am."

"Popeye, will we ever see you again?" Myra curiously asked.

"Probably not, ma'am," Lieutenant McDonald answered.

"Then I thank you now for all that you and your men did for Samir and me," Myra commented. "I wish you and your men a safe journey and may all of you return safely."

"Thank you, ma'am," was all that Lieutenant McDonald could think of to say. "My men and I appreciate your concern for our well-being."

Myra gave Lieutenant McDonald a big hug and then she and Samir Hamidi followed Lieutenant Johnson to the C-130J aircraft and entered. A few minutes later, Lieutenant Johnson exited the aircraft and walked back over to where Lieutenant McDonald and Lieutenant Milestone were standing.

The back cargo door closed and one by one, the pilot fired up the C-130J's four Rolls-Royce AE 2100 D3 turboprop engines. After a few minutes, the pilot throttled up the aircraft's engines, and it began to move. They watched the C-130J aircraft taxi to the runway and take off.

"How long before we can leave?" Lieutenant McDonald inquired.

"The last time I checked the refueling was almost complete," Lieutenant Johnson answered.

"Here comes the crew chief," Lieutenant Milestone pointed out when he noticed the Strike Force assault aircraft's crew chief walking toward them.

"Great, maybe he has some idea how much longer it'll be before we can start to load up," Lieutenant McDonald commented.

"Popeye," the crew chief said when he arrived at the hangar entrance where they were standing. "We are done fueling the aircraft. You can load up whenever you're ready."

"Maverick, let's get this show on the road," Lieutenant McDonald said to Lieutenant Johnson while the crew chief walked back to the Strike Force assault aircraft. "The sun is starting to set, and I want to be in the air when it does."

"Roger that," Lieutenant Johnson acknowledged and hurried into the hangar.

"Crazy Horse, give Maverick a hand," Lieutenant McDonald suggested.

"Roger that," Lieutenant Milestone acknowledged and hurried into the hangar to catch up with Lieutenant Johnson.

Lieutenant McDonald walked over to the Strike Force assault aircraft and walked up the open cargo ramp. A few minutes later, the Strike Force personnel began to load their equipment onto the aircraft while the pilot warmed up the four Rolls Royce AE 2100 D3 turboprop engines.

When the aircraft was loaded, and everyone was properly secured in their seats, the back cargo door closed. The pilot taxied to the runway and powered up the aircraft's engines to full power. The aircraft began to pick up speed as it made its way down the runway. Not long afterwards, the C-130J Super Hercules lifted off the ground and climbed to its cruising altitude.

$* * * * *$

Washington, D. C.
Homeland Security Director Eric Michal's Office

Homeland Security Director Eric Michal was watching the CNN special news report on his television about the aftermath of the bombing in Brussels. "Same old shit," he mumbled as he turned off the television with his remote. Without warning, his office door suddenly opened, and Vice President, James Conrad entered. He closed the door and walked over to Director Michal's desk.

"Mr. Vice President," Director Michal said while he jumped to his feet.

"Eric, we need to talk," Vice President Conrad said as he sat in the chair that was in front of Director Michal's desk."

"About what?" Director Michal asked while he returned to his seat.

"About what happened to Thomas Flowers and Pamela Wells," Vice President Conrad fired back. "I find it hard to believe that some street punk got the upper hand on both of them."

"According to the police report I read, the police believe that there could have been two or more perpetrators involved." Director Michal was quick to point out. "There was nothing in that report to suggest otherwise."

"I still don't like it one bit," Vice President Conrad commented. "Eric, I can't shake the feeling that someone has caught on to our plan."

"Like who?"

"Strike Force for starters or that Deputy Director Hicks."

"Will you stop being so paranoid about this? I assure you that neither one of them has any idea what's going on. Strike Force is too busy with this Kate Livingston business to be of any threat to us. As for Hicks, well, she's still hung up on the fact that her assistant was killed. She's no threat to us either."

"You do know that Wilson and Hicks are sleeping together."

"Yeah, I know."

"That doesn't concern you?"

"Why should it? Maybe Wilson can tame the bitch a little and make her less of a pain in the ass."

Vice President Conrad laughed. "I hope you're right about this."

"I'm telling you there's nothing to be concerned about," Director Michal assured Vice President Conrad. "At least, it'll keep them busy, and out of our hair."

"If you're wrong about this it could cost us dearly," Vice President Conrad remarked as he got up from his seat. "We're too close to achieving our goal for things to unravel on us." He continued while he walked over to the office door and opened it.

Vice President Conrad left Director Michal's office and closed the door. He exited the outer office where two Secret Service agents were waiting. He followed the Secret Service agents to the stairway and down the stairs. They exited the building and hurried to the limousine that was waiting. One of the Secret Service agents opened the back door to the limousine. Vice President Conrad got in, and the limousine drove off.

Seconds later, a Cadillac Escalade pulled up, and the two Secret Service agents got into the backseat, and then it sped off to tail Vice President Conrad's limousine.

Meanwhile, Director Michal got up from his seat and left his office, and walked to the parking garage where his car was parked. He got into his car on the driver's side and closed the door. He started the car and drove off.

Director Michal drove to his house a few miles away. He pulled into the driveway and turned off his car. He got out of his car and started to walk to his front door when a car pulled up in his driveway; and parked next to his. He stopped walking and turned around, and noticed that it was CIA Deputy Director, Karen Hicks' car that had parked in his drive.

*What the fuck does she want?* He thought.

Deputy Director Hicks got out of her car and hurried over to where Director Michal was standing. "We need to talk."

"About what?"

"About Thomas Flowers and Pamela Wells."

"Can't this wait until morning?"

"No, it can't," Deputy Director Hicks fired back. "If it wasn't important, I wouldn't be here."

"Okay, let's go inside," Director Michal said, and they continued to walk toward the front door.

Director Michal pulled his keys from his pants pocket and opened the door, and they hurried inside. Deputy Director Hicks closed the door and followed Director Michal to his study.

When they entered the study, Deputy Director Hicks removed her Beretta M9-A1, with its silencer attached that she had tucked away in the small of her back while she closed the door. She pointed the Beretta at Director Michal and cocked the firing hammer to its firing position.

Director Michal stopped walking and turned around to face Deputy Director Hicks. He quickly noticed that she had her Beretta in her hand and that she was pointing it at him. "What the hell are you doing?"

"Shut up, and turn around." Deputy Director Hicks shot back.

"I have no weapon." He said while he turned his back to Deputy Director Hicks.

"Sit down in the chair, in front of your desk, and put your hands behind your back."

Director Michal walked over to the chair in front of his desk and sat down, and put his hands behind his back. "You're making a big mistake."

Deputy Director Hicks walked over and placed a zip-tie around Director Michal's hands. "You're the one that made a big mistake." She pointed out while she walked around to the front of the chair. "Your friend Pamela Wells told me all about it." She continued while she zip-tied Director Michal's feet together.

"So you're the one that took out Wells and Flowers."

"That's right." Deputy Director Hicks acknowledged while she leaned back against the desk. "I know that you ordered them to kill Carla Garcia. What I want to know from you is who ordered you to have them kill Carla?"

Director Michal laughed. "You have no idea what you're getting into, do you?"

Deputy Director Hicks aimed her Beretta a few inches from

Director Michal's head and squeezed the trigger. The bullet shot out of the Beretta and tore into the wall behind Director Michal. "The next one won't miss. Now tell me, who ordered you to have Wells and Flowers kill Carla?"

"You've gone mad!" Director Michal shouted. "I don't know who ordered it. I got a phone call instructing me to get it done. I have no idea who it was."

"You're lying," Deputy Director Hicks snapped. She walked over to Director Michal and punched him in his mouth with the butt of her Beretta, and his lip began to bleed. "Tell me what I want to know, or I'll put a bullet in your head."

"I've told you all I know."

"Wrong answer," Deputy Director Hicks commented. She aimed her Beretta at Director Michal's leg and squeezed the trigger.

"Jesus Christ, Karen, what the hell was that for?" Director Michal cried out in pain.

"For Carla," She replied. Deputy Director Hicks aimed her Beretta at Director Michal's chest and squeezed the trigger twice. "Say hi to Wells and Flowers for me asshole." Was the last words Director Michal heard.

She searched the pockets of the suit jacket that Director Michal was wearing and discovered that he had two cell phones in his possession. "What are you hiding Michal?" She remarked. She looked through the contact list on the first phone and found nothing out of the ordinary. She tossed the cell phone on the desk and looked through the other cell phone's contact list.

"This is odd," Deputy Director Hicks mumbled when she discovered there were no phone numbers stored in the contact list. She checked the recent call list and found that Director Michal called or received calls from only one number at least once a day. She pushed the send key on the cell phone and put it to her ear.

"Hello," a familiar voice said on the other end.

Deputy Director Hicks was shocked when she realized that the man on the other end was none other than Vice President James Conrad.

*Why the hell would Michal, and the vice president be talking so much?* She thought as she pushed the end key to cancel the call.

"What the hell," she said when the cell phone rang. She looked at the caller ID and saw that it was Vice President Conrad calling back. She pushed the speakerphone on the front of the cell phone.

"Michal, what the hell did you hang up for?" Vice President Conrad demanded to know.

"*Not good Karen.*" She thought.

"Michal, do you have something to report? Is there a problem with the package?"

Deputy Director Hicks pushed the end key to cancel the call. "This is a lot bigger than I thought," she said as she tossed the cell phone on the desk.

Deputy Director Hicks ran out of the room and straight to the front door. She opened the door and hurried to her car, and opened the driver's side door. She got in behind the wheel and started her silver-tone Chevy Cobalt, and backed out of the driveway.

She proceeded down the narrow road and turned onto the main road. After a short drive, she arrived at her residence and parked her car in the drive. She got out of her car and hurried inside. She walked into her bedroom and tossed her purse on the bed.

She walked over to her closet and pulled out her suitcase, and placed it on the bed. She packed a few things inside and closed the suitcase.

Deputy Director Hicks reached for her purse and removed her cell phone. She pulled up the phone number for CIA Director Müller and pressed the send key. After a few rings, Director Müller answered. "I'm sorry to bother you, sir, but something has come up. I need to take the rest of the week off if that's possible," she calmly said.

"No problem," Director Müller said. "If you need more time, let me know."

"Thank you, sir," Deputy Director Hicks pressed the end button to cancel the call. She put her cell phone back into her purse and hung her purse on her shoulder. She grabbed her suitcase and walked out of the room.

Deputy Director Hicks walked to the front door and grabbed her briefcase that was sitting next to the door. She opened the door and stepped outside. She closed the door and hurried to the back of her car; and opened the trunk. She put her suitcase and briefcase inside and closed the trunk lid.

She hurried around to the driver's side front door and opened it. She got in behind the wheel and started the car. She backed out of the driveway and drove away.

# Chapter 17

Arlington County, Virginia
The Pentagon War Room

President Elliot sat at the head of the rectangular table that was in the room along with Vice President, James Conrad, and Secretary of the Navy, John Forsythe. A few minutes later, the Chairman of the Joint Chiefs of Staff, General Thomas Richwood and Secretary of State, George Maxwell, joined them.

"First off, I want to thank everyone for meeting me here on such short notice." President Elliot began when Secretary of Defense, Mark Roberts, entered, and took a seat at the table next to Secretary of the Navy, John Forsythe. The President waited until the Marine, who was assigned to the entrance of the War Room, had closed the double-doors before he continued. "About thirty minutes ago, the President of Iran made a statement on Iranian television that I think we should all hear."

The President pushed a button on the table, and the wall size plasma screen came to life. Everyone watched as the President of Iran stepped up to the podium. "I would like to begin by saying that Iran will no longer tolerate being badgered by the world's superpowers," the translator translated. "With that said, I am proud to announce to the world that Iran was responsible for the Brussels bombing. I would like to conclude that we have several more nuclear weapons at our disposal, and we will not hesitate to use these nuclear weapons to defend ourselves. You have been warned."

President Elliot pushed the button on the table, and the wall size plasma screen went blank."Well, there's no doubt now who's behind the Brussels bombing." He commented, "suggestions anyone."

"Like I've been saying all along, nuke um," Vice President Conrad boldly said.

"We're not going to nuke anyone.' President Elliot fired back. "Has the George Washington and her task group arrived in the Gulf of Oman?"

"They will be there within the hour." Secretary of the Navy, John Forsythe answered. "However, Mr. President, the Washington is within striking range of the shore batteries along the Iranian coast."

President Elliot thought for a quick moment. "John, what's the latest on the Eisenhower?" He asked Secretary Forsythe.

"The fires have been put out, and the flight deck has been cleared, so the wounded can be airlifted off the ship by helicopter," Secretary Forsythe replied. "Mr. President, the Eisenhower is still dead in the water. "Flight ops aren't possible; she's too heavily damaged. She'll need at least nine months in dry-dock to get her back into shape."

"Has any of the Iranian warships left their home ports?" President Elliot inquired.

"No, sir, they have not," Secretary Forsythe assured the president. "I would..." Secretary Forsythe stopped talking when the telephone in front of President Elliot began to ring.

President Elliot removed the telephone receiver from the telephone and put it to his ear. "Yes."

"Mr. President, Ambassador Mitchell at the UN is on the secure line," Mrs. Wyatt began. "He says that he has an urgent message for you from the UN, Iranian Ambassador."

"Put him through."

"Yes, Mr. President."

President Elliot pushed the speakerphone button on the telephone and returned the telephone receiver to the telephone. After a few clicks, Mrs. Wyatt said, "Mr. President, you are now connected with Ambassador Mitchell."

"Sam, what's this about a message from the UN Iranian Ambassador?"

"He handed it to me a few minutes ago," Ambassador Mitchell reported. "I was told that it came directly from the Iranian President."

"Go ahead Sam; read the message.

"The message reads as follows." Ambassador Mitchell began. "The Eisenhower was a warning. Get your ships out of the area, or I will blow them out of the water. You have three hours to comply. That's it, sir."

"Hang tight Sam; I'll get back to you on this," President Elliot said, and then he pushed the speakerphone button on the telephone to cancel the call. "I've had enough of these assholes." He commented. "John, I want everything the Washington has in the air within the hour," President Elliot instructed Secretary of the Navy, John Forsythe. "They are to destroy every missile installation along the coast."

"I understand, sir." Secretary Forsythe acknowledged.

"Mr. President, you don't have the authority to do that without Congress and Senate approval." Secretary of Defense, Mark Roberts was quick to point out. "What you're proposing is an act of war."

"An act of war!" President Elliot shouted back. "Have you forgotten that Iran damn near blew the Eisenhower out of the water? I'd say that was an act of war. I'm well within my authority to retaliate."

"I'm just saying Mr. President that maybe we should wait for the Congress and Senate to approve such a drastic action." Secretary Roberts calmly said.

"The president's right." Secretary of State George Maxwell jumped in. "I don't think we should wait. We need to act now, not later."

"I agree with Secretary Maxwell," General Richwood added. "Now is the time to strike back."

President Elliot sat at the table and thought for a moment. "John, I want you to get with our naval forces in the area and determine what targets we need to hit," President Elliot ordered Secretary Forsythe. He looked at General Richwood. "General, I want all of our armed forces in the region placed on high alert." President Elliot waited for a few seconds before he continued. "If there are no more questions, I suggest we get the ball rolling."

Everyone jumped to their feet when President Elliot got up from his seat. He walked over to the double-doors and opened them. He exited the War Room and the Marine standing guard outside the closed the double-doors.

* * * * *

Oklahoma City, Oklahoma

After countless hours of nonstop driving, CIA Deputy Director, Karen Hicks, was relieved when she finally arrived in Oklahoma City. She exited the interstate not far from the main entrance to Tinker Air Force Base and drove down the service road and turned into the Super Eight Motel. She pulled up to the motel's office and parked. She got out of her silver-tone Chevy Cobalt and went inside. She walked up to the counter and was greeted by a twenty-five-year-old blonde-haired woman. "Hello," the young woman said. "Can I help you?"

"Yes, I'd like a room, please," Deputy Director Hicks answered.

"Would you like smoking, or non-smoking?" She asked as she handed Deputy Director Hicks a registration form.

"I prefer a smoking room with one bed," Deputy Director Hicks said as she began to fill out the registration form. When she was done, she fumbled through her purse looking for her wallet when her Beretta M9-A1 fell out onto the counter.

"Oh, my!" The young woman gasped.

"I'm a federal agent," Deputy Director Hicks said as she pulled out her phony US Deputy Marshall's credentials. "You don't need to worry about me having a weapon." She assured the young woman behind the counter while she put the Beretta back into her purse.

"Wow, a Deputy Marshall." The young woman remarked while she looked at the identification card and badge. "How long will you be staying with us Miss Pamela Carson?"

"Not sure, it depends on how things progress while I'm here," Deputy Director Hicks answered while she put her credentials back into her purse.

"Cash or Credit, Miss Carson?"

"Cash," Deputy Director Hicks answered, and handed the young woman a hundred-dollar bill.

The young woman handed Deputy Director Hicks her receipt and then her change. "You're in room one-forty-six." She pointed out as

188

she handed Deputy Director Hicks the key-card to her room. "It's around back on the bottom level."

Deputy Director Hicks put her change into her wallet and put her wallet back into her purse. She walked back to her car and got in on the driver's side. She drove around to the back of the motel and parked in front of her room. She got out of her car and walked to the back, and opened the trunk. She removed her overnight bag and briefcase from the trunk and closed the trunk. She walked up to the door and swiped the key-card; and opened the door. She entered the room and closed the door.

"I asked for one bed, and the dumbass gives me two," Deputy Director Hicks said softly. She walked over to the bed near the door and placed her overnight bag and briefcase on the foot of the bed. She removed the Beretta M9-A1 from her purse and tossed her purse on the bed. She checked to be certain that the safety was on before she put the Beretta in the small of her back.

She opened her briefcase and removed the laptop, and the small three-ring notebook that she had taken from the house of Thomas Flowers and Pamela Wells. She walked over to the small desk next to the television and placed the laptop down on the desk, and then she laid the notebook on the table next to the laptop.

Afterwards, she hurried back to the bed and opened her overnight bag. She removed a package that contained a prepaid cell phone that she had purchased from a department store the day before; which was already activated and ready to be used. She sat down on the bed and opened the package, and put the battery into the cell phone. She turned on the cell phone and waited for it to power up.

"That'll work," she commented when she saw that the battery was half charged. She dialed the number for Colonel Wilson and waited for him to answer.

"Wilson," Colonel Wilson said when he answered his phone.

"Hey soldier boy," Deputy Director Hicks said in a sexy voice. "What you doing?"

"Who is this?" Colonel Wilson demanded to know.

"How soon you forget," Deputy Director Hicks said in her normal tone of voice. "Are you alone?"

"Yes, I'm alone," Colonel Wilson answered. "I'm sitting at my desk in my office doing paperwork. Where the hell are you?"

"I'm at the Super Eight Motel here in Oklahoma City."

"Which one?"

"The one up from the main gate to Tinker."

"I know the one you're talking about, but why are you here?"

"I have something you need to see. No one knows I'm here, but you and I want to keep it that way."

"What's up?" Colonel Wilson curiously asked.

"Not over the phone." Deputy Director Hicks fired back. "Just get your ass over here. I'm in room one-forty-six." She concluded and canceled the call.

"Doesn't anyone say goodbye anymore?" Colonel Wilson commented when he was disconnected.

"What's up?" Captain Hale asked who was standing in the doorway to Colonel Wilson's office.

"Nothing," Colonel Wilson answered while he returned the telephone receiver to the telephone on his desk. "Any news from Popeye?"

"They're in the air."

"Great!" Colonel Wilson said as he jumped to his feet. "I got to step out for a few. Let me know the minute they land. You can reach me on my cell phone."

*I wonder what's so important that it can't wait,* Captain Hale thought while Colonel Wilson left his office. Captain Hale closed the door and walked toward his office.

Meanwhile, Deputy Director Hicks sat down at the desk and powered down the cell phone. She removed the battery and the Sims card and threw the cell phone into the trashcan that was between the desk and the television. She snapped the Sims card into two pieces and placed it in the ashtray that was on the desk.

She put the battery on the table next to the ashtray, and she then plugged the power cord for the laptop into the outlet that was fastened to the back of the desk. She opened the laptop and entered the password that she had memorized from the small notebook that would unlock the laptop.

She started to sit down in the chair in front of the desk when there was a knock on the door. She hurried over to the door while she removed her Beretta from the small of her back and flipped the safety off. She stood on the side of the door next to the wall. "Who is it?"

"Karen it's John." She heard Colonel Wilson say from the other side of the door.

Deputy Director Hicks remained behind the door. With her Beretta pointed at the door, she opened it, and Colonel Wilson entered. She quickly closed the door and lowered her Beretta.

"Jesus Christ, Karen, what's going on?" Colonel Wilson demanded to know when he noticed that Deputy Director Hicks had her Beretta in her hand. "What the hell is this about?"

"You heard about what happened to Thomas Flowers, and Pamela Wells didn't you?" Deputy Director Hicks asked while she put the safety on the Beretta.

"Yeah, I heard," Colonel Wilson answered while Deputy Director Hicks walked over to the table and placed the Beretta down on the table next to the ashtray. "They were killed when they walked in on a robbery in progress."

Deputy Director Hicks turned to face Colonel Wilson. "It was no robbery. I was there waiting for them." She pointed out.

"Did you..." Colonel Wilson stopped in mid-sentence.

"Yes, I sent those bastards where they belonged, straight to hell." She remarked as tears began to form in her eyes. "They admitted to killing Carla Garcia, and I just pulled the trigger, and Bam, they were dead." Deputy Director Hicks continued as tears began to run down her face. "I don't know what came over me."

Colonel Wilson took Deputy Director Hicks into his arms and hugged her tightly as she wept uncontrollably. "They got what they had coming to them." He whispered, "The world is better off without them in it."

Deputy Director Hicks stopped crying and pulled away from Colonel Wilson. "I'm sorry." She said while she got control of her emotions.

"Never apologize," Colonel Wilson was quick to point out.

"I know; it's a sign of weakness," Deputy Director Hicks said.

Colonel Wilson took out a small package of tissue paper that he kept in his jacket pocket and handed it to Deputy Director Hicks.

Thanks," Deputy Director Hicks said as she took the package of tissues from Colonel Wilson. She opened the package and removed a couple of the tissues; and dried her eyes.

Colonel Wilson smiled. "Feeling any better?"

"Much better," Deputy Director Hicks answered as she handed the package of unused tissue paper back to Colonel Wilson.

"It doesn't bother you that I killed Flowers, and Wells?"

"Why would it bother me? All you did was take out some terrorist."

"Still, I have blood on my hands."

"You need to get over this and move on."

"John, there's something else I need to tell you."

"You mean there's more to this?"

"I'm afraid so," Deputy Director Hicks answered. "When I interrogated Wells, she confessed that Director Michal ordered them to kill Carla."

"Are you telling me that Director Michal of Homeland Security had something to do with Carla's murder?"

"That I am," Deputy Director Hicks replied. "I went to Director Michal's home and confronted him about this. After some convincing interrogation, he admitted that someone higher up the food chain ordered him to have Carla put down."

"You mean you tortured him?"

"You could call it that. Anyway, I was so filled with rage that I put two in his chest."

"You killed the Director of Homeland Security?"

"Yes, I did."

"I got to hand it to you Karen; you got some set on you."

Deputy Director Hicks smiled. "I guess that's why they call me the Ice Queen or the She-Devil. I'm just one cold-hearted evil bitch."

"So, did you search Director Michal's home?"

"I sure did, and I came up with nothing. That is until I searched Director Michal's suit jacket and found that he had two cell phones. The first cell phone I checked appeared to be normal, but the second one was odd. There was only one number that called that phone, and the same number was the only number that Michal called."

"Let me guess; you called the number to see who would answer."

"Yep, I dialed the number, and the vice president answered, so I hung up. A few seconds later, the vice president called back. He thought Michal had hung up on him, and he was pissed. He asked if there was a problem with the package. I have no idea what he was talking about."

"You know it's not uncommon for the vice president and the director of Homeland to be contacting one another." Colonel Wilson was quick to point out.

"That's what I thought at first, but if that was the case, then why are they using a special cell phone to communicate with each other. There's got to be more to this, than what we're seeing."

"Who else knows about this?"

"Just you."

"Good; let's keep it that way." Colonel Wilson thought for a quick moment. "Does anyone know you're here?"

"No one knows where I am. I used a phony name when I checked in here, a name that I set up myself a while back."

"Sounds like you've covered your ass. A fine-looking ass at that I might add."

"I always cover my ass; that's why I'm wearing clothes."

"Smart ass." Colonel Wilson fired back. "I don't know why, but I get the feeling; there's something else you wanted to talk to me about."

"Yes, there is. When I searched Thomas Flowers and Pamela Wells' house, I found a laptop and a code book." Deputy Director Hicks pointed out while she walked over to the desk. "You won't believe what's on this laptop." She continued while she sat down at the table in front of the laptop. "I have gone through most of the files on this laptop and discovered that the list of Red Cell members is bigger than we suspected."

"How many are you talking about?" Colonel Wilson asked while he walked over to the desk and stood next to Deputy Director Hicks.

"It's not about how many names are on the new list, but who is on the list," Deputy Director Hicks answered while she opened the file that contained the list of Red Cell members. "I think you're going to be surprised."

Colonel Wilson leaned forward and looked at the list. "Are you sure about this?"

"Not one-hundred percent sure, but there is a way to verify this list without raising any suspicion," She answered while she opened another file. "I found this e-mail that referred to a meeting; everyone on that list will be there. All we have to do is watch, and we'll see for ourselves if this list is correct."

"So you want me to help you with this?"

"Yes, I could use your help," Deputy Director Hicks answered while she stood up and faced Colonel Wilson. "John, I have no one else I can turn to with this. You're the only person I trust."

Colonel Wilson looked into Deputy Director Hicks' eyes and smiled. "Where and when is this meeting taking place?"

"Three days from now in Baltimore at an abandoned warehouse on Nicholson Street by the docks."

"I can't leave right now," Colonel Wilson pointed out. "I got to see the operation that's in progress through to the end before I can go anywhere."

"You mean Operation Dragonfly?"

"Where did you hear that name?" Colonel Wilson curiously asked. "Very few people know about that operation."

"There was a message on the laptop that referred to that operation."

"Do you know who sent that message?"

"I know it came from Washington."

Colonel Wilson looked at his watch. "There's still time." He mumbled as he rushed over to the door. He opened the door and ran to where his vehicle was parked. He opened the passenger's side door and popped open the glove compartment. He removed the satellite telephone from inside and closed the glove compartment. He closed the door on his car and hurried back into the motel room. He closed the door while he powered up the satellite telephone.

Deputy Director Hicks didn't say a word. She walked over to the other bed and sat down while Colonel Wilson extended the antenna on the satellite telephone. He pushed a series of numbers and waited. "Big Bird, this is Wolverine," He said when the pilot of the Strike Force Delta aircraft answered. "I am declaring an Alfa-Kilo-Mike-one-seven-five. Do you copy?"

"I copy Alfa-Kilo-Mike-one-seven-five." The pilot acknowledged.

"I authenticate Serra-Foxtrot-one-one. We are standing by for instructions."

"Do not enter the playground." Colonel Wilson began. "The mission might have been compromised on our end. Do not acknowledge any transmission from Strike Force Delta Command unless it's from me; do you copy?"

"I copy." The pilot acknowledged.

"Little Joe will contact you on the sat- phone with the new landing site."

"Roger that; I will wait for Little Joe to make sat-phone contact; Big Bird out," the pilot concluded, and the satellite telephone call was disconnected.

Colonel Wilson dialed another set of numbers and waited. "Little Joe, this is Wolverine," He said when Little Joe answered. "How far are you from the LZ (Landing Zone)?"

"About fifteen kilometers;. Why, is there something wrong?"

"I have reason to believe that the primary LZ has been compromised."

"Roger that." Little Joe acknowledged.

"How far are you from the secondary LZ?"

"About twenty kilometers; it's closer to the target than the primary."

"If it's closer than why didn't you use that one as the primary?"

"General Richwood is the one that suggested the location for the primary."

"I see, does anyone here know about the secondary?"

"No, I never mentioned the secondary to anyone until now. Wolverine, is there something going on that I need to be concerned about?"

"I'm not sure at this time," Colonel Wilson answered. "To be on the safe side, I want you to call Big Bird on the sat-phone and give him the necessary information he'll need to get to the secondary. He's expecting your call."

"I understand," Little Joe remarked. "You know General Richwood is going to be pissed when he finds out that you changed the landing zone."

"I'll deal with the general." Colonel Wilson fired back. "Whatever you do, don't use the radio to contact Big Bird or anyone else until I tell you it's safe to do so."

"Roger that," Little Joe acknowledged, and then he ended the call.

Colonel Wilson looked over at Deputy Director Hicks and smiled while he dialed another set of numbers. "We can talk after I make this call." He said while he waited. "This is Wilson," he said when the pilot of the Strike Force Delta Gulfstream G550 twin-engine jet aircraft answered. "I need the aircraft ready for departure in eight hours."

"It'll be ready," the pilot answered. "What's our destination?"

"Andrews," Colonel Wilson answered, and then he canceled the call.

"Now will you tell me what's going on?" Deputy Director Hicks calmly asked.

Colonel Wilson walked over to the bed where Deputy Director Hicks was sitting. "Operation Dragonfly is the operation code name for the operation that's underway to free Kate Livingston from her captors." He said as he sat down on the bed next to Deputy Director Hicks. "The operation is already in motion." He placed his hand on Deputy Director Hick's thigh. "Have I told you how good you look in those tight fitting blue jeans?"

Deputy Director Hicks smiled as she turned to face Colonel Wilson. "Are you sure you want to go another round with the Ice Queen?"

Colonel Wilson smiled. "I can handle whatever you throw at me my lady." He leaned over and kissed Deputy Director Hicks on her lips as his hand made its way between her legs.

Deputy Director Hicks stopped Colonel Wilson's advances and jumped to her feet. "Bring it on Soldier Boy," she commented as she began to unbutton her blouse. She removed her blouse and laid it on the bed next to her overnight bag.

Colonel Wilson removed the lightweight jacket he was wearing, exposing the shoulder holster that held his Glock-19. Deputy Director Hicks looked at Colonel Wilson and smiled. "I never leave home without it," he chuckled as he placed the jacket on the bed, and then he removed his shoulder holster and laid it on top of the jacket. He took off his shirt and tossed it on the bed while Deputy Director Hicks removed her bra, exposing her perfectly shaped breasts, and threw it on top of her blouse.

Colonel Wilson watched with excitement while Deputy Director Hicks unbuttoned her jeans and let them fall to the floor. She picked up her jeans and laid them on the bed next to her other clothes. Colonel Wilson quickly unzipped his pants and carefully removed them.

Deputy Director Hicks smiled when she noticed the bulge in Colonel Wilson's shorts. She removed her panties and laid them on the bed on top of her jeans. She hurried around to the other side of the bed and slipped in between the covers. "What's taking you so long Soldier Boy?" She teased, "It's not polite to keep a lady waiting."

"Well, excuse me my lady," Colonel Wilson said and put his pants on the bed. "I wouldn't want you to get the wrong impression of me." He continued as he slipped in between the covers next to Deputy Director Hicks.

# Chapter 18

Washington, DC
The White House
The Presidential Residence

President Elliot and First Lady Amanda Elliot were sitting at the table in the dining room enjoying their early-morning breakfast together when the red telephone on the wall rang. President Elliot looked at the red telephone, and then he looked at the First Lady. "Duty calls," he remarked as he got up from his seat.

"Maybe it's news about Kate," the First Lady pointed out.

"Not over the red phone," President Elliot said while he walked over to the red telephone on the wall. "I'm afraid it's something else." He removed the telephone receiver and put it to his ear. "Yes." He said.

"Mr. President, we have a situation, sir." White House Chief of Staff, Howard Gordon reported. "Your presence is requested in the Situation Room."

"I'm on my way," President Elliot acknowledged and returned the telephone receiver to its normal resting place. He walked back over to the dining room table where the First Lady was sitting. He leaned down and kissed her on the cheek. "Let's do lunch later."

"That sounds good to me Mr. President," she commented. "That is if you're done with your problem by then."

President Elliot smiled. "We'll see." He commented, and then he walked to the door and opened it. He stepped outside into the hallway and closed the door. He walked to the Situation Room and the Marine, who was standing guard, dressed in his dress uniform and armed with a nine-millimeter Beretta M9-A1 side arm, snapped to attention and saluted the president. "Carry on Marine," President Elliot said and entered the Situation Room, and the Marine guard closed the double-doors.

Everyone in the room jumped to their feet. "Have a seat," President Elliot said while he walked over to the table and sat down in the seat at the head of the table. "Okay, what's up?" He asked while everyone returned to their seats at the table.

"Mr. President, our satellites indicate that the Iranians are setting up more Shahab-3 long-range missile sites along the coast. Sir, their Navy is readying its warships for departure from its naval bases," NSA Director Jack Parkinson reported. "We've also picked up a sudden troop movement by the Iranians. They're building up along their borders."

"So, the Iranians are preparing for war?" President Elliot inquired.

"That would be my best guess," Director Parkinson answered.

"What about their neighbors? How are they reacting to this build up?"

"Mr. President, Turkmenistan, Azerbaijan and Armenia have placed several divisions on their side of the border." CIA Director Robert Müller jumped in. "Iraq and Afghanistan have also increased their troops along the Iranian border, and Turkey is preparing to do the same."

"What about Pakistan?" President Elliot asked.

"It is unclear at this time what they're planning," Director Müller answered. "However, I would like to point out that we have noticed a sudden increase of activity at their nuclear storage facility at Quetta and Multan. I believe they're preparing to deploy their nukes."

"Any idea who they might be targeting with their nukes?" President Elliot asked.

"Not at this time, sir," Director Müller replied. "It's too early to tell."

"Keep an eye on the situation and let me know the minute the situation changes," President Elliot instructed Director Müller. "We don't need any surprises."

"I say nuke the bastards and be done with the problem," Vice President James Conrad remarked.

President Elliot shot Vice President Conrad a cold stare. "You would kill millions of people without any hesitation?"

"The Iranians didn't care about killing millions of people when they set the nuke off in Brussels," Vice President Conrad fired back.

"John, I want you to inform all ships in the area that if they are fired upon, they are to take whatever action, they feel necessary to protect themselves," President Elliot ordered. "If the Iranian Navy deploys, I want our surface ships to be prepared to blow those bastards out of the water if they show any hostile intent. I also want all those new shore batteries targeted and destroyed."

"Yes Mr. President," Secretary Forsythe acknowledged.

"As for the rest of you, I want everyone to keep a watchful eye on the Iranians," President Elliot ordered as he got up from his seat at the table. "Keep me informed of any new developments. I'll be in the Oval Office." He concluded and walked over to the double-doors. He opened one of the doors and exited the Situation Room. The Marine outside the Situation Room snapped to attention and saluted President Elliot. "Carry on Marine," he said and continued to walk toward the Oval Office.

President Elliot entered the Oval Office and closed the door. He walked over to his desk and sat down in the chair behind his desk. He looked at his appointment calendar on his desk in front of him and saw an envelope lying on the desk next to the appointment calendar.

He picked up the envelope and opened it. He removed the paper that was inside and read what was written on the paper.

Time is running out.

Resign, or Kate dies.

President Elliot dropped the paper to his desk and slammed his hands down on his desk. Suddenly, the door to the Oval Office flew open, and two Secret Service agents entered. "No need for alarm," President Elliot explained. "You may go about your business."

"Yes, Mr. President," One of the Secret Service agents said. "We'll be right outside if you should need us, sir." The two Secret Service agents walked out of the Oval Office and closed the door.

President Elliot was startled when there was a knock on the door. The door opened, and his personal secretary, Mrs. Wyatt, entered. She closed the door and walked over to the president's desk. "Mr. President, Pakistani Ambassador Shaikh's wishes to see you. He's on your schedule for later this afternoon, but he says it's important, and that he needs to see you now."

"That's odd," President Elliot commented. "Show him in."

"Yes, Mr. President," Mrs. Wyatt said and walked over to the door. She opened the door and stood in the doorway. "Mr. Ambassador, the President will see you now."

Ambassador Shaikh's entered the Oval Office, and Mrs. Wyatt closed the door on her way out. President Elliot got up from his seat and walked over to greet the Ambassador. "Mr. Ambassador it's nice to see you again," President Elliot said while they shook hands. "Please, have a seat." He continued to say, motioning to one of the sofas in the middle of the room.

"I appreciate you taking the time to see me Mr. President," Ambassador Shaikh's commented while he sat on the sofa, and President Elliot sat on the other sofa across from him. "Mr. President, I know that you're a busy man, so I'll get right to the point. Our intelligence agency has reported that there is heavy activity at Iran's research facility a few kilometers outside of Iranshahr. My government is certain, without any doubt; that Iran has been manufacturing nuclear weapons there for some time now. We fear that Iran is preparing to deploy their nuclear weapons, an action that my government is gravely disturbed by."

"So you're going to target Iran with your nukes?"

"Yes, we are," Ambassador Shaikh's answered. "President Ghasem has declared that Pakistan will protect itself against any kind of aggression from Iran; regardless of the consequences. If Iran attacks Pakistan, we will retaliate with our entire nuclear arsenal, and bomb them back into the Stone Age."

"How can you be certain that Iran has developed nuclear weapons?"

"I cannot tell you how we know, but I can tell you that our source is one-hundred percent accurate. Iran is producing nuclear weapons."

"You do realize that by targeting Iran you're only going to aggravate them and possibly start a war that neither side wants?" President Elliot was quick to point out. "Please convey my objections to this action to President Ghasem."

"I will inform President Ghasem about your concerns," Ambassador Shaikh's commented while he got up from the sofa.

President Elliot stood up and shook hands with Ambassador Shaikh's and then walked over to his desk while Ambassador Shaikh's left the Oval Office and closed the door. He sat down behind his desk and pushed the intercom button on the telephone on his desk. "Mrs. Wyatt."

"Yes, Mr. President."

"Cancel all my appointments for the day," President Elliot instructed Mrs. Wyatt, and then he pushed the intercom button again to cancel the intercom call.

President Elliot stood up and walked over to the side door, and opened it. He stepped into the hallway and closed the door.

∗ ∗ ∗ ∗ ∗

Oklahoma City, Oklahoma
Super Eight Motel
Room One Forty-six

Colonel Wilson was awakened from a sound sleep when his satellite telephone on the nightstand rang. He flipped the covers back and sat up on the edge of the bed. He looked at Deputy Director Hicks, who was still asleep and smiled. He extended the antenna on the satellite telephone and pushed the talk key, and put it to his ear. "Wilson here," he said in a strong voice.

"Wolverine, Dragonfly, is sixty miles (minutes) to touch-down," Captain Hale announced.

"I'm on my way." Colonel Wilson acknowledged and pushed the end key to end the call. He laid the satellite telephone down on the nightstand and began to put his clothes on.

"Leaving so soon?" Deputy Director Hicks asked as she rolled over to face Colonel Wilson.

Colonel Wilson turned around and looked at Deputy Director Hicks. "Duty calls."

"Yeah, I..." Deputy Director Hicks stopped talking when the telephone on the nightstand rang.

"Are you expecting a call?" Colonel Wilson asked.

"No, no one knows I'm here but you," Deputy Director Hicks answered as she began to put on her clothes. "Are you going to answer it?"

"Hell no," Colonel Wilson answered. After a few rings, the telephone stopped ringing. "Call the front desk and see if it was them calling." He suggested as he handed Deputy Director Hicks the telephone receiver. Colonel Wilson pushed zero on the telephone while she put the telephone receiver to her ear.

Three rings later, a young man who was working the night shift at the front desk answered. "Yes, this is Pamela Carson in room one forty-six. Did you call my room a few seconds ago?"

"Yes, ma'am, I did." The young man answered. "Someone called in on the main line and asked if you were staying here. I told them that I couldn't give out that kind of information. I called you right afterwards to inform you of this."

"Did this person identify himself?"

"He said his name was John Wilson. He said he heard you was in town and was trying to locate you."

"How long ago did he call?"

"About five minutes ago. Do you want me to put him through if he should call back?"

"No!" Deputy Director Hicks fired back. "I don't want anyone to know that I'm staying here."

"As you wish ma'am. Is there anything else you need?"

"Not at this time," Deputy Director Hicks answered, and then she handed Colonel Wilson the telephone receiver.

Colonel Wilson returned the telephone receiver to the telephone on the nightstand. "So who's looking for you?"

"You are," Deputy Director Hicks answered.

"Did you drive your own car here?"

"Yes, I did."

"Does your car have any kind of GPS on it?"

"I have an On Star sub..." Deputy Director Hicks suddenly stopped talking. She realized that someone had tracked her down through her On Star connection in her car. "Oh, shit." She remarked.

"Get the rest of your clothes on," Colonel Wilson instructed Deputy Director Hicks while he picked up the satellite telephone from the nightstand. He dialed a number and pushed the talk key. "It's not safe here. You've been compromised." He continued as he put the satellite telephone to his ear.

"Hammer," Second Lieutenant, Daniel Shea, nicknamed Hammer, answered.

"Hammer, I need you, and a five-man security team in full combat dress to meet me at hangar nine in ten mikes (minutes)," Colonel Wilson ordered. "Tell no one where you're going; not even Bulldog."

"Roger that," Lieutenant Shea answered.

Colonel Wilson ended the call and lowered the satellite telephone's antenna; and laid the satellite telephone down on the bed. "Damn that was fast." He commented when he noticed that Deputy Director Hicks was fully dressed. He finished getting dressed while Deputy Director Hicks packed up the laptop and other items from the small desk next to the television into her briefcase.

"Are you ready?" Colonel Wilson asked.

"Yep," Deputy Director Hicks replied as she closed her briefcase.

"Good, let's get out of here," Colonel Wilson commented as he picked up the satellite telephone from the bed. He grabbed Deputy Director Hicks' overnight bag on the bed and walked over to the door.

"I'm right behind you," Deputy Director Hicks commented while she picked up her briefcase from the bed.

Colonel Wilson opened the door and stepped outside, with Deputy Director Hicks following. She closed the door and began walking towards her car.

"We're taking mine." Colonel Wilson pointed out. "I'll send someone to get your car." He continued while he walked to his black colored Cadillac Escalade parked a few feet away.

"Is that your car?" Deputy Director Hicks asked, surprised at the beauty of Colonel Wilson's Cadillac Escalade.

"Yep, I saved for over three years to buy this baby," Colonel Wilson answered as he opened the back door on the driver's side. He laid Deputy Director Hicks' overnight bag on the backseat and closed the door. "I just picked it up a few days ago."

*Sweet ride,* Deputy Director Hicks thought while she walked over to the Escalade and opened the backdoor on the passenger's side. She placed her briefcase on the backseat next to her overnight bag and closed the door. She walked to the front passenger's side door and opened it, and got in. *Nice,* she thought as she closed the door.

Colonel Wilson walked to the front driver's side door and opened the door, and got in behind the wheel. He put the satellite telephone in the console between the front seats and started up the Escalade. He looked at Deputy Director Hicks and smiled. He put the vehicle in gear, and they drove off.

When they arrived at the main gate to Tinker Air Force Base, Colonel Wilson stopped the Escalade at the guard shack and rolled down his window. He and Deputy Director Hicks presented their credentials to the guard and were allowed to proceed.

Colonel Wilson drove to hangar nine where Lieutenant Shea was waiting, and stopped a few feet inside the hangar entrance. "Wait here." He said to Deputy Director Hicks as he opened the door. He got out of the Escalade and closed the door.

Lieutenant Shea hurried over to Colonel Wilson's vehicle "We're all set," he reported. "I have three men patrolling around the hangar, and two at the entrance."

"Sounds like you have everything covered," Colonel Wilson pointed out. "Are the pilots here?"

"They're inside preparing the aircraft for departure."

"Good," Colonel Wilson commented. "Hammer, how's your leg doing these days?"

"Other than not being able to jump, I'm at one-hundred percent."

"Are you ready for some action?"

"I would love to get back in the shit again."

"Are you guys ready?"

"They're ready. Wolverine, what's going on?"

"Something's brewing and I might need a little backup," Colonel Wilson answered. He signaled to Deputy Director Hicks, and she opened the door and got out of the vehicle. Lieutenant Shea was stunned to see Deputy Director Hicks get out of Colonel Wilson's Escalade. He looked at Colonel Wilson dumbfounded. *My god, the rumors are true.* He thought. *You're fucking the Ice Queen.*

"Is there a problem?" Colonel Wilson asked.

"No problem," Lieutenant Shea fired back.

Deputy Director Hicks walked over to where Colonel Wilson and Lieutenant Shea were standing."Karen, this is Hammer. He's one of my team leaders and my training officer." Colonel Wilson pointed out.

"Nice to meet you Hammer."

"The pleasure is all mine, ma'am," Lieutenant Shea kindly commented.

"Hammer, when the aircraft is ready to be pulled from the hangar, I want you and your men to join Deputy Director Hicks inside the aircraft before it's pulled out," Colonel Wilson instructed Lieutenant Shea. "I have a couple of things in the backseat that I need you to load onto the aircraft for me." Colonel Wilson continued as he walked to the back driver's side door and opened the door. He removed Deputy Director Hicks' overnight bag and briefcase and handed them to Lieutenant Shea, and Lieutenant Shea started walking toward the aircraft.

"I don't think he likes being a busboy." Deputy Director Hicks pointed out.

"He'll get over it," Colonel Wilson said as he closed the back door."You need to go grab a seat on the aircraft and make yourself comfortable. I'll be back in a couple of hours."

"Yes, sir," Deputy Director Hicks said, and then she saluted Colonel Wilson. "Right away," she concluded and walked toward the aircraft.

"You asshole," Colonel Wilson mumbled as he walked to the front driver's side door and opened the door, and got in behind the wheel. He closed the door and started up the Escalade. He put the vehicle in gear and drove off. He drove back to the visitor's parking lot and parked next to the Humvee that he had parked there earlier.

He picked up the satellite telephone from the console between the front seats and opened the door. He got out of his Cadillac Escalade and closed the door. Colonel Wilson walked over to the Humvee and got in on the driver's side. He put the satellite telephone in the glove box, and then he started up the Humvee and headed back to the Strike Force Delta facility.

When he arrived at the main gate to the Strike Force facility, he showed his identification badge to the guard and was allowed to proceed. He parked the Humvee in front of the main building and got out. Colonel Wilson entered the building and hurried to the operation center, and entered.

"Wolverine, we have a problem," Captain Hale reported. "Big Bird isn't answering."

"I know," Colonel Wilson said. He walked over to the communications technician who was sitting at his assigned post in front of the communications console. "I want a secured Alfa frequency," Colonel Wilson ordered while he picked up the wireless headset that was hanging on the communications console and put it on his head.

A few seconds later, the communications technician gave Colonel Wilson the thumbs up. "You're good to go Wolverine."

Colonel Wilson pushed the button on the headset to activate it. "Big Bird, this is Eagle Nest; you are Charlie-Tango-Golf, over."

"Roger that; I authenticate November-Mike-Serra."

"Roger Big Bird. You may drive on (carry out the mission) at your discretion."

"Roger that." Big Bird acknowledged. "We are Charlie-Tango-Mike (continuing the mission) Big Bird out."

"Eagle Nest out," Colonel Wilson acknowledged. He pushed the button on the headset to deactivate it and removed the headset from his head. He hung the wireless headset on the communications console and walked over to the mission planning board in the middle of the room where Captain Hale was standing. "All we can do now is wait, and pray that everything goes right."

"Amen." Captain Hale remarked.

# Chapter 19

15 Kilometers east of Khash, Iran

The Strike Force Delta C-130J aircraft touched down and taxied to where Little Joe and his people were waiting. The C-130J came to a complete stop, and the pilot shut down its four Rolls-Royce AE 2100 D3 turboprop engines while the back cargo door opened.

"Secure the perimeter," Lieutenant McDonald ordered his security team while he stepped off the aircraft. "Remember, no chit-chatter over the radio headset. Maintain radio silence, unless we have a breach. Maverick, Crazy Horse, prepare your assault teams and be ready to bug out in five."

"Roger that." Lieutenant Johnson acknowledged. "We'll be ready in three."

Lieutenant McDonald smiled and walked over to where Little Joe was waiting while Lieutenant Johnson and Lieutenant Milestone assembled the Strike Force Assault teams.

"My people will be ready to move out in a few minutes," Lieutenant McDonald said as he shook hands with Little Joe. "I've been told that the mission is still a go."

"Your people have a clean shot to the target," Little Joe reported. "You should have no trouble getting in without being detected. However, there has been heavy activity on the Pakistan side of the border, and there are several Iranian units heading this way. You have about three hours to get in and out."

"A sudden buildup can only mean one thing," Lieutenant McDonald pointed out. "They're preparing to go to war."

"It appears to be so," Little Joe agreed.

"Well, we better get this show on the road," Lieutenant McDonald commented.

"I can have two of my best people drive your people to the target, so they can get to the target sooner."

"That'll work for me," Lieutenant McDonald acknowledged.

Little Joe signaled for Amos Adler and Javad Yousef to join them. "These two men know this area," Little Joe continued while Amos Adler and Javad Yousef hurried over to where Little Joe and Lieutenant McDonald were standing.

"Yes," Amos Adler said when he and Javad Yousef arrived.

"I want the two of you to take the Americans to the place we discussed earlier," Little Joe instructed Amos Adler and Javad Yousef. "You are to help them in any way possible so that they may complete their mission."

"Yes Little Joe," Amos Adler acknowledged.

Lieutenant McDonald walked over to Lieutenant Johnson and Lieutenant Milestone, with Amos Adler and Javad Yousef close behind. "Gentlemen, this is Amos Adler and Javad Yousef. They will drive you to the target. Are you ready to move out?"

"We're ready," Lieutenant Milestone quickly answered.

"I want you to get in and out of there as quick as possible," Lieutenant McDonald continued. "You only have a few hours before you have company."

"What kind of company?" Lieutenant Johnson dared to ask.

"The Pakistani's are building up on their side of the border, and there are several Iranian military units heading this way."

"How long do we have before the Iranian troops get here?" Lieutenant Milestone inquired.

"About three hours."

"All right people listen up. Grab your gear. We're Oscar-Mike (on the move)." Lieutenant Johnson ordered. "Let's go do what we came here to do, so we can get the fuck out of here."

Lieutenant McDonald watched Lieutenant Johnson and Lieutenant Milestone; along with the two Strike Force assault team members follow Amos Adler and Javad Yousef to the two and a half ton truck that was parked a few feet away.

"You got to be fuckin' kidding me," Lieutenant Johnson commented. "You're taking us to the target in a deuce and a half?"

"Yep," Javad Yousef answered.

"I don't like this one bit," Lieutenant Milestone commented. "They'll hear us coming long before we get there."

"Relax my friends. This truck has been specially modified." Amos Adler was quick to point out. "We can drive right up to their front door, and they would not hear us coming. In fact, the truck is idling right now. Can you hear it running?"

"Impressive," Lieutenant Milestone commented.

"Let's climb aboard. We don't have all night," Lieutenant Johnson ordered.

The Strike Force Delta assault teams climbed up into the back of the two and a half ton truck while Javad Yousef walked to the passenger's side of the truck. He opened the door and climbed in, and closed the door.

Amos Adler waited for Lieutenant Johnson, who was the last to climb into the back of the truck before he secured the back gate and then walked to the driver's side. He opened the door and climbed in; and closed the door.

Lieutenant McDonald watched as the two-and-a-half ton truck began to move. A few seconds later, the truck disappeared into the darkness. He walked back over to where Little Joe was standing. "I take it that you have people out there watching for the Iranian troops that are heading this way."

"Yes, I have some of my people watching the advancing Iranians. They check in with me every five minutes," Little Joe answered. "Don't worry, right now, the Iranians are two-hundred kilometers west of here. I will keep you informed of any changes. Now, if you will excuse me, I need to check with my people." Little Joe concluded and walked back to where his people were waiting.

Lieutenant McDonald walked back to the Strike Force Delta assault aircraft. He walked up the ramp at the back of the aircraft and entered. Terminator, Lieutenant McDonald's communications operator, hurried over to Lieutenant McDonald. "Popeye, I just intercepted a priority message over the secured teletype from Fort Fumble (the Pentagon)." He reported while he handed Lieutenant

McDonald the message. "You're not going to like it."

Lieutenant McDonald read the message:

> Be advised that Strike Force Delta might be en-route to your location.
> Arrival time is unknown. Keep me advised of your situation.

## 32

He shook his head in disbelief. "This shit just keeps getting better." He commented as he read the message again. "You're sure this came from Fort Fumble?"

"Without, a doubt," Terminator assured Lieutenant McDonald. "I would like to add that I don't believe the message was received by the intended party."

"Any idea who this thirty-two is at Fort Fumble?"

"No, I don't have any idea, but it would have to be someone who has access to the com-center. However, if I were to guess, I'd have to say that the message was intended for someone at the target fifteen klicks (Kilometers) east of here.

"So what you're saying is that this thirty-two, who is apparently at Fort Fumble, is communicating with someone at our target?"

"That's the only logical conclusion that I can come up with." Terminator pointed out. "Shall I break radio silence and inform Maverick of this new development?"

"Hell no," Lieutenant McDonald fired back. "We can't compromise our location." He continued while he walked over to the plotter board that was set up in the middle of the cargo area of the aircraft. "Show me the latest Looking-glass images (satellite images) of this area." He instructed Terminator while he picked up the satellite telephone that was laying on of the plotter board.

"This is the latest Looking-glass image of the area." Terminator pointed out while he pushed a button on the side panel of the plotter board, and a satellite image of the area appeared. "It was taken twenty-five mikes ago."

"When does our next Looking-glass pass over?" LieutenantMcDonald asked as he began to examine the image on the plotter board.

"In about thirty mikes," Terminator answered. "However, in two mikes, an NSA Looking-glass will be over this area. I can tap into it, and we'll have live sat feed for the next thirty mikes."

"Can you set it up to where only we can see the images, and no one else?"

"I can, but that's going to piss off the NSA."

"Fuck um," Lieutenant McDonald said with a smile on his face. "They'll just have to get the fuck over it, won't they?"

"One hijacked NSA looking-glass coming up," Terminator commented as he walked away from the plotter board.

Lieutenant McDonald turned his attention back to the satellite image on the plotter board. Two minutes later, the live video feed from the NSA surveillance satellite appeared on the plotter board. He touched the area ten kilometers east of Khash, Iran on the plotter board to enlarge the image of the area where the Iranian Secret Detention Center was located. *Looks good to me,* he thought. *All we can do now is wait.*

Terminator joined Lieutenant McDonald at the plotter table. "I have successfully hijacked the NSA Looking-glass. We're the only ones seeing this satellite data."

"Terminator, if I use this satellite telephone to call Maverick can anyone triangulate mine or his position?"

"It is safe to use the satellite telephone. However, I would suggest that you keep your conversation short."

Lieutenant McDonald extended the antenna on the satellite telephone. He dialed the telephone number for the satellite telephone that Lieutenant Johnson had taken with him and put the satellite telephone to his ear.

After a few rings, Lieutenant Johnson answered. "What's up?"

"Just wanted to give you the heads up that I have eyes on the target, and nothing has changed. I will let you know if anything should change. Otherwise, you have the green light to continue, and extract the package."

"Roger that," Lieutenant Johnson acknowledged.

"Maverick, watch your six," Lieutenant McDonald suggested. "This thing could go south without any warning."

"Always," Lieutenant Johnson commented and then he ended the call. He looked at Lieutenant Milestone and gave him the thumbs up, indicating that their mission was still a go.

A few minutes later, Amos Adler stopped the two-and-a-half ton truck and jumped out. He hurried to the back of the truck while Javad Yousef got out on the passenger's side and joined him at the rear of the truck. "This is as close as we dare get you to the target," Adler said while he and Javad Yousef opened the tailgate on the truck. "Your objective is a couple of kilometers down the road."

Lieutenant Johnson was the first to jump off the back of the truck, followed by Lieutenant Milestone and the rest of the Strike Force Delta assault team. "Check your gear," he barked. "We're Oscar-Mike (on the move) in two."

Lieutenant Milestone assembled the Strike Force assault team a few feet away from the truck. Lieutenant Johnson shook hands with Amos Adler. "We should be back within the hour. I'll radio you before we approach."

"We will wait for you here," Amos Adler informed Lieutenant Johnson. "May Allah walk in your footsteps and watch over you and your people."

"Maverick, we're ready to move out," Lieutenant Milestone reported.

"Roger that." Lieutenant Johnson acknowledged while he walked over to where the Strike Force Delta assault team was assembled. "Listen up," He continued in a strong voice. "Remember, you are not to use your headset unless it's absolutely necessary; no chit-chatter; any questions?" He waited for a few seconds before continuing. "Okay, then let's move out. Badger, take point. Ramrod, you bring up the rear."

Amos Adler and Javad Yousef walked to the front passenger's side of the truck while the Strike Force assault force hurried down the road and disappeared into the darkness. Yousef opened a small hidden compartment behind the passenger's side door. He removed two M16-A4 assault rifles, with shoulder straps attached, and handed one of them to Adler.

They checked their assault rifles to ensure that they were ready for action and hung the assault rifles on their shoulders. Yousef removed two ammunition belts and handed one to Adler, and they secured the ammunition belts around their waist. He removed A PRC-25 handheld radio and closed the compartment door. "Now we wait for them to return." He said while he turned on the radio.

* * * * *

Iranian Secret Detention Center
10 Kilometers east of Khash, Iran

Kate Livingston paced around the confines of her small cell, to keep her mind off her current situation. The sound of a woman screaming out in pain was beginning to take its toll on her. She knew that it was only a matter of time before her captors put her through the same painful torture.

She placed her hands over her ears to try to muffle the sound of the woman who was screaming out in pain. When that failed, she walked over to the cot that was in her cell and flopped down on it. Shortly afterwards, the woman's screams had stopped, and Livingston removed her hands from her ears. She listened closely, and all she could hear was the faint whispers from the guards outside her cellblock.

Livingston jumped to her feet when the door to the cellblock opened, and Major Alizadeh al-Shirazi entered. He was followed by two soldiers, both dressed in full combat dress and armed with the Pakistani-made Heckler & Koch G3-A3 assault rifle. The two soldiers remained at the entrance while Major al-Shirazi walked over to Livingston's cell.

"I see that you are awake," Major al-Shirazi remarked. "I hope the noise from down the hall did not keep you from getting some sleep. You are going to need all the sleep you can get."

"What do you mean by that?"

"In time, you will see firsthand what I have in store for you," Major al-Shirazi sarcastically answered. "But for now, if I was you, I would be more worried about what I might have planned for you if your uncle does not meet our demands. If he tries to be a hero, you will pay the ultimate price for his stupidity. You better hope..." Major al-Shirazi stopped talking in mid-sentence when Yasin Abdul Zamani entered the cellblock carrying a newspaper in his hand.

"Is this the woman you told me about?" Zamani asked in Farsi.

"Yes, it is," Major al-Shirazi answered in Farsi.

Zamani walked over to Livingston's cell and looked at her. "Do you know who I am?" he asked in English.

"You're the asshole that killed two of my friends when your townhouse exploded."

"I assure you, Miss, I had nothing to do with that. Your friends' demise was not of my doing."

"Yeah, right. You really expect me to believe that?

"No, I don't, but you should believe this," Zamani said as he handed the newspaper to Livingston. "I'm sure you'll find today's London Times interesting."

Kate Livingston snatched the folded newspaper out of Zamani's hand and opened it. Tears began to run down her face as she read the front-page story about the bombing in Brussels. "You set off a nuke in Brussels?"

"Yes, we did," a familiar voice said as a man entered the cellblock.

"Jacob, is that you?"

"It sure is Kate."

"Harry told me that you were dead."

"Well, as you can see I'm not dead."

Kate Livingston grabbed the top sheet off the bunk and dried her eyes. "You're part of this?" She asked while she tossed the sheet down on the bed. "You helped these idiots kill millions of innocent people? Why would you do such a thing?"

"To show the world's superpowers, how weak, they are," Jacob Calhoun answered. "It's time the world is introduced to Red Cell, an organization that is strong and getting stronger every day."

"You're a member of Red Cell?"

"That I am."

"I don't believe this. You got to..." Kate Livingston stopped talking abruptly when she heard the sounds of automatic weapons fire.

Minutes later, the two soldiers at the cellblock entrance fell to the floor. Second Lieutenant, Rick Johnson, nicked named Maverick, and his teammate Redman, both dressed in black uniforms and armed with the Heckler & Koch MP5-A3 assault rifle, entered. "Don't move," Lieutenant Johnson ordered in Farsi.

"Don't shoot," Yasin Abdul Zamani said in English as he put his hands in the air. "I am unarmed."

Lieutenant Johnson trained his MP5-A3 assault rifle at Zamani. "One wrong move and I'll blow your fuckin' head off," he instructed in English.

Major al-Shirazi, however, reached for his Colt forty-five and Redman shot a three-round burst into the major's chest, and he fell to the floor.

"Secure the prisoners," Lieutenant Johnson ordered.

"I'm CIA operative, Jacob Calhoun," Calhoun said as he put his hands in the air. "I'm a US citizen."

"He's a traitor," Kate Livingston shouted. "He's in with these assholes."

"Really," Lieutenant Johnson commented. He aimed his MP5-A3 assault rifle at Calhoun, while Redman forced Zamani to the floor, and restrained his hands behind his back.

A few seconds later, two of Lieutenant Johnson's teammates, Doughboy, and Badger, entered. "Restrain this man," he ordered while he pointed at Jacob Calhoun. "We'll figure this out later."

"This is bullshit," Calhoun protested.

Doughboy rushed over to where Calhoun was standing and restrained his hands behind his back while Redman pulled Zamani to his feet. Badger and Lieutenant Johnson walked over to Kate Livingston's cell. "What is your full name?"

"Katelyn Amanda Livingston," she replied.

"Where were you born?"

"St. Louis, Missouri."

"What pet name does your uncle have for you?"

"Pickles."

Lieutenant Johnson smiled. "Get her out of there," He said to Badger as he tried to keep from laughing.

"Have you out in a few Miss Livingston," Badger commented as he hurried to the door to Kate Livingston's cell. He took a small explosive charge from his combat vest and placed it on the locking mechanism on the cell door. "Stand back." He said as he set the timer on the charge. Badger stepped back a few feet away from the cell door while Kate Livingston did the same. A few seconds later, the explosive charge detonated, and the cell door flung open.

Kate Livingston ran out of the cell and over to where Major al-Shirazi's lifeless body laid. She stared at the major for a few seconds before she kicked him as hard as she could between the legs.

"Ma'am he's already dead," Lieutenant Johnson pointed out. "He's not going to bother you again."

"What a pity," Livingston commented. She looked down at the floor next to Major al-Shirazi's body and saw the Major's Colt forty-five laying on the floor next to him. She picked up the Colt forty-five from the floor and cocked the firing hammer back. She aimed the Colt forty-five at Major al-Shirazi body and squeezed the trigger. The bullet shot out of the Colt and hit Major al-Shirazi between the eyes. "That's for Harry."

"Crazy bitch," Jacob Calhoun commented. "He's already dead."

Kate Livingston walked over to Calhoun and snatched him from Doughboy; and slammed him against the wall. "So you think I'm a crazy bitch?" She asked as she thrust the Colt forty-five under Calhoun's chin.

"Badger, you and Doughboy, take Zamani back to the entrance," Lieutenant Johnson ordered. "We'll catch up with you in a few."

"Roger that," Badger acknowledged, and he and Doughboy escorted Zamani out of the cellblock.

"We trusted you!" Livingston shouted. "You betrayed the whole team and your country, for what?"

"I'm sure you'll find out soon enough," Calhoun commented with a smirky grin on his face.

"Who do you report to?" Kate Livingston asked Calhoun as she pressed the Colt forty-five harder against his chin.

"What are you going to do, shoot me if I don't tell you? Go ahead, you crazy bitch; pull the trigger. Either way, I'm not telling you a damn thing. I have rights to you know."

"Answer the question," Lieutenant Johnson said as he walked over to Jacob Calhoun. "Because if she doesn't shoot you, I will," he continued while he pointed his Heckler & Koch MP5-A3 assault rifle at Calhoun's foot.

"I don't know who," Calhoun answered. "I send my report to the Pentagon to someone known as thirty-two, and they send me instructions on what to do next."

"What was your mission?" Lieutenant Johnson pressed on.

"I was to use her to distract Elliot long enough to buy them some time."

"Time for what?" Livingston demanded to know. "What are they planning?"

"I don't know, and even if I did..."

"Maverick I found something you got to look at," Lieutenant Milestone said as he entered the cellblock carrying some papers in his hand. "You're not going to believe this shit." He continued while he walked over to Lieutenant Johnson. "We hit the jackpot." He concluded as he handed the papers to Lieutenant Johnson.

Lieutenant Johnson looked through the papers, and then he handed them back to Lieutenant Milestone. "Hold onto this and pass the word that I want everyone back to the rally point A-sap. We'll be right behind you in a few."

"Roger that," Lieutenant Milestone acknowledged and hurried out of the cellblock.

Lieutenant Johnson looked at Jacob Calhoun. "What do you know about Operation Wipeout?"

"I have no idea what you're talking about."

Lieutenant Johnson took aim at Jacob Calhoun's foot with his MP5-A3 assault rifle while Kate Livingston held the Colt forty-five under Calhoun's chin. He squeezed the trigger, and Calhoun screamed out in pain when the bullet tore into his foot. "I'll ask you one more time. What do you know about Operation Wipeout?"

"They're going to set off another nuke."

"What's the target?" Lieutenant Johnson inquired. "When is the bomb going off?"

"I don't know," Calhoun fired back.

"You're lying," Kate Livingston snapped.

"Go to hell bitch!" Calhoun shouted back.

"You first," Livingston said as she squeezed the trigger on the

Colt forty-five, blowing the top part of Calhoun's head off and splattering his brains on the ceiling above. Calhoun's body fell to the floor, and she dropped the Colt forty-five to the floor. "Hope you enjoy the trip."

Lieutenant Johnson and Redman looked at each other dumbfounded. Shocked at the fact that Kate Livingston had just killed Jacob Calhoun.

"Ma'am, we need to go," Lieutenant Johnson said. "We need to get out of here."

Kate Livingston followed Lieutenant Johnson and Redman out of the cellblock. She walked a few yards and stopped. "Is this where they were torturing people?"

"Ma'am, trust me, you don't want to go in there," Lieutenant Johnson answered.

"Perhaps you're right. From the awful screams I heard, I can only imagine what went on in there."

"Please, ma'am, we got to get out of here." Lieutenant Johnson insisted.

Kate Livingston followed Lieutenant Johnson and Redman to the main entrance and exited the building. They walked over to the road where Lieutenant Milestone and the rest of the Strike Force Delta assault team was waiting.

"Where is the other man who was with me?" Zamani asked in English.

"He's lying on the floor in that cellblock that you assholes locked me up in," Kate Livingston snapped, speaking in Farsi. "Do you want to join him asshole?"

Zamani was surprised to hear Livingston speak in Farsi. "I see that we have underestimated you." He said in English.

"Crazy Horse, let's move out," Lieutenant Johnson ordered. "We have a lot of walking to do."

Lieutenant Milestone began barking out orders while Badger escorted Zamani away from Kate Livingston and Lieutenant Johnson. Redman walked over to Lieutenant Johnson and handed him a remote control device. "We're hot Maverick," he said, and then he hurried back to join the others.

"What's that?" Kate Livingston curiously asked.

"It's a remote detonator," he answered. "The building is rigged with explosives."

"Oh, so you're going to blow that shithole up?"

"As soon as we get far enough away," Lieutenant Johnson replied. "Redman take point. Badger bring up the rear."

The Strike Force Delta assault force, along with Yasin Abdul Zamani and Kate Livingston walked down the road about a half-of-a-mile and stopped. Lieutenant Johnson activated the remote detonator. "Miss Livingston would you like the honors?"

Kate Livingston smiled as she took the remote detonator from Lieutenant Johnson. She pushed the red button on the remote detonator and a few seconds later, she could see the flash from the explosion. "That felt good," she commented as she handed the remote detonator back to Lieutenant Johnson.

"Let's pick up the pace people," Lieutenant Johnson ordered. "I don't want to be here when the sun comes up."

# Chapter 20

General Thomas Richwood's Office
The Pentagon
Arlington County, Virginia

General Richwood entered the outer office to his office and was greeted by his assistant, thirty-three-year-old, Major Emily Harris. She handed the general a cup of coffee, and General Richwood continued into his office, with Major Harris a few steps behind him.

"Sir, is it true that Iran was behind the Brussels bombing?" Major Harris asked while General Richwood walked over to his desk.

"I'm afraid so," General Richwood answered as he sat down behind his desk. "Have you heard anything from Colonel Wilson?"

"No, sir, I haven't. Were you expecting him to call?"

"Yes, I am. Let me know the minute Wilson calls."

"Yes, sir," Major Harris acknowledged, and then left General Richwood's Office, closing the door on her way out.

General Richwood took a sip of his coffee and sat his coffee cup down on the desk in front of him. He was startled when his office door suddenly opened, and President Elliot entered his office. "Mr. President," the general said as he jumped to his feet.

"Have a seat general," the president said as he walked over to General Richwood's desk. "I didn't mean to startle you." The president continued as he sat down in the chair, in front of General Richwood's desk. Major Harris closed the office door while General Richwood returned to his seat. " General, A few hours ago, Eric Michal was found dead in his home; he was murdered."

"My god! Any clues as to who was behind this?"

"None so far, but the FBI has taken over the investigation. Until they have concluded that this was an isolated incident, I've ordered added security for all my cabinet members. I strongly suggest that you consider adding some extra security as well."

"Mr. President..." General Richwood stopped talking when the intercom on his telephone beeped. "Excuse me, sir; this must be important."

"Go right ahead," President Elliot remarked.

General Richwood pushed the intercom button on the telephone on his desk. "This better be important," he snarled.

"I'm sorry to bother you, sir, but Colonel Wilson is on the secured line," Major Harris reported. "He says it's important."

General Richwood pushed the intercom button to cancel the intercom call. He then pushed the button on the telephone console that was flashing, and then pushed the speakerphone button. "Wilson, I have you on speaker," the general began. "The president is here with me."

"Mr. President, I've just been notified that Miss Livingston has been rescued from her captors unharmed, and she's on her way back here," Colonel Wilson reported.

"Good work Colonel," President Elliot acknowledged, excited about the news concerning Kate Livingston. "I owe you and your people a debt that I can never repay."

"Just doing our job sir," Colonel Wilson commented. "Sir, I've also been informed that the assault team captured Yasin Abdul Zamani at the same location."

"Any idea what Zamani was doing there? He was supposed to be at the Iranshahr facility." General Richwood asked.

"Unclear, sir. However, we have concluded that Miss Livingston's aduction was a decoy to get Strike Force out of their way. We also believe that the Brussels' bombing was an assassination attempt on the president."

"Colonel, are you sure about this?" President Elliot was quick to ask.

"Yes, Mr. President I am. When the assault team secured the facility and began a routine search, they found several documents that confirmed that Red Cell has been conspiring with Zamani and the Iranian government for several months. They found undisputable evidence that the Brussels' bombing was an assassination attempt on you, Mr. President. Sir, they're also planning to set off another nuke somewhere along our east coast. The nuke is due to arrive at the Port of Wilmington in Wilmington, Delaware in two days."

President Elliot was stunned by Colonel Wilson's report. He looked at General Richwood dumbfounded.

"Wilson, send me the projected course and speed on this freighter," General Richwood ordered.

"Sir, I've already sent you my report," Colonel Wilson pointed out. "You should be receiving it shortly."

"Good; let me know the minute you find out anything else about this Red Cell group." General Richwood pushed the speakerphone button on the telephone to end the call.

"What course of action do you recommend general?"

"Mr. President, I recommend that we stop this freighter from entering the country. No matter what it takes."

"You mean blow it out of the water?"

"Yes, sir, if that's what needs to be done to stop that freighter from reaching our shores."

"Very well general, let's get the ball rolling."

General Richwood removed the telephone receiver from the telephone on his desk. He pushed the red button on the telephone, and then he punched in the extension number for the Pentagon's communication center. He put the telephone receiver to his ear and waited for his call to be answered.

"Communication Center," a young woman's voice said.

"This is general Richwood; I want a secure patch to Admiral McPherson at the submarine base in Groton, Connecticut priority-one."

"Yes, sir general," the young woman said. "Please stand by while I connect you, sir."

General Richwood pushed the speakerphone button on the telephone, and then he returned the telephone receiver to the telephone.

"Richwood you old fart how's it hanging?"

"I have you on speakerphone with the president."

"Admiral, what I'm about to tell you is not to be repeated to anyone," President Elliot began. "We have a situation that requires your assistance."

"Mr. President, what can I do to help?" Admiral McPherson curiously asked.

"There's a freighter bound for the Port of Wilmington in Wilmington, Delaware that is carrying a nuclear device. This freighter must not be allowed entry to our waters. General Richwood will contact you when he receives the detailed information about this freighter. I am ordering this freighter to be stopped at all costs. Even if you have to put this freighter on the bottom of the Atlantic Ocean."

"I understand Mr. President," Admiral McPherson acknowledged. "I'll get the ball rolling while I wait for General Richwood's call."

"Talk to you soon McPherson," General Richwood said, and then he pushed the speakerphone button on the telephone to end the call.

"General I want you to give Admiral McPherson what he needs the minute you receive Colonel Wilson's report," President Elliot said as he got up from his seat. "I'll be at the White House the rest of the day. Keep me updated on this matter."

"Yes, Mr. President," General Richwood acknowledged as he jumped to his feet. He watched President Elliot walk over to the door and opened it, and stepped into the outer office before he returned to his seat.

Major Harris jumped to her feet. "Good day Mr. President."

"It is for some," President Elliot commented and continued to walk toward the exit door. The door suddenly opened, and a young woman stepped inside the office. She snapped to attention and held the door open for the president. "Carry on Miss," The president said as he stepped out of the outer office.

Major Harris returned to her seat while the young woman closed the door behind President Elliot. "I have a priority message for the general from Colonel Wilson." The young woman said, referring to the red folder she was holding in her hand.

"You can leave it with me and I'll see to it that the general gets it."

"No offense ma'am, but I was told to give this to General Richwood personally." The young woman pointed out while she walked over to where Major Harris was sitting.

"Is there a problem?" General Richwood asked who was standing in the doorway to his office.

Major Harris jumped to her feet. "No, sir."

"Sir, I have a priority message from Colonel Wilson." The young woman said as she walked over to the general. "I was told to deliver it to you personally." She concluded while she offered the red folder to General Richwood.

General Richwood took the red folder from the young woman. He opened it and began to read the message from Colonel Wilson. When he was finished reading the message, he closed the red folder. "I'll be in the War Room," he informed Major Harris. General Richwood walked over to the exit door and opened it. He stepped out of the office and closed the door.

"Is there something else you need?" Major Harris asked the young woman.

"No."

"Then why are you still here?"

The young woman walked over to the exit door and opened it. She exited the office and closed the door behind her. *What a bitch,* she thought as she walked toward the Communication Center.

Major Harris picked up the telephone receiver from the telephone on her desk. She punched in the telephone number on the keypad that she wanted to call and then she put the telephone receiver to her ear. After a few rings, a man answered. "We have a problem," she said to the man. "Wilson's people have rescued Kate Livingston."

"Are you sure about this?"

"Yes, I am, but there's more. I listened in on their telephone conversation and learned they know about the package, and that they have captured Zamani alive."

"I thought you warned them that Strike Force Delta was coming?"

"I sent a message to our man there. I guess he didn't get it in time."

"I will pass your information on. Keep me informed of any new developments. I'll see you at our meeting tomorrow night." The man concluded, and the line went dead.

Major Harris dropped the telephone receiver on the desk when the outer office door suddenly opened and General Richwood entered, followed by two MPs. "What's wrong, sir?" She asked while she jumped to her feet.

"Who were you just talking to?"

"No one, sir. I was going to call a friend to confirm our dinner plans."

"Forgive me if I don't believe you," General Richwood pointed out while he motioned to the two MPs. "Place her under arrest."

The two MPs walked over to Major Harris and took her into custody without any resistance.

"Under arrest for what?" She asked while one of the MPs placed her hands behind her back and handcuffed her.

"Treason for starters."

"You have nothing," Major Harris fired back.

"I'm afraid I do," General Richwood snapped. "You see, your last call was recorded. I heard everything you said. Once the techs get done tracing where you called, I'll have your terrorist friend in custody as well."

Major Harris smiled. "Good luck with that."

"Get her out of here before I do something stupid."

"Yes, sir," the MPs acknowledged.

General Richwood followed the MPs and Major Harris out of the office. He slammed the outer office door closed and continued walking.

＊ ＊ ＊ ＊ ＊

Tinker Air Force Base
Oklahoma City, Oklahoma
Hangar Nine

While the ground crew made preparations to pull the Strike Force Delta's Gulfstream G550 twin-engine jet aircraft from inside the hangar. Second Lieutenant, Daniel Shea, nicknamed Hammer, and his assault team, along with Deputy Director Hicks boarded the aircraft. They lowered the window shades to prevent anyone outside the aircraft from looking inside.

"Take a seat people," Lieutenant Shea ordered. "We'll be leaving the minute Wolverine gets here."

Deputy Director Hicks walked to the front of the aircraft and sat in one of the seats while Lieutenant Shea and his assault team sat in the seats at the back of the aircraft.

The pilot and co-pilot were busy going over their pre-flight checklist, preparing the aircraft for departure when Colonel Wilson entered the aircraft, and the ground crew secured the exit door.

"Any news from Popeye?" Lieutenant Shea inquired.

"Operation Dragonfly went off without a hitch," Colonel Wilson answered. "They're on their way back with Miss Livingston. They even managed to capture Yasin Abdul Zamani."

"That is good news," Lieutenant Shea commented.

"That it is," Colonel Wilson said. He walked to the front of the aircraft and entered the cockpit area. "You can leave whenever you're ready."

"Yes, sir," the pilot acknowledged. "We should be in the air shortly."

Colonel Wilson walked out of the cockpit area and sat down in the seat next to Deputy Director Hicks. "I couldn't help but overhear what you told Hammer," she said. "I take it that Kate's okay. And that your people have captured Zamani."

"That's right."

"Is he talking?"

"Not yet."

"Well, at least he's been neutralized, and there's one less terrorist in the world for us to worry about."

"That is true, and the world will be a little safer without that asshole walking around a free man." Colonel Wilson paused for a brief moment before continuing. "Karen, I sent someone after your car like I said I would. When they examined your car, they found a bomb connected to a pressure plate underneath the driver's seat. It would have gone off the minute you sat in the driver's seat."

"I guess I'm getting too close to something," Deputy Director Hicks commented, trying to hide her fear about the car bomb.

"Or, you're getting too close to someone, and they're getting scared that you're closing in on them."

"Yes, but who? I haven't a clue who's behind all of this."

"Don't worry Karen; we'll figure this out."

Deputy Director Hicks took Colonel Wilson's hand into her's and smiled. He smiled back, and then he leaned over and whispered into her ear. "Everything will work out. We're going to get these sons-of-a-bitches."

"I hope so," she whispered back.

Lieutenant Shea was shocked to see that Colonel Wilson sat down next to Deputy Director Hicks and that they were engaged in whisper talk. *Damn, the rumors are true; he* thought. *Wilson is fucking the Ice Queen.*

"You okay Hammer?" Slingshot, one of Lieutenant Shea's team members asked.

"I'm fine," Lieutenant Shea snapped.

"Sorry, I asked," Slingshot commented.

The ground crew pulled the Strike Force Gulfstream G550 twin-engine jet aircraft from inside the hangar and onto the runway. The pilot throttled up its engines, and the aircraft began to move down the runway.

Deputy Director Hicks squeezed Colonel Wilson's hand and began to tremble. "I don't like to fly," she pointed out. "I hope I don't embarrass you in front of your men."

Colonel Wilson put his arm around Deputy Director Hicks and pulled her closer to him. "Don't worry. You'll be fine."

The aircraft gained speed as it traveled down the runway and lifted off the ground. Within a few minutes, the aircraft reached its cruising altitude.

# Chapter 21

Federal Detention Center
Quantico, Virginia

Major Harris paced around her dimly lit cell trying to figure out her next move when she heard someone walking towards her cell. The light in front of her cell went out. *That's odd*; she thought and walked over to her cell door. She strained her eyes to try to see who was walking toward her cell, but all she could see was darkness.

"Hello, Emily," a woman's voice said from the darkness.

"Who's there?"

"You don't know me, but I know all about you," the woman calmly answered.

"How did you get past the guards?"

"Don't worry about the guards. They won't be a problem anymore."

"What do you want?"

"I was sent here by a mutual friend. He wants to know what you've told them."

"I haven't told them anything. They know nothing about Operation Wipeout. You can assure him that I won't tell them anything."

"I believe you," the woman said as she stepped closer to Major Harris' cell. 'However, he doesn't. To him, you're a threat."

The dim light coming from Major Harris's cell revealed the identity of the woman, and Major Harris recognized her. "I know you. Your Second Lieutenant Betty Williams. You're one of Wilson's

*229*

people.""So you do know who I am?" Lieutenant Williams remarked as she stepped closer.

"Tell..." Major Harris stopped talking when she noticed that Lieutenant Williams had a Beretta M9-A1, with its silencer attached, in her hand pointed at her.

"Sorry Emily," Lieutenant Williams said as she pulled the trigger.

Major Harris felt a sudden sting as the bullet from the Beretta slammed into her forehead. A few seconds later, she fell to the floor.

Lieutenant Williams removed the silencer from the Beretta and put it in the pocket of the jacket she was wearing. She put the Beretta in the small of her back underneath the jacket. Afterwards, she removed her cell phone from her inside jacket pocket. Lieutenant Williams dialed a number, and then put the cell phone to her ear. "It's done," she said when her call was answered. She canceled the call and returned the cell phone to the inside jacket pocket. She walked down the hallway and disappeared into the darkness.

She walked to the side exit door and exited the Detention Center undetected. The security alarm sounded while she hurried to her vehicle that was parked a few feet away. *That was quick*, she thought as she opened the driver's side door and jumped inside.

Lieutenant Williams started up her vehicle just as a two-and-a-half ton truck carrying a Marine security force, dressed in full combat dress and armed with the M16-A4 assault rifles pulled up in front of the Detention Center. She put the vehicle in drive and drove off.

* * * * *

Washington, D.C.
The White House Situation Room

President Elliot and Vice President Conrad, along with Secretary of Defense Mark Roberts and Secretary of the Navy John Forsythe were seated at the conference table. General Richwood, followed by NSA Director Jack Parkinson and CIA Director Robert Müller, entered the room. They walked over to the conference table and sat down in their perspective seats at the table.

"How long before we have satellite coverage of the Iranian coast?" President Elliot inquired.

"We should be receiving a picture any minute now," Director Parkinson assured President Elliot.

Moments later, the large plasma screen on the back wall came to life, and the live satellite image of the Iranian coast was displayed on the plasma screen.

Everyone sat in silence and watched as Northrop Grumman B-2 Spirit stealth bombers began their attack on Iranian Air Force installations, and the suspected nuclear research facility at Iranshahr. At the same time, US Naval Boeing F/A-18E Super Hornet jet aircraft from the aircraft carrier USS George Washington commenced their attack on the shore batteries and naval installations along the Iranian coast.

After several minutes of intensive bombardment of their intended targets, the aircrafts broke off their attack. The B-2 Spirit stealth bombers returned to their base, and the F/A-18E Super Hornet jet aircrafts headed back to the George Washington.

"When will we know the extent of the damage from our attack on the Iranian targets?" President Elliot asked.

"It'll take a couple of hours to get an accurate assessment of the damage," General Richwood answered.

"I want that report on my desk as soon as you get it."

"Yes, sir," General Richwood acknowledged. "I'll bring it to you as soon as it comes in."

"John, as a precautionary measure, I want the Washington to keep aircraft in the air patrolling the area," President Elliot instructed Secretary of the Navy John Forsythe. "I know that we've hit them hard, but they're still in the game."

"Yes, Mr. President," Secretary Forsythe acknowledged. "If the Iranians try to launch an attack, we'll be ready."

"We need to stay ahead of this," President Elliot was quick to point out. "The next move is up to them," President Elliot continued as he got up from his seat. "Keep me informed of any new developments."

Everyone jumped to their feet, and President Elliot walked out of the room. He walked back to the Oval Office and entered. He closed the door, and walked over to his desk, and sat down.

President Elliot was startled when the intercom beeped on his telephone. He pushed the intercom button. "Yes."

"I'm sorry to bother you, sir, but Ambassador Mitchell at the UN is on the secure line. "He says that it's urgent."

"Put him through."

"Yes, Mr. President."

President Elliot pushed the intercom button on the telephone to cancel the intercom call. He removed the telephone receiver from the telephone in front of him and pushed the button that was flashing while he put the telephone receiver to his ear. "Sam, what's up?"

"Mr. President, I was getting ready to leave for the day when the Iranian UN ambassador stopped by my office. He says he's been authorized by his government to negotiate a cease-fire. He went on to say that he was personally contacted by the other ambassadors from the neighboring countries and that they have all agreed to sit down and discuss terms for a cease-fire."

"Do you think he means what he says?"

"Yes, Mr. President, I do. I've already checked with the other ambassadors, and they confirmed that the Iranian ambassador has contacted them about a cease-fire. I think that they're waiting to see what we do next."

"Where does he propose we have this meeting?"

"Here at the UN building."

"Very well. Set up the meeting. Tell the ambassador that if Iran wants to talk, I'm willing to listen. However, make it clear to him that if his country fires one more shot at us, I will retaliate with the full force of our military."

"Yes, Mr. President, I'll pass this on to the ambassador."

"Call me the minute the details for this meeting are finalized," President Elliot concluded, and then he returned the telephone receiver to the telephone. *This doesn't make any sense;* he thought. *There has to be more to this. I...* His thoughts were interrupted when the intercom beeped. President Elliot pushed the intercom button on the telephone. "Yes, Mrs. Wyatt."

"I'm sorry to bother you Mr. President, but General Richwood wishes to see you."

"Send him in," President Elliot said, and then he pushed the intercom button to cancel the intercom call.

The door to the Oval Office opened, and General Richwood entered. "Sir, I have the report that you wanted," he said as he closed the door. He walked over to the president's desk and handed the president the folder that he had in his hand. "We've hit them hard," he commented as President Elliot took the folder from him and placed it on his desk. "Will there be anything else, sir?" General Richwood asked while he stood at attention in front of President Elliot's desk.

"Take a seat general," President Elliot said while he motioned to the chair next to his desk.

"Yes, Mr. President," General Richwood acknowledged and walked over to the chair next to President Elliot's desk and sat down.

"General, I just got off the phone with Ambassador Mitchell at the UN," President Elliot began. "He said that the Iranian ambassador approached him moments after our strike on their military installations. The Iranian ambassador claims that he has been authorized to negotiate a cease-fire."

"Let me guess; they want to have the negotiations at the UN building."

"Yes, they do. How could you possibly know that?"

"Just a lucky guess," General Richwood was quick to point out. "Still, I wouldn't trust the Iranians."

"So, you think I should be cautious?"

"I would be;" General Richwood pointed out. "Especially since we know that there's a nuke heading toward the east coast, and we both know that the Iranians aren't afraid to set off a nuke in a populated city. Mr. President, I think we have found their intended target here in the US."

"Those bastards," President Elliot said in anger. "They're planning to set off a nuke at the United Nations building in New York City."

"It looks that way, but we still have time to stop them."

"Do we know the location of this nuke?"

"I talked to Admiral McPherson a few minutes ago. He reported that he has three submarines patrolling the east coast and that the Coast Guard is stopping every ship for inspection. He also informed me that as a precautionary measure, Wilson has had a sub following the freighter carrying the nuke since it left its port in Iran."

"Are you sure the nuke is on this ship?"

"Yes, sir, I am. The freighter left port at the same time the Eisenhower was attacked."

"How can you be sure this freighter is the right one?"

"The intelligence report from an operative working in the area reported that the nuke was loaded onto the freighter that morning and that it was the only freighter that left port that day."

"Do you know where this ship is now?"

"As of twenty minutes ago the freighter was six-hundred miles west of the Canary Islands, and still on course for the Port of Wilmington."

"Does Secretary Forsythe know about any of this?"

"No, sir, he does not. I recommend that until this threat is neutralized, we keep this between us."

"You suggest that I keep this from the Secretary of the Navy?"

"Yes, sir, I do. We can't risk the chance that anyone might find out about us tracking the nuke."

"I hope you're right general. God help us if you're wrong."

"Mr. President, I know I'm right about this. Wilson has been on top of this from the start. I assure you Mr. President; there's no way that nuke is going to reach our shores."

"We got to be…" President Elliot stopped talking when the intercom beeped. He reached for the telephone on his desk and pushed the intercom button. "Yes."

"Mr. President there's an urgent call from Admiral McPherson for General Richwood."

"Put it through."

"Yes, sir."

President Elliot pushed the speakerphone button before he pushed the button on the telephone that was flashing. "Admiral McPherson this is the president. I'm here in the Oval Office with General Richwood."

"Mr. President, General Richwood, we have a situation involving the freighter that the Ohio is following."

"What kind of situation?" President Elliot asked.

"The freighter that they were following has rendezvoused with another freighter. They're sitting side-by-side and dead in the water. The skipper of the Ohio says the freighters appear to be offloading cargo."

"Tell the Ohio I said to send both freighters to the bottom, and that they are to retrieve no survivors," President Elliot ordered. "It's time to end this mess."

"Yes, Mr. President," Admiral McPherson acknowledged. "I'll call you back with confirmation when I receive it."

"I'll be waiting for your call," President Elliot commented, and then he pushed the speakerphone button on the telephone to end the call. President Elliot leaned back in his chair. "All we can do now is wait, and hope that you were right about the nuke being on that freighter."

"Mr. President, I would like to recommend that we continue to search every cargo ship bound for the east coast. It would be to our advantage to keep up the appearance that we're still looking for something."

"You mean in case the Iranians are watching us, or that you're wrong about the whereabouts of that nuke?"

"It doesn't hurt to be cautious, sir."

"Very well general, just keep me informed of any new developments."

"Yes, sir," General Richwood said as he jumped to his feet, and snapped to attention. He saluted President Elliot and then he exited the Oval Office, closing the door on his way out.

# Chapter 22

Joint Base Andrews
Camp Springs
Prince George's County, Maryland

The Gulfstream G550 twin-engine jet aircraft landed and taxied down the runway for a few minutes before coming to a complete stop in front of an empty hangar. The pilot shut down the aircraft's engines, and the hangar doors opened. The ground crew pulled the aircraft into the hangar, and the hangar doors closed.

When the aircraft came to a complete stop, Colonel Wilson got up from his seat and hurried to the back of the aircraft, with Deputy Director Hicks following. "Hammer, I want you and your people to set up a command post as quickly as possible," Colonel Wilson ordered. "Let me know the minute you have something," he continued as he and Deputy Director Hicks reached the opened exit.

"Yes, sir," Lieutenant Shea acknowledged.

Colonel Wilson gave Lieutenant Shea the thumbs up before he and Deputy Director Hicks exited the aircraft. Colonel Wilson was surprised to see Samir Hamidi and Myra. "This is a pleasant surprise," he remarked at the sight of his friends. "I figured you'd be taking it easy after what the two of you have been through."

"Who's your sidekick?" Myra was quick to ask.

"Samir, Myra, this is CIA Deputy Director Karen Hicks."

"You're working with the CIA?" Samir Hamidi curiously asked. "I thought you didn't care much for them?"

"I'm not working with the CIA. I'm protecting her. Someone is trying to assassinate her. I think it has something to do with an operation she stumbled onto called Operation Wipeout; whatever the hell that is."

"How much do you know about Operation Wipeout?" Samir Hamidi asked.

"All I know is that it concerns an operation with a terrorist organization known as Red Cell and that several high-ranking officials in my government may be involved," Colonel Wilson answered.

"Close, but there's more," Hamidi pointed out.

"I've recently found a list of their members," Deputy Director Hicks jumped in. "I think that's why they're after me."

"They must think you have more than a list," Hamidi said. "You most likely have more on them than you realized."

"Samir, I read the report that you recently filed," Colonel Wilson interrupted. "You mentioned nothing about Operation Wipeout. Your report mostly contained information about Yasin Abdul Zamani, and the work he was doing at that research facility near Iranshahr."

"I didn't report about Operation Wipeout because I suspect that someone in your organization is altering my reports," Hamidi began. "I wanted to wait until I saw you in person before I mentioned any of this to you.

"You think Red Cell has someone inside my facility?"

"Yes, I do," Hamidi fired back. "I think it's someone who has access to your decoded messages."

"That would explain how Red Cell has been one step ahead of us in tracking down Zamani," Deputy Director Hicks was quick to point out. "Not to mention the problems you had in locating Kate Livingston."

"I'm positive now that finding Kate Livingston was a diversion," Colonel Wilson remarked. "Red Cell used this to keep us distracted."

"You know who this traitor is?" Deputy Director Hicks curiously asked.

"I have an idea who it might be. I'll look into this when I get back to Strike Force Delta Command."

"Do you still have a submarine following the ship that's carrying the nuke?"

"Yes, I do."

"You never told me about that."

"I'm sorry Karen. I meant to tell you about it, but I couldn't."

"Why not?"

"I had to make sure you were playing on the same team before I could tell you anything about this. I couldn't take the chance that you were working with Red Cell."

"Do you trust me enough to tell me about it now?" Deputy Director Hicks asked sarcastically.

Colonel Wilson looked at Samir Hamidi. "It's your call," Hamidi said. "If you think she needs to know then you best tell her everything."

"Yeah, she needs to know," Colonel Wilson remarked. He waited a few seconds before he began. "Karen, a few days ago, one of Samir's people tracked a nuke to the port city of Bandar Beheshti where it was loaded onto a freighter. That same freighter left port a few minutes after the attack on the Eisenhower. It was the only freighter that left any Iranian port that day. I thought it was odd, so I had the SSBN submarine Ohio secretly follow the freighter and report any suspicious activity directly to General Richwood at the Pentagon."

"So, what you're saying is that you think the attack on the Eisenhower was a diversion, giving the Iranians enough time to get the nuke safely out of the country?"

"Yes, I do," Colonel Wilson answered.

"How can you be certain that this nuke is on that ship?"

"My man helped load the nuke on the truck," Samir Hamidi jumped in. "He rode in the truck to the port and helped load the nuke on the ship."

"You see, Karen..." Colonel Wilson stopped talking when he noticed Lieutenant Shea walking toward him.

"Wolverine, I'm sorry to interrupt you, but General Richwood is on the video-com link," Lieutenant Shea reported. "He says it's urgent."

Colonel Wilson followed Lieutenant Shea to the back of the hangar where Lieutenant Shea and his team had set up a command post. Colonel Wilson positioned himself in front of the plasma screen and waited. A few seconds later, General Richwood appeared on the screen. "General, it's nice to see you again, sir."

"Wilson, what the hell are you doing at Andrews with an assault team?"

"Sir, the team is here to protect Deputy Director Hicks. General, someone is trying to kill her."

"You think it has something to do with Red Cell?"

"Yes, sir, I do."

"Any idea who might want Deputy Director Hicks put down?"

"I have a few leads sir, but I don't think this is the reason why you wanted to talk to me?"

"I wanted you to know that you were right about that freighter. A few minutes ago, it rendezvoused with another ship in the middle of the Atlantic. The president ordered the Ohio to sink both ships. Satellite surveillance of the area confirms that both ships were sunk, but not before the nuke was set off. We haven't heard from the Ohio since. We're still trying to reestablish radio contact with her."

"At least we stopped the nuke from reaching our shores," Colonel Wilson sadly pointed out.

"As a precautionary measure, the president has ordered that all ships bound for the east coast to be stopped by the Coast Guard and searched."

"You think there's more nukes?"

"For our sake, I hope not," General Richwood answered. "All I know for sure is that when we hit that so-called research facility near Iranshahr with several B-2 Spirit stealth bombers, the nukes that they had stored there detonated. No one knows for sure how many nukes the Iranians had at that facility, but our Satellite surveillance of that area shows that everything within a hundred miles of the place was vaporized." The general paused for a moment before he continued. "Wilson, The president wants you to keep looking into this Red Cell matter. Let me know the minute you come up with something useful."

"Yes, sir..." Colonel Wilson stopped in mid-sentence when the plasma screen went blank. *I wish the fuck he'd stop doing that.* He thought as he walked over to where Lieutenant Shea was standing. "Hammer, are your men ready for some action?"

"They're ready Wolverine."

"I want everyone in full assault gear, and ready to move out within the hour."

"We'll be ready."

Colonel Wilson glanced over to where his friends and Deputy Director Hicks were standing. He noticed that Deputy Director Hicks and Myra were talking. *I can only imagine what the two of them are talking about,* he thought as he walked over to where Samir Hamidi was standing.

"Any news," Deputy Director Hicks asked as she and Myra joined them.

"Some," Colonel Wilson reluctantly answered. "None of which is good."

"What's going on?" Myra anxiously asked.

Everyone listened while Colonel Wilson explained what General Richwood had just told him. When he was done, Myra and Deputy Director Hicks had tears rolling down their faces. Samir Hamidi said nothing; his facial expression was blank. Colonel Wilson realized that Samir Hamidi was in a state of shock and dismay.

"There's still much work that needs to be done," Colonel Wilson said to break the silence. "We need to neutralize Red Cell, and put an end to this Operation Wipeout."

"You're right," Deputy Director Hicks agreed as she removed a package of tissues from her purse. She removed a couple of tissues from the package and then offered Myra some tissues. Myra removed a couple of tissues from the package, and Deputy Director Hicks returned the package to her purse. "We need to end this before any more innocent people die," Deputy Director Hicks continued while she dried her eyes.

"Samir, you and Myra can wait on the jet," Colonel Wilson suggested. "We should be back in a couple of hours."

"Roger that," he replied and took Myra by the hand, and they walked toward the Gulfstream G550 jet aircraft.

"Hammer, assemble your people over there by those vehicles," Colonel Wilson ordered, pointing to the four black SUVs parked next to the hangar entrance.

"Roger that," Lieutenant Shea acknowledged.

Colonel Wilson grabbed Deputy Director Hicks's hand and led her over to the four black SUVs. He opened the driver's side door on the first vehicle and removed a map that was on the dash.

"When did you set all this up?" Deputy Director Hicks inquired.

"After I figured out the best way to do this, I called ahead before I left Strike Force Delta Command Center."

"You could have told me."

"With everything that has been going on it slipped my mind. I'm sorry; I forgot."

"Oh my," Deputy Director Hicks gasped. "I never thought I'd ever hear you apologize for anything."

"There's a lot of things you don't know about me," Colonel Wilson snapped.

"I see that now," Deputy Director Hicks fired back.

Colonel Wilson walked to the front of the vehicle when he saw Lieutenant Shea and his team approaching. He opened the map and spread it out on the hood.

He turned to face Lieutenant Shea and his strike team. "Before I go over the operational plan I'd like to point out that this operation has not been sanctioned by anyone. In other words, no one knows that we're doing this. With that said, I want all of you to know that if you don't want to continue with this operation, I will understand. You can get on board the jet, and I won't hold it against you."

Lieutenant Shea looked at his assault team. "We're in Wolverine. What's the plan?"

"Our target is an abandoned warehouse in Baltimore on Nicholson Street by the docks," Colonel Wilson began. "We know that Red Cell is meeting there in a few hours. Deputy Director Hicks and I will take the lead on this one. We will take up a position that will enable us to photograph everyone that enters that building without being seen. The rest of you will be at your assigned locations, and ready to move at a minutes' notice. You will find a map in the vehicle you're assigned to. Stay off your headsets. I don't want to hear any chatter over the radio. One last thing, if you hear me say thunder, everyone is to move in; any questions?"

"What are the rules of engagement?" Lieutenant Shea inquired.

"You are to return fire if fired upon. However, if I call you in, you have the green light for weapons hot, anything else?" Colonel Wilson folded the map and handed it to Deputy Director Hicks. "Hammer, deploy your team."

"Hotdog, you're with me in vehicle two," Lieutenant Shea ordered. "Slingshot, Cobra, you're in vehicle three. Flash, Spirit, you're in vehicle four; questions?" after a few second pause Lieutenant Shea continued. "All right people, let's get moving."

Colonel Wilson got in the first SUV on the driver's side while Deputy Director Hicks hopped in on the passenger's side. He fired up the SUV while Lieutenant Shea and his assault team hurried to their assigned SUV and waited. The hangar doors opened, and they followed Colonel Wilson out of the hangar in a single line.

* * * * *

Baltimore, Maryland
Nicholson Street by the docks

Colonel Wilson parked the black SUV behind the building across the street from the warehouse where they knew the Red Cell members were to gather for a secret meeting. He and Deputy Director Hicks got out of the SUV and hurried inside. They walked up the stairs to the second floor and found a spot where they could see the front of the building across the street. Colonel Wilson was surprised to see that there were two heavily armed guards at the front entrance, and several others patrolling the perimeter of the building. "These assholes mean business," he pointed out.

As the sun began to slip below the horizon, several vehicles began to arrive and unload their passengers. Colonel Wilson carefully peeped out the window to take a look. He couldn't believe his eyes; he recognized some of the occupants that had gotten out of the vehicles. He looked at Deputy Director Hicks. "This is bigger than we thought."

"It would appear so," she commented. "How do you want to handle this?"

"For now, we watch and see who else shows up for this meeting," Colonel Wilson answered. "Once we find out who's involved, we'll know who we can trust, and what type of action we need to take."

They continued to watch, as more vehicles began to arrive. Deputy Director Hicks paid close attention to who was attending the meeting.

An hour had passed before darkness began to set in. Colonel Wilson and Deputy Director Hicks put on their night-vision glasses, so they could see everything that was going on at the front of the building.

"I can't believe the people who have shown up for this meeting so far," Deputy Director Hicks commented. "Bringing them down isn't going to be an easy task."

Colonel Wilson looked at Deputy Director Hicks "Yeah, I think your Intel was wrong about this meeting," he was quick to point out. "This meeting appears to be for high-ranking members; not low-ranking members. However, this might work to our advantage. We can use the information we obtain here tonight to take down their leadership, and hopefully put Red Cell out of business for good."

"Oh my god, look who just showed up."

Colonel Wilson looked back toward the front of the building. "Holy shit. Isn't that..."

"Yep, It's my boss and NSA Director, Jack Parkinson," Deputy Director Hicks interrupted. "Those bastards have been in on this from the start."

"Jesus, how far does this conspiracy go?" Colonel Wilson remarked in disbelief.

"I don't know, but there's two more cars pulling up in the front of the building," Deputy Director Hicks commented.

Colonel Wilson and Deputy Director Hicks watched closely as the occupants exited their vehicles. They were shocked to see Secretary of State George Maxwell, and Vice President James Conrad exit the vehicles and enter the building.

"It's all starting to make sense now," Colonel Wilson commented. "I think they're trying to bring down the president. Those assholes have been planning this for some time. How in the hell could I have been so stupid?"

"They've fooled a lot of people."

"Yeah, but I'm better than that. I should have figured this out sooner."

"John, don't beat yourself up about this. I know you're good at what you do, and so do they. Don't you see? They used Kate Livingston to keep you busy elsewhere?"

"Yeah, I suppose you're right, but..." Colonel Wilson stopped talking when he heard the muffled sounds of gunfire. Seconds later, the men that were standing at the front door dropped to the ground. He turned to face Deputy Director Hicks. "We have company," he said as he put on his radio headset. He touched the button on the earpiece to activate his headset. "Listen up people. We have someone crashing our party. Type of weapons is unknown at this time. They're using silencers. I want everyone to hold their positions, and be ready to move on my command." He turned his attention back to the building across the street while Lieutenant Shea and his team acknowledged receiving his transmission.

Suddenly, four men, dressed in black uniforms with combat vests and armed with a modified Russian-made AK-103 assault rifle to accommodate a silencer, emerged from their position on the street and entered the building. Afterwards, six more men came around the side and stood at the building entrance.

"Something is going down," Deputy Director Hicks said as she watched what was happening across the street. "Got any ideas?"

"We wait."

"You mean we do nothing?"

"I'm not going to risk my people to save those traitorous bastards. That's a ten-man hit squad out there, and they're not here to negotiate. They must have pissed in someone's Wheaties or stepped on the wrong toes. They'd be doing us a favor if they killed all those assholes."

"I see your point," Deputy Director Hicks acknowledged.

"I just..." Colonel Wilson stopped in mid-sentence when he saw the four men that were inside the building join the others at the building's entrance. "Something doesn't feel right," he continued.

"I wonder where they're off to in a big hurry," Deputy Director Hicks said when the men at the building's entrance started to run down the street.

Without warning, the ground started to rumble. "Take cover," Colonel Wilson said as he grabbed Deputy Director Hicks, and they crouched down under the window sill for cover. Seconds later, the building across the street exploded. The concussion from the blast blew out the windows on the building facing the street, covering the room with glass shards and debris.

"Are you all right?" Colonel Wilson asked.

"Yeah, I think so," Deputy Director Hicks answered. "What the hell was that?"

"I think it was a gas explosion," Colonel Wilson replied. He looked up and saw a man standing in the doorway, dressed in a black uniform, and armed with a modified Russian-made AK-103 assault rifle.

"I mean you no harm," the man said with a strong Middle Eastern accent.

"You're Iranian," Colonel Wilson remarked as he got to his feet, and then he helped Deputy Director Hicks get up off the floor.

"Yes, I am," the man acknowledged. "I was sent here to neutralize Red Cell. My job here is done."

"That's funny; I was led to believe that Red Cell was working with your government," Colonel Wilson fired back.

The man removed a bag from his shoulder and tossed it on the floor in front of Colonel Wilson. "Everything you need to know is in that bag. My government has been played in the same manner as yours. I ask that you allow my people and I to leave in peace. I have no quarrel with you. There is no need for anyone else to die this night."

Deputy Director Hicks turned to Colonel Wilson. "You're not buying any of this shit, are you?"

"It makes sense to me," Colonel Wilson answered while he touched the button on the earpiece to activate his headset. "Listen up people. Stand down and return to Andrews." Colonel Wilson turned his attention back to the man in the doorway while Lieutenant Shea and his team acknowledged receiving his orders. "Your people may withdraw from the area. My people will not try to stop you."

"Tell your president that my government wishes to talk peace with him. We will meet with him anywhere he chooses."

"I'll pass it on. Now get out of here before I change my mind."

"I hope you know what you're doing."

Colonel Wilson smiled. He reached down and picked up the bag that was on the floor in front of him. When he looked up, the man in the doorway was gone. "Let's get out of here," he suggested.

Colonel Wilson and Deputy Director Hicks hurried out of the room and down the stairway to the first floor. They exited the building through the back door where the SUV was parked. He jumped in on the driver's side and tossed the cloth bag into the backseat while Deputy Director Hicks got in on the passenger's side.

They removed their night-vision glasses and threw them into the backseat. Colonel Wilson started up the vehicle while he tossed his radio headset in the backseat, and then they drove off.

When they reached the main street, Colonel Wilson headed in the direction for the interstate. He glanced into the rearview mirror and could see the flashing lights of the first responders heading toward the burning building.

When they reached the interstate, he picked up the satellite telephone that was lying on the seat and dialed the number for Lieutenant Shea. "Hammer, where are you?" he asked when Lieutenant Shea answered.

"I just cleared the main gate, and I'm heading to the hangar. The rest of my team is right behind me."

"When you get there, I want you to check our equipment and the jet for bugs. You are to tell no one about what went on in Baltimore."

"Roger that," Lieutenant Shea acknowledged.

Colonel Wilson ended the call and placed the satellite telephone in the inside pocket of the combat vest he was wearing. Twenty minutes later, they arrived at the hangar where the Strike Force jet was parked. Colonel Wilson drove the SUV into the hangar and parked next to the other SUVs. He opened the back door and removed the cloth bag and the night-vision glasses. He grabbed his radio headset from the back seat and closed the door. Colonel Wilson and Deputy Director Hicks walked over to where Lieutenant Shea was standing. "Sit-rep."

"Our gear is loaded on the jet and ready to go," Lieutenant Shea reported. "I did a sweep of the jet, and our equipment like you asked and found nothing."

"Where's Samir and Myra?" Colonel Wilson asked.

"They were gone when we arrived. I asked the hangar maintenance chief if he knew where they went off too, and he said that a woman picked them up a few minutes after we left."

"That's odd," Colonel Wilson commented. "Any idea who this woman was?"

"Not a clue."

"We're ready to pull you out," the hangar maintenance chief said as he walked over to where Colonel Wilson was standing. "The tower has cleared you for takeoff."

"Chief, did you know the woman that my friends went with?"

"All I know is that she was dressed in an Army uniform and that she was an officer. I believe she was a second Lieutenant. I never got a good look at her, so I can't say for sure what she looked like. Is there a problem?"

"No problem," Colonel Wilson answered. "They were probably taken to the Pentagon for debriefing."

"Is there anything else?"

"No, we'll be ready in a few minutes."

The hangar maintenance chief walked away barking orders to the ground crew. Colonel Wilson handed Lieutenant Shea the night-vision glasses and his radio headset. "Stow these for me. We'll be along in a minute."

"No problem," Lieutenant Shea said, and then he hurried over to the boarding ramp. He went up the ramp and entered the aircraft.

"John, I'm staying here."

"Are you sure that's a good idea?"

"I'm going to be needed at Langley. There's a lot of work that needs to be done. Don't worry, I'll be safe there."

"I'll call you when I get back to Tinker," was all Colonel Wilson could manage to say. He kissed Deputy Director Hicks on the lips and walked away.

Deputy Director Hicks watched Colonel Wilson walk up the boarding ramp and enter. The ground crew closed the entry door and removed the ramp. She watched the ground crew hook up to the Gulfstream G550 twin-engine jet aircraft and pushed it out of the hanger.

The pilot began to warm up the jet engines while the ground crew unhooked from the aircraft. A few minutes later, the Gulfstream G550 twin-engine jet aircraft began to move and taxied to the runway. Not long afterward, the aircraft began to pick up speed and leave the ground.

Deputy Director Hicks stood at the hangar entrance and watched the aircraft disappear into the darkness.

"Miss, do you need a ride?" The hangar maintenance chief asked, who was standing behind her.

"Yes, I could use a ride back to Langley."

"Airman Miller, take one of the SUVs and take the Deputy Director to Langley."

"You got it chief."

Deputy Director Hicks followed the airman over to the SUV that she, and Colonel Wilson had used earlier. She got in on the passenger's side while the airman got in on the driver's side and closed the door. He started up the SUV, and they drove off.

# Chapter 23

The White House
Washington, D.C.

President Elliot sat in the sitting room in the Presidential Residence watching his favorite television show on the TV with the First Lady and enjoying a fresh bowl of popcorn. When their program ended, he picked up the remote for the television. He started to turn off the television when a news bulletin flashed on the screen about the incident in Baltimore. He laid the remote down on the coffee table in front of him, and they watched the live footage from the warehouse on Nicholson Street by the docks.

"My God," The First Lady, commented as she watched firefighters pull bodies from the charred remains of the building. "Those poor souls," she continued.

President Elliot remained silent and watched as they showed the bodies being loaded into an ambulance. He jumped to his feet when he noticed the ring on the finger of one of the bodies.

"What's wrong?" Amanda Elliot asked. "You look as though you saw a ghost."

"It's worse than that," President Elliot commented while he hurried over to the telephone on the wall in the kitchen. He removed the telephone receiver and dialed the number for the White House Chief of Staff, Howard Gordon.

"Yes Mr. President," Gordon said when he answered.

"I want you to call the directors of the FBI and ATF and tell them I want them in my office within the hour."

"Yes, Mr. President," Gordon acknowledged. "I'll get right on it, sir."

"Martin what's going on?" Amanda Elliot asked when President Elliot returned the telephone receiver to its resting place.

"One of those bodies they loaded into an ambulance was wearing a ring like this," he answered as he pointed to the ring on his finger. I only gave one person a ring like mine. I think one of those bodies is James Conrad."

"Are you sure about this?"

"That's what I'm going to find out," President Elliot answered as he walked toward the door. "I don't know when I'll be back, so don't wait up for me," he continued as he opened the door. President Elliot exited the Presidential Residence, and the Secret Service man standing outside closed the door.

President Elliot walked to the Oval Office and found Howard Gordon sitting at Mrs. Wyatt's desk. "Where's Mrs. Wyatt?"

"Don't know Mr. President. I've tried calling her several times, but I got no answer."

"Get me the Mayor of Baltimore on the phone."

"Yes, sir, Mr. President."

President Elliot opened the door and entered. He walked over to his desk and sat down in the chair behind his desk. The intercom on his desk beeped. He pushed the intercom button on the telephone. "Yes."

"Mr. President, the mayor of Baltimore, is on line three."

President Elliot pushed the intercom button on the telephone to cancel the intercom call. He removed the telephone receiver from the telephone and pushed the button that was flashing while he put the telephone receiver to his ear. "Mr. Mayor, I must apologize for calling so late in the evening."

"It's no bother Mr. President. What can I do for you?

"I'm calling about the warehouse incident down by the docks."

"Yes, sir, I've heard about it, but I don't understand why you would be calling me about this."

"I have reason to believe that some of my people may have been involved."

"I don't understand Mr. President."

"I believe that some of the bodies recovered are high-ranking cabinet members, including the Vice President."

"Oh."

"I know that your people are capable of handling this, but I'm asking you to allow the FBI and ATF to take over the investigation. We need to contain this until we find out what caused this, and if indeed this was an accident."

"Yes, Mr. President; I'll make the necessary calls at once."

"Thank you, Mr. Mayor. Enjoy the rest of your evening."

"Yes, sir, I will."

President Elliot returned the telephone receiver to the telephone on his desk. He was startled when there was a knock on the door. The door opened, and FBI Director, John Anderson, and ATF Director; Thomas McGrath, entered the Oval Office. Howard Gordon closed the door while they walked over to the president's desk.

"Mr. President, Howard said you needed to see us," Director McGrath remarked.

"There has been an incident near the docks in Baltimore. I need both of you to get your people in there to take over the investigation. I need to know if this was an accident or an act of terrorism."

"Mr. President, the locals aren't going to like having us muscle in on their turf," Director Anderson pointed out.

"I've already talked to the mayor. You should have no problems with the locals," President Elliot fired back. "The situation needs to be handled very carefully. I have reason to believe that some of the dead could be government officials."

"Any idea who the government officials might be?" Director McGrath inquired.

"I believe Vice President Conrad died in that building tonight."

"Oh," was all Director McGrath could say.

"That's why I want you to keep a lid on this until you have completed your investigation," President Elliot explained. "I don't want the press blowing this out of proportion or using the T word until we're sure what really happened."

"Yes Mr. President," they both acknowledged.

Director Anderson and Director McGrath walked toward the door. President Elliot got up from his seat behind his desk while

Director Anderson opened the door, and he and Director McGrath exited the Oval Office.

President Elliot walked over to the opened door and stood in the doorway. "Have you had any luck finding Mrs. Wyatt?"

"No, sir, she's not picking up," Gordon answered as he jumped to his feet. "All I get is her voicemail."

"Go home Howard," President Elliot said as he stepped into the reception area. "There's nothing more that needs to be done here tonight."

"Yes, Mr. President. I'll be in first thing tomorrow morning."

President Elliot watched Howard Gordon walk down the hallway. After a few minutes, he stepped back into the Oval Office and closed the door.

* * * * *

CIA Headquarters
Langley, Virginia

CIA Deputy Director Karen Hicks cleared the main security checkpoint, and the SUV stopped in front of the entrance to the main building. She got out of the SUV and closed the door. She watched the SUV do a U-turn and head back to the main security checkpoint before she walked to the main entrance. She entered the building and walked up to the security desk.

"You may proceed Deputy Director," the woman behind the desk said.

"I can't find my ID," Deputy Director Hicks said while she looked through her purse. "I just had the damn thing a few minutes ago."

"Ma'am, if I may, it's hanging around your neck."

Deputy Director Hicks smiled. "It's been one of those days."

"I know what you mean," the woman behind the desk commented.

Deputy Director Hicks walked to the elevator and pushed the call button for the elevator. When the elevator arrived, the door opened, and she stepped inside. She pushed the button for the floor where her office was located. The elevator door closed and began to move upward.

The elevator stopped on the floor where Deputy Director Hicks' office was located. The door opened, and she exited the elevator. She walked down the hallway and entered the outer office. She looked at the empty desk where Carla Garcia once sat. She waited a few minutes before entering her office. She walked over to her desk and laid her purse on the corner of the desk. She removed her cell phone from her purse and walked to the chair that was behind her desk, and sat down in the chair. She dialed the number for Colonel Wilson and put the cell phone to her ear.

"Wilson."

"Hey, there soldier boy," Deputy Director Hicks said in a sexy voice. "Just thought I'd let you know that I made it back to Langley."

"I figured that you would go home and get some rest," Colonel Wilson commented. "I didn't realize you were going back to your office."

"I think better when I'm working. Besides, I have two stacks of files on my desk three feet high. I'll be here most of the night."

"Well, I better let you go so that you can get started on those stacks of files. We'll be landing soon. I'll give you a call in the morning."

"John, I love you."

"I do you," Colonel Wilson said, and then he ended the call.

*What the hell did I say that for?* Deputy Director Hicks thought. *Now he's going to want to take it to the next level.*

She laid her cell phone down on her desk and began going through the stack of files on her desk when she heard a strange noise coming from the outer office. Reacting to her instincts that something wasn't right, she opened the middle drawer of her desk and removed her Beretta M9-A1 nine-millimeter. She closed the drawer and prepared the Beretta for action, and concealed it in front of her under the desk. The door to her office opened, and Second Lieutenant Betty Williams entered.

"Aren't you…" Deputy Director Hicks stopped talking when she noticed that Lieutenant Williams had a Beretta M9-A1, with its silencer attached, in her hand, and it was pointed at her. Without hesitation,

Deputy Director Hicks raised her Beretta and fired two shots at Lieutenant Williams, striking her in the chest both times.

Lieutenant Williams pulled the trigger on her Beretta and fired three times before she dropped to the floor. Deputy Director Hicks could feel the bullets from Lieutenant Williams Beretta pass by her head, and slam into the wall behind her.

A security officer that was making his scheduled rounds heard the shots. He quickly drew his Glock 19 side arm and keyed his radio. "This is Lewis. I have weapons fire on the third floor near Deputy Director Hicks' office. I'm going in to investigate."

"Backup is on its way," the security officer at the command center said. "Keep me advised of the situation."

"Roger that," Lewis acknowledged.

The security alarm sounded as Lewis neared the entrance to the reception area to Deputy Director Hicks' office. He readied his weapon for action, and then he cautiously entered Deputy Director Hicks' office. *What the fuck,* he thought when he saw Lieutenant Williams lying on the floor, and Deputy Director Hicks sitting in her chair behind her desk, with her Beretta M9-A1 nine-millimeter in her hand.

"Ma'am, are you okay?" Lewis asked while he checked Lieutenant Williams for a pulse and found none.

"I'm alright," Deputy Director Hicks answered. "The bitch tried to kill me."

Lewis keyed his radio. "Central, I have a body in Deputy Director Hicks' office," he reported.

"Is it Deputy Director Hicks?" The man on the other end asked.

"No, it's not," Lewis fired back. "Deputy Director Hicks is unharmed. Central, where's that backup."

"Hang on Lewis. Backup is on the way. They should be there shortly."

\* \* \* \* \*

Tinker Air Force Base
Oklahoma City, Oklahoma

The Strike Force Gulfstream G550 twin-engine jet aircraft landed and taxied on the runway for a few minutes before coming to a complete stop. Colonel Wilson got up from his seat when the pilot shut down the aircraft's engines. He hurried to the back of the aircraft when the exit door opened and exited the aircraft. He was surprised to see Captain Hale standing next to a Humvee parked a few yards away. He could tell by the expression on Captain Hale's face that something was wrong. *Now, what?* He thought.

Lieutenant Shea and his Strike Force team unloaded their gear from the aircraft onto a deuce and a half that was waiting for them while Colonel Wilson walked over to where Captain Hale was standing. "What's up Bulldog?"

"I talked to Popeye a few minutes ago, and he said they'll be leaving Gitmo as soon as he gets Zamani signed in. They should be arriving here in a couple of hours with Miss Livingston. I also got a call from the Marshal, who is handling Samir Hamidi and Myra. He said to tell you that he has securely placed them in an undisclosed location."

"That's great news, but I get the feeling there's more."

"There is. A few hours ago, Deputy Director Hicks shot and killed Raven in her office. Captain Hale waited a few seconds for the news to sink in before he continued. "It appears that Raven was there to kill Deputy Director Hicks."

"Is Deputy Director Hicks alright?" Colonel Wilson dared to ask, fearing the worst.

"She's a little shaken, but other that she's fine," Captain Hale replied. "She was taken to the hospital to be checked out. I talked to the security officer that was first on the scene, and he said that Deputy Director Hicks said she would call you when she got out of the hospital."

"So, Raven was part of Red Cell?"

"It would appear so," Captain Hale answered. "She was their eyes and ears here at Strike Force. They knew every move that we were going to made before we made it."

"That bitch," Colonel Wilson snapped. "We need to find out what she has done to our integrity before this situation gets out of control."

"I'm already on it," Captain Hale assured Colonel Wilson. "I have someone checking to see how bad we've been compromised."

"That was fast," Colonel Wilson commented.

"Actually, I started to have things checked out after the Kate Livingston Op. I wasn't going to say anything to you until I was sure that we had a security problem."

"Smart thinking; who did you get for this job?"

"Navy Lieutenant Commander Emily Jackson. She's been working here on the base at the Joint Services Intelligence Center for quite some time, and she knows her shit when it comes to code breaking and encryption."

"I want her in my office A-sap," Colonel Wilson said as he opened the passenger's side door of the Humvee and then climbed inside. He closed the door while Captain Hale hurried around the driver's side. Captain Hale opened the door and jumped in, and closed the door. He started up the Humvee and drove off, with the deuce and a half following.

# Chapter 24

Strike Force Delta Command
Tinker Air Force Base
Oklahoma City, Oklahoma

Colonel Wilson arrived at his office early. He had with him the pouch that the Iranian operative had given him the night before in Baltimore. The aroma of freshly brewed coffee filled the air. He looked at his watch. *Damn, Giggles is here early;* He thought when he noticed that it was only 0530. He walked over to the coffee pot and poured himself a cup of coffee. He walked over to his desk and put the pouch down on his desk next to the keyboard. He sat down in the chair behind his desk and sat his cup of coffee down on the desk in front of him. He turned on his computer monitor and waited a few minutes before he logged in.

He picked up the cup of coffee and took a sip while he waited for the computer system to boot. *Damn, this is good.* He thought as he returned the coffee cup to his desk. He opened the pouch and removed its contents. Colonel Wilson began to read everything contained in the pouch carefully. He didn't want to overlook anything. When he was done, he put everything back into the pouch and laid the pouch on the corner of his desk. He opened his e-mail program and drank his cup of coffee while he began to read his messages.

"Wolverine, do you have a minute?" Captain Hale asked who was standing in the doorway.

"Sure, what's up?"

Captain Hale entered Colonel Wilson's office with thirty-five-year-

257

old, Lieutenant Commander, Emily Jackson, following close behind him. "This is the code and encryption specialist I told you about," he began. "She has discovered something that you should be aware of."

"By all means Miss Jackson, take a seat," Colonel Wilson said as he sat his cup of coffee down on his desk. "You have my undivided attention."

"I'll wait outside," Captain Hale said, and then he exited Colonel Wilson's office and closed the door. Lieutenant Commander Jackson walked over to the chair that was in front of Colonel Wilson's desk and sat down in the chair.

"Colonel, I found that..."

"Stop right there," Colonel Wilson interrupted. "We don't go by rank around here. We use first names, last names or nicknames. Don't ever address me as Colonel again. I prefer that you address me as Wolverine. Now, what do you have to report."

"I found that your codes and encryption-keys need to be replaced."

"Is it that bad?"

"I'm afraid so."

"How long would it take to do this?"

"Two or three months, maybe longer."

"Then you better get started," Colonel Wilson remarked as he got up from his seat. "I want this done as quickly as possible."

"I'm sorry, but you'll have to find someone else to fix this problem," Lieutenant Commander Jackson pointed out as she jumped to her feet. "I have other obligations at the Joint Services Intelligence Center. I'm needed there."

"I need you here," Colonel Wilson shot back. "I can make the necessary calls to get you reassigned; that is if you're interested."

"Of course, I'm interested," Lieutenant Commander Jackson said with excitement."

"Good, then it's settled. Bulldog, will explain our policies and procedures to you; welcome aboard."

Colonel Wilson returned to his seat while Lieutenant Commander Jackson walked over to the office door and opened it, and exited Colonel Wilson's office.

"Good morning, Wolverine," Second Lieutenant, Samantha

Cooltrain, nicknamed, Giggles said when she entered Colonel Wilson's office. "I see you found the coffee, I made for you."

"Yeah, I did. I must say it tastes pretty good."

"Is it true what they're saying about Raven?" she asked while she walked over to the coffee pot.

"What are they saying about Raven?"

"That she was a rat and a murderer," she answered while she poured herself a cup of coffee.

"I hate to say it, but it looks that way."

"Would you like another cup?" she offered while she had the coffee pot in her hand.

"Yeah, why not," Colonel Wilson answered as he picked up his coffee cup from his desk.

Lieutenant Cooltrain walked over to Colonel Wilson's desk and filled his cup, and then returned the coffee pot to the coffee maker. "So that woman who just left here is Raven's replacement?"

"Yes, she is. She's going to first fix what Raven fucked up, and then she's going to take over Raven's job."

"It's still hard to believe that Raven was a rat and a murderer," Lieutenant Cooltrain commented. "She sure had me fooled."

"Don't beat yourself up about this," Colonel Wilson pointed out. "Raven had us all fooled."

"That she did," Lieutenant Cooltrain commented. "Wolverine, is there anything you need right now?"

"Not that I can think of. I'll call you if I..." Colonel Wilson stopped in mid-sentence when the telephone on his desk began to ring. He picked up the telephone receiver and put it to his ear. "Wilson."

"This is the tower," a woman's voice said. "I've been instructed to tell you that your presence is needed at hangar nine."

"Has the flight from Gitmo arrived yet?" Colonel Wilson demanded to know.

"Yes, it has. They're waiting for you at hangar nine."

"On my way," Colonel Wilson said, and then he returned the telephone receiver to its resting place.

"Is something wrong?" Lieutenant Cooltrain asked.

"Nothing's wrong," Colonel Wilson assured her as he jumped to his feet. "Tell Bulldog I'll be at hangar nine if he should need me," he continued to say while he picked up the pouch from the corner of his desk that he had gotten from the Iranian operative the night before in Baltimore. He hung the pouch on his shoulder and walked to the office door. He exited the office and closed the door on his way out.

Colonel Wilson exited the Strike Force Delta Command building and walked to the Humvee that was nearby. He removed the pouch from his shoulder and placed it on the passenger's seat. Afterwards, he fired up the Humvee and drove to the main gates of the Strike Force Delta facility. He cleared the security checkpoint and continued to hangar nine. He parked the Humvee inside the hangar and grabbed the pouch from the passenger's seat. He got out of the Humvee and put the pouch over his shoulder, and closed the door.

First Lieutenant Mathew McDonald, nicknamed Popeye, ran over to greet Colonel Wilson. "Wolverine, do you have any idea what's going on?"

"No, I don't," Colonel Wilson answered. "I must say that you and your assault team did an excellent job on this one. I'm glad to see that everyone has made it back."

"None of us would have if you hadn't changed the LZ at the last minute. How did you know?"

"I had a gut feeling that it was necessary, and as you can see it paid off."

"Yes, it did."

"Is it true what they're saying about Raven?"

"It looks that way," Colonel Wilson sadly answered. "She betrayed all of us."

"That bitch," Lieutenant McDonald said in anger. "I hope she rots in hell."

"Well, any way you look at it; we're rid of her," Colonel Wilson pointed out. "She won't be hurting anyone else."

"Have you heard from Little Joe since the bombing at Iranshahr?"

"No, I haven't. I fear that he and his people were too close to Iranshahr when the nukes went off."

"There's one thing that doesn't make sense. How in the hell did those nukes detonate when we bombed that facility?"

"We're still trying to figure that out. My best guess is that they were deliberately detonated."

"Well, that's stupid."

"Is that Kate Livingston?" He asked when he saw a red-haired woman walking towards them.

"Yes, it is," Lieutenant McDonald answered. "She insisted on coming back with us to meet you."

"Miss Livingston, it's nice to finally meet you," Colonel Wilson said when Kate Livingston joined him and Lieutenant McDonald. "Welcome home."

"Thank you, it's good to be back."

"I hope…" Colonel Wilson stopped talking when the hanger maintenance chief walked over to where he was standing. "Mr. Wilson, I've just been informed by the tower that Air Force One is landing. I've been instructed to be prepared to receive the president."

"Thanks, chief," Colonel Wilson acknowledged and followed the hanger maintenance chief outside. He watched as Air Force One touched down on the runway, and then he walked back inside the hangar. "Popeye, get everyone ready to greet the president. He'll be here in a few minutes."

"Okay people, I want a row on each side of the hangar entrance," Lieutenant McDonald ordered. "Let's look like the professionals we are."

Still wearing their combat gear, everyone lined up as Lieutenant McDonald had ordered, and waited. Colonel Wilson walked over to the passenger's side of the Humvee. He opened the door and removed the pouch from the passenger's seat, and hung it on his shoulder. He walked outside the hanger and stood at the hangar entrance; and watched as the ground crew prepared for President Elliot's arrival.

Kate Livingston joined Colonel Wilson at the hangar entrance. "You'll be going home soon," Colonel Wilson pointed out.

"Yeah, but their's some people that won't be going home; I can't help but wonder if it was worth the price that so many had to pay."

Colonel Wilson turned to face Kate Livingston. "I've been asking myself that same question for a lot of years, and I still haven't found an answer. It's just something you have to live with."

An Air Force staff vehicle pulled up, and the Base Commanding General got out of the backseat. He walked over to where Colonel Wilson and Kate Livingston were standing. "Wilson, why are you and your people here, and what's she doing here."

"First off, general, she is the reason why the president is coming here and second, the president requested that my people and I be here. Now, if you have a problem with that, I suggest you take it up with the president."

"Smart ass," The Base Commanding General commented, and then he walked away, shaking his head. He walked over to his car and stood in front of it.

When Air Force One reached the hangar area, the ground crew secured the aircraft while the pilot shut down the jet engines. The staircase ramp was then put into place, and properly secured.

The Base Commanding General hurried over to the staircase ramp and stood at the bottom just as the door to Air Force One opened. President Elliot was the first to exit, with the First Lady following. Together, they walked down the staircase ramp.

When President Elliot reached the bottom of the ramp, The Base Commanding General snapped to attention and saluted the president. President Elliot returned the general's salute. They exchanged a few words, and the president and First Lady continued walking to where Colonel Wilson and Kate Livingston were standing. The Base Commanding General walked back to his vehicle and got into the backseat, and it drove off.

"Wilson, it's good to see you again," President Elliot said when he and the First Lady arrived at the hangar entrance.

"It's nice to see you again too, sir."

"Mr. Wilson, I want to thank you for getting Kate back for us," the First Lady said.

"Ma'am, the people inside did all the work. They deserve credit for this more than I."

"Martin, Kate and I will be waiting on board," the First Lady pointed out, and then she and Kate Livingston headed back to Air Force One.

President Elliot and Colonel Wilson stepped into the hangar, and everyone stood at attention. The president shook hands with each member of the assault team and then stood at the hangar entrance facing the Strike Force Delta assault team. "First, as a man I would like to say thank you. Second, as your president, I would like to say that I'm proud of each and every one of you. I wish that I had more people like you that I could depend on to do whatever it takes to complete your assignment. You are a credit to your country and to the US military. Keep up the good work, and God bless all of you, and everyone else like you."

Without saying another word, President Elliot walked out of the hangar, and Colonel Wilson hurried after him. "Mr. President, I have something you should see," Colonel Wilson said, referring to the pouch he had hanging on his shoulder. "Sir, I have information that may be helpful in preventing any more violence in the Middle East; especially where Iran is concerned."

"We can talk in my office on board," President Elliot pointed out and he and Colonel Wilson walked to the staircase ramp.

Colonel Wilson followed President Elliot up the staircase ramp, and into Air Force One. President Elliot entered his office and walked over to the desk, and sat down in the chair behind the desk. Colonel Wilson closed the door and walked over to the chair in front of the desk where President Elliot was sitting. He removed the pouch from his shoulder and sat down.

"Okay Colonel, what do you have for me?" President Elliot calmly asked.

"Mr. President, Deputy Director Hicks and I were in the building across the street from the building that exploded near the docks in Baltimore," Colonel Wilson said while he removed the contents from the pouch. "That explosion was no accident. Sir, I'm convinced, without any doubt, that everyone in that building was top-level Red Cell members."

"So, Colonel, what you're saying is that all those people that died in that explosion were top-level Red Cell members?"

"It appears so, Mr. President."

"I had a conversation with Director McGrath at the ATF before I left Washington. He said that the explosion was an accident. Are you sure it was no accident?"

"Yes, sir, I'm sure. However, by them calling this an accident could work in your favor," Colonel Wilson pointed out. "You could use this to gain public support while at the same time covering up the Red Cell infestation in our government."

"Spoken like a true politician," President Elliot commented. "Have you ever considered running for office?"

"No, sir, not me. I'm a soldier, not a politician."

"Relax colonel; I was only kidding." President Elliot smiled and waited a few seconds before he continued. "What else do you have for me?"

Colonel Wilson opened the pouch and removed its contents. "Sir, I have proof that the Iranian government had its own version of Red Cell, and that they were played just as we were," he continued as he handed President Elliot the content of the pouch. "The Iranians were just as much a victim in this as we were. Red Cell was behind everything that has happened over there in the last six months."

President Elliot looked through the papers and shook his head. "All those poor souls died because of a few power greedy men," he said as he handed the papers back to Colonel Wilson.

"It appears that way Mr. President," Colonel Wilson remarked while he put the papers back into the pouch. "Sir, we have the opportunity to put an end to this mess. We can end this before the region explodes into an all-out war that no one wants," he continued as he sat the pouch down on the corner of President Elliot's desk.

"You're right. I agree. It's time to put this mess to rest," President Elliot said as he got up from his seat. "Enough Innocent people on both sides have died for no reason."

"Yes, sir," Colonel Wilson said as he jumped to his feet. "I'm sure the Iranians feel the same way, sir."

"Colonel, I can't thank you and your people enough for all that you have done for me, and for the country," President Elliot said while he shook hands with Colonel Wilson.

"Just doing our job Mr. President," he remarked. "We'll be ready whenever you need us."

"Let's hope it's not anytime soon," President Elliot commented while he returned to his seat behind his desk.

Colonel Wilson walked over to the door and opened it. He stepped into the hallway and closed the door. He walked to the exit door of Air Force One and walked down the staircase ramp. He walked over to the Humvee that he had parked near hangar nine earlier, and watched the ground crew remove the staircase ramp from

Air Force One.

A few minutes later, the exit door to Air Force One was closed and secured on the inside. The pilot began to warm up the jet engines while the ground crew pulled Air Force One onto the runway. When the tower cleared Air Force One for takeoff, the pilot throttled up the engines. The aircraft began to move down the runway and pick up speed. Not long afterwards, Air Force One left the ground and proceeded to its cruising altitude.

# Chapter 25

The White House
Washington, D.C.

President Elliot sat behind his desk in the Oval Office and watched the news coverage from the United Nations Headquarters in Manhattan, New York on his television set. After three long months of intensive negotiations, a peace agreement was finally reached with Iran, bringing peace to the Middle Eastern region.

The president watched as each ambassador from the nations involved signed the peace agreement. The Iranian ambassador was the last to sign. *Peace at last,* President Elliot thought. He picked up the remote for the television from his desk and switched off the television. He laid the remote back down on his desk when the intercom on his telephone beeped. He pushed the intercom button. "Yes."

"Sorry for the interruption Mr. President, but Colonel Wilson and Miss Hicks are here to see you," President Elliot's new personal assistant, thirty-one-year-old, Megan Parker, announced.

"Send them in," President Elliot said and pushed the intercom button to cancel the call.

The door to the Oval Office opened, and Karen Hicks entered, with Colonel Wilson a few steps behind her. President Elliot got up from his seat from behind his desk while Colonel Wilson closed the door.

"Colonel Wilson, it's nice to see you again. Please, let's sit," President Elliot suggested while he walked over to one of the sofas in the room and sat down. Colonel Wilson and Karen Hicks walked over to the sofa across from President Elliot and sat down. "Let me start by asking both of you a personal question. Are the two of you involved?"

"Mr. President, "I don't understand what our relationship has to do with anything," Karen Hicks pointed out.

"It has a lot to do with everything," President Elliot fired back. "Now, please answer the question."

"Yes, sir, we are," Colonel Wilson said.

"Do you think the two of you can work together without your relationship getting in the way of doing your job?"

"Yes, sir, I do," Colonel Wilson answered.

"Mr. President, I've given you my resignation and my final report." Karen Hicks said. "I don't understand why you wanted to see me."

"Karen, I'm asking you to reconsider your decision to resign," President Elliot said. "I have your resignation on my desk. I would like to give it back to you, and offer you a job that I know is right for you."

"Sir, have you read my report?"

"Yes, I have, and then I put it into the paper shredder. No one needs to know about how you neutralized four dangerous terrorists."

"Mr. President, I killed four people out of revenge," Karen Hicks pointed out."

"You took down four dangerous people," Colonel Wilson jumped in. "Your actions were justified, regardless of your reasons."

"If the truth gets out about why I took them out, it will be a nightmare for all of us," Karen Hicks was quick to point out.

"Karen, the only people that know the truth about this is in this room," President Elliot added.

Karen Hicks looked at Colonel Wilson. "You really think that what I did was justified?"

"Yes, I do."

Karen Hicks thought for a minute and then looked at President Elliot. "What do you have in mind, sir?"

"I want you to take over the position of CIA Director."

Karen Hicks looked at President Elliot surprised. "I thought Mike Hanson filled that position?"

"He's the acting director until I find someone to fill the slot permanently," President Elliot answered. "Mike has accepted the

Director of Homeland Security nomination. He recommended you for the position of CIA Director."

"I don't think the Senate Oversight Committee will approve putting a woman in charge of the CIA."

"Karen, the Senate Oversight Committee has secretly approved your appointment," President Elliot said. "They plan to make the announcement when you accept the nomination for CIA Director. All you need to do is say yes, and the position is yours."

Karen Hicks looked at Colonel Wilson and smiled. She then turned her attention back to President Elliot. She thought for a quick moment. "Mr. President, I accept your offer."

"Great," President Elliot said with excitement. "When can you start?"

"I can start as soon as the Senate Oversight Committee announces the approval of my nomination."

"Excellent," President Elliot remarked. "I will get the ball rolling."

"Excuse me, Mr. President, but what does any of this have to do with me?" Colonel Wilson inquired. "Why did you ask me here?"

"I wanted you here for two reasons," President Elliot answered. "First, I wanted to see if you had a problem with Karen as CIA Director."

"I have no problem with Karen's appointment," Colonel Wilson assured President Elliot. "I assure you, sir, there won't be any conflict of interest."

"I never thought there would be," President Elliot commented. "Now, let's move on to the real reason I asked you here. I want you to expand the Strike Force Delta assault teams to ten members each, bringing the total assault team strength to six ten-man teams."

"Yes, sir. I'll have to get with General Richwood and get the selection process started."

"Okay then, we're done here," President Elliot said as he got up from the sofa.

"Yes, sir, Mr. President," Colonel Wilson said as he and Karen Hicks jumped to their feet.

President Elliot walked to the side door of the Oval Office and opened the door. He left the room and closed the door.

Colonel Wilson looked at Karen Hicks. "Let's get some lunch," he asked, and then smiled.

"Not a bad idea soldier boy," Karen Hicks said as she took Colonel Wilson hand into her's. "After that, what do you have in mind?"

"Oh, I'm sure I will think of something," Colonel Wilson chuckled. "Let's get out of here."

Hand in hand, Colonel Wilson, and Karen Hicks walked over to the exit door, with Colonel Wilson leading the way. He opened the door, and they walked out of the Oval Office. Karen Hicks closed the door, and they continued walking.

To be continued